ON THE RUN

IRIS
JOHANSEN

——

ON THE RUN

——

Bantam Books

ON THE RUN
A Bantam Book

Published by Bantam Dell
A Division of Random House, Inc.
New York, New York

This is a work of fiction. Names, characters, places, and incidents either
are the product of the author's imagination or are used fictitiously. Any
resemblance to actual persons, living or dead, events,
or locales is entirely coincidental.

Book design by Virginia Norey

Bantam Books is a registered trademark of Random House, Inc., and
the colophon is a trademark of Random House, Inc.

ISBN-13: 978-0-553-80343-3
ISBN-10: 0-553-80343-3

Printed in the United States of America

ON THE RUN

1

El Tariq, Morocco

Get the bastard! He's trapped."

The hell he was, Kilmer thought savagely as he gunned the jeep up the hill. He wasn't about to let them catch him when he'd come this far.

A bullet tore past his ear and splintered the windshield. Too close. They were gaining on him.

He put his foot on the brake and slowed the jeep down.

He swerved around a curve in the road, braced himself, and then jumped into a mud-and-sand-filled ditch at the side of the road.

Christ, that hurt.

Ignore it.

He rolled over and dashed into the brush, watching the jeep roll driverless away from him and then veer toward the edge of the road. With any luck they'd think that shot had struck him and not try to analyze why the jeep appeared uncontrolled.

Now wait for the truck pursuing him.

He didn't have to wait long. The Nissan truck roared

around the curve. Two men in the cab. Three in the open back of the truck. The man on the right side of the back was the one with the rifle. He was aiming at the jeep again.

Let them get a little nearer . . .

They were passing him.

Now!

He stepped out of the brush and threw the grenade he'd pulled out of his backpack.

He hit the dirt as the grenade struck the truck and exploded. A second explosion rocked the ground as the gas tank of the truck blew.

His head lifted. The truck was a blackened, flaming ruin; smoke was curling up toward the sky.

And that smoke would be seen for miles.

Move!

He jumped to his feet and started to run toward the glade at the top of the hill.

It took him five minutes to reach it and he was hearing the roar of vehicles behind him when he burst into the glade where the helicopter was hidden. Donavan started the rotors whirling as he caught sight of Kilmer.

"Go!" Kilmer dove into the passenger seat. "Stay away from the road before going south. You might get a bullet in the gas tank."

"I thought from the explosion that you'd taken care of that problem." Donavan lifted off. "Grenade?"

Kilmer nodded. "But there may be more than one truck this time. The first thing they'll do is check the safe when they see that smoke and then they'll call out every man at the compound."

"So I see." Donavan whistled as he saw the line of trucks on the road below. "And one of them has a ground-to-air missile launcher. We'd better get the hell out of this airspace before they spot us. Did you get it?"

"Oh, yes." Kilmer gazed down at the jeweled and embroidered velvet pouch dangling from the gold chain he'd pulled out of his belt pack. The blue sapphire eyes of the two horses whose images were imprinted on the pouch glittered back at him. Deadly. So beautiful. So deadly. He'd already killed seven men today alone to gain possession. Why didn't he feel triumphant? Perhaps because he realized that those lives would probably be only the start of the chaos to follow. "Yes, I got it, Donavan."

Tallanville, Alabama

Talk to him, Frankie," Grace said as she stroked the horse's muzzle. "When you get to the barrier, lean down and tell him what you want him to do."

"And he'll balk just the same." Frankie made a face. "Horses may understand you, but I'm chopped liver to them."

"You don't know until you try. Darling is just having a battle of wills with you. You can't let him have the upper hand."

"I don't care, Mom. I don't have to be boss. If Darling was a keyboard instead of a horse, I might want to assert myself, but I—" She gazed at Grace's face and then sighed. "Okay, I'll do what you say. But he's going to toss me."

"If he does, then fall right, the way I taught you. And then get on him again." She paused. "Don't you know how much it scares me to have you fall? But you love to ride and it was your choice to compete in this show. I don't care whether you win or not, but you have to be prepared for anything that might happen."

"I know." Frankie's smile lit her face. "And I will win. Just watch me." She kicked the palomino and sent him galloping around the ring. She called back over her shoulder, "But it would help if you told that to Darling."

She looked so little on that horse, Grace thought in agony. Frankie was dressed in jeans and a red plaid shirt that made her curly dark hair tumbling out of her helmet look black in the sunlight. She was eight, but she'd always been small for her age and she looked younger.

"She's only a kid, Grace." Charlie had come to stand beside her at the fence. "Don't be so hard on her."

"I'd be hard on her if I let her go through life unprepared." She muttered a prayer beneath her breath as she saw Frankie start the approach to the barrier. "I can't protect her all her life. What if I'm not around? She has to learn how to survive."

"Like you did?"

"Like I did."

Darling was almost on top of the barrier.

Don't balk. Don't balk, boy. Take her over safely.

Darling hesitated, then rose in the air and cleared the barrier.

"Hot dog!" Grace jumped down from the fence as Frankie whooped with glee and then galloped toward her. "I told you that you could do it." When Frankie slipped from the saddle, Grace picked her up and swung her in a circle. "You're incredible."

"Yep." Frankie's grin lit her face. "Maybe you're not the only horse whisperer in the family." She looked beyond Grace to Charlie. "Hot stuff, huh?"

Charlie nodded. "And I thought all that piano playing was ruining you for any decent job." His smile lit his sun-weathered face with slyness. "I might even try to get you a summer job cleaning the stables over at Baker's Farm."

"I get enough of that here." She took Darling's reins and started leading him toward the gate. "And you let me off for piano practice. I don't think Mr. Baker would do that. He likes hillbilly music."

"After you take care of Darling, shower and change your clothes," Grace said. "We have to be at judo class in an hour."

"Right." Frankie took off her helmet and reached up to

4

rumple her curly hair. "And Robert promised to take us out for pizza afterward, Charlie. You're coming, aren't you?"

"Wouldn't miss it," Charlie said. "And if you make it all right with your mom, I'll even put Darling away for you." He grimaced. "Never mind. I'm getting the evil eye for interfering with responsibility."

"She's like that." Frankie led Darling toward the stable. "But I don't mind. I like making Darling comfortable. It sort of pays for all the fun he gives me."

"Like dumping you in the dirt."

"He didn't hurt me."

"Thank God," Grace murmured as she watched Frankie disappear into the stable. "I nearly had a heart attack, Charlie."

"But you made her try again." Charlie nodded. "I know. She has to learn to survive."

"And have a chance at winning. I won't have her beaten down."

"She tickles those keys pretty good. Not everybody has to compete in the ring."

"She's loved to ride ever since you and I taught her when she was three. The piano is her first love and she's brilliant at it. But I'm not having her confined to practice and concert halls. Composing is fulfilling for her too and it doesn't expose her to all the hoopla connected with public life. She's going to have a full, rounded life here before I let her consider whether she wants to see her name in lights." She grimaced. "Who the hell would have dreamed I'd give birth to a child prodigy?"

"You're not so dumb yourself."

"Heredity has nothing to do with a talent like Frankie's. It's one of those freaks of nature. But I won't have her considered a freak by anyone. She's going to have a normal, happy childhood."

"Or you'll blow everybody out of the water." He chuckled. "She is happy, Grace. Don't try so hard. You've done a great job raising her."

"*We've* done a great job raising her." She smiled at him. "And every night I thank God for you, Charlie."

A faint flush colored his lined cheeks, but his tone was rueful. "I hope He's listening. I haven't done much worthwhile in my life and I'm getting pretty old. I may need a few good marks in His book soon."

"Hey, you're only pushing eighty and healthy as one of your horses. In this day and age you've got a lot of good years left."

"That's true." He paused. "But not one of them can be better than the last eight. Frankie's pretty special and you've made me feel as if she belongs to me too."

"She does. You know that." She frowned. "You're very serious today. Something wrong?"

He shook his head. "I got a little scared when Frankie took that jump. It made me start counting my blessings. I was remembering how things were before you showed up that day eight years ago. I was a crabby old bachelor with a horse farm that was going straight to hell. You changed everything for me."

"Yeah, I talked you into a job, moved in, and saddled you with a six-month-old baby. A colicky baby. I'm lucky you didn't toss me out the first month."

"I was tempted. It took two months before I decided that even if I kicked you out, I was going to keep Frankie."

"In your dreams."

"It would have been pretty hard." His blue eyes were twinkling. "Of course, I could have tried to find a bronc tough enough to bust you up a little. But I haven't seen a horse you couldn't break yet. Weird."

"Don't you start. Ever since Frankie saw that horse-whisperer movie, she thinks I'm— I just talk to them, dammit. Nothing weird about that."

"And they understand." He held up his hand. "I'm not accusing you of being a Doctor Dolittle. I've just never run across anyone like you."

"I love horses. Maybe they feel it and respond to it. It's as simple as that."

"There's nothing simple about you. You're tough as nails about everyone and everything but Frankie. You're crazy about the kid. Yet you let her take chances that most doting mothers would never do."

"Most doting mothers never had the experiences I did when I was growing up. If my father hadn't made sure I was able to survive, I wouldn't have made thirteen. Don't you think I want to wrap Frankie in cotton and never let her take a false step? But mistakes are how you learn and get stronger. I'll love her and protect her in the only way I know that works. Teaching her to protect herself."

"I don't suppose you'd care to tell me where you did grow up?"

"I told you, I spent every summer on my grandfather's horse farm in Australia."

"And where did you spend the rest of the year?" Charlie shrugged as he saw her expression close up. "I didn't think so. But you usually don't talk about anything before that day you showed up on my doorstep. I thought I had a chance."

"It's not that I don't— It's better if you don't know anything about—" She shook her head. "It's not that I don't trust you, Charlie."

"I know. I'm just curious why you'd have to trust me to tell me what makes you tick."

"You know what makes me tick."

He chuckled. "Yeah—Frankie. I guess she's enough for anyone." He turned and headed for the barn. "If I'm going to meet you for pizza, I'd better get to my chores. Robert and I are going to play a game of chess after we ship you and Frankie back to the farm. I'm going to beat him this time. He's really better at judo and other martial arts than he is at board games. An unusual man, Robert." He glanced back over his shoulder. "And isn't it also unusual that he showed up in town and opened that martial-arts studio only a few months after you came?"

"Not particularly. The town didn't have any kind of martial-arts center. It was just good business."

Charlie nodded. "Guess it's all in the way you look at it. See you tonight."

She gazed after him as he headed for the barn. In spite of his years, his step was still springy and his wiry body appeared as strong as that of a much younger man. She never thought of Charlie as aging, and it troubled her to hear him talk about it. She'd never heard him speak about age or dying before. He always lived in the moment . . . and these days they were all good moments for all of them.

Her gaze shifted to the hills surrounding the farm. The late-afternoon sun turned the pines in the woods to a deeper shade of green that spread an almost narcotic peacefulness over the hot August afternoon. When she'd first come to Charlie's small horse farm eight years ago, that peacefulness was what had drawn her. The paint on the outbuildings and the fencing had been worn and chipped, and the house had looked as if it had been neglected for years, but that sense of timeless peace pervaded every foot of the place. Dear God, how she had needed that peace.

"Mom."

She turned to see Frankie hurrying toward her. "All set?"

"Yep." She took Grace's hand. "I had a talk with Darling while I was putting him away. I told him what a good boy he'd been and that I expected him to do the same tomorrow."

"Really?"

She sighed. "But he'll probably toss me anyway. I figure today I got lucky."

Grace smiled. "Maybe tomorrow will be lucky too." Her grasp tightened on Frankie's hand. Jesus, she loved her. This was one of the perfect times. No matter what tomorrow brought, today was bright as a new penny. "Race you to the house?"

8

"Right." Frankie broke free and started streaking across the yard.

Let her win? What would it hurt to—

Grace started to run at full speed. It would hurt. She had to be honest with Frankie and never let her doubt that honesty. Someday Frankie would leave her in the dust and then the triumph would be all the sweeter for her. . . .

It's going to rain." Grace lifted her head to the night sky. She and Robert Blockman had stopped outside in the parking lot to wait for Charlie and Frankie, who were finishing their game of pool in the recreation room that adjoined the pizzeria. "I can feel it coming."

"The weatherman says it's supposed to be dry as a bone for the next couple days." Robert leaned on the door of his SUV. "August is usually a dry month."

"It's going to rain tonight," she repeated.

Robert chuckled. "I know, who cares what the weatherman says? You can feel it. You and your horses. They're probably spooked too."

"I'm not spooked. I like the rain." She was watching Frankie cuing up through the glass window. "So does Frankie. Sometimes we go riding together in the rain."

"Not me. I'm like a cat. I like to be dry and cozy inside a house when it's wet."

She smiled. He resembled more a bear than a cat, she thought. Robert was in his late forties, but he was big and burly, with close-cut dark hair and irregular features that included a humped nose that had been broken sometime in the past. She always told him that he looked more like a prizefighter than a martial-arts instructor. "Oh, I think you could survive a patch of rough weather. How's your week gone, Robert? Any new customers?"

"A couple. You might have seen them when you came into the studio this afternoon. I was just finishing signing them up. Two boys whose truck-driver father thinks they should be as tough as he is." He grimaced. "They wouldn't have to learn much. You could take their papa with one hand tied behind your back. Hell, Frankie could probably make short work of him. No finesse. Sometimes I wonder why I don't pull up stakes and go somewhere away from small-town rednecks and gossipmongers."

"I thought you liked Tallanville."

"I do. Most of the time. Slow living appeals to me. Just every now and then I get fed up." His gaze shifted to Frankie. "Why don't you bring her in tomorrow and let her show those boys a few moves."

"Why should I do—" Her gaze narrowed on his face. "What's this about, Robert?"

"Nothing."

"Robert."

He shrugged. "I just heard Papa asshole muttering to his sons after you drove up. Even after eight years in this town, they still talk about you and Frankie."

"So?"

"I just don't like it."

"Frankie's illegitimate, and even in this day and age there will always be someone who wants everyone to go by their own standards. Particularly in a small town like this. I explained that to Frankie and she understands."

"I don't. I want to punch someone."

She smiled. "Me too. But the kids are much more open than their parents, and Frankie's not hurting. Except for me."

"I bet she wants to punch someone too."

"She already did and I had to have a talk with her." She shook her head. "So we're not going to have Frankie beat up any of your clients just to make you feel better."

"What about making you feel better?"

"Catering to ignorance and intolerance wouldn't make me feel better. And it might make things difficult for Charlie. He can be very defensive and he's not a young man. I'm not going to take a chance on him getting hurt."

"He can hold his own. He's a tough old bird."

"He's not going to have to hold his own. Not about me and Frankie. He's done too much for us to have a payback like that."

"It's pretty even-steven. You've done a lot for him too."

She shook her head. "He took me in and gave Frankie a home. All I did was work my rump off to keep the farm showing a profit. I would have done that anyway."

"I don't believe he has any regrets."

She didn't speak for a moment. "And what about you?"

He lifted his brows. "What?"

"You've spent eight years here. You said yourself that you have your moments when you're fed up with small-town life."

"I'd have my moments even if I lived in Paris or New York. Everyone has their time of discontent."

"I don't."

"But then, you have Frankie." He looked down at her. "And so do we. I've never regretted being sent here to watch out for you. For all of us that's the bottom line. It's all about Frankie, isn't it?"

Frankie was putting up her pool stick, her face alight, her dark eyes glowing with laughter as she talked to Charlie.

"Yes," Grace said softly. "It's all about Frankie."

How about me driving you home, Charlie?" Robert opened Charlie's car door. "You're a little on the tipsy side."

"I'm legal. I only had two drinks. I don't need any young whippersnapper chauffeuring me."

"Whippersnapper? You flatter me. I'm too close to the big five-O for comfort." He grinned. "Come on. You may have had only two drinks but you were weaving a bit when you got up from the table. Let me drive you."

"My truck knows the way home." He made a face. "Like old Dobbin." He started the engine. "If I'd beat you that last game, I might let you drive me home in style, but I reserve that right for our next session." He smiled. "I was close this time. You're going down next week."

"Just be careful."

"I'm always careful. I've got a lot to lose these days." He tilted his head, listening. "Is that thunder?"

"It wouldn't surprise me. Grace said it was going to rain tonight. How the hell does she know?"

Charlie shrugged. "She told me once she was a quarter Cherokee. Maybe it's in the genes." He waved as he backed out of the parking lot.

Robert hesitated, gazing after him. Charlie seemed to be driving okay and it was almost all back roads to his farm. He'd give him a call when he'd had time to get home, just to ease his own mind. He turned and started back toward his SUV.

It had been a good night and he was filled with warm contentment. Even if it hadn't been a part of his job, he'd have enjoyed these evenings with Grace, Frankie, and Charlie. They were as close to family as he'd ever possessed. When he'd taken on this assignment, he'd never dreamed it would last this long, and now he'd be disappointed when it was over.

If it was ever over, he thought ruefully. He'd been told Grace Archer was too important for them to take a chance with her safety. The fact that they'd kept him here for eight years in this little Podunk of a town only underscored that fact.

Not that he'd take that chance even if she was considered dispensable by the agency. Grace had become a personal mission. He liked her, dammit. She was smart and strong and she never let anything get in the way when she was going after something. She was also one hell of an attractive woman. He was surprised that he found her appealing. He'd always liked cute, cuddly women, and his first wife had fallen dead center into that category. There was nothing cute or cuddly about Grace. She was tall, slim, and graceful, with curly, short chestnut hair that framed her face, big hazel eyes, full lips, and spare, elegant bone structure that was more interesting than conventionally pretty. Yet there was something about her confidence, quiet strength, and intelligence that turned him on. There had been times when he'd had to backpedal, but she was so completely absorbed by her daughter and the life she'd carved out at Charlie's farm, he doubted if she'd even noticed.

Or maybe she had and chose to ignore it. He knew she liked being his friend, and she probably didn't want to jeopardize that relationship for a less calm, volatile one. God knew her life had been volatile and violent enough before she came here. When he'd read her dossier, he'd had trouble connecting the Grace he knew with that woman. Well, except for the fact that she had little trouble putting him down during their workouts. She was strong and skilled and went for the jugular. Who knew? It could be that that hint of danger was why he found her so interesting.

He'd reached his SUV and he clicked the remote to unlock the door. It would take Charlie twenty minutes to get home. He'd give him another five minutes to get in the house and then call him and—

A large brown envelope was on the seat.

He stiffened. "Shit." There was no question that he'd locked the SUV.

He glanced around the parking lot. No one suspicious. But whoever had put the envelope on the seat had had all evening to do it.

He slowly picked up the envelope, opened it, and took out the contents.

A photo of two white horses in profile.

Both horses had blue eyes.

Mom. May I come in?" Frankie stood in the doorway of Grace's bedroom. "I can't sleep."

"Sure." Grace sat up and patted the bed next to her. "What's wrong? Stomachache? I told you not to eat that last piece of pizza."

"No." Frankie was cuddling underneath the covers. "I was just lonesome."

Grace put her arm around her. "Then I'm glad you came. Being lonely hurts."

"Yeah." Frankie was silent a moment. "I was thinking maybe you probably get lonesome too sometimes."

"When you're not around."

"No, I mean what about all that love and marriage and stuff on TV? Do I get in the way?"

"You're never in the way." She chuckled. "And I promise I'm not missing all that 'stuff.' I'm too busy."

"Sure?"

"Sure." She brushed her lips across Frankie's temple. "This is enough, baby. What I have with you and Charlie makes me very, very happy."

"Me too." Frankie yawned. "I just wanted to let you know that I wouldn't mind if you decided that you—"

"Go to sleep. I have a two-year-old to break tomorrow."

"Okay." She nestled closer. "I heard the music again. I'm going to get up early and try to play it on the piano."

"Something new?"

She yawned again. "Mm-hmm. It's just a whisper now but it will get louder."

"When you're ready, I'd love to hear it."

"Uh-huh. But it's just a whisper. . . ."

She was asleep.

Grace moved carefully to shift her so that she was lying more comfortably on the pillow. She should send her back to her bed, but she wasn't going to do it. Frankie was so independent, she seldom came to Grace to be cuddled anymore, and she was going to enjoy this. There was nothing more endearing than the soft, warm weight of a beloved child.

And God knew there was no child more beloved than this child in her arms.

It was odd that Frankie had started worrying about Grace's solitary status. Or maybe not so odd. Frankie was older than her years and extremely sensitive. Grace hoped she'd convinced her that this life at the farm was enough for her. She'd told her the truth. She kept herself so busy that there was no room for worrying about sex or any other intimate relationship. Even if a relationship hadn't posed a threat, she was not about to be pulled down into that whirlpool of sensuality that had almost destroyed her. When she had conceived Frankie, she was totally immersed in a physical obsession that had made her forget everything she should have remembered. That couldn't ever happen again. She owed it to Frankie to keep a cool head.

The rain was pounding against the window and the rhythmic sound only added to the sweetness that was enveloping her. She wanted it to go on and on. To hell with the horse she had to break tomorrow. She was going to lie here with Frankie and savor this moment.

W hat the hell is it?" Robert asked when he got through to Les North in Washington. "Horses? This county is full of them, but no one's ever seen fit to break into my car and put a photo of them on my seat."

"Blue eyes?"

"Both of them. What is it—"

"Get out to the farm, Blockman. Check and see if everything's okay."

"And wake her up? I just saw her and the kid tonight. They're fine. It could just be some practical joke. I'm not the most popular person in this town. I'm not a Southern Baptist and I have nothing to do with horses, their feeding or well-being. That guarantees I'll stay an outsider."

"It's not a joke. And it's not one of your neighbors down

there. Get out there. Try not to scare her, but make sure the place is secure."

"I'll call Charlie on his cell phone and make sure everything's okay." Robert was silent a moment. "This is serious stuff, isn't it? Are you going to tell me why you're bent out of shape?"

"You're damn right it's serious. This may be the reason you've been parked on her doorstep all these years. Get out there and earn your salary."

"I'm on my way." Robert hung up.

Northpressed the disconnect and sat there thinking.

Warning? Probably. And if it was a warning, who had given it?

Kilmer.

He muttered a curse. Kilmer surfacing after all these years was the worst-case scenario. They'd made a deal, dammit. He couldn't show up and throw the setup into chaos. If there was a problem, Blockman could handle it.

Maybe it wasn't so bad. Maybe he wasn't in Tallanville. Maybe he'd hired someone to leave the photo.

And pigs could fly. Even if that warning hadn't been delivered in person, he wasn't a man who'd let anyone else handle a dangerous situation that concerned Grace Archer.

He had no choice but to call Bill Crane, his superior, and tell him Kilmer was probably back on the scene. Hell, Crane was one of the new wonder boys who'd been brought in after 9/11. He'd bet Crane didn't even know Kilmer existed.

Well, he was about to learn. North wasn't going to handle this hot potato by himself. Wake the wonder boy up and make him see what he could do with Kilmer.

He quickly dialed the number and waited with malicious satisfaction for the ringing to jar Crane from sleep.

2

The tires of Charlie's truck rattled the loose wooden slats of the old bridge as he started across the river. He'd been meaning to fix those slats. . . .

Almost home.

Charlie turned the radio up as a Reba McEntire song came on. He'd always liked her. Pretty lady. Pretty voice. Maybe country music wasn't as deep as the stuff Frankie wrote, but it made him feel comfortable. No reason why he couldn't like both.

The rain was splashing hard against the windshield and he turned the wipers on full blast. He didn't need to cope with rain as well as being tipsy. Getting old sucked. Two drinks and he was woozy. He used to be able to drink all his buddies under the table and still be clearheaded enough to—

His cell phone rang, and it took a minute to get it out of his pocket. Robert. He shook his head and smiled as he punched the button. "I'm fine. I'm almost home and I'll thank you to not treat me like a doddering—"

Something was on the road directly ahead.

Light!

Grace was still not sleeping when her cell phone rang on the bedside table.

Charlie? She hadn't heard his truck and he sometimes stayed with Robert if he drank too much.

"Mom?" Frankie murmured drowsily.

"Shh, baby. It's okay." She reached over her daughter and picked up the phone. "Charlie?"

"Get out of there, Grace."

Robert.

She sat bolt upright in bed. "What's wrong?"

"I don't know. And there's no time to explain. North told me to come out there, and I'm on my way. But I might be too late. Get out of there."

"Charlie?"

He was silent a moment. "He was on his way home. I talked to him a few minutes ago. I lost him. I think something happened."

"What? Then I have to go find—"

"I'll find him. You get yourself and Frankie out of there."

"What's wrong?" Frankie was sitting up in bed. "Is Charlie okay?"

Oh, God, she hoped so, but she had to trust Robert. She had to take care of Frankie. "You find him, Robert. And if you're having me take Frankie out in this storm for no reason, I'm going to strangle you."

"I hope there's no reason. Keep in touch." Robert hung up.

"Charlie?" Frankie whispered.

"I don't know, baby." She flung off the covers. "Go to your room and get your tennis shoes. Don't turn on the light and don't bother getting dressed. We'll grab a rain poncho in the mudroom downstairs."

"Why am I—"

"Frankie, don't ask questions. We don't have time. Just trust me and do what I tell you. Okay?"

Frankie hesitated. "Okay." She jumped out of bed and ran out of the room. "I'll be quick."

Bless her. Most kids jarred from sleep in the middle of the night would have been too scared to even function.

Grace went to the closet and pulled out her knapsack from the top shelf. She'd packed this knapsack eight years ago and updated the contents periodically. She hoped the clothes she'd packed for Frankie would still fit. . . .

She was unfastening the lockbox she'd put in the knapsack when Frankie ran back in the room. "Good. You were very quick. Go to the window and see if it's still raining so hard."

While Frankie was crossing the room, Grace took out the gun and dagger. She quickly stuffed them and the papers she'd placed in the box eight years ago in the front pocket of the knapsack, where they were readily available.

"Maybe the rain's a little lighter." Frankie was looking out the window. "But it's so dark it's hard to see— Oh, there's someone with a flashlight coming across the yard. Do you think it's Charlie?"

It wasn't Charlie. Charlie knew every inch of his farm and wouldn't need a flashlight. "Come on, baby." She grabbed her arm and pulled her down the stairs. "We're going out the kitchen door. Be very quiet."

A sound of metal on metal at the front door. She inhaled sharply. She had jimmied too many locks herself not to know that sound.

She had changed Charlie's flimsy locks when she came here, but it wouldn't take an expert long to break in. And if they couldn't force the lock, then they'd find another way.

"Out," she whispered, and pushed Frankie toward the kitchen.

Frankie flew down the hall and threw open the kitchen

door. She looked back at Grace, her eyes wide. "Robbers?" she whispered.

Grace nodded as she grabbed a rain poncho for Frankie from the mudroom hooks, threw it to her, and then grabbed one for herself. "And there might be more than one. Head for the paddock and then the woods on the other side. If I'm not right behind, don't wait for me. I'll catch up."

Frankie was shaking her head.

"Don't say no to me," Grace said. "What have I always taught you? You have to take care of yourself before you can take care of others. Now do what I say."

Frankie hesitated.

Christ, Grace could hear the creak of the front door as it opened. "Run!"

Frankie ran, streaking across the yard and into the paddock. Grace watched for a second, waiting. There was almost always a lookout man.

She didn't have to wait long. A tall man had come around the house and was running after Frankie.

She took off after him.

No gun. She didn't want to bring the others in the house out here.

Run. The rain and thunder would mask the sound of her footsteps behind him.

She reached him as he entered the woods.

He must have heard the sound of her breathing. He whirled, gun in hand.

She sprang, the side of her hand numbing the wrist of his gun hand. Then her dagger sliced across his jugular. She didn't watch him fall to the ground. She turned, searching the shadows. "Frankie?"

She heard a low sobbing. Frankie was huddled at the base of a tree a short distance away. "It's okay, baby. He can't hurt you now." Grace fell to her knees beside her. "But we have to leave. We have to run. There are others."

Frankie's hand reached out and touched a smear on Grace's poncho. "Blood. There's blood . . . on you."

"Yes. He would have hurt you. He would have hurt both of us. I had to stop him."

"Blood . . ."

"Frankie . . ." She stiffened as she heard a shout from across the paddock. She stood up and pulled Frankie with her. "I'll talk to you about it later. They're coming. Now do what I say and *run*. Let's go."

She half-pulled Frankie deeper into the woods. After only a few steps Frankie was running, stumbling with her through the brush.

Where to hide? She had scoped out and planned bolt-holes in these woods over the years. Choose one.

She couldn't count on Frankie being able to keep this pace for long. She was a child and almost in shock. Grace had to find a close place to hide and wait them out. Robert was on his way.

Or at least find a way to hide Frankie. She could decide after she saw how many were after her whether she could handle the situation alone.

The blind.

Charlie had a hunting blind in a tree not far from here. He hadn't used it for years, claiming he couldn't climb the damn tree anymore.

Well, she could climb. And Frankie was as agile as a monkey.

"The blind," she gasped. "Get to the blind, Frankie. Hide there."

"Not without you."

"I'm coming."

Frankie glared back at her. "Now."

"Okay, now." Grace grabbed her hand and tore through the underbrush. The wet foliage slapped her in the face and her tennis shoes sank deep in the mud with every step.

She listened. Could she hear them?

Yes, but she couldn't tell where they were.

Flashlights.

Christ.

The blind was just up ahead. She put on speed and reached the tree. "Up," she whispered, and gave Frankie a boost. Frankie was halfway up the tree when Grace started. Her daughter crawled out on the branch holding the blind a moment later.

Grace joined her in seconds and pulled her down flat on the wooden platform. "Quiet. In a hunt like this no one expects you to be above them. They're focused on straight ahead." The rain was making a slapping noise on the camouflage drape. It was different from the sound of the rain on the leaves, she realized. It would be a dead giveaway. She jerked the drape down.

She hoped she was telling the truth about them not looking up. It was generally a fact, but who knew how experienced the leader of this particular team was? "Keep down," she repeated. She could feel Frankie trembling with fear against her.

Damn them. Damn them to hell.

Grace drew Frankie closer as she pulled the gun out of the pocket of her poncho.

The men were calling back and forth to one another as they searched the brush. They weren't afraid she'd hear them. She and Frankie were the prey, the hunted. She listened. At least three different voices. If there were no more than that, then they wouldn't be impossible targets. She knew these woods and they didn't, and they wouldn't expect—

But she couldn't leave Frankie.

And one of the men was now directly below the tree with their blind.

She held her breath. Her hand covered Frankie's lips.

The beam of his flashlight was skimming the mud, looking for footprints.

She aimed the gun at his head. He was on the wrong

side of the tree, but if he moved a few feet to the left he'd
see the place where they'd climbed—

An explosion shook the earth.

"What the hell!" The man below her whirled in the direction of the farm. "What the devil was—"

"The car. I think it was the car, Kersoff." Another man
had run up to stand beside the one below their tree. "I saw
a flash and fire and it came from down the road where we
left the car. Maybe the gas tank."

"That bitch. How did she get out of these woods?"

"How did she kill Jennet?" he asked. "You warned us she
wouldn't be easy. He's not going to like—"

"Shut up." Kersoff turned away and started toward the
paddock. "If she blew up our car, she can't be that far away.
She's probably trying to get to her own car now. We can
block the road and wait for her. Locke! Where are you?
Have you seen Locke?"

"Not for a couple minutes. Shall I look—"

"No, we have to get to the road. Move."

A moment later the sound of their passage through the
brush faded.

Frankie was turning her head to escape Grace's hand
on her lips. Grace moved it but whispered, "It's still not safe.
We don't know where that other man is, baby." She listened.

No sound but the rain on the leaves.

And when they didn't find them back at the farm, they
might come back and begin to search the woods again.

"I'm going down to look around. You stay here and wait
until I come back for you."

Frankie was violently shaking her head.

"Yes," Grace said firmly. "You can't help. You might hin-
der. Now, stay here and be quiet." She was already climbing
down the tree. "It shouldn't take long."

She heard a stifled sob, but Frankie wasn't trying to follow her, she realized with relief.

She moved quietly through the brush.

As quietly as she could, pushing through this wet brush

and mud sucking at her shoes, she thought bitterly. But if the missing Locke heard her, she should be able to hear him.

She stopped. Listened. Moved on.

Two minutes later she saw him.

A small man lying on the ground, half-pushed beneath a bush. His eyes were open and the rain was falling on a face twisted in a death rictus.

Locke?

She could only guess at his identity. She could make no guess on who had taken him out and destroyed that car.

Or maybe she could.

Robert had promised her he was on his way.

So grab the chance he'd given her and get Frankie away from the farm.

Where?

Baker's Horse Farm was five miles from here. She'd follow the woods until she was a few miles from the farm and then hit the road. She could hide in the barn at Baker's place until she could contact Robert.

She turned and ran back toward the blind.

She caught glimpses of the burning car on the road as she and Frankie ran through the woods. No sign of the bastards who had driven it.

"Mom." Frankie's breath was coming in gasps. "Why?"

Why had her life been turned upside down? Why had she been forced to witness her mother killing another human being? Why was she being hunted like an animal?

"I'll talk to you later— I can't— I'm sorry, baby. I'll try to make it right." They had reached the curve of the road that couldn't be seen from the farm. Grace glanced both ways. No one. "Come on. We can travel quicker on the road. We have to move fast and—"

Headlights were suddenly bearing down on them.

She reached for her gun and pushed Frankie to the side

of the road. Grace followed her, fell flat, and lifted the gun, trying to see past the glare of lights to get a good shot.

The car was stopping. "It's okay, Grace."

She froze. She couldn't see the driver, but God help her, she knew that voice.

Kilmer.

"Get in. I'll make sure you're safe now."

She closed her eyes. Get over the shock. She'd always known it would happen. "The hell you will." She opened her eyes to see him kneeling beside her. The headlights were behind him and she couldn't make out anything but an outline. She didn't need to see him; she knew every line of his body, every feature of his face. "Your fault. This is all your fault, isn't it?"

"Get in the car. I have to get you out of here." He turned to Frankie. "Hello, Frankie. I'm Jake Kilmer. I'm here to help you, and I promise no one will hurt you as long as I'm here."

Frankie shrank closer to Grace.

Kilmer turned back to Grace. "Are you going to let her stay there in the mud or are you going to let me take care of her? I'm not the threat here."

No, he wasn't. Not the immediate threat. But Kilmer was more dangerous than—

Kilmer stood up. "I'm going to get back in the car. I'll wait two minutes and then I'm leaving. Make up your mind."

He'd do it. Kilmer always did what he said he was going to do. That was one of the things that had drawn her to—

He was getting into the driver's seat.

Two minutes.

Make a decision.

She got to her feet. "Come on, Frankie. Climb in the backseat. He won't hurt us."

"You know him?" Frankie whispered.

"Yes, I know him." She took her daughter's hand and led her toward the car. "I've known him for a long time."

* * *

There's a blanket on the seat, Frankie," Kilmer said as he stepped on the accelerator. "Take off your poncho and wrap up."

"Should I?" Frankie was looking at Grace, who had climbed into the backseat with her.

Grace nodded. "You're sopping wet." She reached for the blanket and wrapped it around her. "We have to get you dry, honey." She turned to Kilmer. "Take us to town and drop us off at a motel."

"I'll take you to town." He glanced at her. "I'm not sure any motel would take you in. You look like you've been buried in a mudslide for a month."

"Then you can check me in before you leave us." She was reaching for her phone. "I don't need you for anything else."

"You're calling Robert Blockman?"

No time to wonder how he knew about Robert. "I have to make sure he's all right. He was back at the farmhouse and I don't know what kind of spot—"

"He wasn't at the farm."

She looked at him. "How do you—" She stopped. "You blew up that car."

"It was the easiest way to draw them away from you. They weren't very woods-savvy, but I wasn't sure that they wouldn't stumble across you. I took one of them out in the woods, but there wasn't time to stalk down the other two when you and Frankie were so close. So I drew them back to the farm."

"Then I'll have to warn Robert that they're still there. He was on his way to—" She stopped again as she saw Kilmer shaking his head. "Has something happened to Robert?"

"Not that I know about. But I resolved the problem at the farm before I came after you."

Resolved the problem. She'd heard Kilmer say that so many times before. "You're sure?"

"You know I'm always sure." He smiled. "You don't have to worry about your watchdog."

"Yes, I do." She dialed Robert's number. "If he didn't get to the farm, I should have heard from him. He was going to try to find Charlie."

She got Robert's voice mail. She hung up without leaving a message. "He's not answering." She turned to him. "Tell me what's happening, dammit."

"Later." He glanced at Frankie, who was bent over drying her hair. "I think she's had enough for one night. You don't want to worry her any more than she is already."

Frankie's head lifted and she glared at Kilmer. "That's pretty stupid. How can I help worrying about Charlie? And Mom's worried too."

Kilmer blinked. "Sorry if I treated you disrespectfully. I obviously didn't realize who I was dealing with." He paused. "I'm concerned about your friend Charlie too. I know you're probably scared and confused, and I believe I'll let your mother discuss the matter with you. It's difficult to give anyone a clear picture unless they have a background in the problem." He glanced at Grace. "Does she?"

"No."

"I didn't think so." He gazed gravely at Frankie. "I'm sure your mother will rectify that omission as soon as she can. And you'll trust her and know that it's the truth. Okay?"

He was talking to Frankie as if she was an adult, Grace thought. It was the right way to handle her. But then, Kilmer was very smart about people.

Frankie was nodding slowly. "Okay." She curled up on the seat and wrapped the blanket around her again. Her face was pale and her hand clutching the blanket was shaking. She had been through a nightmare tonight and Grace wanted desperately to hold her, rock her. Not now. Not until she was sure they were somewhere safe. Frankie was holding on to her composure by a thread. One touch might break her.

"Smart kid." Kilmer's gaze was on Grace's face in the rearview mirror. "She'll deal with it."

"How do you know? You don't know anything about her." She crossed her arms over her chest. It was weird to be so cold on this hot August night. She hadn't been chilled before, but now that the adrenaline was subsiding, she was shaking as badly as Frankie. "Turn on the heater."

"It's on," Kilmer said. "You'll feel it soon. I thought you'd have your usual reaction. Just relax and let the— Shit!" His brakes screeched as he stopped on the side of the road beside the river. "Stay here." He jumped out of the car and was running down the incline toward the riverbank. "I think I caught sight of a truck down there in the water. Do what I say. You don't want to leave Frankie alone."

But Frankie was already out of the car.

Grace caught her before she could follow Kilmer down the incline. "No, Frankie. We've got to stay here."

"Charlie has a truck." Frankie was fighting to get free. "It could be him. We've got to help him. It's in the water."

"Kilmer will tell us if we can help." Grace was in an agony of frustration as her gaze followed Frankie's. The river water was up to the windows of the cab and she could see very little else through the rain. It might not be Charlie's truck.

Hell, who else could it be on this stretch of road? She wanted to be down *there.* But there was no way she could have Frankie go with her if it was Charlie's truck. She put her arm around her daughter's shoulders. "It's better if we stay here. If Charlie's there, Kilmer will get him out."

"He's a stranger. You don't even like him. I can tell."

"But he's very good in emergencies. If I was in that truck, there's no one I'd rather have go after me than Kilmer."

"Is that the truth?"

"That's the truth. Now let's get closer so that we can see if there's anything we can—"

Kilmer was coming up the bank, half-leading, half-carrying someone.

She stiffened, her heart jumping with hope. Charlie?

"Charlie!" Frankie was running toward them. "I was so scared. What—"

"Easy, Frankie." It was Robert, not Charlie, who was being helped up the bank. He was soaking wet and dragging his left leg. "Be careful, this muddy bank is slippery."

She skidded to a stop. "Robert? I thought it was—"

"No." Robert met Grace's eyes. "God, I'm sorry. I dove in and managed to get him out of the cab, but when I got him to the bank, I found out it was—" He shrugged helplessly. "I'm sorry, Grace."

"No! Don't you tell me that." She was running past him down the incline.

Not Charlie.

He was wrong.

Not Charlie.

He was lying on the bank. So still.

Too still.

Grace fell to her knees beside him.

Don't give up. Drowning victims sometimes could be brought back.

She felt for his pulse.

Nothing.

She bent over him to give him mouth-to-mouth.

"It's no use, Grace." Kilmer was standing beside her. "He's gone."

"Shut up. Drowning victims can be—"

"He didn't drown. Look closer."

How was she supposed to look closer when she couldn't see through the tears brimming from her eyes and running down her cheeks? "He . . . was in . . . the river."

"Look closer."

She wiped her eyes with the back of her hand. She saw the hole in Charlie's temple.

She bent over double as the pain jagged through her. "No. It didn't happen. Not to Charlie. It's not fair. He was—"

"Shh." Kilmer was kneeling beside her. "I know." He pulled her into his arms. "God, I wish—"

"Let me go." She pulled away from him. "You don't know. You never met him."

"I know your pain. I'm feeling it, dammit." He stood up. "But you won't believe me right now." He looked down at her. "I'll leave you alone with him for a few minutes, but you'd better get back to the car. Frankie's pretty upset. I left Blockman with her, but she needs you."

He didn't wait for an answer but started up the incline.

Yes, Frankie would need her. Frankie loved Charlie. Frankie wouldn't understand the death of a loved one.

Neither did Grace. Not this loved one . . .

She reached out and gently pushed back the damp hair that was clinging to Charlie's forehead. He was always very neat about his hair. She had often teased him about how much he combed—

The tears were coming again. Try to stop them. Frankie needed her.

Jesus, Charlie . . .

3

Frankie tore away from Robert and hurled herself into Grace's arms when she opened the car door. Tears were running down her cheeks. "They wouldn't let me go. Tell them I have to go see Charlie."

"No, baby." Grace hugged her close and buried her face in her daughter's hair. "You can't see Charlie right now." And never again. But how to say those words?

"You're crying." Frankie pushed her away and looked at her face. She reached out with a tentative hand and touched Grace's cheek. "Why?"

She drew a shaky breath. "Why are *you* crying?"

"Because I'm scared and they wouldn't let me go down—"

"And I'm crying because they did let me go to Charlie." She cupped her hands around Frankie's face. "And I knew I had to tell you something terrible."

"Terrible," Frankie whispered. "About Charlie?"

"He's gone, baby." Her voice broke and she had to stop. Get through it. She tried again. "Charlie's not going to be with us any longer."

"Dead. You mean he's dead."

She nodded jerkily. "That's what I mean."

Frankie stared at her in disbelief.

"It's true, Frankie."

"No." Frankie buried her face in Grace's chest, her little body convulsed with sobs. "No. No. No."

"Get into the car with her," Kilmer said as he opened the driver's door. "I'll drive you to that motel and get you settled."

"Maybe I should have told her, Grace," Robert said as he moved over on the seat. "I thought you'd want to do it yourself."

"You were right." She sat down and pulled Frankie closer in her arms. She rocked her back and forth in an agony of sympathy. "It was my job. Shh, baby, I know none of this makes sense and it hurts. It hurts. . . . But I'm here and it will get better. I promise it will get better."

"Charlie . . ."

Just let her mourn and hope the tears would bring some sort of closure. She didn't know what else to do. God, she felt helpless.

And in pain. The world seemed full of pain.

Pain for Frankie, pain for herself. Pain and regret that Charlie's life had been ended so brutally.

"I'm sorry." Frankie was looking up at her, the tears still running down her cheeks. "You're hurting too. Am I making it worse for you?"

Jesus, who could have expected Frankie to think of anyone else at a time like this? Grace shook her head. "You're making it easier. Sharing always makes it easier." She pressed Frankie's head back on her shoulder. "We'll get through it together. Just like we always do."

"Is the Holiday Inn okay?" Kilmer asked as he turned the car and drove back onto the road.

"Yes, it doesn't matter."

"You could stay at my place," Robert said.

Grace shook her head. "Thanks, maybe later." She leaned back in the seat. "Not tonight."

"You're afraid my apartment might not be—" He looked at Frankie. "Maybe you're right. I'll check in next door."

"I'll take care of it, Blockman," Kilmer said.

Robert shook his head. "You don't stay anywhere near her. Not until I do some checking with Washington."

Kilmer shrugged and didn't pursue it.

But he wouldn't let Robert stop him from doing anything he wanted to do, Grace knew. He would just go around the corner of the obstacle and slip in another way. Kilmer was relentless.

"It's okay, Grace." Kilmer was gazing at her in the rearview mirror. "I'm not going to make trouble for you."

"You bet you're not." Her arm tightened around Frankie. "I have only one thing to ask right now. Is Frankie in any immediate danger?"

He shook his head. "We have a few days."

She breathed a sigh of relief. If Kilmer said it was safe, it was safe. "Good. But you're not going anywhere until I talk to you."

He nodded. "Agreed." He looked at Frankie. "After you get her through this."

Yes, after she got her through this horror of a night she would deal with him.

Kilmer's hands tightened on the steering wheel as he watched Blockman usher Grace and Frankie into the lobby of the motel.

Christ, he wanted to go with them.

It didn't matter what he wanted. It would be the worst possible move to crowd Grace now when she was in the throes of grief and anxiety. Let her come to terms with Charlie's death before he piled more stress on her.

He dialed Donavan's number. "Any news?"

"Other than Marvot's people buzzing around like hornets ready to sting? No. How is it there?"

"Shit. But Grace and Frankie are still okay." He paused.

"Kersoff's boys found her. They work strictly on the bounty, so I figure I have a day or two before someone else comes after her. But they will come. There has to be a leak."

"You told me that the Company buried her records."

"If there are enough people looking, then the chance of an information buy goes up astronomically." He paused. "I have to get her out of here. It's not going to be easy."

"I'd think she'd want to get out."

"Not with me. Never with me. But I can't give her a choice if she won't see reason."

"Grace is smart. She's not going to risk that little girl."

"But which way will she choose to save her?" Kilmer stared at the entrance through which Grace had disappeared. "In her eyes, behind every door there's a tiger. And I'm the tiger who savaged her before. Keep me posted." He hung up the phone. He should check in and get a few hours' sleep. Blockman was with her and they should be safe. Blockman impressed him as being efficient, and he clearly cared for Grace and Frankie.

Screw it. He'd stay here and keep watch. He made a habit of trusting only his own people, and Blockman was a Company man. He could pull in Cam Dillon, the only one of his men he'd brought to town, but he'd planned on sending him to the farm to keep an eye on things there. The Company would probably rush in a crew to clean up things, but, if not, Dillon would take care of it.

No, he'd stay here himself and make sure Grace and Frankie stayed safe.

It was about time he stepped up to the plate, he thought grimly.

Grace quietly swung the adjoining door almost shut, but left it cracked so that she could hear Frankie if she stirred.

"Is she asleep?" Robert asked.

She nodded wearily. "I thought it would take longer.

She probably went to sleep because she couldn't stand being awake. Escape. You were limping. Is your leg all right?"

He nodded. "I twisted it when I was trying to get Charlie out of the truck."

She flinched. "What did you do about him? Did you call the sheriff?"

"No, I had some of our boys come down from Birmingham to take care of him, along with the bodies you and Kilmer left at the farm. The site's probably clean as a whistle now. Washington thought it best."

"I don't care what happens to the bodies of those other bastards. Probably one of them killed Charlie. But I do care about Charlie's remains. Why did they include Charlie in the cleanup? Because they don't want anyone to know he was murdered? Erase and cover?" Her hands clenched. "Charlie's not just going to disappear. He lived his whole life in this community. He had friends here. He would have liked to have them say good-bye."

"Hold it, he's not just going to disappear. He'll be listed as drowned in the river, and the CIA will provide suitable witnesses to state they saw the body—without the bullet wound. After that, we'll move quickly to obey the instructions in Charlie's will. He wanted to be cremated and have his ashes spread over the hills on his property. We'll just do what he asked and then have a memorial service."

"How convenient for the CIA. How do you know he wanted to be cremated?"

"For God's sake, Grace. I liked that old guy. I wouldn't lie to you."

"How do you know what was in his will?" she asked again.

"Because I was a witness when he changed it three years ago," Robert said gruffly. "He trusted me, even if you don't. Do you want to call his lawyer?"

Robert was obviously hurt, and for the first time she remembered that Charlie had been Robert's friend too. She shook her head. "No, I'm sorry. But you work for the Company, and they've been known to arrange matters to suit themselves."

"Not this time. Anyway, he asked me to take care of his arrangements and make it easy for you and Frankie."

"You can't do that." The tears were stinging her eyes again. "They killed him, Robert. He wasn't involved in this at all. He was in the way and they killed him. That's no reason for a man to die."

"No, it's not." He paused. "What are you going to do now, Grace?"

"I don't know. It's too soon. I always made plans for different scenarios, but I never planned on this happening to Charlie. Or maybe I blocked it out because I couldn't bear thinking I'd be responsible for him dying."

"You're not responsible."

"The hell I'm not."

"Because he owned the farm you worked at? You couldn't live in a vacuum. Your life had to touch someone. And in this case it touched and enriched Charlie more than you knew. These last years were probably the best ones of his life."

She shook her head.

"Grace. I know what I'm talking about." He paused. "He left the horse farm to Frankie and appointed you as guardian."

She stiffened. "What?"

"He loved that little girl. He loved you. He didn't have any close family, but he thought of you as that family."

"Oh, shit." The tears that had brimmed were running down her cheeks. "We loved him too, Robert. What the hell are we going to do without him?"

"What you always tell Frankie after a fall. Get up and get back on the horse." He smiled faintly. "And when you're more yourself, you're going to hate me telling you something you know anyway."

She shook her head. "My head's messed up right now. I'm grateful for any help I can get."

"Is there anything else I can do for you?"

She tried to think. "Have a rental car waiting for me tomorrow morning. I left my car at the farm."

"I'll take you anywhere you want to go."

"Just get me the car." She smiled without mirth. "Don't worry. I'm not going to run right now. Kilmer said I had a little time."

"Good." He didn't speak for a minute. "Because when I called Washington, Les North told me he's bringing his superior, Bill Crane, down here to talk to you." He glanced at his wrist. "It's three-forty A.M. now. He should be here by noon."

"No."

"You can tell him that. I don't have anything to say about it. I'm very low on the totem pole."

"Let him talk to Kilmer."

"I'm sure they're very eager to do that. North perked up when I mentioned Kilmer's name. Would you care to tell me how he's involved in this? I'm really tired of acting as bodyguard without knowing who I'm guarding you against. This 'need to know' basis is bull."

She rubbed her temple. "Not now."

"But you don't feel threatened by Kilmer?"

She did feel threatened. The moment she had seen him again, every instinct had started vibrating like a fire alarm. "No, I'm not afraid of him." It wasn't exactly what Robert had asked but it was all she would allow herself to admit. "Where is he?"

He shrugged. "After he dropped us at the lobby, I guess he took off." He paused. "When I told North that Kilmer had taken out those three bastards at the farm, he said he wasn't surprised. Is Kilmer really that good, Grace?"

"Yes." She turned and gently opened the adjoining door. "He's very, very good. Good night, Robert."

A moment later Grace was staring down at Frankie. Still sleeping, thank heaven. Her face was swollen from weeping and her tousled curls were a silky mop on the pillow. She had been too exhausted and broken to ask questions when Grace was putting her to bed, but they would come when she woke.

And Grace had to be ready for them.

She sat down in the chair by the bed. She wasn't ready. But then, she'd never be ready. She had to decide what facts to tell and what to leave for another time when Frankie was more able to accept them.

It was going to be a long night.

We'll have to get a rental car from here. I've already had it taken care of," Les North told Crane as they strode through the airport terminal in Birmingham. "Tallanville has no air service. It's just a small Southern town, a dot on the map. That's why we steered Grace Archer there eight years ago."

"Well, evidently someone found that dot," Crane said grimly. "Why wasn't I informed of this situation?"

"After Congress tied his hands, your predecessor, Jim Foster, was hoping it would just go away. Marvot had a few senators in his pocket and he'd manipulated several lobbyists to persuade more members of the House to come down on us like a ton of bricks," North said as they exited the terminal and headed for the rental-car parking lot. "Foster wasn't much for initiative." He added with no expression, "I'm sure you would never have let it slide."

"You're damn right I wouldn't. I would have pushed ahead and brought everything out into the open. They love to blame the agency for their own waffling. That's the only way to keep our butts from getting spanked by those politicians." He got into the passenger seat of the Buick North indicated. "I'm a firm believer in Murphy's Law. Something was bound to happen if the situation wasn't resolved." He opened his briefcase and pulled out the dossier he'd had his assistant dredge out of the files. "Archer should have been forced to work with us and not allowed to opt out."

"That's easy to say. And how were we supposed to do that?"

"Threaten to take away her protection."

"And lose any hope of having her assistance. She'd already lost a hell of a lot and was pretty bitter."

"It's astonishing how bitterness can fade away when you put their life on the line."

What a son of a bitch, North thought. "Do I have to remind you that she was working with us, Crane?"

"According to her dossier there was some doubt about that. Her father was a double agent and she worked hand in glove with him." He was scanning the dossier. "Born in Los Angeles, California, to Jean Dankel and Martin Stiller. Mother died when she was three, and her father pulled up roots and went to Europe and took the child with him. He moved in and out of several criminal enterprises and got his hands very dirty indeed. He traveled around Europe and Africa doing gunrunning and whatever other scam he could promote." He shook his head. "He took the kid with him wherever he went, and it's a wonder she lived to grow up. At one point they were in Rwanda and she was shot by the rebels and left for dead. The Red Cross worker who found her tried to take her away from her father, but Grace refused and ran away when she got the chance."

North nodded. "Martin Stiller was a complete charmer and he evidently loved her and was good to her." He added sarcastically, "Not good enough to give her up and send her to live with her maternal grandfather in Melbourne, Australia. She spent her summers with him on his horse farm, but every fall Stiller was there, picking her up and taking her back to whatever hellhole he was living in at the time."

"And how did he come to our attention?"

"He came to us and peddled us some information about Hussein. It turned out to be legitimate and we used him for the next few years. We suspected he was double-dealing but we couldn't prove it. So we were just careful what information we gave him."

"And the woman?"

"She wasn't much more than a kid at the time. Agent Rader was the contact with Martin Stiller, and he said Stiller's daughter was a pleasant enough kid. She took correspondence courses and was bright enough to be accepted at the Sorbonne."

Crane was still scanning the dossier. "No criminal background on her. We accepted her for agent training when she was twenty-three years old." He glanced up. "With a background like that, why the hell was she hired?"

"We justified it on a special-case basis. She spoke eight languages fluently, she was bright, psychologically sound, and seemed genuinely patriotic. She also had one valuable qualification we needed at the time. She was amazingly good with horses from the years spent with her grandfather. We needed her for one specific job and we figured we could get rid of her later if she didn't work out." He paused. "She did work out. Her marks on the initial training were some of the highest ever posted. But we needed to mature her fast for this job. So we sent her to Kilmer."

"My assistant couldn't find a dossier on this Kilmer." He frowned. "But I found one of the old fogies in the office who'd heard of him. He was very vague."

Old fogy? Jesus, North was only fifty and had just a few gray hairs. But he was also probably an old fogy to Crane, who was in his thirties and sleek and tanned as a tennis pro. He tried to keep the irritation out of his voice. "Kilmer was a very valuable asset to the CIA, and everything he did was top secret. Some of his missions would have been considered questionable to the administration, and Foster decided that if there was no record of him, there'd be no leaks. The people who needed to know knew who he was and how he could be contacted."

"That's absurd. Foster must have been an idiot. It's no

wonder the agency was in such chaos before the shake-up. Operating like that could cause mass confusion."

"Oh, I believe we managed to keep confusion to a minimum." He added, "And Kilmer didn't end up dead in the water."

"Who is this Kilmer? The agent who knew about him spoke of him as if he was some freakin' legend."

"A legend?" North repeated as he drove out of the parking lot. "Yeah, I guess that's as good a description as any."

"Legends are fairy tales. Talk to me."

He shrugged. "I'll tell you what I know. He was born in Munich, Germany. His father was a colonel in the U.S. Army; his mother was a translator. His parents were divorced when he was ten, and his father got custody. He believed in the iron hand and raised Kilmer in that school. He went to West Point and did well but quit when he was in his third year. He was a brilliant strategist and his teachers were sorry to see him go. He batted around the world for a while and invariably ended up in a guerrilla unit of some sort wherever he was. He finally formed his own military unit and hired himself out for special jobs. He earned a fine reputation. Years after he formed his team we hired him for a number of tricky missions and found him invaluable."

"Until the Marvot job."

North nodded. "Until the Marvot job."

Wake up, baby." Grace shook Frankie gently. "It's time to get stirring."

"It's too early," Frankie said drowsily. "Ten more minutes, Mom. I'll do my—" Her lids flew open. "Charlie!" Her eyes filled with tears. "Charlie . . ."

Grace nodded. "It's true. There's nothing either one of us can do to change it." She wiped her own eyes. "I wish there was. But we have to go on, Frankie." She tossed the covers aside. "Go wash up and brush your teeth. There's a change of clothes for you in my knapsack. We have to get going."

Frankie gazed at her in bewilderment. "Where are we going?"

"Back to the farm. It's almost ten now. We have livestock to feed and water. Charlie wouldn't want them to suffer, would he?"

Frankie shook her head. "I forgot about them."

"Charlie wouldn't forget. We have to do what he would have wanted." She brushed her lips across Frankie's nose. "I know you want to ask questions, to talk, and we will. But there are chores to do first."

Frankie nodded. "Chores. Darling." She headed for the bathroom, and her movements held a hint of purpose. "I won't be long, Mom."

"I know you won't. We'll grab a muffin downstairs in the coffee shop and be on our way."

The door slammed behind Frankie, and Grace drew a breath of relief. So far, so good. If she could keep Frankie busy, it wouldn't heal the pain but it would keep her from remembering every single moment. It was the same remedy she should prescribe for herself. But there was no question that she was going to be busy. She was being sucked back into that horror she thought she'd escaped nine years ago. But she'd not really thought it was over. Why else had she prepared, packed the knapsack, scouted out those woods? She'd known it wasn't finished.

She sat down in the chair to wait for Frankie to come out of the bathroom.

It's . . . different." Frankie's eyes were fixed on the stable. "I keep expecting to see Charlie walking out of the barn or the stable and teasing me because I got up late."

"Me too." She got out of the car. "But he's not going to be doing that, baby. So we have to get used to it. Why don't you run and start your chores? I have to go in and do a few things inside the house."

Frankie's gaze shifted to her face. "What things? Something to do with Charlie?"

"Partly. I have to gather all his important papers together and send them to his lawyer."

"And what else?"

"I have to pack our clothes."

Frankie was silent a moment. "That's right; we won't be able to live here anymore. This was Charlie's place. I'm going to miss it."

"We'll come back. Charlie would want us to come back."

Frankie was shaking her head.

"Frankie, listen to me. Things are going to change for a while, but I promise you that you'll still have this place and the animals. Do you believe me?"

Frankie nodded. "You don't lie to me." She headed for the stable. "I've got to go see Darling. He's smart, but he won't understand either."

Either. Frankie didn't understand, but she was trusting Grace to make things right. She couldn't disappoint her. "I'll be there in an hour and we'll start exercising the horses."

Frankie lifted her hand in acknowledgment before disappearing into the stable.

Grace stared after her for a moment before turning and going up the front steps. She'd promised her she'd be there in an hour, and it was going to be tight. But she didn't want Frankie to be alone any longer than she had to be.

"Grace."

She stiffened and turned to face Kilmer, who was walking down the road toward the house. "I don't want you here."

"But you need me."

"The hell I do."

"Then Frankie needs me." He'd reached the porch.

"You can be as independent as you like, but you won't jeopardize Frankie."

"Don't you tell me how to take care of my daughter." Her hands clenched into fists at her sides. Christ, he was just the same. In character and appearance. He must be in his late thirties now, but the years had been kind to him. Tall, lean—deceptively lean, she knew, because no one was more aware than she of the strength and stamina that lay behind that slenderness. But it was his face that she had found so riveting nine years ago. His features weren't actually good-looking. His dark eyes were deep-set, his cheekbones high, his lips thin, tight. It was his expression that she had always found fascinating. Or lack of it. There was a quietness, a wariness, a containment that had been a challenge from the moment she had first seen him.

"I wouldn't presume." He smiled. "Not when you've done such an excellent job. She's quite wonderful, Grace."

"Yes, she is."

"I'm only suggesting that you take advantage of my help in getting her out of this predicament. After all, it's your right to make a few demands on me."

"She's not in any predicament I can't get her out of. And I've no intention of making any demands. I don't want you involved in her life."

"Then I'll have to insist." His voice was soft but there was a thread of hardness running through it. "I've left you alone as long as I could because it was safer for both of you. But the situation has changed. I have to step in."

"Insist all you please. You've no right to—"

"I'm Frankie's father. That gives me a hell of a lot of rights."

The words struck her like a slap in the face. "You don't know that. And I'll swear in any court that you're not her father."

"DNA, Grace. The magic of DNA." His gaze narrowed on her face. "And the timing is right. I don't think you'd be capable of taking another lover and conceiving in the short

44

time between the time you left me and the time she was born."

"You're *not* taking her away from me."

"That's not my intention." He paused. "Look, I promise that I won't try to take her away. I won't even tell her that I'm her father. I only want to make sure you're both safe."

"Go to hell." She turned on her heel and opened the front door. "We don't need you. We have Robert and the CIA to protect us."

"And they'll protect you as long as you're useful. But you're soon going to prove an encumbrance."

"Why?"

"Because I've broken my deal with them." He made an impatient gesture. "Look, the important thing is that Marvot's turned his dogs loose. He's put a five-million-dollar bounty on your head. And a three-million-dollar bounty on Frankie."

"What?" she whispered.

"Dead or alive on Frankie. He prefers you alive because you could prove valuable, but he doesn't care about Frankie."

She shook her head in disbelief. "No."

"Yes. You know he's been looking for you since the raid. But when I came back on the scene and became a threat, he decided to pull out all the stops. He put the word out a month ago, and every bounty hunter and cheap hood in Europe and the U.S. is scrambling to find you. Kersoff must have paid off someone at the CIA and hit the jackpot. Donavan got word through one of his contacts that Kersoff had gotten lucky and was on his way to you." His lips tightened. "I decided it was time to check out Tallanville."

"Three million dollars on Frankie." The horror of it was overpowering. "A little girl . . ."

"You know that wouldn't make a difference to Marvot. You haven't been away from the action that long."

"Long enough." She shuddered. "Why?"

"I stole something away from him that he valued. He

knew it was only the opening foray and wanted to punish me. You know Marvot. He believes in a clean sweep. The Mafia has nothing on him."

"Frankie . . ."

"I know it sucks. I didn't know he'd find you or her," he said roughly. "The Company was supposed to be protecting you. They screwed up."

"And it's not your fault," she said sarcastically.

"I didn't say that. I take the full blame. I'm just giving you my reasons for thinking it wouldn't affect you. I was wrong and I have to correct it."

"Tell that to Charlie. Correct that, Kilmer."

"I can't." He paused. "But I can keep you both alive if you'll let me." He held her gaze. "And you know I'm your best bet, Grace. You may believe I'm a son of a bitch, but nobody's better than me at what I do."

She shook her head and opened the door.

"Don't be scared if you run into Dillon inside," Kilmer said.

She froze. "Dillon?"

"You've never met Cam Dillon, but he's very efficient. I had him put a photo of 'the Pair' in Blockman's truck while I hurried on here."

"Why? How melodramatic. Wouldn't it have been simpler to just have Dillon talk to him?"

"No, there wasn't time and I knew Blockman would contact North when his truck was broken into. Orders from headquarters are quicker than long, drawn-out explanations. Anyway, Dillon's been watching this place since last night, and when I saw you take off in this direction, I told him to start packing for you."

"What?"

"You don't have much time and you won't want to spare the time from Frankie. I told him to pack up your and Frankie's things. You'll have to grab Charlie's documents and any mementos. Dillon wouldn't be able to decide what you'd value. He should be almost finished by now. If you want him to do anything else, just tell him." He paused. "He's only obeying orders, Grace. Go easy on him." He turned away. "I called your neighbor, Rusty Baker, this morning and arranged for him to send two of his hands from his horse farm to take care of your horses and keep this place clean. They'll start tomorrow."

She started to open her lips to speak, but he was already walking away from her.

He glanced back. "Admit it, that's what you'd do. That's what would make Frankie happiest when she knows she has to leave here."

It was what Grace would have done, what she'd been considering doing since she'd realized they couldn't stay. He'd just beaten her to the punch. "Perhaps."

He smiled faintly. "You know it. I'll stick around and talk to you later. Consider what's best for Frankie. Three million dollars is a lot of money, and there are a lot of money-hungry bastards out there. You need me, Grace." He strode toward the paddock.

She didn't need him, she thought as she went into the house. She didn't want him in her life. He'd brought her nothing but trouble in the past, and now he'd brought her another tragedy. The CIA would relocate her and protect her. They owed her big-time and they wouldn't let Marvot kill her.

Three million dollars.

But, if there was a leak at Langley that had led those bounty hunters here, then who was to say it wouldn't happen again?

If North knew there was a leak, then he'd plug it. She had to—

"You're Ms. Archer?" A tall, sandy-haired man was coming down the stairs. "I'm Cam Dillon. Glad to meet you. I packed a pretty wide selection of clothing for you and your daughter. The suitcases are in your room." He smiled. "But I didn't know whether to pack your daughter's teddy bear or the *Star Wars* collection. Or both. Kids' favorite toys change from year to year. I don't get to see my son very often, and I'm always behind the eight ball."

"You have a son?"

He nodded. "But I'm divorced. My wife has custody of Bobby." He looked around the living room. "This is a nice place. Homey. And I bet your daughter loves being around the horses."

"Yes, she does." She started up the steps. "I'll finish packing her things. She likes the teddy bear, but she doesn't need to take it. As long as she has her keyboard and books, she'll be fine."

"I can squeeze it in. Her keyboard is already in its case with the suitcases. Anything else I can get from the other rooms in the house?"

"No, it's my job. Kilmer shouldn't have involved you."

"I was glad to help." His smile faded. "I saw the picture of the old man on the piano. I'm sorry we didn't get here in time. Kilmer was hopping mad. He looked like a nice old guy."

"He was more than nice." She had to steady her voice. "Now, if you don't mind, I have things to do. I have to get back to my daughter."

"Sure. I'll be outside on the porch if you need me. Just give a call."

"You don't have to stay."

"Yes, ma'am, I do. Kilmer's orders." He moved toward the door. "And that means I stay."

Her lips twisted. "It seems discipline is on the same level as when I was working with him."

He grimaced. "He cracks a mean whip. But it's worth it. It's a good feeling to know you're the best." He headed for the front door. "I'll put the bags in your car when you finish."

It's a good feeling to know you're the best.

That was how she'd felt when she was working with Kilmer. He was tough, painstakingly thorough, and pulled every bit of talent and skill from those who worked for him.

Yet his team had shone like diamonds when he'd finished training them. You could always count on the man or woman next to you. And you could always count on Kilmer to get them all through. He had never failed them.

Except for the last mission at El Tariq.

Don't think about it. She'd learned from that night and moved on. It had not been easy. For years afterward she'd had moments filled with fury and a desire to murder that son of a bitch Marvot. Yet she'd been forced to put it behind her when she found she was pregnant with Frankie. At first, she couldn't risk her unborn child, and it was even more impossible after Frankie had come into the world. She'd hoped as time went by that she'd be able to forget and live a normal life. It wasn't happening. Kilmer was here, bringing back the past.

And all hell was going to follow.

4

I want to jump the barrier, Mom," Frankie said as she rode Darling back toward where Grace was sitting her mare. "Is that okay?"

Grace searched Frankie's face. "Why?"

"I just do. Okay?"

She nodded her head. "If that's what you want. Be careful."

"He won't toss me." Frankie turned Darling and started around the ring. "I'll be right back and then we'll put him up."

A last good-bye to the horse? No, Grace had an idea it was more than that. Frankie wanted to be in control of something, anything, in this life that had been turned upside down. Grace could understand that feeling. She was feeling the same sense of inadequacy herself. Only pushing a stallion over a barrier wouldn't help her.

"Come on, Darling," she murmured. "Give her what she needs."

No hesitancy this time. Darling soared over the barrier with room to spare and appeared very pleased with himself.

"Good boy."

She watched Frankie ride back toward her. No joy or exultation this time. Just satisfaction and determination.

"Very good, Frankie."

Frankie lifted her shoulders. "Darling's the one who jumped. I just went along for the ride."

"And a very good ride."

Frankie turned Darling toward the stable. "Which one of the wranglers from Baker's Farm will be riding Darling?"

"Who do you want to ride him?"

"That Viennese girl is pretty good. I think her name's Maria. I saw her ride in a show at Compton and she was kind to the horses."

"Then Maria will take care of Darling. I'll see to it." She added gently, "But it's only for a little while, Frankie. You'll be back."

"Yeah." She was looking straight ahead. "But it won't be the same, will it? There won't be Charlie. And I don't know if I'll ever be able to— I can't look at it in the same way. I'll see . . . those men."

Grace felt the anger sear through her. Christ, so much had been taken from Frankie last night. Grace had worked hard to give her a golden childhood and now it was tarnished. "Then you'll have to forget them and think of Charlie. It's what he'd want you to do. It would be your gift to him."

She shook her head doubtfully. "I'll try, Mom." She dismounted and started to lead Darling into the stable. "I'll say good-bye to Darling and be right with you." She looked back over her shoulder. "It may happen again, right? That's why you want to run away."

What should she tell her?

The truth. She wouldn't lie to Frankie. She'd always been honest with her and she wouldn't let that trust be damaged. "It might happen again."

Frankie stopped and turned to face her. "Why?"

Grace had known it would be coming and now it was here. She was almost relieved. "A long time ago I was working for a government agency and I made a very powerful criminal angry with me. I did something he didn't want me to do and I had to hide to keep him from killing me."

"It's like something in the movies," Frankie said.

"Not the G-rated ones you're supposed to be watching." She tried to smile. "I always told Charlie not to let you watch those action movies."

"Can't the police or someone keep him from hurting you?"

"They're trying. There are problems. He's very important."

"I don't understand."

How could she? Grace thought. Bribes and deals and corruption were outside her realm of knowledge. "Sometimes I don't either. But the bottom line is that we have to run."

"But you didn't do anything wrong." Frankie was frowning. "Can't we fight them?"

Three million dollars on Frankie's head.

"No, we can't. But I'll try to work out a way that will keep us from having to run again." She shook her head. "I'm sorry this happened, Frankie. I wish I could have stopped it."

Frankie turned. "Charlie would have wanted you to fight. He was in World War Two, and he said if they hadn't fought those Nazis they would have run all over this country. Even here in Alabama . . ."

Grace watched her lead Darling into the stable. She'd taken it as well as Grace could expect. It was probably not real to her, as that remark about the movies proved. But Charlie's death was real; that terror she'd experienced last night was real. Given time, she'd accept the reality of the story Grace had told her. She dismounted and started to follow Frankie.

"Grace." Robert was coming toward her. "I'll take care of your horse. North and Crane are here. They're in the car outside the paddock. They want to talk to you."

"I don't want to talk to—" She stopped. She had no choice. She had to talk to them. She'd need help to relocate and protection for Frankie. She tossed Robert the reins of her horse. "Frankie will help you. Stay with her until I get back."

He nodded and led the horse into the stable.

She glanced at the blue Buick outside the paddock. No one else had gotten out of the car. They were making her come to them. A psychological move? If it was, it didn't bode well.

She started across the paddock toward the Buick.

Hell, no!" Grace opened the door of the Buick and got out. "You're nuts if you think I'd let you use me or Frankie for your games."

"You'd be quite safe," Crane said. "We'd see that you were protected. We just need to draw Marvot out of his lair, and you may be the ticket."

"And put Frankie at more risk? No way. Find us a place to dig in until Marvot forgets about us."

Crane shook his head. "Unfortunately, we can no longer fund your protection. After all, we gave you eight years."

"And my father gave his life."

"I know nothing about that. It was before my time. My job is to put this business to rest, and I expect your help in doing it."

"By letting you stake us out like a goat for a tiger."

"Or perhaps take a more active role. I understand you might be able to—"

"Screw you."

Crane flushed. "Understand me. Cooperate or you're

on your own. You've had a free ride long enough. I'm leaving for Washington this evening. I'll expect your answer."

She turned to North. "You're not talking. Is Crane speaking for both of you?"

He shrugged. "He's my superior, Ms. Archer."

"And that's my answer?" She slammed the car door. "Get your butts off this farm. That's your answer." She strode away from them toward the paddock.

"You were tough on her," North said. "She can't be pushed, sir."

"Everyone can be pushed," Crane said. "You just have to press the right buttons. She has a child to protect, and she'll give in eventually. Start the car. Let's get back to town. I want her to see us drive off. The finality will frighten her."

"Don't count on it." North glanced after Grace as he started the car. She was staring straight ahead, and her body language was angry and defiant. She did not look back. "She doesn't look at all frightened."

Bureaucratic bastard.

There was no question Crane had wanted to scare her. How dare he use Frankie's safety as a bargaining chip to get his way. She wanted to strangle him. No, that was too good for him. Roast him over a slow—

"I take it that it didn't go well." Robert was standing in front of the stable. "Crane's pretty much of an asshole."

"You'd better call them and tell them to come back and pick you up," she said curtly. "I told them to get off the farm."

"I drove my own car. I didn't want to be any closer than I had to be to Crane." His lips twisted. "That was fine with him. He doesn't like dealing with us peons."

"He's not in touch with the human race. He wanted to stake me and Frankie out. Frankie!"

"Shit." Robert frowned. "As God is my witness, I didn't know anything about that, Grace. I guess I should have suspected something when North brought him into the picture. But North's not a bad guy. I didn't think he'd go along with—"

"Well, he did," she interrupted. "And you're probably out of an assignment. Do me a favor and say good-bye to Frankie before you leave. She's had enough loss without you disappearing on her."

"I wouldn't do that. And I wouldn't go along with Crane shafting you. You should know better than that. I care about you guys."

A little of her anger faded as she looked at him. This was Robert, her friend. He wasn't to blame for Crane's decisions. "I know," she said. "But you're an agent and you have to go along with them. It's hard for me to forget that."

"Then work on it. Now, how can I help you?"

"I don't know. I'll have to think about it. Where's Frankie?"

"She's still in the stable with Kilmer."

She froze. "What?"

"He came into the stable right after you left and said he'd take over putting up your horse." He made a face. "I made a token protest, but you know I'm really not into working with horses. I knew Frankie would be safe with him and he seemed to know what he was doing."

She nodded. "Yes, he knows horses." But she didn't want Frankie around him, dammit. She knew how magnetic the bastard could be, and she didn't want Frankie influenced.

Robert was studying her expression. "It seemed okay. She is safe, isn't she? I called a buddy in Washington this morning and did a check on Kilmer. There wasn't much on file, but Stolz said he heard rumors Kilmer used to be hot stuff with the agency."

She glanced at him. "Used to be?"

"He severed relations with the CIA eight years ago."

"What?"

"You didn't know?"

"No, I didn't want to know anything about him except that he was out of my life. The CIA took care of that. They gave me a new identity and you." She glanced longingly at the door of the stable. She wanted to go running in there but she had to be more composed before she faced Frankie again. She was still angry with Crane and she didn't want Frankie to sense her urge to jerk her away from Kilmer. She'd stay here with Robert until she was calmer. "What's Kilmer doing now?"

"Search me. You know him pretty well. You guess. What's he qualified to do?"

Anything he wanted to do. She'd never met anyone more capable of manipulating circumstances to suit himself. He was a natural commander and his people were fanatically loyal. "When I met him, he was running a special commando team for the CIA. He specialized in guerrilla raids and complex operations. The CIA sent him in when the situation was too hot for the usual commando teams."

Robert gave a low whistle. "Impressive."

Yes, that's what she'd thought when she had first met Kilmer. His manner was quiet, offhand, but his presence dominated effortlessly. "Occasionally, North would send him an agent he wanted to season."

"And he sent you?"

"He sent me."

"How was it?"

"As heady as drinking straight whiskey. As scary as walking a tightrope over the Grand Canyon. He knew exactly what he was doing and swept us along with him. I was only twenty-three and he was larger than life. I was almost as dazzled as the rest of the team when I was around him."

"But you got over it."

"Oh, I got over it." She couldn't wait any longer. She was getting Frankie away from Kilmer. "I'll go get Frankie." She headed for the stable door. "Stay here and I'll bring her out to say good-bye."

"Don't be in such a hurry. They're going to have to pry me away from the two of you."

"You have a job, Robert. Don't risk it. I understand." She added ruefully over her shoulder, "When I'm not mad as hell."

She heard Frankie's voice as soon as she entered the stable. "Darling is really my favorite. It doesn't seem fair to have favorites, but Charlie gave Darling to me, and Mom says that some horses have a special understanding."

"I'm sure she's right," Kilmer said. "She knows a good deal about horses. He's certainly handsome."

"I like palominos. Darling reminds me of Roy Rogers's horse, Trigger. Did you know that Trigger knew fifty tricks?"

"No. I heard he was smart but that's amazing."

Grace was close enough now to see Kilmer and Frankie in Darling's stall. Frankie's expression was animated as she looked up at Kilmer, and Kilmer was smiling at her. It was a wonder that Kilmer had been able to stir Frankie out of her depression, if only for the moment.

"Frankie."

Frankie nodded as she glanced at Grace. "Just finishing, Mom. I had to help Mr. Kilmer. He didn't know where anything was."

"Jake," he told Frankie. "We can't shovel manure together and still be on formal terms."

She smiled. "I guess not."

"Robert is waiting for you, Frankie," Grace said. "He'd like to say good-bye."

Frankie's face fell. "That's right. We'll have to leave Robert. I didn't think about that."

"He's just as sad as you are, Frankie. It's not forever. Good friends stay good friends."

"Yeah, I guess so." She wiped her hands on the towel draped over the door of the stall. "It's just that everyone seems to be . . . going." She didn't wait for an answer but ran down the aisle toward the door.

Grace gazed after her. "Dammit to hell."

"They're not assigning Blockman to you again?" Kilmer asked. "Can you request him?"

"No."

Kilmer's gaze was narrowed on her face. "Why not?"

She was silent.

"Why not?"

"Because I told North and Crane to go to hell."

"Interesting." He was perfectly still, but she could feel the storm beneath the calm. "May I ask why?"

"Crane wanted to play goat and tiger with me and Frankie as the price for continuing protection. I told him to stuff it."

He was silent. "I believe I may have to pay a visit to Crane at the earliest opportunity." He added, "Though his stupidity may work to my advantage if it drives you toward me. Does it?"

"No."

"Tell me that after you've had time to consider all the consequences." He turned and headed for the door. "I'll leave Dillon here to play night watchman and horse sitter until Baker's people take over in the morning. Are you going back to the motel?"

"For tonight." She gave Darling a final pat and followed him. "After that I'm gone. As soon as I firm up a plan, I'll go to the bank and take out money. You said I had a couple days. Does that still hold?"

"As far as I know. Donavan is keeping his finger on Marvot's pulse at El Tariq and I'll have notice." He paused. "I already have a plan, Grace. And I have a good team to protect you."

"Robert said you weren't with the CIA any longer."

"You know half my people weren't CIA even when you were with me. It wasn't difficult to replace the government agents. And a lot of them chose to stay with me."

She could believe that. Kilmer inspired loyalty without even making the effort. "To do what?"

He shrugged. "To do what I'm hired to do. There's always use for a well-oiled military machine in this world. I've done everything from rescuing kidnapped oil executives in Colombia to ridding the U.S. Army of terrorist snipers in Afghanistan. Nothing much changed when I quit the CIA."

"Then why did you quit?"

He met her gaze. "The same reason you quit. It all went bad."

"And you didn't help."

"I'm not going to justify myself," he said quietly. "I did what I had to do. I'm not a miracle man. I had to make a choice."

"Your choice sucked." She looked away from him. "It might have killed my father."

"It didn't, but there was that possibility. I had to move fast to save the four other men on my team who we had to leave at El Tariq that night. Your father was in Tangiers. I wouldn't have had time to reach him before Marvot could set up a trap."

"And you didn't let me go to him." Her hands clenched into fists at her sides. "You knocked me out and then locked me in that damn cellar. I didn't ask for your help. I didn't need you. I could have reached my father on my own."

"Marvot would have been waiting for you. I sent your father a warning just in case I was wrong. He didn't leave Tangiers. Does that tell you anything?"

"Maybe he didn't get the warning."

"He got it." Kilmer shook his head. "But he didn't need a warning. He knew what had happened at El Tariq."

"He *didn't* know. He was the one who told the CIA about Marvot in the beginning. He got me the job at El Tariq. It wasn't his fault that Marvot was tipped off."

"I've told you before. Your father tipped him off, Grace."

"No, that's a lie. He wouldn't do that. He knew I was there. He loved me."

Kilmer didn't answer.

"He *loved* me," she repeated.

"Maybe he thought he could get you out before the sky fell in. But we were moving very fast toward the end of the mission." He shrugged. "We've gone through this before. You didn't believe me then. You won't believe me now. So let's put it behind us and deal with what's happening. You need me to protect Frankie, and I have the means and the willingness to do it. Let me help you."

She tried to control the anger and sense of betrayal those memories had brought flooding back. She jerkily shook her head. "I can do it myself." She gazed across the stable yard at Frankie and Robert. "I have to get over there. Frankie doesn't look too upset, thank God."

"She's very close to him?"

She started across the yard. "Yes."

"Close to you too?"

She glanced at him over her shoulder. "What?"

"Do you sleep with him?"

She stopped. "That's none of your business."

"I know. It doesn't seem to make any difference."

His tone was quiet, but it was charged with all the intensity she remembered.

Oh, my God, and her body was readying, responding, as if their intimacy had been yesterday instead of nine years ago.

No!

"It won't matter what I feel, Grace," he said. "You'll be totally in control if you decide to trust me to take care of the problem."

She'd never been in control with him. He'd only had to touch her and she'd melt. That sexual attraction had bewildered and frightened her. At first, she'd thought it was just hero worship but it had become like a drug in those following weeks, totally out of control.

It couldn't be the same feeling. She was older now and she had every reason not to feel anything but anger and bitterness toward him.

His smile held a slight element of sadness. "It doesn't

seem to make any difference to you either, does it? Don't feel bad. Hormones have nothing to do with cool logical thinking." He turned away. "I'll be close to your motel tonight. I gave Blockman a card with my cell number to give you. If you need me, call." He strode away from her toward the road.

She was glad he was gone. That moment had shaken her and she didn't want to deal with him right now. She had thought she had put him out of her life but evidently that didn't include physical instincts.

She could handle it. Maybe their affair had ended too abruptly for there to be closure. Some remaining tendrils of emotion were probably natural in situations like this. Maybe the next time she saw him it would be with no sexual tension at all. She had to remember who he was and what he had done and everything would be back to normal.

Normal?

What was normal in this world where sweet guys like Charlie could be killed for no reason?

I like Mr. Kilmer," Frankie said as she settled down in bed that night. "I mean Jake. He told me to call him Jake. I think he's cool. But you don't like him, do you?"

"I used to like him," she said noncommittally. "Why do you think he's cool?"

"He listens. Most people don't really listen to kids. But he does." She yawned. "And I think he's smart. He doesn't say much but he sort of— Is he smart, Mom?"

"Very smart."

"And you worked with him when you were a super-duper spy?"

"I wasn't a super-duper anything. I just did a job." She kissed her forehead. "Are you feeling any better, baby?"

"I don't know. When I was in the barn, I started crying again."

"That's natural. You think you're okay and then something happens and you're crying again."

"You too?"

"Me too. But the important thing is that we did what Charlie would have wanted today. And that we remember him every day with love. And we can do that, can't we?"

"Sure." Frankie reached up to brush Grace's lashes with a gossamer touch. "They're wet." She suddenly buried her head in Grace's breasts. "It hurts me when you hurt. What can I do?"

Grace's throat was tight as she hugged her close. "Love me. And I'll love you. That's the cure for almost everything." She pushed her back down on the pillows. "Now go to sleep."

"Everything's going to be okay, isn't it?" Frankie whispered. "Nothing bad is going to happen to us again?"

Grace nodded. "Nothing will happen to you. I promise I'll keep you safe."

"And you," she insisted.

"And me." She tucked the blanket around her. "I have to keep myself safe so that I can keep you safe. It's a package deal. Good night, baby."

"Good night, Mom."

Grace turned out the bedside light and turned back the sheet on the other bed. She doubted if she could sleep, but she wanted Frankie to have the comfort of someone in the room if she woke in the night. Her daughter had had enough insecurity and terror in the past few days to last her for a lifetime.

Frankie was already asleep. She could hear her steady, deep breathing.

Grace went over to the window and looked down at the parking lot two floors below. What did she expect to see? An elite militia force invading this small town? Perhaps. Marvot could afford an elite force if he could afford that bounty he'd put on their heads.

But no force he could hire would be as good as Kilmer's team.

Her hand clenched on the drape. Her lack of shock at that thought demonstrated that it hadn't come too far out of left field. No matter how she wanted to push his offer of help away, it kept returning. Kilmer was qualified to help Frankie on a scale that no one else could come near. If Grace went off on her own, it would mean being on the run and a million times more vulnerable. She'd scoped dozens of possible bolt-holes, but none of them was as safe as being under Kilmer's wing.

Frankie was murmuring in her sleep. Dreaming?

And would that dream become a nightmare? Grace had promised her she would be safe. Did she have the right to turn down Kilmer when he could guarantee Frankie her best chance?

Yes, blast it, Grace was intelligent and capable, and she didn't want interference from—

Screw it. It was what Frankie needed, not what Grace wanted. Let Kilmer bust his butt protecting Frankie. She deserved everything he could give her.

She reached for her cell phone and dialed Kilmer's number written on the card Robert had given her. She said as soon as he picked up, "I don't have a choice, dammit. She's got to be safe."

"Clarify."

"The answer is yes. But it's going to be on my terms, and if I don't like how you're handling anything, I'm going to bail. Understand?"

"Understood. I'll get cracking. Have her ready to leave by five in the morning."

"Don't run in here like a steamroller. I don't want her scared."

"I'll surround her with all the familiar comfort I can. But you'll be the deciding factor. You're the center of her life. You're the one who'll have to give her confidence in what we're doing."

"You've already made inroads," she said sarcastically. "She thinks you're cool."

He was silent a moment. "Does she?"

"She's a kid and she doesn't know you."

"I'm properly deflated." He paused. "She's extraordinary, Grace. You've done a remarkable job."

"I did my best. She's very special." She added harshly, "And nothing's going to happen to her. So you'd better do a damn good job of planning *and* executing." She hung up.

It was done. She was committed.

She went back over to Frankie's bed and looked down at her. Beautiful. Sleeping, she still had the glowing vulnerability of a much younger child. "We're on our way, baby," she whispered. "It's not what I wanted, but I think it's best for you. Jesus, I hope it's best for you."

5

R eady?" Kilmer asked when Grace opened the
door.

She nodded. "Frankie's in the bathroom. She'll be right
out."

"How's she taking it?"

"Good. She's very resilient. I told her we had to find a
place to go that would be safe, and she accepted it." She
made a face. "I think she's more worried about me than she
is about herself."

"It wouldn't surprise me." Kilmer flipped open his
phone. "Dillon, come up and get the bags. It's a go."

"Did you think I'd back out at the last minute?"

"There was a possibility. You weren't too enthusiastic
about—"

"Hi, Jake." Frankie had come out of the bathroom.

"Hi, Frankie. I was glad to hear you're going with us.
We're going to need your help."

She frowned. "Doing what?"

"Taking care of the horses at the ranch."

Her eyes widened. "Horses? How many?"

"Three. I didn't get the particulars, but I imagine they're going to need plenty of exercise and care."

"Horses always do. Mom didn't tell me we were going to a ranch. Is it your ranch?"

"No, I'm just leasing it for the next few months. I hope by that time you'll be able to go back home."

"Where is it?"

"Outside Jackson, Wyoming. It's supposed to be a nice place."

"Out west. A ranch . . ." Frankie's eyes were shining. "Like Roy Rogers."

He smiled. "But I'm afraid there's no Trigger. If you want a wonder horse, you'll have to train him yourself."

"Can't we take Darling? I've already started to train him."

"Not right now. Maybe later." There was a knock on the door and Kilmer opened it. "Frankie, this is my friend Dillon. He's going with us to the ranch. Will you show him where your bags are?"

"Sure." She led Dillon through the sitting room. "Are you a cowboy?" she asked as she pointed out the bags beside the bed. "You don't look like one."

"I'm a cowboy in training," Dillon said. "Maybe you can give me a few pointers."

"Maybe." She looked doubtful. "But I don't know much about cows. Charlie didn't like cattle. Only horses. Are there any cows, Jake?"

"Not that I know about. We'll have to find out together." He grabbed one of the duffels. "But that will only make it more of an adventure." He looked at Grace. "Okay, so far?"

"We'll see once we get to this ranch. How do we get there?"

"We drive to a private airport outside Birmingham and board a jet to Jackson Hole. We take a rental car to the ranch from there."

"No trail?" she asked.

"No trail," Kilmer said. "You know me better than that."

"I knew you nine years ago."

"I haven't changed." He met and held her gaze. "Not about the important things."

With an effort she pulled her gaze away from his.

He turned back to Frankie. "Go on down to the car with Dillon, Frankie. We'll do the usual check of the drawers and closets and be right behind you."

She looked at Grace. "Okay?"

Grace nodded and Frankie took her overnight case from Dillon. "I'll carry this one. . . ."

Grace picked up her jacket from the couch as Frankie left. "Talk to me. How safe is this place?"

"As safe as I can make it. I'm bringing most of the team to the ranch to protect the two of you. I've buried the paperwork; except for the horses, the ranch is self-sufficient, so there won't be any locals around."

"Why a ranch?"

"I told you I'd make Frankie as comfortable as possible."

Her gaze narrowed on his face. "But there's something else, isn't there?"

His lips turned up at the corners. "You know me too well."

She stiffened. "My God, you're actually going to try for the Pair."

"Not while it will impact you."

"You're crazy. You lost three men at El Tariq nine years ago. Isn't that enough?"

"Too many. Even one would have been too many. That's why I won't give up. They were my men and I didn't get them out in time. You did get out but you've spent years hiding from the bastard, afraid to have a normal life. Any minute he could show up and take everything you've built away from you. Including your life, Frankie's life. I'm not going to have that threat hanging over you any longer." He paused. "I'm not going to let Marvot sit fat and sassy running his little empire. He's going to lose everything and then I'm going to kill him. And I'm going to start with the Pair." The last words were spoken without expression but with absolute conviction.

Marvot dead. A surge of fierce satisfaction exploded through her at the thought.

"You still hate the son of a bitch." Kilmer was studying her expression. "I remember at the time you couldn't decide who you wanted to kill more. Me or Marvot."

"Marvot. By a hair. He killed my father, but you kept me from saving him."

"And I'd do it again. How did you manage to keep yourself from going after Marvot all these years?"

"Frankie." She tried to suppress the emotional turmoil that anger against Marvot had ignited. Nothing had changed. The reason she had run and hidden and let Marvot go his way was still present and valid. "I'm out of it. I won't help you."

His brows lifted. "Who asked you?"

"Crane."

"I'm not Crane. I don't want your help." He gestured for her to precede him. "I just want the two of you safe. I've taken care of business quite well without you all my life, Grace. The Pair will be no different."

"Good." She passed him and walked toward the elevator. "Because the moment I see any sign of you going after the Pair while Frankie is at that ranch will be the moment we're gone."

Robert!" Frankie jumped out of the car and ran across the tarmac to where Robert Blockman stood beside the hangar. She hugged him boisterously. "Why are you here? I thought you—"

"So did I." He picked her up and swung her in a circle. "But then I thought about how much you need me to get you from brown belt to black belt. If I let it go too long, you'll lose all your moves. So I decided to come along."

"Great." She hugged him again and turned to Grace. "Isn't it great, Mom?"

Grace nodded. "We wouldn't want you to lose your moves." She met Robert's gaze over Frankie's head. "But you have a lot more to lose than Frankie. Unless Crane changed his mind?"

Robert shook his head. "I was told to go mind my own business when I tried to talk to him." He smiled down at Frankie. "And since I'd recently received a business offer difficult to refuse, I took his advice." He glanced at Kilmer. "I called Stolz—my contact at the head office at Langley—and he's trying to track down the leak that led Kersoff to Grace."

"Time frame?"

Robert shrugged. "I don't know." He took Frankie's hand. "Let's get on the plane. I brought along a DVD of Sarah Chang's latest concert. I thought you might want to see it."

"I do." Frankie nodded eagerly as she walked beside him toward the plane. "You know, she started young like me. But she actually performed with the New York Philharmonic when she was eight. I don't think I'd like that. It would get in the way. Maybe later . . ."

Grace turned to Kilmer as soon as they were out of earshot. "Why?"

"I promised you a comfort cushion for Frankie. He's part of her life."

"So you lured him away from a government pension?"

"He won't suffer for it, and all I did was dangle the carrot. He's the one who grabbed it. He cares about you and Frankie and he was ready to try something new and different."

"Being on your team will certainly fill that bill," she said dryly. "If you don't get him killed."

"I promise I won't play David to his Uriah," he murmured. "No matter how tempted I am."

"David and Uriah." Her forehead wrinkled in puzzlement. "Who were—"

"Never mind." He was striding toward the plane. "Let's get out of here."

David and Uriah.

Then it came to her. The biblical King David and Uriah, Bathsheba's husband, who had been sent to his death by David because the king had lusted after his wife.

Lust.

No, she wouldn't think about Kilmer's words.

Jesus, but how the devil could she stop thinking about it? It had triggered memory followed by tingling sensuality, as dark accompanied night.

He'd meant her to remember. Subtle son of a bitch. He'd wanted her to know that it wasn't over for him. He'd dropped that reference to the biblical passion that had been all-consuming and then made her associate it with the sexual frenzy that had—

Stop it.

He wasn't David and she wasn't some biblical bimbo who took baths on rooftops. What they'd had together was over.

She just had to make sure it stayed over.

The ranch was the Bar Triple X. The name was emblazoned on the wooden post beside the gate.

"Let me undo the gate." Frankie jumped out of the car. She stopped, her head lifted. "It's cooler here than home." Her gaze shifted to the stark grandeur of the Grand Teton Mountains. "And pretty. Real pretty. But it's different. . . ." She frowned, trying to get it right. "Charlie's place was like a gentle pony, and this is . . . a bucking bronco." She chuckled. "That's it." She opened the gate wide, waited for the car to drive through, closed the gate, and got back into the car. "But different is interesting, isn't it, Mom? And you've broken a lot of bucking broncos. You were going to break that two-year-old, but you—" Her smile faded. "Everything happened."

"I'll do it when we go back." Grace slipped her arm around Frankie. "But you're right, it's different here. We'll just have to see what we can make of it." She turned to Kilmer. "I haven't seen any security."

"They're flying in tonight." He glanced down at Frankie and smiled. "You'll have a lot of cowboys wandering around tomorrow."

She smiled back at him. "But no cows. I didn't see any cows."

"I'd bet a few of those cowboys have never even been on a horse," Dillon said with a grin. "I hope so. I don't want to be the only one." He pulled up in front of the two-story brick house and jumped out of the car. "I'll get the bags. At least I'm good as a pack mule."

"I'll help you." Robert grabbed a duffel and two suitcases and followed Dillon up the steps. "What bedrooms, Kilmer?"

"Frankie and Grace have the first one at the top of the stairs. The others are up for grabs. After you finish, will the two of you check out the stable? Don't forget the hayloft."

"Sure." Robert disappeared into the house.

Frankie got out of the car and ran to stand on the porch. "Pretty," she murmured. "And listen to the wind. It . . . sings."

"Does it?" Kilmer squatted down beside her. "And what's the song?"

"I don't know." She gazed dreamily out at the mountains. "But I like it. . . ." She sat down on the steps. "May I stay out here for a little while, Mom?"

"If you don't wander off." Grace rumpled her curls as she passed her. "Thirty minutes."

"Okay."

"If you like, we'll go take a look at the horses as soon as the stable's checked out," Kilmer offered as he took Frankie's keyboard out of the backseat, where she'd insisted on keeping it, and climbed the porch steps.

Frankie shook her head. "Not now." She leaned against the porch rail, her gaze on the mountains. "I just want to sit out here and listen. . . ."

"By all means," Kilmer said as he held open the door for Grace. "Getting acquainted with the horses can wait."

The decor of the interior of the house was more mellow, fine-hewn craftsman than western, Grace thought. A huge stone fireplace occupied one wall, fronted by a comfortable beige corduroy-covered couch. Several leather easy chairs were scattered about the room, and a splendid Tiffany floor lamp loomed over one of them. "Nice."

"I'm glad you approve." He was heading up the stairs with Frankie's keyboard case. "There are four bedrooms. I've put you and Frankie in the first one."

"You might as well leave the keyboard down here. She's going to want it pretty soon."

He looked back at her. "The wind singing?"

"Maybe." She shrugged. "Or maybe it's about something else. She was talking about needing the piano the night before last, even before we knew about Charlie."

"It's the first time I've seen this side of her." He glanced thoughtfully back at the door. "It's interesting. One minute a horse-crazy kid and the next . . . interesting."

"It's all Frankie. I've tried to make sure one side of her doesn't unbalance the other." She started up the stairs. "For instance, she's not allowed to shirk her chores just because she's toying with a melody."

"Heaven forbid."

She glared at him. "It's important. Yes, she has to be encouraged, but building a strong character is just as vital."

"I'd say she has a damn strong character." He held up his hand. "I'm not criticizing you. You've done an incredible job and I've no right to interfere."

"That's the truth."

He smiled. "But may I say I feel a certain amount of

pride that my share of genes gave you the material to work with?"

"You can say it to me. As long as you don't say it to Frankie." She passed him and continued up the stairs. "Is Donavan coming tomorrow too?"

"No, I have him staking out Marvot. He's the one who tipped me about Kersoff being one of the players who showed up at Marvot's compound. I won't pull him until I need him here."

"And who else was invited by Marvot to try for the bounty?"

"Pierson and Roderick. Those were the big players, but I'm sure Marvot threw the game open to a number of smaller fish too. He wanted to stimulate enough competition to make sure he got what he wanted."

"Bastard."

"Yes. But by making them compete, it turned out lucky for us. No one was going to risk one of the others discovering they'd found you before they'd actually caught you and turned you over to Marvot."

"Or gave him our heads in a basket."

Kilmer nodded. "At any rate, it gave us time to get out, since no one was reporting directly to Marvot." He turned and headed back downstairs with the keyboard. "I'll put this by the couch in the living room. I guess I should have arranged for a piano."

"She's fine with the keyboard." Grace paused at the top of the stairs to look back at him. "You told me the amount of the bounty Marvot put on Frankie and me. What's the price on your head?"

"Enough to set up a small kingdom." He straightened and headed back to the porch. "He's a little irate with me. Imagine that."

A shudder ran through her. Why the hell hadn't he just turned his back on Marvot as she'd done? No, he'd had to dig in and bide his time and risk everything.

But had she really turned her back on Marvot? That

surge of sheer ferocity she'd felt had taken her again by surprise.

Feelings weren't actions.

It was Kilmer's decision to go forward. The only thing she cared about was keeping Frankie safe.

The bedroom Kilmer had indicated had two queen-size beds covered with embroidered floral quilts. The picture window across the room revealed the same breathtaking mountain view that had enthralled Frankie.

She went over to the window and looked down at the paddock. A gray and a chestnut were ambling lazily around the area. Handsome horses. Small bone structure. Arabian blood?

The blue-eyed Pair at El Tariq were white Arabians, she suddenly remembered. Splendid in every physical detail, and those blue eyes made them even more unusual.

And smart. Very smart. She'd never handled smarter or more responsive horses. They'd seemed to sense her every thought, every emotion.

And she'd *known* them. It had been totally exhilarating being with the Pair. At first, it had been impossible to think about them singly. They were always just the Pair to her and everyone else at El Tariq. But toward the last she'd been able to start separating them, make them respond as individual beings. They'd been frisky and high-strung and totally fascinating. Would they still be that way? They were almost ten years old now. . . .

Stop thinking about them.

She'd told Kilmer she wanted nothing to do with the Pair, and she meant it. It was too dangerous and they had already cost her too much.

She turned away from the window and lifted her duffel to the bed and unzipped it. After she'd finished unpacking the bags, she'd take a shower and then go down to the kitchen and see what she could find to fix for Frankie's supper. Her daughter was usually a healthy eater, but during these periods of creating she was a bit abstracted and had to be reminded to eat.

On second thought, she'd unpack one bag but leave the other one packed and ready to go. She trusted Kilmer's efficiency, but not the kindness of circumstances. It was always best to prepare for the worst and hope for the best.

El Tariq, Morocco

We think Kersoff located the woman and child," Brett Hanley said as he came into the sunroom. "Alabama."

Marvot looked up from the game of chess he was playing with his ten-year-old son. "When may we expect them?"

"Well, it's not exactly . . . It wasn't an entirely successful mission."

Marvot moved his piece. "Checkmate." He frowned. "Guillaume, I've always told you to watch your queen. Now, run along and think about what mistakes you've made. This evening I want you to tell me how you could have won this game."

"I'm not sure—" Tears filled Guillaume's eyes. "I'm sorry, Papa."

"Sorry isn't enough." He cupped the boy's cheek with a gentle hand. "Listen, you must concentrate and get better so that I may be proud of you. That's what you want, isn't that so?"

Guillaume nodded.

"And I will be proud. You do better with every game." He hugged the boy and then swatted him on his rump. "Now go do as I told you." He watched the boy run away. "What absurdity are you trying to hand me, Hanley?"

"Kersoff has disappeared."

"Then how do you know he found her? More to the point, how do you know he failed?"

"Kersoff's wife, Isabel, called me an hour ago. She said he'd found the woman and planned on completing the job two nights ago. But she hasn't heard from him since early that evening. I followed up and found there were a woman and a child of the appropriate age living on a small farm in Tallanville, Alabama. The owner of the farm met with an automobile accident on the night in question and the woman, Grace Archer, and the child have disappeared."

"And Grace Archer is supposed to be our Grace Stiller?"

Hanley nodded.

"Then perhaps Kersoff is on his way to deliver them to me."

"Kersoff's wife was—she was most concerned." He smiled sarcastically. "She asked if you'd pay for information about her husband's informant who'd located this Grace Archer. She evidently was more afraid that she was missing out on the gravy train than that her husband had disappeared. What shall I do?"

"Go to see her. You have good judgment; use it. You can tell whether she's just trying to squeeze me. If you think she knows something of value, find out what it is."

"And if she doesn't?"

"You know I hate people who try to gouge me. As I said, use your own judgment." Marvot gazed down at the chess pieces. "How many men did Kersoff have?"

"Three."

"And do you believe Grace Archer could have taken care of them by herself?"

"She was very good. You told me so yourself."

"But four men, presumably taking her by surprise. It would be difficult unless she had help."

"Kilmer?"

"It's what I hoped would happen. It's possible. When I found out that the bitch had given birth to Kilmer's child, it opened a door for me. I know the power a child can have over a man. If anything could bring him out in the open, it would be that."

"But it's the woman you really want?"

"It's the woman I have to have. She was truly incredible with the horses. For a while I thought she was going to be my answer to the puzzle. I still believe there's a chance. I've had to be patient for a hell of a long time, but I knew I'd find her eventually. And evidently she's just as deadly as she was nine years ago." He picked up the chess piece that had lost Guillaume the game. "But then, you always have to watch out for the queen."

May I help?" Kilmer stood in the doorway of the kitchen. He looked at the soup simmering on the stove. "I guess not. You seem to have everything well in hand. I don't remember you knowing how to cook."

"I learned. Frankie had to eat." She got bowls from the cabinet. "And anyone can open a can of soup and put garlic bread in the oven."

"She's still sitting out on the porch. Do you think you can get her inside for a meal?"

"Yes. I'll tell her she has to eat because we have to go to the stable and check out the horses. Do you know anything about them that I can tell her?"

"The gray stallion is a two-year-old and has never been broken. The chestnut is supposed to be gentle and will probably be a decent mount for her. The black is a little temperamental but not vicious."

"What are their names?"

He shrugged. "I didn't ask. I could call the owner and—"

"Never mind. Frankie will probably like naming them herself." She started for the door. "Where's Robert? I haven't seen him since we got here."

"I told him to take the jeep and do a little reconnoitering of the area. I figured it couldn't hurt."

"No." She took the tray of garlic bread out of the oven. "What did you promise him to get him to quit his job?"

"A clear conscience about you and Frankie." He handed her a plate to put the bread on. "And enough money to make sure his old age would be very comfortable."

"Then you must be doing very well."

"Yes, I always do well when left to my own resources. It's only when I put my trust in others that I have problems."

"My father didn't—"

"I wasn't referring to anyone in particular. Actually, I was thinking about the three years I was linked with the CIA. There were several times when they tied my hands." He smiled into her eyes. "And wasted my time sending me greenhorns to train."

She pulled her gaze away. "How sad."

"Not at all. It was worth it. You made up for all of them."

"Really?" She forced herself to look back at him. "I take it you couldn't persuade any of the others to go to bed with you."

"I didn't try. North sent me only male trainees before you, and I'm not of that persuasion." His smile faded. "I didn't try with you either, Grace. It just happened. It was like an underground explosion. The first time I saw you I felt the ripples, and then all hell broke loose."

It had been like that for her too. She had been so cocky, so sure of herself and what she wanted out of life. Then she'd met Kilmer and been swept out to sea. "Yes, it did. But I felt the ripples after I left you too. I was pregnant. It wasn't over for me."

"Grace, I thought it was safe. You told me—"

"I know what I told you. I lied. I was crazy. I wanted it and nothing else mattered to me at that moment."

"I'm sorry, Grace."

She lifted her chin. "I'm not. I got Frankie. How the hell could I be sorry about that? You're the one who should be sorry. You spent those eight years without her and didn't even know what you were missing."

"I knew. North told me you were pregnant a day after you told him."

Her lips twisted. "And you rushed to my side."

"No. Would you like to know why?"

"It was inconvenient. You didn't want a pregnant lover."

He ignored the bitterness of her answer. "Marvot wanted you. You'd accomplished more than anyone else with the Pair. He was searching for you in every corner of the globe. I couldn't find a place that would be safe for you. I was on the run and I'd lost half my team on that raid to get the Pair. I knew it was going to take a while to build it again. So I made a deal with North."

"A deal?"

"He promised me witness protection treatment for you and the baby, with a bodyguard parked on your doorstep. The CIA was able to offer more protection than I could at that time. So I took the deal."

"And what did you give him?"

"I did one very dirty job for him in Iraq and made him a promise I wouldn't go after Marvot as long as they kept you under protection."

"Not go after him?" She frowned. "The CIA wanted to stop him. They gave us permission to take him out if he tried to stop us from stealing the Pair."

"But the winds of political opinion had changed even before the raid took place. Marvot clearly had several politicians in Congress on the payroll who were putting roadblocks in the way of the agency."

"Politicians? What the devil did Congress have to do with a crook like Marvot?"

"Evidently quite a bit, from what I've found out from Donavan's sources. Marvot was pouring lucre into several senators' campaign funds to influence them to go over to the dark side. There was a big struggle going on in Congress and it centered on what was happening at El Tariq. The power kept shifting back and forth, and during one of the shifts the CIA was pushed by several members in Congress to raid El Tariq." He held up his hand as she started to speak. "I know. It doesn't make any more sense than anything else about the raid. We both wondered why the CIA wanted the Pair when we got orders to go after them. But like dutiful drones, we obeyed orders."

"There's nothing dutiful about you."

"On the contrary, I consider doing my job well an irrevocable duty. I'm not saying I wouldn't have asked questions after I had possession of the horses." He shrugged. "But I didn't have the chance. Everything was blown to hell. I wasn't in a position to pursue the matter for a number of years." He paused. "But I never forgot, Grace."

No, he wouldn't forget, and he would be relentless in getting what he wanted. "And Congress just changed their minds about Marvot?"

"Probably with the help of a stupendous increase in bribe money. All Donavan found out was that there was a final shift for Marvot's benefit at the time. Then a few years later there was 9/11 and everything was in turmoil. I'm slowly putting the pieces together. I'm sure North thought that if he showed Congress a fait accompli they'd go along with him. It didn't happen. We failed. So Marvot was allowed to continue at El Tariq and keep his fingers in a dozen dirty international pies."

She shook her head. "No."

"It's the truth. Ask North. Though I'm not sure how much truth he'd be allowed to tell you these days."

"It couldn't be the truth. Crane wanted to set me up as bait for Marvot."

"Then Crane may be Marvot's man and wanted to turn you over to him. Or he doesn't know how strong the congressional lobbies are that could topple him from his job." Kilmer shrugged. "Either way I couldn't let him get his hands on you again."

"Let? It's my choice, Kilmer."

"No, I leave you free choice where Frankie's concerned." He made a face. "Though I'm finding it increasingly difficult. You have no choice whatsoever about whether the two of you are going to live or die. I'll fight you tooth and nail on that score. You're going to live." He moved toward the door. "I've waited too long to be cheated now."

"What the hell do you think you're—"

He was gone.

And she was shaking. Anger? Indignation? Shock? Her reaction was a mixture of all three. All these years she'd thought the CIA had protected her because they were responsible for her being on the run from Marvot. That it was because a deal had been struck with Kilmer came as a shock. She didn't want to be beholden to him for anything, dammit. And he had no right to think he could step in and run her life. She'd accepted his protection for Frankie, but there would be no—

She drew a deep breath. Calm. Kilmer had always been able to arouse a response no one else could. She couldn't allow that to happen again. She had to think clearly about the content of his words. If what he said was true, then she couldn't trust the CIA even if she made a deal with them.

And she didn't doubt it was the truth. Kilmer had never lied to her. It was one of the attributes she'd admired the most about him. She could always count on blunt honesty if she asked for it. It had once made her feel secure to know that honesty was a rock she could cling to in the violence that surrounded them.

"Is that for Frankie?" Robert stood in the doorway, looking at the plate. "Would you like me to go get her?"

Grace shook her head. "I'll go myself." She paused. "Well, did you find any wolves in those hills?"

"Only the four-footed kind. And I saw those at a distance. Kilmer didn't really expect anything else. He's just being careful."

"And you're taking his orders. Doesn't that bother you?"

He thought about it. "No. He's polite and he knows what he's doing. He paid me a whopping big bonus to come over to his team. He's got a right to give the orders." He tilted his head. "I understand he once gave orders to you. Did you mind?"

She looked away. "No, you're right. He knows what he's doing." She moved toward the door. "I'd better get Frankie. Her food will get cold."

"It won't matter. She won't taste it. I remember she had that same look on one of our pizza nights. We might as well not have been there." He paused. "I'm glad she's got something to occupy her mind. I thought she might brood."

"She's still thinking about Charlie. She's just dealing with it in her own way. That's what we all have to do, isn't it?" She passed him and a moment later she was out on the porch. It was sunset, and the pink-and-lavender-tinged clouds hovering over the mountains were magnificent. "Frankie?"

Frankie glanced over her shoulder. "Nice, huh, Mom?"

"That's an understatement." She sat down on the step beside her. "Beautiful. But it's time to get something to eat, Frankie. Soup and garlic bread okay?"

"Fine." Frankie looked back at the sunset. "We don't have mountains like this back home. I bet Charlie would have liked it here."

"I'm sure he would. But Charlie was all for gentle ponies, not bucking broncos. He always left the broncs to me."

"I was thinking. I bet he wasn't like that all his life. He went through World War Two, and that must have been like riding a bronc."

"Worse."

"So maybe he only wanted the gentleness when he got old. Maybe when he was younger he wanted crashing cymbals instead of violins, Tchaikovsky instead of Brahms."

"It could be." She slipped her arm around Frankie's shoulders. "Where is this going, baby?"

"I just have to be careful. It's got to be right for Charlie.

Do you remember when I told you I heard the music again that it was just a whisper?"

"Yes."

"I think it might have been Charlie."

Grace went still. "Charlie's not with us anymore," she said gently.

"But maybe he's like the music. You don't know where it comes from but that doesn't mean it's not there. Do you think maybe that could be true?"

"I believe anything is possible." She cleared her throat. "And I think Charlie would like the idea that you're comparing him to your music."

"No, not mine; this one is Charlie's." Her gaze shifted back to the sunset. "That's why it's got to be right. Broncos and gentle ponies and cymbals and everything that Charlie— It's got to be right."

"I can see that." She could see more than the picture that Frankie was drawing for her. She'd told Robert that Frankie would deal with her grief in her own way, but she'd never dreamed it would be with this gift to Charlie. Or maybe it was Charlie's last gift to Frankie. Either way, it was moving and beautiful and right. "Can I help?"

Frankie shook her head. "It's coming slow. It's a whisper, but it's louder now." She jumped to her feet. "I'm hungry. Let's go in and eat supper and then look at the horses."

Frankie was back in child mode and Grace accepted it gratefully. She didn't know how much longer she would have been able to keep her composure. "That's a great idea. We'll have to do some heating in the microwave."

"I'll do it. I kept you out here." She headed for the door. "I just wanted to talk to you. It makes things clearer. . . ." The last words drifted off as Frankie ran into the house.

Clearer?

It seemed to her that Frankie saw things with crystal clarity. There was no truth like that seen through the eyes of a child.

She glanced at the sunset one more time. It was almost gone, disappearing in a maze of deep purple. There was no longer a wind. At least, she couldn't hear it. Perhaps it was there, still singing through the pines.

And probably Frankie could hear it.

6

_____

"Which one do you like?" Frankie asked as she stared eagerly at the horses. "I like the gray."

"He's beautiful. But he's not been broken, so you'll have to wait until I can get around to it."

"That's okay. I like them all." She cautiously reached up her hand to stroke the chestnut. The mare lowered her head to Frankie's touch and neighed softly. "And this one likes me too."

"Then we'll have to make sure that you get better acquainted."

"What's her name?"

"Kilmer didn't know. So we'll name them again ourselves. What do you think suits her?"

Frankie tilted her head. "She has soft eyes and she looks like she knows things. Like that gypsy we saw at the carnival."

"Gypsy?"

Frankie nodded. "Gypsy."

"Do you want to start taking care of her in the morning?"

"First thing. May I ride her then?"

"As long as I'm there to watch."

"Pardon me, ladies." Dillon was coming down the aisle toward them. "But you're not going to have to take care of the horses. Kilmer took pity on me and is bringing in some of the team who are familiar with our equine friends." He grinned. "Thank God."

"Frankie will still take care of the horse she chooses as her mount."

Frankie nodded solemnly. "It's the way you have to do it. The horse rewards you by letting you ride her and you reward the horse by caring for her. Gypsy will have to get used to me and know I care about her."

"I apologize," Dillon said. "I didn't understand. Is it okay if the guys take care of the other horses?"

"Until Mom breaks the gray." Frankie gave Gypsy a final pat. "Have you named the gray yet, Mom?"

"I'm still thinking about it. Maybe you can help me. It's a big responsibility giving a horse— What's that?" At a raucous sound, her gaze flew to the stall at the end of the row. "That's no horse."

"No," Dillon said. "It's a jackass. He's supposed to keep the horses calm, but they don't seem to know that. From what I've seen this afternoon they pretty much ignore him."

She stiffened. "A jackass," she repeated. She started slowly down the row. It didn't have to be Cosmo. A jackass's braying was pretty much the same from animal to animal. "Kilmer didn't mention a jackass. Did he lease it with the rest of the livestock?"

"I guess so. Or maybe not. He only talked about the horses. Maybe the jackass is a new addition."

"I don't think there's any doubt about that." She was standing in front of the small gray jackass. "The question is, how new?"

The jackass was staring at her belligerently. He pulled back his lips and brayed, spraying her with saliva.

Damn him. It *was* Cosmo.

She turned on her heel. "I have to see Kilmer. Stay with Frankie and bring her to the house when she's ready. I'll see you back at the house, Frankie."

"Okay." She turned back to Gypsy. "I think she's got eyelashes like a movie star. Maybe Julia Roberts. What do you think, Mr. Dillon?"

"I can't see the resemblance," Dillon said. "But then, I'm a fan of Julia Roberts, and I wouldn't want to compare her to a horse face."

"Just the eyelashes," Frankie said. "And maybe the teeth. She has fine, big teeth too."

They were the last words Grace heard as she tore out of the stable and headed for the house. Damn Kilmer. He'd promised her, and there was Cosmo in that stable.

She flew up the porch steps and toward the front door.

"May I help you?"

She whirled. Kilmer was standing in the far corner of the porch, a dim figure in the darkness.

"Cosmo, dammit. Did you think I wouldn't recognize him?"

"No, I knew that you'd know him right away. That's why I was waiting for you."

"When did you get him?"

"I liberated him six months ago."

"How?"

"It wasn't easy. I had to wait until they took the horses and Cosmo to the Sahara for their yearly jaunt. They put him out to graze at an oasis when they took the Pair into the desert. I had to grab him and then I had to keep him quiet until I got him away. Damn ass has the loudest mouth on the planet."

"You could have been killed."

"I considered the risk worth taking. I wasn't ready to take the Pair, but I could get their stablemate. Cosmo is the only quieting influence that the Pair would accept, except you. Without him, I'm sure that the handlers are going through hell with the Pair."

She was sure of it too. "Six months. Then you didn't lease this ranch for Frankie. You were getting ready for the Pair."

"I hoped I'd never need a hiding place for either of you," he said. "But it would have been stupid for me to not take advantage of a place that I'd made safe for the Pair."

"There's no place safe for the Pair." She shook her head in frustration. "I can't believe you're going to try for them. Marvot obviously knows you're coming. He'll be waiting for you. You can't do it."

"I can do it. I just have to take it one step at a time."

"And Cosmo is a step."

"A completely obnoxious one." He smiled. "But a step nonetheless. Don't worry, I'm not taking any other steps at the moment. It would be too dangerous for you."

"Am I supposed to be grateful?"

He shook his head. "I'm the one who's grateful to you. I just wanted to put your mind at rest about Cosmo."

Her mind wasn't at rest. Cosmo might be a small step, but it indicated the relentless drive that was pushing Kilmer. He'd even gone to the trouble of stealing the Pair's stablemate. He was getting ready. And as soon as she and Frankie were out of the picture, he was going to go for it.

And probably get himself killed.

"Fine." She turned and headed for the door. She stopped. "You told me that you'd taken something from Marvot that made him mad enough to start after us in high gear. Cosmo?"

"No, it was a little more important than Cosmo. One of the items of information that Donavan uncovered for me." He smiled. "But there's no need for me to share it with you. You're not interested in all this."

"No, I'm not." And she wouldn't worry about him. He'd opted out of her life and it was just as well. He was still running around blowing up ammo depots and rescuing kidnap victims and putting himself at risk in a hundred different situations. Her life was completely different. It was centered around Frankie and life, not death. If he was still fanatical about getting the Pair, then good luck to him.

He'd need it.

Kilmer's team arrived in a helicopter the next morning.

"Who are they?" Frankie whispered as Kilmer went out to meet them in the stable yard. "They look like—" She frowned. "I don't think they're cowboys."

"I'm sure a few of them are," Grace said. "Remember? Dillon said they'd help with the horses." She knew only two of the team, Luis Vazquez and Nathan Salter. The rest were strangers to her, but she recognized the quiet, understated air of confidence that Kilmer seemed to instill in every man he accepted for his team. "That tall man in the orange shirt is Luis. He knows a lot about horses. He grew up on a ranch in Argentina. He was a vaquero. Do you remember I told you about vaqueros and their bolos?"

"May I meet him?"

"As soon as Kilmer gets finished talking to them." It was almost over now. The men were separating, moving quickly and with purpose as they received their orders. A few minutes later the yard had emptied. "Well, I guess they're busy now."

"Not cowboys," Frankie repeated positively. "And not soldiers. But they kind of look like both of them."

"No, they're men who know how to protect us. That's what they do for a living. You can count on them. I'll introduce you later today."

Frankie nodded. "But not now. I have to sit down and work with my keyboard."

"By all means. I'll go down to the stable and make sure they know how to properly take care of the horses." She held up her hand. "Except Gypsy. You and she seemed to get along fine this morning."

"Yeah." Frankie's response was abstracted as she opened the screen door. "See you later, Mom."

"Right." Frankie wasn't seeing much of anything right now. She was concentrating on the music. Grace could already see her mentally toying with the notes running through her mind. "Later."

Kilmer was coming back up the steps.

"Donavan didn't come?" she asked.

"I told you he was keeping an eye on Marvot."

"Have you heard from him lately?"

"Not since we got here. That might be a good sign. I'll call him tonight if there's no word." He studied her. "You're worried about him."

"I always liked Donavan. He saved my life once in Libya."

"Really?" His brows rose. "He never told me."

"It wasn't your business. It was between the two of us."

"It was my business if it endangered the mission. Did it?"

"Go to hell."

He smiled. "I take it that it did. I'll have to talk to Donavan."

"For God's sake, it was nine years ago."

"And Donavan always did have a soft spot for you."

Friendships weren't encouraged on Kilmer's team, but it was difficult not to form attachments when you were depending on each other for your life. "Not that you could tell. You had him put me through my paces until I dropped when I first came to you."

"And you toughened up nicely. I was proud of you."

And his pride in her had meant everything. She had been willing to do anything, work her body to the breaking point, to get his approval. God, she had been naive. "I was young and stupid. I thought doing well for you meant something. I suppose I had a king-size case of hero worship."

"I know."

Her cheeks flushed. "Conceited bastard."

"Why do you think I had Donavan work with you? We'd have been in bed the second night after you got there if I'd handled your training myself. Hell, I couldn't wait to touch you from the moment I saw you. I was being bloody ethical." He turned away. "It didn't matter. It ended the same way a week later. I'm not one to resist that kind of temptation for long."

She watched him walk away. She'd always loved the way he moved, every muscle response graceful and coordinated. Now she couldn't tear her gaze away. God, it was happening again. She could feel the tingling heat in her palms, the shortness of breath, the urge to go after him, touch him.

He looked back over his shoulder. "Me too," he said softly. "Hell, isn't it?"

She opened her lips to speak and then closed them again. She turned on her heel and went into the house.

She stopped inside and tried to steady her breathing. Jesus, she didn't want this. She had a good, steady life with Frankie. She didn't want to dive into that pool of sensuality that had given her only one golden gift. The rest had been crazy, animal-like need that had made her question her own will and strength. She had wanted to give everything, take everything, and she hadn't cared about the consequences.

She cared now. She owed Frankie a mother who had the strength to fight that weakness that had conceived her. And she wasn't sure she would be able to do it if she stayed here close to Kilmer. She needed time to build her defenses.

Christ, how much time did she need? she thought in disgust. She'd had nine years, and the barrier she'd built had been torn down in a matter of a few days. Then start again and don't stand around and think about Kilmer and how he looked, and moved, and—

Keep busy. She had a horse to break. The gray would

make her pay attention to something besides the way she felt.

And if she didn't pay attention, the stallion would break her instead.

What a pretty boy you are," Grace said softly as she gently stroked the gray. "You've had a great life, haven't you? Running and kicking up your heels with no one able to touch you. I wish I could let you go on like that. There's nothing more beautiful than a horse in the wild. It would fill my heart just watching you. But life isn't always that good for horses. You're safest if you learn how to get along with us. You can pretend it's a game. You do what we want you to do for a little while every day. Then you get to go back to doing what you want to do. Fair?"

The gray backed away from her.

"Maybe not so fair. But that's the way it has to be. And I'll make sure you're safe and happy. We don't have a name for you yet. Shall I call you Samson? He was strong and didn't want to be tamed either. But you'll be smarter than he was." She stepped closer and rubbed his nose. "Now listen to me and I'll tell you what we're going to do together. Can't you feel how much I want you to be happy? You will, Samson. You will. . . ."

I thought she was going to break the horse." Robert came up to stand beside Kilmer at the corral fence. "I've been watching from the porch and she hasn't done anything but stand and look at him."

Kilmer felt a ripple of annoyance. He might have to have Blockman here but he didn't have to like it. And he didn't want him hanging around when he was trying to concentrate on Grace and the stallion. "She's doing something." He didn't take his gaze off Grace standing in front of the horse, her lips moving with words he couldn't make out from this distance. "Haven't you ever seen her break a horse before?"

Robert shook his head. "I'm not exactly the bucolic type. I never went to the farm except when I was invited for a meal. I know Charlie thought she was some kind of voodoo priestess where horses were concerned."

"Smart man." Kilmer climbed the fence and threw his leg over the top bar. Patience. It had been his choice to bring Blockman here. Now he'd have to accept and work with it. "I've seen her at one or two truly amazing sessions. Horses seem to understand her."

"Does that mean they won't buck?"

Kilmer shook his head. "She says that's very rare. Every horse hates to have its independence curtailed. But it makes the process very short if they've reached an understanding before she actually gets on them."

"Understanding?"

Kilmer shrugged. "Ask her."

"If we're not going to see any fireworks, why are you here?"

He was silent a moment. "Because if there are fireworks, the gray could kill her. I have to be here." He glanced at Robert challengingly. "And why are you here?"

"The same." Robert's lips tightened. "But I wasn't sure that the gray really posed a threat. Grace always seems so confident around horses."

"He's a threat. Grace wouldn't have it any other way. She says a horse without spirit is a horse without heart."

"You seem to know her very well," Robert said slowly. "How long was she on your team?"

"Six months."

"Not long."

Kilmer felt a surge of irritation. He gave him a cool glance. "Long enough."

Robert studied his expression. "Look, I don't know what was between you two, but I'm not getting in the middle. I take it that whatever you had going was pretty heavy. If I thought I had a chance with Grace, I'd step in. She's special. But I don't have a chance or I'd have done it before this. I might compete with you, but not with Frankie. She's too much to—" He broke off. "Is Frankie your kid?"

Kilmer's gaze flickered warily. "Why would you think that?"

"The age is right. Eight years. And you were together sometime in the months before she came to Tallanville. I started adding up the possibilities. And after I came up with that one, I took a good look at Frankie. She resembles Grace, but there's something of you in the shape of her eyes."

"There is?" Kilmer stiffened in surprise. "I didn't see that."

"I did." He smiled. "My God, I believe I've caught you off guard."

He had done just that, Kilmer thought. He had been careful to keep from thinking about Frankie as belonging to him. He had given up that privilege when he'd left Grace to raise Frankie by herself. Even though he hadn't been able to smother the possessiveness he still felt for Grace, that would necessarily be an equal passion. In the end, it would be her free choice. Frankie was . . . different.

"She really looks like me?"

Robert nodded. "She really does."

"Hot damn," Kilmer murmured. "Not that it changes anything."

"No." Robert glanced at Grace. "I think she's going to mount him."

Kilmer's gaze swung back to Grace. She was still talking, her foot in the stirrup.

The gray shied, almost pulling her from her feet. She freed her boot just in time. She was shaking her head and laughing. The gray stared at her indignantly. She started to move toward him again.

Three times she tried to mount him.

Three times he shied.

She kept talking.

Two more times she made the attempt.

He shied.

The next time he only moved slightly, as if bored with the game.

The following time he let her slowly, painstakingly, swing into the saddle.

Kilmer held his breath.

The stallion wasn't moving, but Kilmer could see the muscles of his haunches tense.

Grace was bent over his neck, talking, murmuring, letting him get used to her weight.

"Look at his eyes. He's going to blow," Kilmer whispered. "Watch him, Grace."

She didn't appear to be worried, dammit. She was stroking the gray and seemed perfectly at ease. Kilmer tensed and found himself preparing to slip off the fence and go to her. No, that would only startle the horse and make Grace furious. Let her do it. She would know what—

The stallion exploded!

Bucking, gyrating, making Grace's slim body jerk and toss back and forth like a puppet's.

"Jesus," Robert said. "Hold on, Grace."

She rode him.

It went on for minutes, and a dozen times Kilmer was sure she'd be tossed.

"Can't we get her off of—" Robert broke off. "Stupid. Of course we can't. It's— He's stopping."

The stallion was standing still, shaking. Grace bent over him and murmured something. Then she gently kicked him.

He didn't move.

She nudged him again with her boot.

He took a step forward, then another.

Grace took him around the corral, gently asserting, never forcing.

She finally stopped him and slid from the saddle.

Kilmer let his breath out. Christ, he hadn't realized he'd been holding it.

"Shit." Robert jumped down inside the fence and headed toward Grace and the stallion. "That was damn scary."

Kilmer started to follow him and then stopped. He'd been crowding Grace, and she wouldn't appreciate having him near her at this moment. He watched Blockman laughing and ruefully shaking his head as he fell into step with her while she led the horse from the corral.

He didn't like it. It stung like hell.

It didn't matter what Blockman had said. Kilmer was experiencing the same primitive response that had stirred him since the moment he'd realized what a big role Blockman was playing in Grace's life.

Then get over it. There were more important things to deal with than the—

His cell phone rang. Donavan.

"Problem?"

"Maybe," Donavan said. "Hanley left the compound last night. I had Tonino follow him. He went to Genoa to see Kersoff's wife."

"Why?"

"I don't know. We weren't able to bug her place before he got there. Hanley stayed two hours and then flew back to the compound."

"Information?"

"That's my bet. Kersoff's wife might have had an ace in the hole she wanted to barter."

"Can you have Tonino verify? If Marvot has a chance at finding out Kersoff's informant, we want to get to him before Marvot."

"I've already sent him back to Genoa. I wanted him to make sure that Hanley wasn't stopping over anywhere else before he went back to Marvot." He paused. "How's Grace doing?"

"Fine. I just watched her breaking a damn stallion."

"And the kid?"

"Kids are kids."

Except this one looked like him. . . .

"Yeah, nothing special about any of them." Donavan chuckled. "Tell Grace I can't wait to see her again." He paused. "And it may not be too long. I have a hunch. . . ."

"You said nothing was happening there except with Hanley."

"It's not. Maybe I've been doing this surveillance too long. Don't pay any attention to me."

"Be careful," Kilmer said. "If you see even a sign that puts you on edge, get your butt out of there."

"I will. I want to stay alive to see that kid of yours." He added slyly, "Even though she's nothing special, just another kid." He hung up.

Bastard. Kilmer was smiling as he pressed the disconnect button.

His smile faded. But that bastard had great instincts that had saved both their necks any number of times. If he thought there was something brewing, then the chances were that he was right.

And Kilmer wasn't ready for the game to start. Not with Grace and Frankie tying his hands right now.

It could be that Donavan was wrong. Maybe camping out on that hill by himself was making him edgy.

It wasn't likely. There were few situations that made Donavan edgy. He ambled along until the situation exploded, and then he acted with deadly skill and swiftness until it was under control.

But Kilmer hoped to hell Donavan was wrong.

Genoa, Italy

Isabel Kersoff lived on a winding street two blocks from the waterfront. It was a decent house, Mark Tonino thought as he knocked on the front door. Clean and freshly painted, with that red door to give it a little style.

No answer.

He knocked again. It could be that Hanley had given her money and she had left this little house flush with success.

Still no answer.

Even if she wasn't there, it didn't necessarily mean that there was no information to be had. She might have left papers, cards, telephone numbers.

He pulled out his skeleton keys and tried two before the door swung open.

He turned on his pen flashlight as he entered the living room. A small desk was set against the wall. He went through it carefully. Nothing but unpaid bills and brochures for cruises. Kersoff evidently had had big dreams and no funds.

And his wife might not keep valuable information in a desk drawer. It had been Tonino's experience that women were more inventive when hiding treasures. They stored items in freezers or in hollow curtain rods.

Bedroom first. There were more places to—

Oh, shit.

He reached for his cell phone. "Donavan, it's a wash. She's dead."

"How?"

"Tied up, throat cut." He shone the beam of his flashlight on her face. "Cuts, lots of cuts all over her face and upper body. Nasty. Hanley spent a long time with her. Evidently she wasn't being cooperative. What do I do?"

"Get out of there."

"Do you want me to keep looking around the house?"

"No, she wouldn't be dead if they hadn't got what they wanted. Hanley would have kept at her." Donavan paused. "She's been dead how long?"

"I'm not a medical examiner, but I'd guess about twelve hours if we're to assume it was Hanley."

"Then Marvot's known what Kersoff's wife was selling for almost a full day. Not good. Get rid of any fingerprints and any other evidence you were there and come back here. I have to call Kilmer."

7

——————

Twelve hours," Kilmer repeated. "It may not make any difference. If Kersoff's leak was someone in the CIA, he'd be useless to Marvot as long as no one at Langley has information about Grace."

"If," Donavan repeated.

"They're out of the loop. Grace has broken with them."

"They've still got contacts with the FBI. What's to stop the FBI from pulling strings with local cops to get information?"

"Nothing." And the FBI and CIA were supposed to be much more cooperative these days. Kilmer hadn't seen much sign of it, but this might be a different situation. Congress could inspire an amazing amount of togetherness when they talked budget cuts. "I'll get Blockman on it. He hasn't come up with anything yet, but it's only been a couple days."

Donavan was silent a moment. "Are you going to tell Grace about this?"

"Why? So that she can get more worried about something she can't do anything about right now?"

"Grace wouldn't like to be kept in the dark about anything that would affect her or the kid."

"Grace isn't liking much that's happening. That's why I'll pick and choose until you bring me something I can get my teeth into."

"You'll be lucky if she doesn't get her teeth into you. I'll call you when I hear more." He hung up.

Donavan was right; Grace wouldn't appreciate having anything kept from her, even in the name of protection. Well, to hell with it. He'd been forced to stay on the sidelines and let Grace take megapunishment and hardship in the past. He wasn't going to opt out now. He would do what he—

Music.

Radio? No, tentative, delicate strains. A keyboard.

He glanced at his watch: 1:40 A.M. and the music was coming from the front porch. He crossed the living room and stood at the screen door looking out.

Frankie was sitting on the porch in front of her keyboard. She was dressed in a white flannel robe and fuzzy pink slippers, and her expression was intent as she bent over the instrument. She had a penlight beside her but she wasn't using it.

She must have sensed him standing there, because her head lifted swiftly. "Mom?"

"No." He opened the door and came out on the porch. "Do you know what time it is, Frankie?"

She sighed. "Busted. But at least it's not Mom. I didn't want to wake her. It always makes her tired when she breaks a horse."

"Couldn't this wait until morning?"

She shook her head. "Sometimes the music doesn't stop just because it gets dark and it's time to go to bed. And this one belongs to Charlie; I didn't want to lose it."

"I see." Yeah, just an ordinary kid. Not. "But I'm in a bit

of a predicament. I don't believe your mom would want you to be out at this hour alone. And it's very chilly. What would she do if she found you out here? Would she make you go to bed?"

"No, that's why I sneaked out after she was asleep." She made a face. "She'd stay down here with me until I was ready to come in. She knows about the music." She frowned. "You going to tell her I'm down here?"

"No." He smiled. "And I may not know about the music or bucking broncos, but I'm pretty good at keeping watch. Suppose I stay there in the living room until you're ready to go up?"

Her expression brightened. "You're not sleepy?"

He shook his head. "I never go to bed until the wee hours anyway. It would be kind of nice to sit in there and relax and listen to you play."

She stared at him doubtfully. "Truly?"

"Absolutely," he answered solemnly.

"Okay." She bent over the keyboard again. "Thanks, Jake . . ."

"You're welcome." He went into the house, grabbed a chenille throw from the couch, and brought it back to her. "But you have to wrap up as part of the deal. You're not in Alabama, and the nights here are chilly even in August."

"Yeah, I noticed." She let him wrap the throw around her, but she didn't take her gaze off the keyboard. "Funny . . ."

He stood looking at her. She was so absorbed he doubted if she heard him. With her curly hair and loose robe she looked like a little girl from a Shirley Temple movie. Yet there was nothing childlike about the intensity that was gripping her. Her lashes were shadowing silky cheeks and he couldn't see her eyes, which Robert had said were shaped like his.

Did Frankie look even a little like him?

And what if she did?

He . . . liked it.

Stupid ass. He turned and opened the screen door. A few seconds later he dropped into the easy chair close to the open door. He relaxed and closed his eyes.

And listened to Frankie create her music.

The Pair were running toward her. Their white coats shone silver in the moonlight. Their blue eyes glittered wildly as they tore across the field.

They meant to kill her.

She had to stand still, Grace told herself. If she turned and tried to run away, they'd be after her, stomping her. She'd seen them trample a stable man to death this morning when he'd panicked and tried to bolt for safety.

I know you have to do it.

I know you're afraid too.

I'm no threat to you.

I'm no threat.

I'm no threat.

The horses were close enough that Grace could smell their sweat.

Don't move, she told herself.

Her heart was beating so hard that it hurt. A few more yards and they'd be on top of her.

She held her arms out to her sides, careful not to put them in front of her in what they might perceive as an aggressive move.

No threat.

They were thundering toward her. She wanted to close her eyes. Keep them open. There might be some way she could avoid those hooves when they were—

Please, no threat.

She wasn't making contact. Whatever was driving them was too strong. In seconds they'd be knocking her to the ground.

She was going to die.

One more try. All her strength. All her will.

No threat!

The Pair parted at the last moment and passed on either side of her!

She could feel the wind, the dirt churned up by their hooves striking her.

Triumph.

And relief. My God, the relief.

No time for this weakness. She had to move fast. Start the approach. She couldn't let the Pair have time to recover. . . .

But there was something wrong. She couldn't hear them. Movement, but not the sound of hooves. Soft, quiet movement . . .

A dream, she realized hazily as she opened her eyes. She was reliving that night in the field with the Pair. No wonder, after her afternoon with the gray.

And it was Frankie moving, climbing into her own bed, Grace thought drowsily. "Frankie?"

"It's okay, Mom." Frankie was pulling the covers up around her. "Go back to sleep."

"Did you have to go to the bathroom?"

Frankie didn't answer.

"Frankie?"

"I wanted— The music wouldn't go away. I went down to the porch."

Grace was suddenly wide awake. "Alone? You shouldn't have done that. You should have wakened me."

"You were tired."

"That doesn't matter."

"It does matter. It was okay, Mom. I wasn't alone. Jake was there."

"What?"

"He never goes to bed early. When he found me on the porch, he gave me a throw to wrap up in and stayed in the living room until I was through."

"Oh." She was silent. "You still should have wakened me."

"Next time." She yawned. "When you're not so tired."

"I'm never too tired for you."

"But Jake wasn't tired at all. He told me so and I could see he was telling the truth. And he's a grown-up, so it was okay that he stayed with me. Right?"

"Not all grown-ups—" But Frankie had been given the usual generic warnings, and Grace didn't want her to mistrust Kilmer when there might be a moment that it was important she obey him without questioning. "Yes, it was okay. Just wake me next time. It's not as if—"

Frankie had fallen asleep.

Why hadn't Grace roused when Frankie had left the bedroom? She always slept lightly and she was attuned to every change of breathing.

But not tonight, when there was imminent danger on the horizon. It didn't make sense.

Unless she was trusting that Kilmer would keep them safe. Frankie certainly seemed to have that confidence.

Frankie was a child, and Kilmer managed to inspire confidence in even hardened mercenaries. It was a gift.

And after people gave him their trust, he never betrayed it. At least, that's what she'd thought until the night they'd gone after the Pair. Her father had given him his trust. . . .

She turned over and gazed at the moonlight pouring into the window. It seemed peaceful, but she knew Kilmer's team was moving, shifting, watching.

Where was he? Had he gone to bed after Frankie had come upstairs? He never slept much. He'd told her once that he was afraid he'd miss something if he slept more than five hours. That life was too short and they had to squeeze every moment of pleasure from every minute.

They'd been in bed together when he'd told her that, she remembered. It had been an unusual moment of confidence in a relationship that had been more concerned with sex and emotion than personal philosophies. She'd felt . . . close to him.

Then he'd rolled over and mounted her and she'd forgotten about everything but sex and need. She could see him now, his dark hair falling on his forehead, his chest rising and falling with each breath, each movement. The power and the precision and the—

Stop thinking about him. If she was feeling this vulnerable, it was because it had been a long time for her. It wasn't Kilmer, it was sex itself. He'd just ignited the embers that she'd kept low and under control all these years.

And they were still under control. She just had to make a greater effort to keep them that way.

You're riding him." Robert propped his elbows on the top of the fence. "It was only yesterday that I watched you break him. Didn't he buck today when you got on him?"

"Of course, but Samson thought about it last night and decided that cooperation made sense. So he let me off with three minutes of bucking to prove his independence. Tomorrow it will be less." She got off the gray and patted his neck. "He's got a nice gait. Smooth." She glanced at Robert. "In a week or so he might be ready for another rider. Want to try him?"

"No, thank you. I've told you that I like comfy, sleek cars, preferably convertibles. Your Samson doesn't appeal to me."

"I wanted to give you your chance. There's nothing like the feeling of riding a horse across a meadow or by the shore."

"If you can stay in the saddle," Robert said dryly.

"Practice."

"I think I'll stick to Lamborghinis and Corvettes. You can't fall off them." He paused. "Kilmer was a little on edge while you were riding that monster yesterday. I took the brunt of it."

She glanced at him. "And that means?"

"He wanted to help you fight the stallion. He was frustrated and decided I was a prime candidate on whom to vent."

"And did he?"

"I beat him to the punch. I knew what was bothering him and I jumped in first. I had to clear the air if I was going to work with him."

She opened the gate and led Samson toward the stable.

"Aren't you going to ask how I cleared the air?"

She didn't want to talk about Kilmer. It was difficult enough just seeing him every day, and last night had proved that she was thinking about him entirely too much. "You're evidently going to tell me anyway."

"I told him I hadn't gone to bed with you." He chuckled as he saw her expression. "I thought that would get your attention. It's hard to read Kilmer, but I'd bet that made him feel a whole lot better. He didn't like the idea at all."

"No wonder. The idea is ridiculous."

"I didn't think so. I thought about it, but I knew that wasn't the role you'd cast me in. And that's okay. I like being your friend. I like being Frankie's friend." He paused. "But I'd have appreciated it if you'd told me Kilmer was Frankie's father."

Her gaze flew to his face. "He told you?"

He shook his head. "I put the numbers together, and Frankie does have a look of him."

"She does *not*."

"Have it your own way," Robert said. "And it's only the tip of the iceberg anyway. I've been left in the dark about a hell of a lot of things. North only told me what I needed to know to protect you, and Crane wouldn't give me the time of day. I'm tired of it, Grace. I'm not going it blind any longer."

He was right. They hadn't been fair to him. She couldn't speak for the CIA, but she and Kilmer were responsible for their own actions. She hadn't told Robert anything because dredging up the past hurt. Kilmer never confided in anyone as a matter of policy. "What do you want to know?"

"What did you know that made you important enough for North to keep you under longtime surveillance?"

"It's not what I knew. None of us on the team knew why we were going after the Pair. We were just ordered to get them. I thought Marvot wanted to kill me just because I was one of the people on the raid we'd made at El Tariq. Marvot's famous for his vendettas, and he knew my face because I worked on his horse farm. It was logical that I'd be a target."

"Who is this Marvot?"

"Paul Marvot. Half French, half German. He inherited a criminal empire from his father, a kingpin who operated in North Africa and Southern France. He took over when his father was murdered by a rival mob leader and is every bit as lethal and as much a scumbag as his father. He lives in Morocco and has a palatial horse farm at El Tariq near the coast."

"And this bastard wants you dead?"

"That's what I thought." She paused. "But Kilmer told me he'd had to make a deal with North. Marvot wanted me alive, not dead. And the CIA wasn't protecting me out of the kindness of their hearts. They wanted to keep a rein on Kilmer. He promised them he wouldn't go after the Pair."

"El Tariq. What was this raid at El Tariq? What the devil is this Pair? What were you after? Prisoners? Money?"

"Horses."

"What?"

"There were two white horses in Marvot's stables at El Tariq. White Arabians with blue eyes. A stallion and a mare. Marvot guarded them as if they were the English crown jewels."

"Why?"

"I don't know. North never told us. Personally, I think they were some kind of hostages." She held up her hand. "I know. It's crazy. But it was true. Marvot was fanatical about them. I was there. I saw them trample a stable man, and Marvot was only concerned about whether the death had upset the Pair. The horses were fed and watered and allowed to run wild on the farm. Except occasionally they were taken to a place in the Sahara. I wasn't allowed to go along, but I was at El Tariq once when it happened. And when they were brought back to the farm Marvot was in a terrible temper."

"Why?"

She shrugged. "I listened, but I wasn't about to ask questions that would arouse suspicion."

"Weird."

"Yes, but the CIA wanted those horses, so they must have known why Marvot thought them so valuable. North told Kilmer to go in and get them. And they sent me to him to help."

"Why you?"

"My father was the one who went to the CIA and told them what was happening at El Tariq. He'd been doing some minor dealing with Marvot and knew Marvot was under surveillance. He thought he could sell the tidbit of information about the Pair to the CIA. North jumped on it. Evidently they knew something about what was going on. He wanted my father to go back and find out more."

"And Papa sent you instead?"

"I wanted to go," she said defensively. "I was tired of trailing my father around the world and he knew it. I'd never spent more than a few months in America. I wanted to know what it felt like to belong to a place. My father told North about my way with horses and they took me as a CIA trainee. We were a little surprised they were willing to wait to go after the Pair until I was ready, but my father said that it only proved how important the raid was to them. I didn't care. I was going to have my chance. Do you know how difficult it would have been for me to be accepted if my father hadn't asked North to take me on?"

"Lucky you."

"I *was* lucky. You don't understand. Everything would have been fine, but— It wasn't my father's fault."

"The raid was a bust?"

"It was hard as hell, but we got the horses out of the stable and into the truck. Marvot's men were waiting for us on the road. We barely made it out of there."

"Sounds like a tip-off."

"It *wasn't* my father."

"Whoa. I didn't say it was." He studied her face. "But maybe Kilmer did?"

"My father died. He was killed later that day in Tangiers by Marvot's men. Does that sound like he betrayed us?"

"No." He held up his hand. "Look, I don't know anything about this. It's between you and Kilmer."

"No, it's not." She led Samson into the stable. "There's nothing between Kilmer and me. That ended a long time ago." She glared at him over her shoulder. "And Frankie does *not* look like him."

"My mistake," Robert murmured. "Sorry."

She drew a deep breath. "No, I'm sorry. I had no right to snap at you. It's not been a good few days for me. I don't like relying on Kilmer for anything." She tried to smile as she changed the subject. "Did you know that the music Frankie's doing now is for Charlie?"

"No." A smile lit his face. "He'd like that."

She nodded. "She was talking about how she had to make sure there were plenty of cymbals. That Charlie's life wasn't always slow and easy."

"From what he told me, she's right," Robert said. "She's just a kid. How does she understand stuff like that?"

Grace shook her head. "I don't know. She's a miracle." She started to unsaddle Samson. "Now, if you don't have any more questions, I've got work to do."

"In other words, I've wasted enough of your time."

"No, you had a right. Have you gotten anywhere on tracking down that leak at Langley?"

"Not yet. Stolz is working on a lead. There's a young kid

who's a computer whiz in records. He's a possible. If not, Stolz will keep searching. I talk to Stolz at least once a day to keep him hopping."

"But Stolz doesn't know where you are?"

"Of course not. For God's sake, do you think I'd risk leading anyone to you? I trust Stolz, but Kilmer told me up front that I didn't have the right to trust anyone while I was being paid by him. That wasn't in our deal. I told Stolz I was in Miami."

"I had to ask." She stared him in the eye. "Frankie's my responsibility, and I don't have the right to take anything for granted."

He nodded. "Not me. Not Kilmer. You're not great on trust. Tell me, Grace, did you trust your father?"

"Of course I did." She shook her head wearily. "Most of the time. When it was about him and me. He wasn't very reliable and, yes, he wasn't particularly honest, but he loved me. He wouldn't have done anything that would have hurt me. And he knew I was going to be at El Tariq that night. He wouldn't have sold me out."

"It doesn't seem likely."

"Likely, bullshit—he wouldn't have done it."

Robert grimaced. "I seem to be saying the wrong things. I'm out of here."

Grace watched him walk away. She shouldn't have been sharp with him. He'd only asked questions that anyone would have asked. He hadn't known how defensive she was about her father. Since earliest childhood she'd had to defend her dad from people who didn't understand that her life with him wasn't what they thought. He'd made life an adventure for her. Sometimes a terrifying adventure, but he'd always shown her love and kindness. In all the loneliness of her childhood she'd never doubted that he cared about her. That knowledge was important to her. In a world that changed every day, when she hadn't been able to count on anyone or anything, she could count on her dad loving her.

And Kilmer had tried to take that certainty away from her.

Damn him.

Tonino showed up at Kersoff's house last night," Hanley said. "I was having her place watched by Lackman until the body was discovered. The woman seems to have had few friends, because her body was still undisturbed after twelve hours."

"Tonino," Marvot repeated, thinking. "One of Kilmer's men."

Hanley nodded. "He must have been sent by Kilmer to find out how Kersoff located Grace Archer."

"Or you might have been followed when you visited the lady."

"I was careful," Hanley said quickly. "I'm a professional. I would have known."

It was true Hanley made few mistakes, Marvot thought, but Kilmer had an extraordinarily skilled team. "I believe we'd still better scour the perimeter here for any surveillance. What was Lackman's report?"

"Tonino was there for less than ten minutes. He evidently found the body and then flew the coop."

"And you're sure you left no evidence after you dispatched Kersoff's wife?"

Hanley shook his head. "I went through the desk and her bedroom. No paperwork."

"Then it seems we've got a jump on Kilmer." He smiled. "And all we need is a small head start. Have you made contact with Kersoff's informant in the CIA yet?"

"I've sent a man to Langley to make contact personally. If Kilmer knows about the leak, then we have to gather in the source before he gets ahold of him." Hanley shrugged. "And there's nothing more persuasive than cash in hand. Unless it's fear. Fear is good."

Marvot nodded. "So it is." He stood up. "Either way I expect an answer by tomorrow night. You'll remember that, won't you?" He stared Hanley in the eye to instill a little fear of his own. "I've waited a long time to get my hands on this woman, Hanley. My patience is almost at an end. I won't take it kindly if we lose her now."

"You don't have to tell me that." Hanley's gaze slid away. "We won't lose her."

"Excellent. Now, you contact Langley and stir them up a little." He headed for the door. "I expect a report when I get back from my evening walk. I've promised to take Guillaume down to the paddock to look at the Pair as a special treat."

Hanley shook his head. "Why is the boy so besotted with those horses? He has a fine horse of his own."

"Children are always fascinated by the forbidden. He knows the Pair have killed before."

"Aren't you afraid Guillaume will sneak down and try to ride them?"

"He almost certainly will at some point. That's why I've told everyone in the stable that if he's permitted near them without me, I'll tie them down in the stall with one of the Pair." He shrugged. "But by giving Guillaume a taste every now and then, it will put off that time." He opened the door. "Ah, there you are, Guillaume. Ready?"

"Yes, Papa." Guillaume's eyes were shining. "I brought my camera. I want to take photos of them for my room."

"What a good idea." He took Guillaume's hand and glanced back over his shoulder at Hanley. "And if you bring me Grace Archer to work with the Pair, there may not be any reason for me to be concerned about my son. A twofold reason for you to do your job with utmost dispatch."

Hanley nodded. "Of course I will."

Marvot smiled down at Guillaume. "Hanley is going to bring us a playmate for the Pair. A young woman. Won't that be interesting?"

Guillaume looked doubtful. "But they don't like to play."

"Perhaps they will with her." He led Guillaume toward the paddock fence and motioned the stable hand to let the horses out into the paddock. "Climb up and watch them. They move like silk."

"Or fire." Guillaume's eyes were fixed on the two white streaks that bolted into the paddock. "White fire. Lightning, Papa. Could this woman tame the Pair for me? Could I ride them then?"

Marvot thought about telling him yes but then thought better of it. After he got what he wanted from the Pair, it was quite probable he'd dispose of them. "Sometimes it's better to enjoy a treat at a distance. Like this. Look at them run."

The moonlight was shimmering on the horses as they ran around the paddock. It had been a bright, clear night like this that he had first seen Grace Archer working with the Pair. He had been sure that the Pair would kill her, and he had been curious to see how she would behave in the face of death. He could still remember how slim and fragile she had looked in comparison with the brute strength of the horses. She had not died that night, and he had been filled with hope as he saw how the Pair responded to her.

Bitch.

"Aren't they pretty, Papa?" Guillaume's eyes were focused on the horses. "Look at the way they arch their necks."

"Magnificent," he said. And totally useless to him. As useless as they had been for these many years.

But perhaps for not much longer. He had thought to rid himself of a possible encumbrance by putting a death bounty on the child. He'd thought perhaps the woman would be better able to concentrate on the Pair without the girl. But he was glad that Kersoff had not killed her. Now that he had a line on Kersoff's contact, he could take over the operation himself.

And mothers were notoriously malleable when one used their children.

"They're coming toward us," Guillaume whispered. "Perhaps they want to be friends."

"Get off the fence," He told Guillaume. "That's not affection you're seeing. You have to learn to recognize and interpret."

"What?"

Hatred. He stared at the horses as they ran toward the fence. The Pair never lost an opportunity to try to savage him. They had hated him from the moment he'd brought them here. He wondered why when he had never personally mistreated them. Was it some deep instinct that recognized that he controlled the pain and whether they lived or died?

He jumped down off the fence as the horses reared only feet from his head.

"Papa!"

He turned to Guillaume, who was staring at him with fear—and feverish excitement. For a moment he was filled with anger, and then it vanished. Guillaume was his son, and Marvot would have felt that same excitement if it was his father who had been at risk. Love sometimes existed side by side with the desire for the one in control to be knocked from the throne. It was his own nature that he'd bequeathed to Guillaume. "You thought I might die." He clapped his son on the shoulder. "Not me. Never. I won't be beaten. It won't happen. Accept that."

"I only thought . . ."

"I know what you thought. I'll always know." He looked back at the Pair. "But I believe you need to witness what death means. It would be a good lesson for you. I've protected you too long. I saw my first violent death when I was your age. A young man annoyed my father and he had to be punished. My father didn't know I was awake and watching, but he found out later and asked me how I felt. I told him that I was proud of him, proud of his power, proud of him being able to lift his hand and crush anyone who disobeyed him. I was much closer to my father after that. He sent me to fine schools and gave me an education of which any scholar would be proud, but I never learned anything as important as I learned that night." He didn't take his gaze from the Pair. "Yes, we definitely need a lesson for you, Guillaume."

8

The blood wouldn't stop. . . .

No time to do anything but keep his hand pressed above the wound to try to stem the flow, Donavan thought as he tore through the shrubbery and jumped into the shallows of the river. They were right behind him.

He was going to die.

Screw it. This was no place for a good Irishman like him to bite it. Keep going. He knew a cave behind the waterfall a half mile from here where he could hide. He'd scouted it out the first week he'd set up surveillance of El Tariq.

If Marvot didn't know about that cave. It wasn't on his property, but close enough. If he did, then Donavan would be caught like a fox in a trap.

Worry about that later. Get to the cave and then stop this damn blood. Call Kilmer and tell him what had happened. He'd come or send someone.

If it wasn't too late . . .

* * *

I'm supposed to help you with the horses."

Grace turned away from brushing Samson to see Luis Vazquez grinning at her. "Hello, Luis. How have you been?"

"Well." Luis came into the stall and took the brush away from her. "You have been doing well too. I saw your daughter. She's very beautiful."

"Yes, if I remember you have a daughter too." Her brow wrinkled. "She was three. . . . How is she?"

"Mercedes? An angel." He grinned over his shoulder. "But she's becoming a young lady. It frightens me."

"You were going to go home to Argentina when you had enough money for a horse livery shop. Yet here you are."

"I tried to go home five years ago." He shrugged. "It didn't work out. I couldn't settle. It's difficult becoming a shopkeeper after you work with Kilmer. There was no excitement, no edge. I was bored and boring. My wife was glad to see me go." He chuckled. "Now we have great homecomings every few months and don't have to put up with each other for the rest of the time. A perfect arrangement."

"And Mercedes?"

"I'm a warrior, a hero. I bring her presents and tell her tales and I dazzle her. Every man needs to be a hero to someone." He took a step back from the stallion. "This is a fine animal. Good lines."

"Yes." She paused. "Did you go along when Kilmer stole Cosmo?"

He nodded. "Very scary. I thought Kilmer was dead meat. It was lucky the bullet bounced off his canteen and went into the rib cage instead of his heart."

She went still. "He was shot?"

"Didn't he tell you? He was bringing up the rear and one of Marvot's men got off a round before we were out of range."

The bullet bounced off his canteen and went into the rib cage instead of his heart.

A chill went through her. So close. Christ, he might have died and she would never have known.

"No, he didn't tell me."

"Donavan poked fun at him for a month. He said it would have served Kilmer right to die because he stole the blasted jackass. Kilmer didn't think it was funny. He had the devil of a time getting that jackass here."

"I can see how he would."

"But if he's going for the Pair, he had to have Cosmo. And now he has you, Grace. Everything's falling into place for him."

"He doesn't have me," she said coolly as she turned away. It was idiotic to feel this shocked. Kilmer lived with death every day of his life. There had been several close calls when she had worked with him.

But that had been different. She had been there, she had shared the danger.

"No offense," Luis said. "I thought that was what this was all about. We were going to get that bastard Marvot and take the Pair. When I saw you, I knew that—"

"Luis!" Dillon was standing in the doorway of the stable. "Front and center. We're heading out. The helicopter will be here in ten minutes. Get your gear."

"Right." Even as he spoke he was throwing down the brush and heading at a dead run for the door. "See you, Grace."

Grace stood watching, stunned, as he disappeared. How many times had she answered that call and responded in the same way? But that call shouldn't have happened here.

Not here.

She strode out of the stable and headed for the house. The stable yard was filled with Kilmer's men, moving, gathering equipment, but silent, swift, efficient. Kilmer was on the porch talking to Robert and looked up as she came up the steps. He made a motion to Robert, who disappeared inside the house.

"What's happening?" Her hands clenched into fists. "Where are you going?"

"I'm not leaving you and Frankie unprotected," he said quietly. "I've ordered Blockman and four of the team to stay here. I should be back in two days, tops. If I'm not, I'll call you. If there's a problem, Blockman will take you and Frankie to another safe house in the mountains near here that I've told him about."

"What's happening?" she repeated.

"Donavan's down. He's still alive, but I don't know how long he'll stay that way if I don't get him out. He says he's lost a lot of blood."

"Donavan," she whispered. "Where?"

"El Tariq. Or near there. Marvot's men surprised him. One of Marvot's scouts must have spotted him and then brought back the troops."

"It will be hours and hours before you can get to El Tariq. Can't you arrange for someone closer to go after him?"

"Not at El Tariq. The risk is too high. I checked with Tonino and the hills are crawling with Marvot's men." He checked his watch. "I'll call when I reach El Tariq, but after that you won't hear from me until we're on our way back. Marvot's men may be able to pick up the signal. I told Donavan not to call me again unless he changed locations." He looked up at the sky. "There's the chopper." He started down the steps. "Don't worry, you'll be okay. I've given instructions that—"

"You're damn right I'll be okay. I can take care of Frankie. I've done it all her life." She glared at him. "And why do you think I'm such a bitch that I wouldn't want you to go after Donavan? Are you supposed to leave him to bleed to death? Get the hell out of here."

He smiled. "I'm going, I'm going. What a nag."

She watched him trot across the yard toward the helicopter that had just landed. The wind from the rotors was blowing his hair and pressing his khaki shirt against his lean body. He motioned the team to board the helicopter and stood there until every man was on board. That was Kilmer's standard operational procedure, Grace remembered. He was always the last man out.

And it was probably why Kilmer had almost bought it when he'd stolen Cosmo.

And why he'd gone back to El Tariq that night nine years ago to get his men out of the hills around the estate.

Always the last man out.

She'd understood that he had to go back and retrieve the rest of his team. She hadn't understood why he didn't let her go to Tangiers to get to her father when there was a chance she could have saved him.

"Where are they going, Mom?" Frankie was standing beside her.

"One of the men who works for Kilmer is hurt and in trouble. They're going to help him."

"Could we go?"

Grace glanced down and saw Frankie's troubled expression. "Why? You don't even know this man."

"I don't want Jake to get hurt too. Maybe we could make sure he didn't. Don't you want to go?"

"No, I—" She *did* want to go, she realized suddenly. She wanted to be one of the team jumping into that helicopter. She wanted to be part of the teamwork that would bring Donavan to safety.

If he was still alive when Kilmer got to him.

"Yes, I'd like to go," she told Frankie. "The man who's hurt is a good friend of mine. But sometimes you can't do what you want. Sometimes it's better if you stay at home and don't get in the way."

"I wouldn't get in the way."

"You might not mean to." She paused. "Remember when we went to see *The Nutcracker*? All those dancers were used to doing exactly what they were taught to do. What would happen if someone from the audience got up on stage and tried to dance with them?"

Frankie chuckled. "It would be funny."

"But it would cause the real dancers to make mistakes because they'd be trying to get out of the way. Can you see that?"

Frankie's smile faded. "I guess so. I wouldn't know the steps."

Grace nodded.

"But you'd know the steps, Mom."

Grace watched the helicopter leave the ground. Yes, she'd know the steps, and she wanted to execute them, dammit. "I might have forgotten a lot. It's best that I stay with you." She forced herself to turn away and not watch the helicopter disappear. "Let's go inside and find Robert. It's almost time to make supper."

But Frankie was still staring at the helicopter. "I like Jake. He'll be okay, won't he, Mom? He won't die like Charlie?"

How could she answer that without risking lying to Frankie?

Last man out.

"He has a great chance." Her arm slid around Frankie's shoulders. "Jake has dealt with situations like this for years and he's very, very clever."

Frankie didn't speak for a moment, and Grace knew that she realized her mother hadn't given her a positive answer. Then she said, "And he knows the steps. Right?"

"He knows all the steps. Every one." She brushed a kiss on Frankie's temple. "In fact, he invented a few himself."

"That's good." Her expression was still troubled. "But Charlie wasn't young like Jake. And he was smart too. He should have learned a lot in those years. But he died, Mom."

Trust Frankie to come up with the comparison with Charlie's death that was uppermost on her mind. And that comparison was sending a chill through Grace as well. She drew a deep breath. "Look, if Jake gets in trouble and needs help, I promise I'll go and get him out. Okay?"

"And not get hurt yourself?"

Jesus, so much for not making promises she couldn't keep to Frankie in the name of honesty. "And not get hurt myself. Now, may we go and get something to eat?"

Frankie nodded. "Sure." She glanced back at the sky, but the helicopter had disappeared over the horizon. "Helicopters are kinda neat, aren't they? When the propellers go around, it's like the sound of a whip. Kind of sharp but there's still a rhythm. . . ."

Don't be stupid. Leave me," Donavan whispered. "It's too late. Get the team out of here."

"Screw you." Kilmer tightened his hold around Donavan's waist as he dragged him through the muddy water. "Do you think I came all this way and got these blasted bloodsucking leeches on my legs to let Marvot have you for breakfast? This isn't about you. It's about my goddamn ego."

Donavan started to laugh but ended in a cough. "Bastard."

"Yes." Kilmer moved quicker, his gaze searching the woods on either side. They had eliminated four of Marvot's patrol when they came in an hour ago, but there could be more. "Now shut up. If I can get you through this creek and the woods, we'll have a chance. We'll rendezvous with the rest of the team at the road. And the chopper's five miles on the other side of the road."

"Five miles or five hundred. It's still not—"

"Look, it's going to happen. Now, put one foot in front of the other and keep your lips closed. I'm not going to die in this stinking river and I'm not going to leave you. That leaves only one other choice. I have to be a damn hero."

"I'd never be able to stand it if you saved my life. You'd

never let me hear the end of it. I'd rather give up the ghost now."

"Donavan."

"Okay, okay. I'll shut up. I'm feeling a little weak anyway. If you don't get me out of here soon, I may faint and make you carry me."

"Don't you dare."

"I believe . . . it's happening. . . ." His words were coming in gasps. "If you're going to be a hero, I should make sure you . . . do . . . it . . . right. . . ."

You okay?" Robert asked as he came out on the porch. "You were quiet at supper."

"Was I? Do you think Frankie noticed?" Grace grimaced. "God knows I'm trying to act normal."

"Frankie was quiet herself. I think she's absorbed in her music," Robert said. "You're worried?"

"He said he'd call by last night. Hell, yes, I'm worried."

"Things happen."

"I know that," she snapped. She took a deep breath and then let it out slowly. "And I know that some of those things that happen are bad. The entire team could be wiped out. Kilmer could be dead." She crossed her arms across her breasts to stop their shaking. "We should have heard from him."

"What do you want to do? Should I call North and see if he's heard any word of a disturbance at El Tariq?"

"No. It's dangerous for Frankie if we make any contact when we know there was a leak before. We wait."

"Not long. I promised Kilmer I'd get you and Frankie away from here by tomorrow if he didn't get back. He was afraid one of the team would be caught and forced to talk."

"We'll wait until day after tomorrow." She shook her head. Christ, what was she thinking? "No, you're right. We have to get Frankie away. I'll have her ready to leave by dawn tomorrow." She added wearily, "Dammit, I hate to have her forced to go on the run again."

"I do too." Robert turned away and opened the screen door. "But that's life."

Or death, she thought with a shiver. Kilmer's death.

She looked out at the mountains. Why was that possibility hurting her so badly? She'd gone for nine years without even thinking about him, and now it—

No, that was a lie. Kilmer had always been there in the back of her mind in spite of her trying to deny it. How could it be any other way? He'd been the prime sexual experience of her life. She'd admired him and respected him. She'd given birth to his child.

And he'd kept her from going to her father when he'd needed her. It didn't matter that she would have been too late to save him. Kilmer had taken away the choice.

Certainly that knowledge was still angering her, but the stark possibility of Kilmer's death seemed to dwarf everything else.

She could hear Frankie playing the keyboard inside the house. She wasn't composing right now. She was taking a break and playing Mozart. Beautiful. So beautiful. And Kilmer had never had the opportunity to realize just how beautiful she was in every way.

And now he might never know.

Her cell phone rang at three forty-three in the morning.

She jumped for the phone on the nightstand. "Hello."

"We're coming home," Kilmer said. "We're boarding the plane now outside Tangiers."

Thank God.

She couldn't speak for a number of seconds. "You said you'd call last night." Jesus, that was an idiotic thing to say.

"I was a little busy," he said dryly. "And I couldn't use the cell phone anywhere near El Tariq. Marvot's men were all over the area and I couldn't risk them picking up the signal. I'll be home tomorrow."

"Donavan?"

"Alive. We patched him up and got him a transfusion, but he's not good. I picked up a doctor here in Tangiers to take with us on the plane. I can't put him in a hospital. Marvot has too many local contacts. Everything okay there?"

"Yes."

"Good." He hung up.

She slowly pressed the disconnect. Dear God, her hand was trembling. She was almost dizzy with relief . . . and joy.

"Mom?" Frankie had raised up on one elbow. "Was that Jake?"

"Yes." She had to clear her throat. "He's safe. He's coming home."

Frankie sat upright, her face alight. "When? May I go tell Robert?"

"He'll be back tomorrow." She steadied her voice. "And I believe that letting Robert know would be a very good idea. Go on."

Frankie jumped out of bed and streaked out of the room.

She should have gone to tell Robert herself, but she didn't want to face anyone now. She was too shaken. Christ, she'd thought it was over. How could it not be over?

It might be over, but this emotion she was feeling was too strong to ignore. It had to be identified and resolved. She couldn't go through the rest of her life like this. In a state of denial but torn to pieces by memories and feelings that she couldn't banish. The sensible thing would be to face it and rid herself of any lingering emotion for Kilmer she'd suppressed. Yes, that would be the logical, sensible thing.

Oh, God, he was *alive*.

She heard the throb of the helicopter rotors an hour after she had gone to bed the following night. She jumped out of bed and ran to the window. Blue-white light was spearing down from the helicopter as it slowly descended.

"Is it Jake?" Frankie asked.

"I think so." She grabbed a robe and headed for the door. "Stay here until I'm sure." She met Robert on the stairs. "Kilmer?"

He nodded. "He called me ten minutes ago and told me that he was coming in and to get a room ready for Donavan." He jerked his head. "I'm giving him my room. I'll bed down with the rest of the team in the bunkhouse. I changed the sheets. . . ." He ran down the steps and out the door.

She followed him and reached the porch in time to see the helicopter doors open and Kilmer jump out. "Get Donavan inside." He turned to Blockman. "Everything okay?"

Robert nodded. "My room. Second on the left. How is he?"

"Dopey. Dr. Krallon has kept him under sedation from the time he left Tangiers." His gaze shifted to Grace as two of his men carefully lifted Donavan out of the helicopter on a stretcher. "He's going to make it, Grace. The big threat was the shock."

"Thank heaven." She looked down at Donavan's face as he was carried past her. "Jesus, he's pale."

Donavan opened his eyes. "Kilmer's fault," he whispered. "He let all those leeches suck the blood out of me."

"Ungrateful bastard," Kilmer said. "I'm the one who got eaten alive." He gestured to the men carrying him. "Get him inside and up to bed before I open those stitches and let him bleed to death."

"Too late," Donavan said. "I have Grace to protect me." His eyes focused blearily on her. "Hi, Grace, how you doing?"

"Better than you." Nevertheless, she was relieved to see that he was well enough to joke with Kilmer. "But we'll take care of that," she called after him as he was carried up the stairs. "So give Kilmer hell whenever you feel like it."

"Thanks a lot," Kilmer said. He turned to the short, dark-skinned man who had come to stand beside him. "Grace Archer, this is Dr. Hussein Krallon. He's taking care of Donavan."

"My pleasure, madam." The doctor bowed politely. "And now I must get to my patient. With your permission?" He didn't wait for her assent but hurried after Donavan.

"Is Donavan safe with him?" Grace asked as she watched him disappear down the hall. "Marvot wields a lot of influence in Morocco."

"I've used him before. He hates Marvot's guts. His son was murdered in a drug-related crime by one of Marvot's thugs five years ago. He won't smother Donavan in his sleep and he'll get him well just to spite Marvot." He paused. "How's Frankie?"

"Fine." Lord, he looked tired. "When did you get any sleep?"

"I dozed on the plane." He rubbed his jaw. "But I need to get rid of this stubble."

"Jake!" Frankie was at the top of the stairs. "You look like a pirate." She ran down the stairs, her wary gaze on her mother. "Sorry I didn't stay in my room. But I saw Jake get out of the helicopter and I knew it was all right. I think you forgot me."

"I think you're right." She smiled. "So I'm the one who should be sorry. As you can see, Jake's safe and sound."

"Good. We were worried about you, Jake."

"Were you?" His gaze went to Grace. "Both of you?"

"Naturally. I was worried about you getting Donavan out."

"What a cut." He grimaced and then smiled at Frankie. "Since you don't know Donavan, may I assume you were worried about me alone?"

"Of course. I like you." She glanced at Grace. "Could I get Jake some hot chocolate? He looks like he needs... something."

"It's late."

"I can't go back to sleep now. I'm too excited."

"Jake can take care of—" She saw the disappointment in Frankie's face. "Sure, go ahead. I'm going up to make sure Donavan's settled. I'll be down in fifteen minutes and then you go to bed. Deal?"

"Deal." She ran down the hall toward the kitchen.

Grace started back up the stairs. "If you don't want to bother with her, send her up. She just wants to do something for you."

"Not in a million years. I'm honored." He paused. "I'm just curious as to why you're letting her associate with me."

She looked back over her shoulder. "It must have been rough over there. She's right; you look like you need something. Maybe it's not hot chocolate, but Frankie is a great healer. When I'm hurting, just being around her makes me feel better."

"I can see how that would be true." He turned away. "Thanks, Grace."

His tone was filled with weariness, and she stopped on the stairs. "How close was it, Kilmer?"

"Close enough for me to regret a lot of things I haven't done in my life. And close enough for me to regret not having a will made up to protect you and Frankie." He smiled faintly. "But I guess that would have offended you too."

"We don't need it. Charlie left Frankie the horse farm."

"Good. But that doesn't mean I don't have an obligation."

"It's a little late."

He nodded. "I know. But I have to play the cards the way they're dealt. Good night, Grace." He started down the hall. "If you want to go on to bed, I'll make sure Frankie gets back to you."

"I'll do it." She didn't want to leave him, she realized, shocked. She wanted to stand there and look at him. She wanted to do something, anything, to smooth away those lines of exhaustion on his face. Christ, she was as bad as Frankie.

No, worse.

Because it wasn't a hot chocolate she wanted to offer him.

"Grace?" He had stopped and was looking back at her, his gaze reading her expression.

"No." She shook her head, panicky. "It doesn't mean anything. I'm just grateful about Donavan. It's crazy to think—"

"Easy," he said quietly. "I'm not thinking anything. I'm too scared to even hope. I just want you to know if you want to use me in any way, I'd be happy as hell. I wouldn't expect more than you want to give. I wouldn't ask more than—" He shook his head and said roughly, "The hell I wouldn't. I'd devour you and ask for more. It was always that way with us."

His words sent a jolt of tingling electricity through her body. Yes, they had always been insatiable where sex was concerned. "No." She moistened her lips. "There are too many years, too much else between us."

"It wouldn't get in the way of sex. I guarantee it."

"You couldn't guarantee— Why am I even talking to you?"

"Because you're looking for a way to take what you want. Take it, Grace. No consequences. I promise."

She shook her head and hurried up the stairs. She was running away, she thought in exasperation. So much for coming to terms with what she was feeling for Kilmer. She'd only had to see him and she was caught up in that intensity that made her dizzy and weak in the knees.

And heat. She felt as if she had a fever, tingling, her breath coming short and shallow.

As it had been nine years ago.

But she wasn't that woman. She was Frankie's mother, and that was enough.

No, dammit, at this moment it wasn't enough.

Take what you want.

That would be too dangerous, too all-consuming. She'd

been satisfied before he came back. She'd be content again after he was gone.

Content. What a puny word.

Happy. She was always happy with Frankie. She didn't need that madness she'd experienced with Kilmer. . . .

9

"Did you have a good night, Donavan?" She smiled as she opened his door the next morning. She glanced at Dr. Krallon, who rose quickly from his chair. "Has he been a bad patient?"

"Terrible." The doctor shook his head. "He curses me and refuses to do what I tell him. He has no gratitude."

"A bedpan, Grace." Donavan shook his head. "He wouldn't get me up to go to the bathroom. It was humiliating."

"And practical." She sat down in the chair the doctor had vacated. "Go get your breakfast, Doctor. I'll stay with him."

"Gladly." The doctor headed for the door. "And if I can bring myself to forgive him, I'll get him breakfast when I return."

Donavan smiled as the door closed behind him. "He's a nice little guy. And stubborn, damn stubborn."

"Then stop giving him a bad time. And you know that

you can't get out of bed to go to the bathroom yet. Give it a couple days."

"A man has to make a dignified protest."

"A man has to be reasonable and stop making trouble." She studied his face. "You have more color this morning. I was worried about you last night, but today I can see that you're as mean as ever."

"Certainly. I was only playing on your sympathies when they toted me off that helicopter. It was the dignity thing again. Kilmer comes striding in like a conquering hero and there I was lolling on that stretcher, weak as a kitten. I had to work it for all I could get."

Her brows rose. "It was all an act?"

"Well, perhaps I was a little out of sorts. It was a night-mare trip." His gaze fastened on her face. "You look older, Grace."

"Thanks a lot."

"No, it's becoming. You were always interesting, but now you have a . . . depth. I want to keep on looking at you to see what's hiding beneath the surface."

"Nothing's hiding. I'm as uncomplicated as I've always been."

He shook his head. "Uncomplicated my ass. You were a mass of contradictions from the moment you got off the plane almost nine years ago. You were patriotic and yet you'd seen too much to totally trust any government. You were brave but you were scared to commit. You wanted friends but you were afraid to reach out and take them for fear they'd go away."

"Good God, Donavan. Since when did you become a psychologist?"

"Just one of my minor talents." He smiled. "But I only use it with people I like. And I don't voice my opinions un-less asked."

"I didn't ask."

"And when I want to butt into something that's none of my business."

She stiffened. "What are you talking about?"

"I thought I was going to die in that river."

"So?"

"Kilmer saved my bacon. It's not the first time. There's not much he'll let me do for him, so I decided to take matters into my own hands."

"What matters?"

"He cared about you, Grace. I don't know how much. He won't talk about it. But I know that he was crazy about you."

"Sex."

"Yeah, I know that had a lot to do with it. But there was more."

She shook her head.

"See, you always saw things the way you wanted to see them."

"You're tired. I'm going to leave and let you rest." She started to get up.

"Don't you dare move." He coughed. "You'll cause me to have a relapse."

"You're not recovered enough to have a relapse."

"Then be still so that I can reach that happy state. I'm about to be profound. I need an audience."

She slowly sat back down. "You're taking advantage of that blasted wound."

He nodded. "Why not? It hurts like hell. I should get something positive out of it."

"We'll talk later."

"What if I get a blood clot and die? It happens. No, it's got to be now. It's perfect timing. I'm too pitiful for you to slug me. And by the time I'm well you'll have had time to get over it."

"Get over what?"

"Your defensiveness when I tell you that you've been a close-minded bitch where Kilmer's concerned."

She went still. "I don't have to take this, Donavan."

"Yes, you do." He coughed again. "See, you're upsetting me. I can feel that clot forming."

"Liar."

"You can leave me alone. But the doctor may find me dead as a doornail when he comes back."

"Bluff."

"But it's working." He added slyly, "You've gotten softer over the years. It must be that motherhood thing."

"Talk," she said through her teeth.

"You cheated Kilmer. You had something special going. I've never seen him like that with any woman. Kilmer never lies. Why the hell didn't you trust him instead of running away?"

"You know why. He kept me from going to help my father." Her hands clenched on the arms of the chair. "He's lucky I didn't strangle him."

"He kept you from walking straight into Marvot's hands."

"You don't know that."

"Yes, I do. Kilmer sent me to Tangiers to contact your father that night. Your sweet papa wouldn't leave. He told me that it was better that you work with Marvot, that there was big money to be had if you left the agency and concentrated on gentling the Pair for that bastard. That's why he made a deal with Marvot and tipped him about the raid."

"No." She glared at him. "You're lying."

"I don't believe he wanted you hurt. He said he'd gotten a guarantee that you wouldn't be killed in the raid. He honestly believed that what was best for him was best for you."

"Three men died in that raid. You're saying he as good as murdered them?"

He was silent.

"I don't believe you."

"Why should I lie to you? I have nothing to gain."

"How could he expect me to work with Marvot? I'd never do it."

"Not even if you thought that your father was being held hostage?"

"But you'd tell me differently."

"If I was alive. I escaped being caught by the skin of my teeth when he called one of Marvot's hoods from the next room. I got a bullet in the leg and I was on the run for two days. I did manage to call Kilmer and tell him to keep you the hell away from Tangiers."

"My father was killed by Marvot."

"Marvot obviously thought the trap was blown and your father wasn't of use any longer. But he could kill your father as punishment for your part in the raid. It would be a warning to you when he caught up with you."

She shook her head. "No."

"Yes."

"If it's true, why didn't Kilmer tell me any of this?"

"He told you that your father tipped Marvot. But that was the night your father died. Was he supposed to elaborate on what a scumbag your father really was and that he had proof? You loved your father. You trusted him. He was the only person you had in the world. I think Kilmer was planning on trying to talk to you later, but there was no later. You ran away. Kilmer got word that Marvot was after you and he had to find a way to protect you. Then North told him you were pregnant. That cinched it. He couldn't be there to protect you and he wasn't going to strip you of the little comfort you had."

"My father loved me." Her voice was shaking. "He did love me, Donavan."

"Maybe. There are a lot of funny kinds of love in the world. He didn't love you enough to keep you out of Marvot's hands if it meant money in his pocket. I was there, Grace. You were being set up." He met her gaze. "You know I don't lie. I've got a scar in my left thigh as a souvenir of that night. Do you want to see it?"

She shook her head.

"You believe me?"

"I don't know. Oh, God, I don't want to believe you, Donavan."

He nodded. "You believe me. I'd bet you knew in your heart that Stiller had betrayed us. You just couldn't admit it to yourself. Now you have to admit it. Come to terms with it." He closed his eyes. "Now I have to rest and fight off that blood clot so I can use it again sometime when I need blackmail. Do you think it would work with Kilmer?"

"No."

"You can never tell. He's not as much of a hard-ass as you'd think. . . ." He opened his eyes. "It's the truth, Grace. As God is my witness, every word is true. Now tell me you believe me."

"I can't," she whispered.

"Tell me."

"I won't." The tears were brimming. "It hurts."

"Tell me."

"All right, dammit. I believe you." The tears were running down her cheeks. "Satisfied?"

"Yes." He closed his eyes again. "Go away. Nothing like a weeping woman to make a man feel bad. I mean worse. I want to meet your daughter, Grace. Will you let her come to see me?"

She didn't answer as she headed for the door.

"I'd be a good friend to your daughter. Don't let your bitterness hurt her."

"I wouldn't do that." She opened the door. "I'll bring her to see you tonight." She rested her head on the door-jamb. "And I'm not . . . bitter with you. You did what you thought best. I'm just raw and hurting. And I know Frankie needs friends."

"Kilmer could be a good friend to her too."

"Back off, Donavan."

"Just thought I'd strike while the iron is hot."

"Hot enough to burn me alive." The door shut behind her and she took a moment to try to compose herself. She wiped her eyes and took a deep breath. She couldn't go down to breakfast with Frankie when she could barely cope. She'd expected to comfort Donavan, not be savaged by him.

Jesus, she was hurting. Was Donavan right? Had she known that her father had betrayed them but refused to admit it? Had she clung to the security of having just one person in the world she could trust to love her? Was she that weak?

Truth.

Think about it. Come to terms with it as Donavan had told her to do.

Go downstairs. Have breakfast. Don't let Frankie know she was upset. Then go off by herself as soon as she could to get her mind clear and straight. Right now that seemed an impossible task. She was shaking and she had to stop these damn tears from falling.

She started down the stairs, pasting a smile on her face. Don't let Frankie know. . . .

Frankie was sitting on the top bar of the corral, her gaze on the mountains. Waiting.

Kilmer watched her for a few moments before he left the porch and walked across the stable yard. "What are you doing here?"

"Nothing."

"Mind if I join you?" He climbed the fence to sit beside her. "I haven't done nothing in a long time. I want to see if I've been missing something."

She smiled. "It's pretty boring."

"That's what I thought. So why are we doing it?"

She didn't speak for a moment. "Mom's been gone a long time. I wanted to be here when she got back."

He stiffened. "How long?"

"A couple hours. She rode out on Samson and hasn't come back."

"Did you see her go?"

She nodded. "She was acting . . . funny. It bothered me."

"Funny?"

She shrugged. "Something like that." She frowned. "Like she does when she has a headache or a cold and doesn't want to worry me."

"You mean when she's hurting."

"I don't know. It bothered me."

"She's probably fine." He paused. "Would you like me to go after her?"

"She wouldn't like it. She never wants me to worry about her. That's why I didn't take Gypsy and go myself."

"But I don't have to worry about what she thinks of me. Most of the time she's mad at me anyway. So I think I'll borrow Gypsy from you and go find her. Okay?"

She nodded, relieved. "It's not that I think she's hurt or anything. I've never seen her thrown, and Samson loves her now. It's just—"

"She was stiff." Kilmer got down from the fence. "And you'll feel better when you have her back." He headed for the stable. "Which direction?"

She pointed to the west. "The foothills."

"I have men patrolling the foothills, Frankie. If anything had happened to her, we'd know about it. But I'll take a look anyway."

"And you won't tell her I was worried?"

"No, I won't promise that. Sometimes it's a comfort to know someone loves you enough to worry about you. Your mother probably feels pretty much alone since your friend Charlie died. Maybe that's why she wasn't feeling very happy today." He smiled. "At any rate, we'll ask her and then make it right. That's the best way of handling it. Much better than ignoring it. Why don't you go to the house and work on your music until I get back? I'm sure she'd rather hear that when she comes home than see you perched on that fence."

Frankie nodded and climbed down. "I'll try. But it's hard to concentrate when something's wrong with Mom."

"I'll make it right, Frankie."

She studied him and then slowly nodded. "Okay." She smiled. "I believe you." She ran toward the house. "Gypsy doesn't like to be near fences. She shies. Be careful."

Kilmer watched her disappear into the house.

I believe you.

Be careful.

Christ, he felt like some medieval warrior knighted by his queen. Proud and full of hope and the fire of purpose to go out and battle dragons.

Is that how most fathers felt about their children? Probably. But for him it was new and fresh and made him remember a time before he was the cynical son of a bitch he was now. How long ago was that? Perhaps when he was younger than his daughter.

When you were eight like Frankie, anything seemed possible.

And when you had a Frankie in your life, you tried to make sure that even the impossible became possible.

Don't you think it's time you started back?"

Grace whirled away from the stream where she'd been watering Samson to see Kilmer on Gypsy a few yards away. He was the last person she wanted here right now, she thought in frustration. She was still too upset, still on that emotional roller coaster started by Donavan. "Not unless there's a reason why I should. Is this area hazardous to my health?"

"No, it's safe." He got off Gypsy and led her toward the stream. "But Frankie's not too happy. She thinks there's something wrong with you."

"Oh, shit."

His gaze searched her face. "Is there?"

She didn't answer. "I'll go back."

"Is there?"

"Nothing that should affect Frankie."

"Everything you are and do affects Frankie. I promised her I'd make it right. How do I go about doing that?"

"You shouldn't make promises you can't keep."

"I'll keep this one." He smiled ruefully. "I can't do anything else. I've never made a promise to a child before. It's a big responsibility. You already know about that but I'm just finding out. So tell me how I can make her stop worrying."

"Leave it to me."

His smile faded. "I've left too much to you. I'm not doing it again."

She looked away from him. "Until Frankie and I are out of sight, out of mind."

"You were never out of mind. And you're never going to be out of sight again."

"I don't believe you."

"You will if you'll stop looking at everything but me."

She didn't take her gaze from the pines in the glade in front of her. "I don't want to look at you."

"Because you're a pretty good judge of character and you know that I'll never lie to you. Even when I told you about your father, you—"

"Shut up." Her gaze flew to his face. "Why didn't you and Donavan come after me and make me listen? Why did you let me go on lying to myself?"

He went still. "Donavan talked to you."

"This morning," she said curtly. "He couldn't wait."

"Sorry. I thought I could get to him first. You didn't need to have to handle this now."

"When did you intend to tell me? Another nine years?"

He shook his head. "I'm no masochist. I was just going to give you a little more time."

"For God's sake, I'm not a helpless idiot." She tried to steady her voice. "So I wanted to believe something that wasn't true. So it hurts me and makes me feel a little empty. I can handle it."

"I know you can." He paused. "But I don't know if I can. Maybe you can give me some advice."

"You don't need advice." She gathered the reins and prepared to mount. "As I told Frankie, you know all the steps."

"The hell I do." His grasp on her shoulder spun her away from Samson. "I've been stumbling blind since the moment I met you." His eyes were glittering with intensity as they stared into hers. "I didn't know what hit me."

"Sex."

"Hell, yes. But there was something else. Sex just got in the way. We didn't have time to find out if we had a chance for something— It was my fault. I should have— But every time I started to talk to you about—" He shrugged. "Maybe if we'd had a few more months. I couldn't keep my hands off you. That was the only thing that seemed important. That's the bottom line."

And she hadn't been able to keep her hands off him. "Maybe that was all there was."

"We didn't get a chance to find out." His lips twisted. "And when I found out you were pregnant, I felt angry and cheated. I didn't even think about the kid. I admit it. I just knew that there wasn't a hope for me. You were angry with me about your father, and I'd knocked you up and burdened you with a child you didn't want. All I could do was damage control."

"I did want Frankie."

"When you first found out?"

She shook her head.

"See?"

"That's all in the past." She tried to move away from him. "I don't want to talk about it now."

"I know. You're hurting." His hands moved slowly, almost yearningly, on her shoulders. "I'll leave you alone. Soon."

She was aware that her breathing was becoming shallow. His touch was spreading tingling sensations through her body. Jesus . . . She swallowed. "Now."

"Yeah." He didn't release her. "But it's no good, you know. We have to find out. It ended too soon. It wasn't fair to— We have to find out."

"I found out eight years ago when Frankie was born. It's over."

"Liar. Then why is your heart beating so hard I can see it in the hollow of your throat?"

She took a deep breath and jerked away from him. She turned and hurriedly got on the horse.

"Be honest with me and yourself," he said quietly. "It will be safe for you. Your choice. I'm not backing you into a corner." He smiled. "Though I may back you toward the nearest bed given the opportunity. That wouldn't be so bad. You know you'd like it."

Yes, she'd like it. She'd probably go crazy if what she was feeling was any sign. "I can't deal with this now."

He nodded. "I'm not being fair. If I was the kind of man Blockman is, I'd back off. You've just had a shock and you're upset. But I'm not like Blockman. You've got to deal with me as I am."

"I don't have to deal with you at all."

"Yes, you do. I'm not opting out again. Choose the role you need from me, because I'm not going away."

A wild mixture of emotion was tearing through her as she stared at him. Crazy. She mustn't feel like this. She had come out here to get her head straight, and now it was spinning.

"Frankie's waiting for you," he said quietly.

Yes, Frankie was waiting. It was Frankie who was important, not this inner turmoil. She kicked Samson into a gallop that sent them racing across the fields toward the ranch.

* * *

Hi, Mom." Frankie met her as she came up the porch steps. Her gaze searched Grace's face, and then she gave a relieved sigh. "You're okay again."

"I was always okay." She gave her a hug. "Why would you think I wasn't?"

"You weren't . . . right." She shook her head. "I don't know. But Jake fixed it. He said he would."

"Oh, he did? How do you know he fixed it?"

"You look like you do when you've had a good ride. Sort of glowing."

"You've got a great imagination." She kissed her cheek. "But if you're worried again, you come to me and talk about it. Don't go to strangers."

"Jake doesn't feel like a stranger," Frankie said. "I have to go to the barn and work out with Robert now. He said I haven't practiced my martial arts enough since I've been here. Want to come and watch?"

"I wouldn't miss it. You go on. I'll be there as soon as I go to the bathroom and grab a bottle of water."

"Okay." Frankie looked back at her as she ran down the stairs. "You do look pretty, Mom. Sort of . . . young."

"Thank you, I think."

She watched Frankie run across the yard toward the stable before she went inside and headed for the bathroom. Robert was doing just the right thing, keeping Frankie busy and focused on the ordinary tasks that had been her life before it was disrupted. They all had to concentrate on—

My God.

She had caught a glimpse of her face in the mirror of the medicine chest. She reached up and tentatively touched her cheek, which was flushed with color.

Glowing, Frankie had said.

Young, Frankie had said.

Twenty-three again, when every minute of life was exciting.

No, she didn't want that time back. And she didn't want to look this vulnerable and full of hope and dreams.

And she didn't want Kilmer to have the power to bring about that metamorphosis. She'd spent only a short time with him, and yet the result of the emotion he'd ignited was staring at her from the mirror.

Lord help her. Twenty-three again.

I'm not pleased, Hanley," Marvot said. "How did Kilmer get his man through our lines?"

"There was a distraction from another group he'd stationed to the west. By the time we realized it was a false alarm, he was—"

"Making me look foolish." Marvot's hand clenched into a fist on the desk. "My father taught me that dignity was everything, and you've let Kilmer humiliate me three times. First he stole the pouch, then he took that blasted jackass, and now he plucks a wounded man away from within ten miles of El Tariq. And you were in charge on two out of three of those occasions." His tone took on silky venom. "I believe it's time you made restitution, don't you?"

"I accept full blame," Hanley said. "I thought— It was unfortunate that—"

"Unfortunate? That's not a word I accept. Now tell me how I'm going to keep my associates from thinking I'm a soft touch and trying to move in on my territory?"

"We'll find Kilmer and Grace Archer."

"When?"

"The negotiations with the man at Langley are proceeding slowly. He's playing very coy." He added quickly as he saw Marvot's expression, "But I intend to fly out tonight and take over myself to make sure that we get what we want. I won't come back until I have Kilmer's location."

"No, you won't come back until you have Kilmer—and Grace Archer. I'm going to have to set an example to erase the taint of your failures. No one is going to be allowed to think that I'm less than my father. I'm not going to have my son hear rumors that I'm a weakling and a fool." His lips tightened. "I'll give you seven days to give me Kilmer and Archer, Hanley. No delays, no excuses. Seven days. After that I start the example with you."

10

"Donavan, this is my daughter, Frankie," Grace said. "She's been anxious to meet you. What's your first name, Donavan? I don't think I've ever heard it."

"And you're not about to. My mother made the mistake of giving me a name unfit for my gigantic strength and talents. Donavan is just fine."

"How intriguing. It tempts me to do a little in-depth exploring," Grace murmured. "Frankie, Donavan and I used to work together a long time ago." She closed the door of the bedroom. "He taught me a lot."

"Yes, I did." Donavan held out his hand. "And I'm very pleased to meet you, Frankie." He frowned. "But a beautiful lass like yourself should be called by a beautiful name. Your true name is Francesca, isn't it?"

Frankie nodded. "But that's too fancy. I like Frankie better."

Donavan glanced at Grace. "Why Francesca, Grace?"

"I spent a few years in Italy as a child and I always liked it." She grinned at Frankie. "But I didn't want to hang a big name on a little girl, so Frankie seemed a good compromise."

Donavan shook his head. "She could carry Francesca off with style."

"What did you teach my mother?" Frankie asked. "Spy stuff?"

"Well, a little more basic training. You can't spy or steal secrets until you know how to protect yourself and get in and out of tight corners."

Frankie frowned. "You didn't get out of your tight corner very well. You got shot."

"True." Donavan chuckled. "But I assure you that I wasn't that clumsy when I was teaching your mother." He looked at Grace. "And she was one of my best pupils. I was proud of her. Of course, Kilmer would have strangled me if I hadn't done a good job. He was very particular."

"Jake?" Frankie smiled. "Mom says he's clever. I like him."

"So do I."

"Frankie, we have to let Donavan get to sleep," Grace said. "You can visit him another time."

"I feel a relapse coming on," Donavan said. "Don't cut me short. I want to get to know your daughter. You run along and leave her with me to get acquainted."

"Donavan, the doctor—" Grace shrugged and gazed at Frankie. "What do you say?"

"She wants to stay and have me tell her all about her mom," Donavan said. "Isn't that right, Francesca?"

"Frankie," Frankie corrected. But she looked intrigued. "Yes, if it wouldn't hurt him. Could he really have a relapse?"

"No, he was joking, Frankie."

"It would hurt me not to talk to you." Donavan glanced at Grace and his tone became wheedling. "Maybe not *all* about her mom. Thirty minutes, Grace?"

In other words, he wouldn't mention Kilmer and Grace's relationship. Donavan could be discreet when he chose. But it was only when he chose. She nodded as she opened the door. "Thirty minutes. Then get to bed, Frankie."

"Right." Frankie settled in the chair next to Donavan's bed, her eyes fixed intently on Donavan's face. "Why was it you who taught my mom instead of Jake?"

"Because I was smarter, naturally."

Frankie shook her head. "If you were smarter, Jake would be working for you."

Grace smothered a smile as she closed the door behind her. Donavan would get to know Frankie, all right, and she might give him a few surprises. Her daughter seldom held anything back unless she thought it would hurt someone's feelings. She'd instinctively realize Donavan was fair game. She'd be gauging him at the same time he'd be gauging her.

"How's Donavan?"

She stiffened as she turned to see Kilmer at the head of the stairs. "He seems fine. Better than I thought he'd be. What does the doctor say?"

"That he's bouncing back at an unbelievably fast rate. Dr. Krallon's having a hard time making him rest." He paused. "I saw you take Frankie in to see him."

She nodded. "He wanted to get to know her and shooed me away."

"And you let him get away with it?"

"I want him to get to know her. I want him to care about her. I want the whole world to care about her. Maybe that way I can keep her safe."

"Very smart."

She shook her head. "Desperate." She started to pass him, and he reached out and grasped her arm. She froze. "Don't do that."

"I'll keep her safe, Grace. Ask me why."

"Let me go."

"Because I care about her. She's got me hook, line, and sinker."

"You can't have her."

"For God's sake, I told you I wouldn't try to steal her away from you. But can't you give me as much as you give Donavan?" His hand tightened on her arm. "Let me get to know her without worrying that you're going to panic and snatch her away. Your reasoning should apply to me too. The more I care about her, the harder I'll work to keep her safe."

She wasn't reasoning at all where he was concerned. She was only feeling. "It's . . . different. There's too much in the way."

"Then knock it down," he said roughly. "Knock it all down. And you know what would do it. I'm not saying sex would clear away everything between us, but it would let us get close enough to see the problems from another perspective. Shit, what am I saying? If I'm that close to you, I won't be able to think about anything but what I'm doing to you." His hand dropped away from her. "Hell, and maybe I was using Frankie to get you in bed. God, I hope I'm not that much of a son of a bitch." He turned away. "Maybe you're right. Maybe I shouldn't even get near Frankie."

She'd never seen Kilmer like this. He was always so sure, so confident. She felt a sudden surge of sympathy mixed with exasperation. First he'd thrown her off balance with that burst of sheer sexual attraction, and then made her feel bewildered and sorry for him. "For heaven's sake, I didn't say you shouldn't get near her."

He looked back at her, waiting.

"I just said I didn't want—" She went past him down the hall toward her bedroom. "Just don't get her confused. Don't make her like you too much and then leave her. She's had enough of that."

"What did you tell her about her father, Grace?"

"Nothing. I told her I'd made a mistake, but that I'd do it over again if it meant having another child like her."

"No blame?"

"Why should I blame you? I was a grown woman and I

made the choice. I didn't protect myself. I was to blame." She opened her door. "You were out of it."

"Jesus, that hurts."

"Not as much as missing Frankie's first steps. Or her first words, or singing her to sleep at night. You have no idea."

"Yes, I do."

She looked back over her shoulder and went still as she saw his expression. Perhaps he did realize what he had missed and was hurting because of it. There had been moments when they were together that she had seen glimpses of the Kilmer behind that contained exterior. She had admired him to the point of hero worship, and she had loved his body and everything he did to her. What if she'd really known the entire man? Would she have chosen to trust the affection of her father over Kilmer's word?

His gaze narrowed on her face as he read her expression. "Grace . . ."

She quickly went into her bedroom and shut the door. She closed her eyes as she leaned back against it. She felt as if she was tingling, melting. Her heart was pounding fast, hard. This crazy response had to stop.

It wasn't going to stop. Not as long as she was in the same house as Kilmer, seeing him every day. And there was no question she had to stay here with Frankie until it was safe. She couldn't close him out, and every time she saw him the tension increased.

She could ignore it. Keep busy. Spend time with Frankie.

She had a sudden memory of the way Kilmer had looked at her in that last moment before she had gone into the bedroom. Raw, basic, hot, and so intense she had panicked because it had been like looking into a mirror.

Lord, she hoped she could ignore it.

Do you like your Gypsy as well as you do Darling?" Frankie looked up from brushing Gypsy to see Jake leaning on the stall door. "I like them the same. It wouldn't be fair to have a favorite. They might know and get their feelings hurt."

"I see." He smiled. "Not even in your heart of hearts?"

She thought about it. "They're different, you know. Gypsy is solid and gentle, and Darling is nervous and . . . fun. I want to be around them at different times. I wish I could have Darling here."

"It seems to me you have enough to do. Your music and Gypsy."

"But you're never too busy for a good friend." She started brushing Gypsy again. "And I don't have many friends."

"Why not?"

"I don't like the same things as most kids. They think I'm weird."

"And it bothers you?"

"A little. Sometimes. The riding is okay. Lots of kids in Tallanville ride. But not many play an instrument, and none of them hears the music."

"Would you rather have the friends and skip the music?"

"Don't be silly."

"I take it that's a no?"

"It's part of me. How could I just stop? And it makes me feel . . . I don't know . . . as if I were an eagle flying or maybe Darling when she jumps high and—" She shook her head. "No, Darling is scared, and I'm not scared of the music. I guess I've never seen a horse who's like the music."

"I believe I have."

Her gaze flew to his face. "Where?"

"Two horses, really. In Morocco. Your mother's seen them too."

"She never told me about them."

"They're not the kind of horses that she'd want you to ride. They're full of thunder and lightning. But when you see them run, they might remind you of the music."

"Thunder and lightning . . . Tchaikovsky?"

"Or Chopin."

"I want to see them."

"Perhaps someday."

"What are their names?"

"They call them the Pair. I've never heard them called anything else."

She shook her head positively. "If Mom saw them she would have named them. She says every horse has to have a name. If they have their own soul, they have to have a name."

"Well, if she's named them, she hasn't told me." He smiled. "And she wouldn't like me talking about them to you. As I said, they're not the kind of horses she'd want you associating with. Definitely from the wrong side of the tracks."

"She doesn't let me ride some of her horses, but she doesn't mind me looking at them and talking to them. She says it's important to make friends with horses." She gave Gypsy a final pat. "Like she does. Mom always works and works until the horses love her."

"I've seen her make friends with animals. She's pretty special."

Frankie nodded and then turned to look at him. "She's my best friend. I don't need any of those kids at school."

"I can see how you'd feel like that. I admire her very much."

"But she's mad at you. She's better than she was the night Charlie died, but she still acts funny around you."

"I did some stupid things a long time ago. I've been trying to make it right, but it may take time. I'm glad you think she's not as mad at me as before."

She nodded. "Don't feel bad. I don't think Mom would have let you bring us here if she really didn't like you."

"That's comforting." He paused. "And do you like me a little, Frankie?"

She smiled. "Sure." She opened the stall door. "You're kinda different. I think maybe you're like Trigger. You know

all the tricks, but you don't show off until someone signals.
'Til then, you just stand around and look pretty."

"Pretty?" He started to laugh. "Good Lord, no one ever
called me pretty before."

"Well, something like that." Her grin widened. "But it's
true. You're always walking around giving orders. What are
you doing just standing around talking to me?"

"Enjoying myself. But maybe if you signal, I'll start paw-
ing my foot."

She chuckled with delight. "Would you? I'd like to see
that. Do it."

He pawed the floor with his left foot. "Dear God, how
the mighty have fallen. But I refuse to neigh on command."

"Then you're not Trigger."

"No." His smile faded. "But I could be a better friend to
you than Trigger. Maybe not as good as your mother, but I'd
like to try."

"Why?"

"You're tough. Couldn't you just accept me on face
value?" He studied her face. "No, I guess you couldn't.
You're too much like your mom." He paused. "I like you.
I've never been around kids much. These days are like a gift
to me. Okay?"

"Maybe." She lowered her lashes, but he could see a glint
of mischief. "I don't have a lot of time. There's the music."

"I wouldn't interfere with the music."

"And I have my chores." She said slyly, "Of course, if
you'd shovel the manure for me like you did at Charlie's
place, it would give me— Ouch." He'd swatted her on the
rump and she broke into giggles. "Well, you didn't seem to
have anything else to do."

"Brat." He took her by the hand and pulled her out of
the stall. "You should be honored I'd make time for you in
my busy schedule. And contrary to your judgment of my
character, I don't have to wait for a signal to do tricks. I'm a
veritable circus jester, a miracle man."

She was staring at him with an expression that was suddenly grave. "I heard the doctor say that it was a miracle Donavan was alive. You brought him here and he's going to be fine. That's almost a miracle."

"I was joking, Frankie."

She nodded. "Yeah." A smile lit her face. "But maybe I'll help you shovel the manure."

You have to understand I'm taking a big chance." Carter Nevins looked nervously around the bar. He'd chosen to meet Hanley at this bar on the outskirts of Fredericksburg because it was frequented by blue-collar workers and not anyone from Langley. But you could never tell who might wander into any watering place. Yet at first glimpse of Hanley, he'd known it was better than meeting him at a deserted location. Brett Hanley was tall, muscular, with black hair and brown eyes, and his suit probably cost more than Nevins made in a year. He'd smiled a lot in the first five minutes after he sat down at the table, but he wasn't smiling now. Screw him. Nevins had something Hanley wanted, and the bastard was going to pay through the nose. "I could lose my job. You've got to make it worth my while."

"I'm sure Kersoff paid you less than I'm offering you." Hanley's tone was silky. "You mustn't be greedy, Nevins."

"All I had to do was bypass a password lock and access computer records to find Grace Archer. There aren't any records about her location now. And I don't think North knows either. That makes it a different ball game."

"Then how do you intend to find out where Kilmer and Archer are?"

"I have a contact."

"Who?"

Did this Neanderthal think he was an idiot? "Someone who's been in touch with them since they left Tallanville. But I have to have enough money to make it worth his while."

"How much?"

"Five hundred thousand." Hanley didn't blink, and Nevins cursed under his breath. He should have asked for more. "For him. The same for me."

"You're crazy."

"If he doesn't come through, I have another way to find Archer. I just have to have one little kernel of information and I'll be home free."

"How?"

Nevins smiled. "The magic of computers. It makes a small man a giant. I'm a giant, Hanley. Hear me roar."

Hanley gave him a cold glance. "You're a punk and a nerd. You're holding a weak hand and you're trying to bluff. I hate bluffers."

Nevins felt a chill. He'd better not push him. "I'll take two hundred thousand now and the rest when I give you the information you need. And you're the one who's bluffing. If you had a better source to tap, you wouldn't be here."

Hanley gazed at him for a long moment. "How long?"

Nevins tried not to let him see his relief. "Two weeks?"

"I have five days. Get it for me in five days."

"That's not much time."

Hanley smiled without mirth. "I know. Five days." He got up from the table. "There will be two hundred thousand dollars deposited in your bank account tomorrow. If you don't come through for me, I'll be very displeased. And my employer will be even more irate. You really don't want to make him irate, Nevins." He turned and walked out of the bar.

Nevins drew a deep breath. Christ, he was shaking. What was he getting himself into? Kersoff had been tough, but he had an idea that Hanley was big-league poison. It would be okay. So he had been bluffing a little. He didn't have Stolz in his pocket yet. Stolz had been very nosy, and he had an idea that Nevins was stalking him. Maybe money could swing him. Money could do anything. But now that Nevins had found out he could get more money from Hanley, he wanted it all for himself.

And plan B was a definite possible. He was smart, and

he knew the way to access the mysteries of the universe. Or at least his universe.

But he'd better get back to Langley and put in some long and productive hours at his computer tonight. Hanley hadn't believed him when he'd told him that he was a giant. Well, it was true. He'd make it true.

Hear me roar, Hanley.

They were riding together again. It was the third morning in a row.

Grace watched Frankie and Kilmer take off across the field toward the foothills. Frankie was laughing and talking to Kilmer, and he was listening to her with that quiet intentness so characteristic of him.

Isolation.

Grace shook her head and tried to lose that sudden sweeping, empty feeling. It wasn't as if she hadn't given permission for Kilmer to spend time with Frankie. And it was to be expected that Frankie would grow to like Kilmer more every time she was with him. At twenty-three Grace had been dazzled by Kilmer herself.

But she had seen him in hero mode, a leader of men, smart and savvy. Frankie was seeing him without the bells and whistles. She liked the man, not the larger-than-life warrior, and the intimacy growing between them was more powerful for being stripped to the basics.

"They look good together, don't they?" She turned to see Donavan being wheeled out onto the porch by Dr. Krallon. "When are you going to tell her?"

"Shut up, Donavan." She turned to the doctor. "Are you sure he shouldn't be back in bed? Preferably with adhesive over his mouth?"

The doctor shook his head. "Too late. He's well on the mend." He paused. "That's why I'm going to be leaving tonight. He no longer needs me. Mr. Kilmer's assigning someone else to help him around."

"I'm sure you're relieved."

"Yes, as I told you he's a very bad patient." The doctor smiled at Donavan. "But I'm happy to see him getting well. It's a feather in my cap that I saved his unworthy neck."

"It's not unworthy," Donavan protested. "And you should be glad that I gave you the chance to practice. You probably need it."

"Ingratitude." Krallon shook his head. "I believe I'll go inside and get another cup of coffee. Would you like one, Ms. Archer?"

She shook her head. "And I'll make sure Donavan is taken care of. I'm grateful to you even if he isn't." She watched the doctor go inside before turning to Donavan. "Is he going back to Morocco?"

Donavan shook his head. "Too dangerous for him. Megadangerous for you and Frankie. Kilmer's flying him to a cabin near Yellowstone until the situation cools down."

"Why not let him stay here?"

"Kilmer doesn't want to reward a favor by putting him into jeopardy. The farther away from us, the safer he is." Donavan's gaze shifted back to Kilmer and Frankie. "It wouldn't hurt to tell Frankie he's her father."

Grace shook her head.

He shrugged. "It's your call."

"Yes, it is." With an effort she pulled her eyes away from her daughter and Kilmer. "I don't mind her being friends with him, but fathers are different. Frankie's not going to get her hopes raised that Kilmer is a permanent fixture. I won't let him hurt her when he walks away."

"Did he hurt you, Grace?"

She didn't answer. "I didn't expect anything from him. I'm the one who walked away."

"And he came after you. Not right away, but when he saw you needed him, he was there."

"Donavan, why are you pushing?"

"Kilmer's my friend. These last nine years haven't been easy for him either. I've never seen him as upset as the day he found out you were pregnant. But he did what he had to do to protect the two of you, and some of the missions North forced on him were ugly. He wouldn't have taken them if he hadn't had to think of you."

"Are you trying to make me feel guilty?"

"Hell no, I'm trying to make you see that Kilmer was caught in the same net you were and he didn't try to cut himself free. Now give him a little slack. He deserves it."

"I'm giving him slack. I'm letting him have his time with Frankie. Back off, Donavan. Or I'll push that wheelchair off the porch and watch you skid down to the corral."

"Ah, you're a tough woman, Grace." Donavan tilted his head. "Could I use the relapse ploy again?"

"No."

"Then I guess I'd better close my mouth. Pity. It's not often I choose to utter such pearls of wisdom. Will you wheel me into the house, or do you want to stay out here and enjoy your hair shirt?"

"Donavan, I'm—" she said through her teeth. "I'm not tormenting myself. I'm doing what's necessary. Stop talking about Frankie."

"Oh, I wasn't talking about Frankie this time. I watched you last night when the good doctor brought me down to dinner. You and Kilmer. It was very familiar. I had a flashback to nine years ago. But maybe it's a bit stronger now?"

Jesus, had she been that obvious?

"Hair shirt, Grace . . ." Donavan murmured. "I can see why you'd have a conflict about Frankie, but why deny yourself the fun of—"

"That's enough. I'll tell the doctor to bring you in." She turned and walked into the house.

Y ou ride pretty well," Frankie told Kilmer. "I didn't think Samson would let you on him. Does Mom know that you're riding him?"

"I told her." Kilmer grimaced. "Well, I asked her. I think she thought that Samson would toss me in the dirt."

"But she told me that you knew about horses."

"What she taught me in a crash course nine years ago. I think I was a fair rider then, but I wasn't sure it would come back to me." He patted Samson's neck. "I'm not like your mom. I can't read their minds. But I know the basics, and it turned out I can ride horses that are a little skittish. Grace says they feel safe with me."

"Mom taught you?" Frankie kicked Gypsy and sent her galloping across the field. He galloped after her. "Why?"

"We weren't sure if I'd need to have a working knowledge of horses. The mission we were on might have called for it."

"Mission." Frankie giggled. "That sounds important . . . and funny."

"I guess it does."

Her smile faded. "But it's not funny. Donavan was on a mission, wasn't he? He almost died. You could have died too. Mom was worried."

"Was she?"

She nodded. "So was I. But she promised to go and get you if you got into trouble."

"That's . . . interesting."

"That means she does like you after all, doesn't it? And you must have been friends once if she taught you to ride."

"What are you getting at, Frankie?"

"Sometimes I have to leave Mom alone. I mean, not exactly alone. I don't mean to do it, but when the music . . . I can't bring her with me into the music." She bit her lower lip. "She told me she wasn't lonely, but that was before Charlie died. I don't want her to be lonely, Jake."

"And?"

"I . . . like you. You came to help her when we were in trouble. You must like her too. I just want you to keep her from being lonely. You don't have to be around all the time, just now and then."

Christ, how touching could you get? He couldn't speak for a minute. "I like you too, Frankie. But I'm not sure your mother would want you to be talking to me about this."

She grinned. "Me either. She'd say it was none of my business. But she is my business. Just like I'm her business."

"You're a great team."

She nodded. "Yeah. Look, I don't want to make you feel bad if you don't want to stick around, but I've got to look out for Mom." She had a sudden thought. "When Mom taught you to ride, were you supposed to ride one of those white horses you told me about? The ones you said were like thunder and lightning?"

"Yes."

"But it never happened. . . . I was thinking about those horses after we talked. White horses are beautiful. Did you ever hear about the Pacing White Mustang?"

"I'm afraid not."

"No one knows if the Mustang is a legend or not, but it's been seen from the Rocky Mountains to the Rio Grande. Some say it saved the life of a little girl who got lost from her family."

"You know a lot about famous horses, don't you?"

"Sure. Mom told me a lot about them and she gave me a book about them when I was six. One of my favorite stories is about Shotgun. He was just a small pony, but he went into a raging sea to pull out a lifeboat filled with stranded men. And then there was Bucephalus."

"What?"

"Did I pronounce it right? He was the black stallion owned by Alexander the Great. Alexander even named a city after him. Isn't that cool?"

"Very cool."

"And we don't know the name of Paul Revere's mare. Though some people think it was Brown Beauty. But I think she was just as much a hero as Paul Revere. After all, she's the one who . . ."

* * *

Blockman followed Kilmer out to the porch after dinner that night. "Stolz says Nevins may be the leak."

"The computer nerd?"

Blockman nodded. "It's possible. He said he was looking around and seeing if he could find anything definite and he'd get back to me tomorrow. But it's not urgent, is it? There's nothing to leak. North doesn't know where we are."

"It's urgent. Anyone looking for Grace and Frankie makes it urgent."

"I'm checking every night." He changed the subject. "I saw you with Frankie this morning. Great kid, isn't she?"

Kilmer nodded.

Blockman chuckled. "I take it you don't want to elaborate." He started down the steps. "And there's a little too much tension in the air. I believe I'll go down to the bunkhouse and find a game of poker. Your guys always have one going."

Tension? Damn right, Kilmer thought as he watched Blockman stroll across the yard. He seemed to be living with tension these days. Tension about Marvot, tension about the Pair, tension about Grace.

Music was beginning to drift from the living room. Frankie was starting to play a sonata. Nice. She usually played in the evening if she wasn't composing. He'd grown accustomed to sitting out here by himself and listening until she went to bed. He would have liked to watch her face when she was playing, but it was becoming difficult as hell to—

"Frankie wants to know if she's driving you away."

He turned to see Grace standing in the doorway. "What?"

"She's not dumb. She notices things. You always come out here right after supper. She's wondering if she should be playing her keyboard if it bothers you."

"Of course she should play. I'll talk to her tomorrow."

She hesitated. "You talk a lot, don't you?"

He smiled. "I guess I'm trying to make up for lost time. Not that that would be possible."

"No, it's not." She paused. "That's why I said it was okay for you to get to know her. You have no idea what you've missed."

"Yes, I do." He paused. "But you could tell me a little. When did you find out that Frankie wasn't a usual kid?"

"I don't know. When she was three, probably. That's when she discovered the old piano in Charlie's living room. Even when she was younger, she'd seem to be listening to something we couldn't hear. But then she found out that what was inside her could come out. Charlie and I were dumbfounded. We didn't know what to do. Then I decided that what wasn't natural for other people was perfectly natural for Frankie, and I had to accept it and keep her happy and comfortable with it."

"You did a good job."

"I tried. I hope I did."

He didn't speak for a moment. "She worries about you. She thinks you're lonely."

She stiffened. "She told you that?"

He chuckled. "I think she's looking for a mommy-sitter while she works on her music. She assured me that it wouldn't be a full-time job."

"Oh, you're elected?"

"I was honored she thought of me. I was surprised she didn't choose Blockman. I guess she thought he was too busy. And everyone knows I just stand around and give orders." He held up his hand as she opened her mouth to speak. "I know. You don't have to say anything. I realize you don't think I'd qualify."

"I don't need you. I can take care of my own life. And you've made it clear that you don't want the responsibility."

"The hell I have. You haven't been listening lately." His gaze narrowed on her face. "Or you haven't wanted to hear.

I can't blame you, but don't give me that bullshit. I'm back on the scene and willing to take all the responsibility you'll let me take." He added roughly, "And the reason I don't stay in there when Frankie begins to play is that I can't keep my eyes off you. You say that Frankie notices things. Do you want her to notice that I want to drag her mother into bed? I don't think she's ready for that degree of education yet, do you?"

"No, of course not. Frankie wouldn't realize that—"

"Not at first. But you'd better realize that she's going to notice eventually anyway. I can't keep it under wraps, and you're not much better. Not as long as we're both aching to— Why the hell don't you just let me—" He drew a deep breath. "I wasn't going to say that. It just came out." He started down the steps. "I think I'll go down to the bunkhouse before I really put my foot into it." He glanced back over his shoulder. "But it's true, and it's time we did something about it. We'd both be a helluva lot calmer and better able to function if we didn't have to deal with this." He paused. "I'm going to be in the barn tomorrow afternoon at three."

She stiffened. "What's that supposed to mean?"

"It means that I know you won't want to let me have you here at the house. Not with Frankie around." His lips twisted. "And we don't need a bed. As I remember, we did it everywhere we could find a flat surface. From a muddy ditch to the table in the kitchen of that little hut outside Tangiers. Nothing got in the way." He walked away before she could answer.

Nothing got in the way.

Grace was trembling as she watched him stride across the yard. That single sentence brought back too many memories, too many wild couplings, too many crazy— Stop thinking about it. She could feel her body readying, the tingling at her wrists and the palms of her hands. She was finding it hard to breathe and her breasts felt swollen, sensitive.

My God, she wanted him.

Hair shirt, Donavan had said.

He was right, it had been torture to look at Kilmer, watch him, listen to him, and smother the sexual need. She was a woman, for God's sake. It was natural to have desires and needs. It was unnatural to keep herself from satisfying them if it hurt no one.

Go to bed. Think about it. Consider the consequences.

She didn't want to think. She wanted to follow Kilmer now, this minute.

We don't need a bed.

She closed her eyes. Fight it. If she had enough time, she'd get over this weakness. Tomorrow she'd keep busy and block Kilmer from her mind.

Tomorrow . . .

The barn, tomorrow at three.

11

The sun was hot on her back as Grace walked slowly toward the barn.

This was a mistake.

No, it wasn't a mistake.

Or if it was, she was going to do it anyway, she thought recklessly. She'd tossed and turned and fought with herself all night long and come to that conclusion. She was a mature woman and she could handle a sexual encounter. She had the sense to protect herself this time. It didn't have to mean anything more than the physical madness that had been between them all those years ago. It had been a long time for her, and she was probably suffering from withdrawal. Kilmer was right, they would both function better once that need had been satisfied.

Jesus, she didn't know if she was rationalizing. But she knew that her knees felt weak and she could feel the flush burning her cheeks as she opened the barn door.

Dimness. The smell of hay and horses.

"I was afraid you weren't going to come." Kilmer came

out of the shadows. "God, I was afraid." He stood there look-ing at her.

Why didn't he touch her?

And then he did.

He put his hand on her throat. His palm was hard and callused against her softness. Her pulse leaped in the hol-low of her throat. She shuddered.

"Say it's okay," he said roughly. "For God's sake, tell me it's okay."

She couldn't speak. Hell, she couldn't breathe. All she was aware of was the hard texture of his hand on the soft flesh of her throat.

"Grace."

"Shut up." She buried her face in his shoulder. "Just *do* it."

"Hell, yes." His hands were all over her, rubbing, stroking, squeezing. He was making low sounds that were wild and almost animalistic. "Good. You feel so—"

"So do you." She was unbuttoning his shirt so that she could get closer, skin to skin. Lord, she'd forgotten the smell of him. Basic and spicy and as erotic to her as an aphrodisiac.

He had her shirt off and was unfastening her bra. He jerked it off and pulled her toward a stall. "Come on. Now. I have to get *in* you."

She was vaguely aware of a pile of hay covered by a blan-ket in the stall before he pulled her down, frantically strip-ping her.

Naked against him. The feel . . .

She arched up, trying to get more of him.

"Yes." He was moving between her thighs. "Take— Let me—"

She was going to scream.

She dug her nails into his shoulders. "Kilmer, it's—"

"Shh, it's right. It's right. Just let me—"

"Let you?" She was panting. "No, let me." She rolled over. "I can't be still. I have to—"

"Whatever you want." He pressed a spot at the base of her spine and a shudder went through her. "Whatever . . ."

Crazy," she whispered as she tried to get her breath. "I thought it would be different. I hoped it would be different, but it was just the same. You'd think that older would be wiser."

"Pleasure is wise. We can't live without pleasure." Kilmer was holding her spoon fashion, his hand stroking her stomach. "It makes up for all the bad times and keeps us sane."

"There wasn't anything sane about what just happened." She tried to steady her voice. "It was crazy. I can't figure out why I react like this with you. It just happens."

His lips brushed her temple. "And I thank God for it."

"Chemistry."

"Maybe."

"What else?"

"I've no idea. And I'm not going to tear apart something fantastic to see how it's put together. I'm going to accept and enjoy the hell out of it." His tongue stroked the lobe of her ear. "I suggest you do the same."

"We're not the same."

"Oh, I noticed that."

"Bastard." She sank her teeth playfully into his upper arm. "I mean women worry. It's the way we are. We can't enjoy a roll in the hay without thinking of the consequences." She shook her head. "What am I saying? That's exactly how Frankie was conceived. I was really careful then, wasn't I?"

"It was my fault too."

"Bullshit. You asked me and I lied. That makes it totally my responsibility, with no demands on you."

"I could have wished you'd been a little more demanding when you found out you were pregnant. I felt helpless. I wanted to do something, anything, and there was nothing I could do that wouldn't put you at risk." His palm moved down to caress her belly. "I used to think about you, wonder how you looked when you were big with child, how you'd feel if I stroked you like this."

"I was big as a house and waddled like a duck. You would have laughed."

"No, I wouldn't have laughed."

She was silent a moment. "Perhaps you wouldn't. People change when a baby's involved. I know I did." She stiffened. "Stop petting me."

"Why? I'm trying to be tender, dammit."

"It's not having that effect."

He laughed and rolled over on top of her. "Why?"

"Because I keep thinking of being pregnant, and that leads to how I got that way. And that makes me remember how we—"

"I get the connection." He slowly rubbed against her and smiled when she inhaled sharply. "I gave orders that no one was supposed to come in here for the next three hours. How much time do you have?"

"I don't know. I asked Donavan to keep an eye on Frankie. She's working on her music." Her hands were tightening on his shoulders. "Stop asking questions. Don't waste a minute, dammit. I *need* it."

"Not a minute," he whispered. "Not a second . . ."

W ait."

Grace turned at the door of the stall to look back at Kilmer still lying naked on the blanket. God, she wanted to go back to him. She should be sated, but it was as if she hadn't already coupled with him innumerable times already. "What? It's almost five; I've got to get back to the house."

"I'm not arguing with you." He smiled. "There's straw in your hair. I'd help you get it out but that would lead to problems."

She quickly ran her fingers through her hair. "Okay?"

"Beautiful."

"Sure."

"I'm not lying. You look flushed and tousled and soft . . . beautiful." He paused. "When?"

"What?"

"Don't stall. You know it's going to happen again. It's better if we plan it so that it's easier for you. Tomorrow this time?"

She nodded jerkily. "If it works out with Frankie."

"I'll wait." He sat up and began to put on his clothes. "But it's probably not going to be enough for either of us. You've got to be prepared for that."

"I won't let Frankie think her mother's some bimbo who—"

"I wouldn't let her think that of you. I'm just saying that I'm not going to be able to keep my hands off you. And even when I'm not touching you, you'll know what I'm thinking."

And she'd want his hands on her, she thought. There wasn't any question that she'd want him. This encounter had been every bit as heady and desperate as the sex they'd had nine years ago. She knew it would prove just as addictive. "I can't think that far ahead."

"It won't be that far ahead." He fastened his belt. "I guarantee. But let me take care of it. I'll make it easy for you, and Frankie won't know."

She made a rueful face. "But everyone else on the ranch will know."

"Yes, but if they even raise an eyebrow, I'll make them wish they'd never been born. It never bothered you that the team knew about us nine years ago."

"I wasn't thinking enough to be bothered by anything. I was just feeling."

"I can't keep this secret," he said quietly. "We're all living too close together."

"I know that." She opened the stall door. "I made a decision and I don't have any right to expect anything else. Just make sure Frankie doesn't know."

* * *

Langley, Virginia

What are you working on?" Stolz stood outside Nevins's cubicle gazing curiously at Nevins's computer screen. "I thought we were supposed to go to dinner together."

"You're early. I thought we'd agreed on seven-thirty." Nevins quickly blanked out the screen. "Just a little project North gave me to do. He said he wanted it right away." He got to his feet. "Where do you want to go? The cafeteria or off site?"

"Off. The Italian restaurant we went to day before yesterday. I don't want to even think about work for the next hour. Sometimes I wonder why I put up with all this bureaucratic bullshit."

That lead was supposed to make him think of Stolz as a buddy, Nevins thought scornfully. Not likely. Stolz didn't have half his ability or brains. But he was still going to need him to get the fix. "The benefits are good." He smiled. "Maybe we'll take a look at the private sector."

"What's Ops 751?"

"Nosy." Thank God he'd blanked the screen before Stolz could get the rest of the ops number. He'd better not work on it until he could get a little more privacy. Everyone had gone home in his section and Stolz wasn't supposed to be here for another hour. But he'd only risked it because the time was getting short. Only a few more days until Hanley would be on his ass. "I told you that I was on a North assignment."

"What's North up to?"

He lowered his voice melodramatically. "Confidential. Top-secret." He laughed. "All that crap. I'll tell you all about it over dinner." Which meant he'd better start concocting the fable right now to make it plausible. "Let's get out of here."

* * *

Grace stood on the porch and looked out at the mountains, waiting.

Frankie was playing in the living room after supper. Tonight the music was lively and light, and Grace could hear her chatting with Donavan as she played.

She should be in there. No, she shouldn't. She had a few minutes.

The screen door opened and she tensed.

Kilmer came out of the house to stand behind her. His hands slid around to cup her breasts. "Thank God. Jesus, I couldn't wait to get that damn meal over with."

Neither could Grace. She arched back against him as sensation tore through her. "It's not— I have to go back in."

"Not yet." He was squeezing and releasing. "I told Donavan to keep her busy. The barn. Give me thirty minutes. I'll be quick."

Hell, they'd both be quick. These days by the time they got to each other they were almost exploding.

"Come on. Would you rather lie in bed all night and think about it?" He took her hand and pulled her down the steps. "Thirty minutes, Grace."

She shouldn't go. So far she'd managed to keep control when Frankie was around.

Not tonight. Those hours of waiting had made her frantic.

She started to run toward the barn. "Hurry."

They were walking quickly back to the house forty-five minutes later. Grace could hear Frankie playing, still laughing at Donavan. She hadn't been missed.

Kilmer said the same thing. "She didn't miss you. Stop worrying. It wasn't that long." His lips tightened. "Not nearly long enough. But it was enough so that we won't go crazy."

"We're acting like animals."

"Yes, and there's nothing wrong with that. It's clean and hot and beautiful."

"It's wrong if I can't control it."

He stopped her with his hand on her arm. "If all you're worried about is Frankie, then we can fix it. You don't want to sneak around? Then make it legitimate."

"What are you talking about?"

"Marry me."

She stared at him. "What?"

"We could sleep in the same bed. No more barn."

"I'm not marrying anyone so that I can have sex with him."

"Why not? If we had enough of each other, you might get bored with me and send me on my way. Isn't that what you want?" He paused. "And Frankie likes me. I think she'd accept me."

"And then have her fall apart when you left us?"

"I wouldn't leave her. I'll never leave you again. If there's any leaving to be done, you'd leave me. There's a difference and I'd make sure she knew it. Will you consider it?"

She shook her head.

He shrugged. "I didn't think you were ready. There's still too much bitterness lingering because I made you raise Frankie alone."

"I told you that's not true."

"I believe it is. No matter how much you tell yourself that you don't blame me, there has to be a little bitterness. That's okay. I'll work around it."

She shook her head again.

"Then we'll leave it at status quo." Kilmer stepped aside for her to precede him up the porch steps. "But it's going to get worse instead of better. You can bet on it."

* * *

Time for bed, Frankie." Grace got up from her chair. "It's almost ten."

"Okay." Frankie made a face. "But I hate going to bed. It's such a waste of time."

Donavan laughed. "You remind me of my friend Kilmer here. He's always afraid he'll miss something if he sleeps more than a few hours."

"Really?" She looked at Kilmer. "Is that true, Jake?"

He nodded. "We're definitely soul mates, Frankie."

Grace had heard Frankie complain about having to go to bed hundreds of times. She had never connected that dislike with Kilmer's aversion. Did Frankie take after Kilmer, or was it only a child's worry that she might miss something? "Soul mates or not, you'll be dragging by morning. Kilmer already has his growth." She jerked her thumb at the door. "Move it. I'll be right up."

"I'll go with you." Donavan got slowly to his feet. "You can keep me from falling on those stairs."

Frankie was immediately by his side, handing him his crutch. "You'd better not fall. You're so big you'd probably smush me." She put his other hand on her shoulder. "Lean on me."

"I'll do that." He smiled down at her as he started across the room. "And I'll try not to smush you. Is that a combination of smash and crush?"

"I think so." Her brow was knitted in concentration as she helped him toward the stairs.

Grace followed them to the hall and watched them start upstairs. They seemed to be managing very well, and it was touching to see the small child and the giant of a man together.

"It's fine, Grace," Donavan said. "She's taking good care of me." He smiled down at Frankie. "I may hire her until I get back on my feet."

Frankie shook her head. "I'm too busy. And you don't really need me. You're just a little stiff from sitting tonight."

"I'm glad that your diagnosis is so positive," Donavan

murmured. "Then Kilmer will be putting me back to work in no time."

"I'll send Luis up to help you undress," Grace said.

"I can do it myself. As Frankie says, I'm getting past the point of needing anyone."

Grace watched them disappear down the hall. Life for Frankie was so different from the existence she'd lived before coming here. Kilmer, Donavan, Blockman, and even several of Kilmer's men were with her constantly. She never got a chance to be lonely. It wasn't an ideal situation, but it wasn't all that bad.

She turned and went back to the living room.

Robert had come into the room and was talking to Kilmer. He broke off when he saw Grace. "Hi. Got Frankie to bed?"

"No, I'm going up in a few minutes."

"Then I'll just say good night." He started for the door. "See you in the morning."

"Wait." Her gaze was narrowed on him. "What's happening, Robert?"

"Everything's fine."

Her gaze switched to Kilmer. "What are you keeping from me?"

"Evidently nothing," Kilmer said. "Though I was hoping. Tell her, Blockman."

Robert shrugged. "My guy Stolz, at Langley, thinks he's narrowed in on the man who sold your location to Kersoff. He's a computer guru named Nevins, and Stolz believes he's negotiating again."

Grace's heart leaped with panic. "What?"

"Easy," Kilmer said. "He doesn't have anything to sell. He has no idea where we are."

"Then why the devil would he be negotiating?"

"A double-cross?" Robert suggested. "Stolz isn't sure. But Nevins has been working on something on his computer for days. He says it's a project for North, but Stolz has doubts."

"You think North is tracing us?"

"That's not logical," Kilmer said. "I was damn careful."

"Stolz caught a partial number on Nevins's computer before he blanked out the screen. Ops 751. He tried to access it later but came up with zilch."

"Ops 751," Grace repeated, and then shook her head. "Maybe it is a project for North."

"We're not letting it go without checking," Kilmer said. "I'll let you know as soon as we come up with something."

"Will you?" she asked coolly. "You wouldn't have said a word to me if I hadn't interrupted your tête-à-tête."

"I admit it," Kilmer said. "Don't blame Blockman. It was my decision. There's no clear threat and I didn't want you worrying for nothing."

"It was a bad decision. I want to know everything you know." She met his gaze. "And from now on it had better be that way."

He nodded. "It will. I know when I'm pushing my luck."

"Good. Then don't do it again." She turned and headed for the door. "Good night, Robert."

"Good night." Robert hurriedly exited the room.

"Good night, Grace." Kilmer was ignoring the obvious omission. "Sleep well."

"I'll sleep very well. No problem."

He laughed. "Liar."

She looked back to see him walking out onto the porch. Cocky bastard. No, not cocky. He'd have to be in a coma not to know how she felt about him. Even though she was angry, it wouldn't change the sexual charge between them that interfered with sleep, thought, and every waking action.

Marry me.

The proposal had stunned her and then panicked her. Because for the first few seconds the words had sent joy and hope ringing through her. Totally unreasonable, totally without a trace of practicality. Yet the joy had been there.

She had reached her room and paused outside the door to gather her composure before facing Frankie. She seemed to be having to do that constantly these days. Hiding her fear, hiding her affair with Kilmer, hiding her worries about the future.

Frankie was getting into bed as Grace opened the door. "Hi, Mom." She pulled up the covers and nestled her head on the pillow. "I think Donavan is going to be able to walk without that crutch pretty soon, don't you?"

"Probably. He seems to have made an amazing recovery." She crossed to the bed and tucked the covers around her daughter. "And it's nice of you to help him."

"I like him. I like everyone here." She yawned. "But I like Jake best. Soul mates . . . that's a nice thing to be, isn't it?"

"Very nice." She turned out the lamp on the nightstand. "Now go to sleep, baby."

"You like him much better now. I can tell." She huddled on her side. "You spend a lot of time together. . . ."

Grace stiffened. She should have known a kid as sharp as Frankie would have noticed. "Do we?"

"Sure, like tonight when you were out on the porch."

"Oh."

"You must have a lot to talk about."

"Uh, sometimes."

"I'm glad. Like I told you, talking to him makes you look . . . happy. All shining and pink and soft."

"Sounds like a newborn baby," she said dryly.

Frankie giggled. "That's silly."

"Yes, it is. Now, go to sleep."

"I will." Frankie nestled deeper. "But when I'm as old as Jake I'm not going to sleep more than a couple hours a night. I'm going to play my piano and write music and go for lots of rides."

"Horses have to sleep too."

"I'd let them sleep. After all, I wouldn't need to ride all

the time." She yawned again. "There's too much else to do. . . ."

Yes, for children, life was exciting and new and filled with anticipation. Particularly for her Frankie.

And her Frankie had fallen asleep.

She sat down on the other bed, gazing at her. Frankie had been hinting very broadly, stressing her liking for Kilmer, tacitly giving her approval of the time they spent together. Her daughter knew nothing about him except what was on the surface, what her instincts told her.

And did Grace know any more than that? She knew his background, but he'd never talked about anything in the past. She knew he was clever and dynamic, fair to his men and lethal to his enemies.

And, God help her, she knew his body intimately and wanted him with a voracious appetite that was close to addiction. Just thinking about sex with him was arousing.

Then don't think about it. Go to bed and try to get to sleep. Don't dwell on that impossible proposal. The only things Kilmer and she had ever done together were sex and military operations.

Wait. That wasn't so bad. On missions they had meshed like a finely tuned Swiss clock, supplying each other's needs before being asked. And sex was the same. Perhaps she did know Kilmer and the way he felt and thought. Perhaps they were instinctively attuned to each other. If that was true, then the learning process might not be as difficult as—

Good Lord, she was actually considering the possibility. Insanity.

No way.

She stood up, drew back the covers, and started to get undressed.

12

"Hanley, I need you to have your men ready to move," Nevins said. "I'm very close. But I won't get more than a few minutes or North may find out what I'm doing."

"You've found out where Kilmer and Archer are? Someone there knows where they're—"

"No, I told you. No one knows. But there's a man who's in touch with them and I can get the information from him."

"Give me his name. I'll find out."

"I don't believe he knows. He's in communication with them once every evening, but I've tapped his phone and Blockman's not giving him any information."

"Trace the call."

"No way. Blockman's not an amateur. He's using equipment to block a trace."

"Then how are you going to get me the information?"

"Try an unusual method. The eight-hundred-pound gorilla."

"What?"

"Just get your men positioned in the center of the U.S. so that they can move in any direction fast. I'll notify you when I can give you a definite time when I'll know. I'll expect you to transfer the remaining money into my account before I give you the location."

Hanley didn't speak for a moment. "If you're wrong or you're crossing me, you'll regret it."

"I'm no fool. And I won't be wrong. I just want to be paid for my work. This is chancy, and I may have to leave my job and get out of here quick. I'll need that money. It may be as early as tomorrow, so position your men accordingly." Nevins hung up the phone and leaned back in his chair, his gaze on the computer screen. Close. He'd have been able to tap the password days ago if he hadn't had to be so careful. His computer could be monitored by his superiors, and he'd had to mask where the program originated by cloning the node while he was working on it.

His superiors. He had no superior here at Langley, he thought scornfully. Would North or Crane ever be able to infiltrate a program like Ops 75132? No, they used men like him, who had the brains they didn't.

And he'd spoken the truth about the chance he was taking. Stolz was suspicious and was stalking him even as Nevins was stalking Stolz. And Ops 75132 probably had a hundred different alarms. The percentage was high that he'd miss disarming one.

Maybe not. He'd be careful and he only had to have control for a minute before scooting out of the program. Then he'd be on his way, phoning Hanley from his car as he headed for the bank. Seven hours later he'd be in Guatemala. A day later he'd arrive in Brazil with new ID papers and enough money to set up his own computer operation. He'd have everything. Money, women, and the respect he deserved.

He eagerly leaned forward and started working again on tapping the eight-hundred-pound gorilla.

* * *

Ops 751?" Donavan repeated. "It's not much to go on."

"It's all Stolz saw before Nevins shut down his computer. He said he didn't catch the entire number."

"I'll get on it right away." Donavan reached for the phone. "But it might be useless. It could be anything."

"Try. You have enough contacts in Washington to find out who the President is sleeping with. You should be able to decipher an ops number."

"I didn't say it was impossible." Donavan grinned. "And I'm glad to have something to do besides distract your daughter. She's a great kid, but she's too sharp. She keeps me on my toes and I'm a sick man."

"She keeps us all on our toes."

"And it wouldn't surprise me if she knew what was going on."

Kilmer frowned. "She'd better not. She may be old for her age, but she's not ready for that."

"The G-rated version." Donavan waved him out of the room. "Let me get to work. I'll try to have something for you by tomorrow."

You're sure that Nevins will come through?" Marvot asked. "I'm becoming a little impatient, Hanley."

"Tomorrow. He'll come through. I know it," Hanley said. "I told you I'd take care of everything."

"Yes, you did. I consider that a promise. Don't break it." He hung up and turned to Guillaume. "We're getting close. In a few days the Pair should have their playmate. Won't that be exciting?"

I have to go," Grace whispered as she raised herself on her elbow. "It's after five. Frankie will be—"

"Expecting you," Kilmer finished for her. "You're safe.

You shouldn't worry. You know Donavan isn't going to let her run down here."

"I still have to leave." She started to dress. "And some-one has to worry. You don't seem to care if she finds out or not."

"I don't." He leaned back on the straw. "I'm beyond that. I've already offered to make an honest woman of you. Maybe if Frankie knew we were . . . close, it would tip the scales in my direction."

"She does know."

He went still. "What?"

"At least she notices we want to spend time together. She's not unobservant."

"Donavan said she was too sharp to be fooled entirely. I'm surprised you didn't panic and throw me out."

"I would if it hurt her. It doesn't seem to bother her if I take this little time for myself."

"And you need it."

She didn't answer.

He was suddenly on his knees before her, unzipping her jeans.

"No."

"Tell me you need it." His lips were on the soft skin of her belly, and she could feel his warm breath as he said, "Give me that much."

Oh, God. She was surrounded by the headiness of sight, scent, and touch. The dimness of the barn, the smell of hay and Kilmer. Kilmer's tongue . . . "I have to go."

His tongue licked delicately, sending a hot shiver through her. Her hands closed tightly on his hair.

"Only that much, Grace."

Only that much wasn't enough for her. She wanted him to pull her down again and—

She tore away from him and backed against the stall door. "Damn you, Kilmer."

He sat back on his heels. "I have to make you want to

come back tomorrow. Since you won't simplify things and let us sleep together with all the proper sanctions."

"Stop talking about it." She zipped up her jeans and thrust her shirt into the waistband. "Frankie wouldn't understand a marriage made so that two people could make out. And I don't want her to understand. It should mean something."

"Then stop being stubborn. Let's give it a chance to mean something. Do you think most of those teenage kids who line up at registry offices know what marriage is all about? All they're thinking about is sex. We have a lot better chance of making it work, because we have the maturity to fight for it."

She shook her head and turned away. "I'm going to the house. Give me fifteen minutes before you come after me."

"I'm in no hurry." He stretched out on the blanket. "I believe I'll lie here and listen to Cosmo's melodious braying. It says something that when we're making love I never even hear it. It has to be the most raucous sound on the face of the earth."

"I think that's why the Pair like him so much. He's an outcast like them."

"I never considered that possibility. Thanks for the insight."

"You're welcome. That's all the help you're going to get from me with the Pair."

"You're not thinking I'm seducing you because I want your help? No way."

She looked back at him as she opened the stall door. He was still naked and looked tough, lazy, and completely sensual. She glanced quickly away. "No, I'm not thinking that. You're not that good an actor. I'll see you at dinner."

I've *got* it," Nevins said. "Transfer the money, Hanley. I'll call the bank in an hour and, if it's there, by tonight you'll have your location."

"You'd better be right," Hanley said. "I have men in St. Louis waiting for the go-ahead and I wouldn't like to appear foolish." He hung up.

That last sentence had been another threat, Nevins thought. But he didn't have to worry about that son of a bitch's threats any longer. He had control. The only thing that could go wrong was if Blockman didn't phone Stolz tonight. But Blockman had been regular as clockwork checking in with him so far. Nine o'clock Eastern time. A conversation that seldom lasted more than two minutes and then the disconnect.

But two minutes would be enough for him.

He was ready.

There's no Ops 751," Donavan said when Kilmer came into the house. "But the army has several ops programs. I have my contact going through the list to see what he can come up with. It's not easy. The 75 series are supposed to be classified."

"You can do it?"

"Sure. There aren't any secrets these days that can't be brought to light. But classified takes longer." He grinned. "Maybe another day. Top-secret could take a week."

"The army . . ." Kilmer frowned thoughtfully. "What could Nevins be doing messing around with army records? I don't like it."

"If you could get Blockman to put a spur under his man Stolz to get me the rest of those numbers, I might be able to tell you."

"He's doing all he can." He checked his watch: 6:15 P.M. "But I'll talk to him before his nine o'clock call to Stolz."

Almost time. Eight fifty-nine EST.

Nevins tensed, his eyes on the screen where he'd programmed Stolz's number.

Come on, damn you. Ring.

The phone rang at 9:02 P.M.

He went into action. His fingers flying over the keyboard.

Bring it in. Bring it in. Bring it in.

Locked!

Yes.

His eyes were glued to the screen. There it was, whirling, zeroing in.

Just another minute. Stay on the phone one more minute, Stolz.

He didn't need another minute!

He bent forward over the keyboard.

Got it.

No more information," Blockman told Kilmer. "Nevins is being elusive. A week ago he was on Stolz's heels, nosy as hell. Now he's practically ignoring Stolz and being very cagey. Every time Stolz gets near his cubicle, he's doing everything from making North's and Crane's hotel reservations to answering North's interoffice memos for him." He added dryly, "But curiously enough, Nevins is always in the first stages of the job. Fancy that."

"I don't fancy it at all," Kilmer said. "If he's not trying to get information from Stolz, then he has another source."

"Ops 751?" He shrugged. "You said Donavan is working on it."

"If he's not going down a blind alley. His source says it's probably an army designation. It doesn't make sense that they'd have any information about Grace."

"Stolz is doing all he can," Blockman said. "Nevins is a wizard and is covering his tracks. Even if I dropped an anonymous tip to North about him, I doubt if he'd be able to catch him."

"If you can't get more information from Stolz, then

we'll try it anyway." Kilmer turned to go into the house. "Catch him or not, I want the bastard's hands tied."

Wake up." Donavan threw open the door and hobbled on his crutch into Kilmer's room. "I just got a call from my source in Washington. He gave me a list of Army Ops 75 projects." He thrust the piece of paper at Kilmer. "Take a look at it and see if the same one strikes you in the gut."

The list had seven project numbers on it. Kilmer's gaze scanned them quickly until he came to number five: 75132.

"Holy shit."

"That's what I thought," Donavan said grimly. "The question is, could Nevins pull it off?"

"Stolz says he's a wizard. I wouldn't want to take the chance." His mind was quickly going over the possibilities. "He's not interested in Stolz anymore because he realized he could approach the problem in another way. But he already had what he needed from him. He probably knew what time Blockman was making the calls. Even if he couldn't trace them, he could latch on to the signal."

"And let Ops 751 take care of it. Is it too late?"

"It may be." Kilmer was throwing on his clothes. "It depends how far along Nevins was at nine this evening. Call the bunkhouse and get the guys moving. Tell Blockman I want him up here quick."

"Grace and Frankie?"

"I'll wake them. Jesus, I'm sure as hell not looking forward to it." He went to the window and gazed out into the darkness. "No headlights on the road. But they could be coming by air. Get moving, Donavan."

A hand was covering Grace's mouth!

Her lids flew open at the same time the edge of her

hand aimed at the throat of the blurred figure bending over her.

Kilmer caught her hand before it reached his throat. "Shh," he whispered. "Try not to scare Frankie. Just wake her and tell her we have to move out. Now."

Her heart jumped with panic. She tore his hand away from her lips. "How can I not scare her? Marvot?"

"Mom?" Frankie was sitting up in bed. "Something wrong?"

"Yes." She was out of bed and throwing on her clothes. "Get dressed. Hurry."

Frankie threw back the covers and jumped out of bed, her gaze on Kilmer. "What's happening, Jake?"

"I'm not certain. Maybe nothing. I just want to take precautions." He squatted in front of her. "There's an old hunters' cabin in the mountains. I'm going to send you and your mother and your friend Robert up there for a day or so. Nothing's going to happen to you, I promise."

"Why aren't you going?"

"It's better if I stay here to let you know when you can come back." He stood up. "Now, hurry up. Robert should be waiting for you downstairs."

"Okay." Frankie ran to the bureau and started pulling out clothes.

Frustration was battling with panic as Grace got her knapsack down from the closet. Dammit, she'd done this only days ago. When would it stop? "Why are we on the run?" she asked Kilmer in a voice inaudible to Frankie. "What's happening?"

"Ops 751 is probably Ops 75132," he said. "It's a satellite sent up by Army Intelligence two years ago. Presumably to gather military information to save the U.S. from terrorist attacks. A beautifully crafted spy vehicle with all the bells and whistles. It's fully capable of grabbing a signal and zeroing in on any location in the world if pointed in the right direction." He paused. "And like everything else in our modern-day world, it's controlled by computers."

Computers. "Nevins," she whispered. "But how could he gain control of it? How would it be possible?"

"He's brilliant. High-school hackers have broken into top-secret war rooms with no problem. Nevins is smarter, more experienced, and motivated. It's definitely possible. I just don't know if he's done it yet or if we got lucky. I'm not taking any chances." He started for the door. "Get out of here, Grace. I don't know how much— Shit!"

She heard them too.

Rotors. A helicopter.

"Out!" Kilmer grabbed Frankie up in his arms and started at a run for the door. "Drop everything. Move."

Grace was already running through the hall and down the stairs.

Robert was waiting at the foot of the stairs. "The jeep's parked in back." He grabbed Frankie's hand as Kilmer set her down and strode toward the kitchen door. "Kilmer, how safe is that cabin?"

"It's in the backwoods. A day or two. I should be able to reach you by then."

The rotors were louder, lower as they reached the jeep.

"I won't count on it," Robert said. "If you don't call me within twelve hours, I'm going to find another place to take them."

He meant that Kilmer might be dead within twelve hours, Grace thought, chilled. She looked up at the night sky and saw the blue-white lights of the helicopter. She turned to Kilmer. "What are you going to do?"

"Take them out." He lifted Frankie into the jeep. "What else?" He stepped back. "Move it, Blockman. Don't turn on your lights. Get out of here before they see you. And no matter what happens, keep on going."

A spatter of bullets splayed over the house from the helicopter.

A bedroom window shattered and glass showered down on the roof of the jeep.

Take them out? Grace thought frantically. That was military artillery the helicopter was firing. They had to dodge those bullets while waiting for the helicopter to get close enough to take their shot.

She glanced back over her shoulder as Robert tore down the road. The helicopter's bullets were strafing the stable yard, and by the beam of the helicopter she could see men moving, running, ducking.

"Mom . . ." Frankie cuddled closer. "What about Jake?"

"He'll be fine." God, she hoped she was telling the truth. She wanted nothing more than to jump out and run back to the house that was now riddled with bullet holes. "He knows what he's doing."

"But I don't see him."

Neither did Grace. And the helicopter was lower now, the lights illuminating the scene with daylight clarity.

Where was Kilmer?

D o you want me to take the shot?" Donavan asked.

"No, I'll do it." Kilmer sighted down the barrel of the Springfield. "Of course, if you want to help, you could distract them by running across the stable yard."

"Very funny. It better be soon. I figure that they'll make one more pass to do as much damage as they can. Then they'll land out of range in one of the paddocks and pour out of that tin can like gangbusters."

"How remiss of me to not have a ground-to-air missile launcher. Sorry to keep you waiting."

"You should be. After my recent experience at El Tariq, my nerves are in a very delicate state. Just get it—"

"They're coming back."

Smart. They were moving fast and changing directions with every assault. This time they were coming in from the north. If the helicopter didn't swerve from its present course, he should get a clear shot at the gas tank.

One shot.

"It better be good," Donavan murmured. "Or you'll never hear the end of it from me."

"So what's new?"

Coming fast. Make the shot a little ahead of the target. . . .

The helicopter exploded in a fiery detonation that lit up the night sky.

Grace's arm tightened fiercely around Frankie. "Got them."

Frankie was staring at the flaming wreckage plummeting to the ground. "Is Jake safe now?"

"I think so." She supposed she shouldn't display this barbaric satisfaction in front of Frankie. To hell with it. It was what she was feeling. She could explain later. "At least, safer."

"Then can we go back?"

"You heard Jake," Robert said. "We're not to come back until he phones us and gives us the okay. I doubt if that's going to happen. He's probably going to arrange to meet us somewhere."

Frankie obviously couldn't take her eyes from the wreckage. "Because there will be someone else coming to the ranch," she whispered. "Another helicopter?"

"I don't know," Grace said. "But, yes, someone will be coming."

"I hoped maybe after Charlie—" Frankie's hands clenched at her safety belt as she was flung about the jeep. They had reached the foothills and the jeep was bouncing over the rutted road. "We have to hide again?"

Grace nodded.

"That man must hate you to want to hurt you this much," Frankie said.

"Marvot? Yes, he doesn't like to be beaten. He wanted something from me and didn't get it."

"Then I hate him too. I hope he was on that helicopter."

"He wasn't. Marvot hires people to do his dirty work. That's why we have to keep on running. There's always someone else for him to pay."

"It shouldn't be that way." Frankie's voice was shaking with anger. "He should be punished. Someone should make him stop. Why don't we do it?"

"I've told you that—"

"Jake could do it. Is he going to try?"

"Perhaps."

"Then we should help him."

God, this was hard. "Frankie, Marvot could hurt you. It's crazy, but it's not only me; he wants to hurt you too. I can't let that happen. Even if it means hiding for a while. It can't last forever."

"It's wrong, Mom. We shouldn't let him—"

The jeep veered wildly to the left as the front tires blew!

"Christ." Robert fought wildly for control as the jeep jolted down the incline. "Hold on. I can't keep it on—"

A pine was looming dead ahead!

"No!" Grace released her seat belt, grabbing Frankie closer, trying to protect her from possible flying glass. "Keep your head down. Close your eyes, baby! It will be—"

Pain.

Darkness.

Move out," Kilmer called as he watched the burning helicopter hit the ground. "Donavan, tell Estevez to get the equipment and men in the truck. I want to be heading for those mountains in five minutes. Set up the helicopter to land near the cabin in thirty." He turned to Dillon, who had run up to him. "Casualties?"

"No deaths. Vazquez has a splinter piercing his left shoulder. I stopped the bleeding."

"Can he function?"

Dillon nodded. "No problem."

"Then go help Donavan round up—" His head suddenly lifted to the sky. "Christ, *no.*"

"What is it?" Dillon asked.

"Rotors. Another damn helicopter."

"I'll tell the men to take cover." He sprinted away.

"Yeah." But the rotors didn't sound close. What the hell? And he should be seeing lights.

Then he saw them in the distance. Not heading in this direction. The helicopter was circling, coming down somewhere in the foothills.

"No!" He ran toward the truck. "Donavan!"

The helicopter was ascending again by the time they reached the foothills.

"Shall I try to take it down?" Donavan asked. "The distance isn't too—"

"No." His gaze was searching the sides of the road. "It's not safe. Where the devil— Blockman didn't have time to reach the cabin when the helicopter popped up. He has to—"

"On the slope," Dillon yelled from the back of the truck. "I see something on the—"

Kilmer screeched to a halt and jumped out of the driver's seat. "Fan out. Look sharp."

It could be a trap. A decoy. But he could see the outline of the jeep ahead.

No shots.

The terrain was bare and stark except for his men heading down the slope. The moon was bright and full, and he should be able to see anyone lying in wait.

"I see something," Dillon called softly. "On the ground by the driver's seat."

Kilmer saw him too. Blockman was lying on his back, blood pouring from his leg. He couldn't see Grace or Frankie.

Shit. Shit. Shit.

He skidded the rest of the way down the slope. "Block-man, what the hell happened?"

Blockman opened his eyes. "Trap. They must have guessed you'd try to send Grace away from the ranch and dropped some men down here in the foothills. Tried to stop them. Grace . . ."

"They took Grace?"

Blockman shook his head. "Took Frankie. Didn't get . . . Grace. The ravine. Bastards. I tried to stop them, but they—"

He stiffened. "Stop them from doing what?"

"Hurt her . . ." His eyes closed. "Tried to—"

"You said the ravine?"

Blockman didn't answer.

Kilmer jumped to his feet and glanced in the wreckage of the jeep on the way to the ravine on the other side of the road.

No Grace. No Frankie.

Maybe Blockman was out of his head. Why would they leave Grace instead of taking her with them?

Don't think about it.

Search for them. Find them.

"Donavan, turn the truck and beam those lights down in the ravine."

She was lying on her side at the bottom of the ravine like a crumpled doll.

"Christ. Get me a first-aid kit." He was skidding down the thirty-foot embankment. He fell, got up, and fell again before he finally reached her.

He dropped to his knees and shone his flashlight on her face. Unconscious.

So still.

He checked her pulse.

Alive.

He was dizzy with relief.

"Okay?" Donavan was beside him with the first-aid kit.

"No," Kilmer said unevenly. "She's not okay. I don't

know how bad it is. But she's alive and I'll keep her alive."
He turned to Dillon as he checked Grace for broken bones.
"Search the area to make sure Frankie's not here. Blockman
said they took her, but he could be out of his head."

"The helicopter should be here within five minutes,"
Donavan said. "We'll get her fixed up, Kilmer."

"You're damn right we will." He rose to his feet. Concussion? Internal injuries? "Phone them and tell them we're
going to need medical help. How is Blockman?"

"Okay. The bullet passed through and he's not bleeding
much now."

"No Frankie." Dillon was back. "It's pretty clear terrain
up beyond this ravine. We'd see her if she—" He bit his
lower lip. "But the guys don't want to give up. Could we stay
and keep on looking for her?"

All the guys cared about Frankie. They didn't want to let
there be even the tiniest chance that she might be alone in
these hills.

Or not alone.

Kilmer felt the same way. But Blockman had said they'd
taken Frankie. The chances were almost nil she'd still be
around here.

He pushed Grace's hair back from her forehead.
Dammit, why didn't she wake or at least stir?

Screw it. He had to stay with Grace, but he wasn't going
to think logically and miss the slightest chance of finding
Frankie.

"You and Vazquez stay behind and keep looking. I'll
send the helicopter back for you in the morning."

13

Kilmer's face was a swimming blur before her as Grace slowly opened her eyes. He was bending over her. . . . Had they just made love? Love? She mustn't confuse sex for love, but sometimes it was difficult to—

The jeep crashing into the pine tree.

"Frankie!" Grace sat bolt upright on the bed, her gaze frantically searching the room. "Where's Frankie?"

"Easy." Kilmer's hand tightened around hers. "Frankie's alive."

"But she's hurt? I tried to keep her from—" She swung her feet to the floor. "I've got to see her."

"That's not possible."

Her gaze flew back to his face. "You lied to me," she whispered. "She's not alive. She was killed in that crash."

"I'm not lying to you, Grace. Blockman says she was alive and conscious the last time he saw her."

"The last time he saw her? What the hell are you talking about?"

"I'm trying to tell you. Calm down. Be quiet and listen to me. Okay?"

She wanted to scream at him, tell him that she couldn't be calm, not when Frankie was— She drew a deep breath. It wasn't going to do Frankie any good if she was hysterical. "Tell me. Where's Frankie?"

"I'm not sure." He paused. "Probably El Tariq."

"Oh, my God."

"I'll get her back, Grace."

Don't fall apart. Keep control. "No, I'll get her back. What happened? The last thing I remember was Robert crashing into that pine tree."

"There was another helicopter. It landed in the foothills. The first helicopter must have dropped men on the mountain, and they worked their way down and were waiting for you. They shot out the front tires and you went off the road and banged into the tree. You were tossed out of the car and rolled down a steep slope to the bottom of the ravine. Blockman said Hanley sent a few men down to get you, but he called them back when he saw the headlights of my truck in the distance. He was cursing a blue streak, but he grabbed Frankie and took off for the helicopter."

"Hanley," she repeated. "Marvot's number-two man. How did Robert know it was Hanley?"

"Hanley wanted to make sure he knew. He told him before he shot him in the leg to drive it home. He gave Blockman a message to give to you. He said Marvot would be in touch."

"Why Frankie?" she whispered.

"I'm sure Marvot will give you the opportunity to ask that question." He paused. "I can guess. So can you."

Yes, she could guess. "He's going to hold Frankie as a hostage." She could feel the waves of anger and terror wash over her. "Son of a bitch."

"I'll get her back, Grace."

"You won't do anything that will give that bastard an excuse to hurt her." She closed her eyes tightly. "What if she's hurt now? Robert said she was conscious. He wouldn't know if she was hurt or not. They wouldn't care if they hurt her."

"Blockman said Frankie kicked Hanley in the nuts as he dragged her into the helicopter. I'd say she's in pretty good shape."

"She'll fight them." She opened her eyes and brushed the hair back from her face with a shaking hand. "I taught her to fight. But what if she makes them angry? She's only a little girl."

"Grace, you're not thinking. If they're holding her hostage, they won't want her hurt."

"Damn you, how do you know? And no, I'm not thinking, I'm feeling. She's my daughter. You couldn't possibly realize how scared I am."

"Maybe not." He looked away from her. "But I know how scared I am. You don't have the monopoly on loving Frankie. I may not have the right to feel possessive of her, but I have the right to love her. She gives me that right by being what she is, not who she is." He added roughly, "And I'm going to keep on loving her and doing what's best for her. So don't you dare try to shut me out of getting her away from Marvot. It's not going to happen."

"You . . . love her?"

"For God's sake, Grace. How the hell could I help it? Did you think I just wanted to be with her out of some sense of paternal pride? She's bloody wonderful."

"Yes, she is." The tears were running down her cheeks. "And she's probably scared. She won't let them see it, but she'll be scared."

He sat down beside her and pulled her into his arms. "I know." He rocked her back and forth. "It's killing me."

The comfort of his arms didn't stop the terror, but the knowledge that she wasn't alone in that terror helped. Her arms tightened around him. "Why take a helpless little girl?"

"Who managed to kick one of his men in the nuts. I bet

he's not thinking she's so helpless." He pushed her back to look down at her. "And we're not helpless either just because he found a way to take Frankie. We'll get her back well and safe." He brushed a kiss on her forehead. "I have to leave for a few moments and talk to Dr. Krallon. He should have a report for me on Blockman and Vazquez."

"Vazquez was hurt too?"

He nodded. "But it wasn't bad enough to keep him from searching the site of the wreck all night on the chance of finding Frankie. He doesn't believe affection should be dictated by blood either."

Another name hit home. "Dr. Krallon." She looked around her at the rough but comfortable furniture of the living room. "Is this the place where you sent him?"

"It was convenient. I needed medical help and this place is safe. The ranch is closed down, and I'm transferring the horses to Charlie's farm in Alabama."

Her lips twisted. "I'm so upset, I didn't even notice where we were."

"You're a little preoccupied." He headed for the door. "And you didn't even ask about your own injuries. You have a banged-up right knee, a bruised rib cage, and a minor concussion. The knee may cause you the most trouble. It will heal, but it's going to hurt like hell." He opened the door. "And it would be smart to try to get some rest. You were out for the last eight hours and that will help, but you're nowhere near normal. You may have to be a hundred percent pretty damn quick."

She didn't want rest. Her nerves were screaming and she wanted to throw on her clothes and go after Frankie.

"I know." His gaze was reading her expression. "I feel the same way. But we have to wait. It's not our move."

"Wait for Marvot to call me." That would be the next move.

"Yes."

"How will he know how to reach me?"

"Blockman said that Hanley scanned his number into

his cell phone. Marvot will be using that number. But I don't believe he'll be in any hurry. He wants you to be frantic. He wants you to think about all the things he can do to hurt Frankie."

"I will think about it," she whispered. "I can't help it."

"Neither can I." The door shut behind him.

She hesitated and then forced herself to lie back down on the bed. Rest, heal, and wait.

And pray.

The phone call came from Marvot over twenty-four hours later. "How delightful to hear your voice again, Grace. I was very disappointed when you deserted me all those years ago. I had great plans for you."

"Where's my daughter?"

"Charming child. So deliciously lethal. I'd know she was your daughter if I ran into her in the middle of the desert."

"She's a frightened little girl."

"Tell Hanley that. She bit his wrist so badly that he had to have it cleaned and bandaged. Did you know that human bites are particularly subject to infection? He was very angry."

"He deserved it."

"I had a good deal of trouble convincing him of that. He wanted to tie her legs together and throw her into the sea. He doesn't admire spirit the way I do."

"Don't hurt her."

"Are you pleading?"

Her hand tightened on the phone. "Yes, I'm pleading."

"I thought you'd be willing to beg for the sake of your child. I have a child of my own and I know how they have a tendency to weaken us. I fight it all the time. Tell me, is Kilmer equally upset?"

"No. Why should he be?"

"Really, Grace, do you believe I wouldn't pay to know everything about you? Including the name of the father of your child? But it wouldn't surprise me if he didn't have the same pain as you. He hasn't had the experience of raising a child that we have. It's different seeing a baby born and knowing that your blood flows through his veins."

"How can I get my daughter back?"

"You have to complete the work you started. I believe you're aware that would be the price."

"I don't know what you want from me. I've never known."

"I want you to tame the Pair. I want them to love you. I want them to obey you. I want them to be happy to take you wherever you wish."

"Why?"

"That's none of your concern."

"What if we work a trade? I give myself up and you turn Frankie over to Kilmer."

"No deal. I'll have you both. At first, I was very angry with Hanley for not getting the two of you. But on consideration I believe it may be better this way. If he'd taken both of you, then I'd have had to deal with Kilmer. He'd have come roaring after you. He's a man with warrior instincts and his own agenda. He might weigh that agenda against your daughter's life. I understand that conflict. But you won't permit that to happen. You'll be the one to control Kilmer. You won't let him be unduly precipitous and force me to kill your little girl. Isn't that true?"

"Yes, it's true."

"Then we can proceed with our plans. You'll come to El Tariq immediately. Kilmer will do nothing. Is that clear?"

"It's clear."

"If there's any sign of him or any of his men, I'll give your little Frankie to my men to rape and then I'll kill her myself. Do you understand?"

She closed her eyes. "I understand."

"Then I'm looking forward to seeing you and introducing you to my son. He can't wait to see you with the Pair."
He hung up.

* * *

Well?" Kilmer asked.

"I'm to go to El Tariq immediately. If you interfere in any way, Frankie dies after being gang-raped."

Kilmer muttered a curse. "You can't go. Leave it to me."

"The hell I'll leave it to you. Marvot doesn't bluff." She met his gaze. "You know that as well as I do."

His hands clenched into fists at his sides. "I know you'll both die if you walk into that trap."

"Kilmer."

He drew a deep breath and then nodded jerkily. "Okay, we have to protect Frankie. I'm not arguing that."

"You'd better not. Marvot said you had warrior instincts. He's right. But you're going to suppress them or so help me God I'll kill you myself." She got to her feet. Her knees were shaking and she had to reach out to grab the back of the chair to keep from falling. "Nothing's going to happen to Frankie."

Kilmer gazed at her for a moment before he said quietly, "You know that your going will only be a temporary reprieve. He's not going to let either one of you live after you give him what he wants."

"He didn't even make the offer," she said bitterly. "He knew I'd come because there was a chance I could delay the inevitable."

"Or in the hope that you could save her."

"It's not a hope. It's going to happen." Jesus, she was sick to her stomach. She kept picturing Frankie with those bastards. She had to stop it. She couldn't think when she was this scared. "It has to happen."

"You're shaking. Would you like me to fix you a drink?"

She shook her head. "Coffee. Black. I'm going to go to the bathroom and splash water on my face."

He nodded, his gaze on her face. "Good idea."

Frankie . . .

She made it to the bathroom just in time before she threw up. Oh, God . . .

"Okay." Kilmer was beside her, holding her steady as she heaved.

"Go away."

"No way." His grasp tightened. "Never again. Finished?"

She nodded.

He turned her toward the sink. "Lean." He flushed the toilet and grabbed a washcloth and dampened it. He gently washed her face before throwing the washcloth down and gathering her in his arms. "Hold on to me."

She shook her head. "I'm not weak. I can't be weak."

"Who said you were? I need someone to hold on to." His voice was husky. "Do you think you're alone in this? I . . . love that little girl. And I've got a good chance of losing both of you."

He was shaking. She'd never known Kilmer to be this traumatized. Her arms slowly slid around him. "I'm so scared, Kilmer," she whispered.

"So am I." He buried his face in her hair. "Warrior, shit. I'm not going to make a move that could hurt her, Grace. I just want to keep you both alive."

She wanted to stay here, held safe and secure against the harshness that lay ahead. But Frankie wasn't safe or secure.

She pushed him away. "Then we'd better find a way to do that." She tried to steady her voice. "Get out of here and let me wash my mouth out."

He hesitated, staring at her. Then he turned away. "Ten minutes."

You were longer than ten minutes." Kilmer looked up as she walked into the kitchen.

"I was upstairs throwing things into a suitcase."

He poured her coffee. "Gun?"

She shook her head. "Marvot will have me searched. I'll leave that to you to plant when I need it."

He went still. "Me? I'm going to be allowed to help?"

"Don't try to con me. You know you wouldn't stand by if you could find a way to make a move."

"A safe move," he corrected.

"I trust you." She moistened her lips. "I have to trust you. I can't get her out by myself. But I'm the one who has to call the shots. You don't do anything until I let you know it's safe for her."

"And how are you going to do that?"

"You're going to have someone watching me. I've packed four blue chambray shirts and one khaki shirt. If I wear the khaki shirt it will signal that something's going to happen, a change, maybe an escape attempt. It will signal you to be on the alert."

"An escape attempt? At El Tariq?"

She thought about it. "Maybe. But after you plucked Donavan out of his hands, it's going to be difficult. Maybe it will be to signal you we're going to that oasis in the desert. I can't be sure that Marvot won't take us there."

"And what if Marvot decides to leave Frankie at El Tariq?"

She shook her head. "I won't let him. I'll find a way. Just be ready."

"I'll be ready." He looked down into his coffee cup. "Anything else?"

"Yes. I need to know everything you've found out about the Pair. No more secrets, Kilmer."

"No secrets. I would have told you anytime you asked. You weren't interested."

He was right. She hadn't wanted to know anything about the Pair. She hadn't wanted to be involved. "I'm interested now. I'm not working blind like I did all those years ago. I have to have all the weapons I can beg, borrow, or steal. And knowledge is a very powerful weapon."

"Then ask away."

"What did you steal from Marvot that roused him enough to go after me?"

"A map. It was tucked into a very fancy pouch with the heads of the Pair embroidered on it."

"What kind of map?"

"A map of a general location in the Sahara. I'd judge it to be within fifty miles of the oasis where Marvot sets up camp with the Pair."

"What location? What's there?"

"Something Marvot wants very badly."

"What, dammit?"

"A prototype of an engine built by a British inventor over fifteen years ago. His name was Hugh Burton, and he lived in the Sahara most of his adult life. His father was an archaeologist, but he was an electrical engineer. He was a genius at his profession and he was equally clever at training horses. He had a passion for his horses and had a small stable near Tangiers. Owners came from all over Europe to pay him to train their horses."

"Get back to the engine."

"It's all part of it. It seems that the father and son's vocations became a complement to each other at some point."

"What do you mean?"

"Hugh's father unearthed a battery pack in an ancient tomb in Egypt. It wasn't the first time that such a device had been found, but this one was incredibly efficient. It made the advances Detroit has made in fuel-free engines look like kindergarten toys. Hugh persuaded his father not to report the find to the Egyptian government and began to work on creating the perfect engine. An engine that would eliminate the need for oil and revolutionize the world economy."

"And he succeeded?"

"Oh, yes. It took him over seven years but he did it. Then he took it to the U.S., one of the biggest gas guzzlers in the world. He demonstrated it for a select number of congressmen who were big on environmental issues. They were impressed and were starting to negotiate with Burton for the rights. Then Burton quit the negotiations cold and went back to the Sahara."

"Why?"

"While he was in Washington his father had been tortured and murdered by Marvot. Marvot had found out about the discovery and was trying to stop the negotiations until he could gain control of the engine from Burton. Can you imagine the power that would give him with the Middle Eastern oil states? If he released the engine to the Western world, it would destroy the oil cartel. Liquid gold would become dross."

"If Burton broke off negotiations, then Marvot must have succeeded."

He shook his head. "He loved his father and there wasn't any way he'd let Marvot have anything he wanted after the murder." He grimaced. "Marvot had pretty much butchered the old man. Burton went off his head when he saw him."

"Then he should have made a deal with Marvot's enemies."

"At that point Burton thought the whole world was his enemy. He wanted nothing to do with anyone. He'd always been an odd bird, and that was enough to send him around the bend. He packed up and took off into the desert. He didn't take much—the engine and several of his horses."

"And Marvot followed him?"

"Yes, but Burton had lived in the desert, knew the people, and was able to lose himself by hooking up with a nomadic tribe. He'd known the Sheikh, Adam Ben Haroun, at school in England and they had common interests. The Sheikh's tribe also raised fine Arabian horses."

"How long was he with them?"

"It was four years before Marvot caught up with him. But Burton didn't have the engine. He'd hidden it somewhere in the desert."

"Didn't Marvot force him to tell him where?"

"No, Burton died trying to escape. But Marvot managed to torture some information out of him before he was killed. He said he'd buried the engine in the dunes near the oasis and that he'd trained the Pair to find it."

"The Pair?"

"They were born while Burton was on the run—a mare and a stallion. He broke them to be one-rider mounts and to kill anyone but him who tried to ride them. Evidently, he also taught them the way to his greatest treasure. It was a complicated business because the horses were trained never to go near the stash unless they were together. That way if someone stole one of the horses or killed one, no one would be able to retrieve the engine."

"And that's why Marvot had to find someone to ride the Pair?"

"You saw them. They wouldn't be ridden. He had a choice of risking killing them or finding someone they would accept. He's tried drugs, imported a truckload of horse breakers, but if they mount one of the Pair the horse freezes. Or tries to kill the rider. And they don't quit. One of the Pair almost died before Marvot pulled the rider off him."

"It's bizarre. I can't believe Marvot would believe all this."

"Oh, he believes it. He doesn't think Burton would lie while undergoing the kind of punishment Marvot was dealing out. He's been hedging his bets by searching the desert on his own for the last decade. But, yeah, he thinks the Pair can find it."

"How did you find all this out?"

"I've been looking for answers for eight years. Donavan tapped some contacts in Washington for some of the info. I went searching in the desert until I found the nomad tribe that sheltered Burton. The Sheikh is very interesting but not very forthcoming. I had to live with them for over six months before they trusted me enough to talk."

"What about this map you stole?"

"It was in a pouch taken off Burton when Marvot captured him. Very vague. Burton probably made it that way on purpose. He had the Pair; he only needed to know where to take them. It contained only the general area of about seventy-five miles where Marvot has been searching for years. Hell, when you're dealing with dunes that shift with every storm, it could be buried anywhere. That's probably why Burton trained the Pair to find it. He was afraid he might not be able to find it himself after a few years of having landmarks destroyed and shifted." He shrugged. "But I hoped for more when I stole the map from Marvot."

"Couldn't Marvot use some kind of aerial or metal detector to locate the engine?"

"You'd think so. Burton must have found some way of masking any signal. There's no question he was brilliant."

"So Marvot is left with only the horses as a clue. No wonder he takes such good care of them."

"Considering they could make him one of the most powerful men in the world."

"Providing it's true that the horses can lead anyone to that engine." She looked him in the eye. "Do you believe it's possible?"

He shrugged. "The Sheikh said it was true. I believe I'd be willing to take a chance on it panning out if it meant I'd rake in that kind of return. But then, I don't know much about horses. What do you think?"

She frowned. "I know that wild horses have an instinct that keeps them coming back to certain areas as the seasons change. And there's the old true story about Dobbin always knowing his way home. Animals' homing sense is definitely keener and more highly developed than ours. Look at all the stories of dogs and cats finding their way home across entire continents. Could Burton train those young horses to not only do it, but to do it only when there are two of them?" She shook her head. "I don't know. If he was as brilliant as you say, it's possible." Her lips tightened. "But he must have been a cruel son of a bitch if he taught those horses to hate everyone but him."

"He was a bitter man. He probably enjoyed the idea of balking Marvot even after he was dead. Dangling the carrot and then making it impossible for him to reach out and grab it."

"But it was the Pair who suffered." She rubbed her temple. So much cruelty. Not only from Marvot but from this Hugh Burton, who had been full of hate and left it as a legacy. "And Marvot expects me to make them do what no one else can do? Jesus."

"You don't have to do anything but pretend to make progress until we can get Frankie away from him."

"Pretend? Marvot's not stupid." She shook her head. "But I can't think of that now. I'll face the problem when I'm at El Tariq. Be sure to assign someone good to watch me. Marvot will be expecting some move from you and will be on the alert. Whoever is doing surveillance will have to get close, and if he's caught, Frankie's dead."

"He'll be good."

"Donavan?"

"Yes." He inclined his head. "Or me. Am I good enough for you, Grace?"

She met his gaze. "Yes, you're good enough." She turned toward the door. "Drop me off at the airport. I'll go the rest of the way to El Tariq alone."

"That would be best. Marvot's going to be on the lookout." He paused. "We're going to do this, Grace. Don't doubt it."

"I don't." She had to smother the panic. Take every minute one second at a time. "I *can't* doubt it."

I didn't think you'd let her go." Donavan watched Grace disappear into the terminal.

"No choice." Kilmer pulled away from the curb. "She was right. She had to go. And I have to stay in the background until I see a way to get them out."

"And it's killing you."

"It's not easy."

"So when do I leave for El Tariq?"

"If you've had enough of El Tariq, I'll go instead."

"Don't be an ass."

"I'll come as soon as I can. I need to go back to the Sahara."

"What?"

"I'm almost certain we're not going to be able to get close to her at El Tariq. There will be guards all over the place. I can prepare the way at the oasis."

"You think that's where they'll end up?"

"Grace is going to try to do what Marvot wants with the Pair. If she does, then he'll take them to the desert to try to find that engine."

"What if you're wrong? What if she needs you at El Tariq right away?"

His hands tightened with white-knuckled force on the steering wheel. "Then I cut my throat."

14

El Tariq

The ropes around her wrists chafed as Frankie tried to loosen them by rubbing them against the side of the stall.

No good.

She gave up and leaned back to get her breath. The stall was dark and stank of manure and straw. Funny how stables always smelled the same. She would have thought that this foreign one would be different.

"She's younger than I am, Papa." Her head lifted to see a boy peering down at her. He was older than her but not by much. He was standing beside the man to whom Hanley had brought her, Marvot. "The Pair will kill her."

Marvot chuckled. "Perhaps. That would make Hanley very happy. But it's her mother who I'm bringing here to work with the Pair. Our little Francesca is just a means to an end." Marvot lifted the flashlight to shine it into her eyes. "I've brought my son, Guillaume, to meet you. He saw Hanley carry you into the stable and he was curious. Say hello, Guillaume."

"Hello." The boy's tone was absent. "What's going to happen to her?"

"What do you want to happen to her?"

Guillaume shook his head. "I don't know."

"I believe you do know. You mentioned the Pair."

Guillaume moistened his lips. "I just thought . . . she's like me. I didn't think you'd hurt her."

"But you were curious to see if I'd treat her as I would anyone else. The answer is yes. Just because she's a child doesn't exempt her. You must remember that." He said to Frankie, "And you must remember that too. When your mother comes, you must convince her she must do as I tell her."

"Are you going to leave her here?" Guillaume asked. "She's all dirty." He wrinkled his nose. "And she smells."

"So do you," Frankie said fiercely. "You stink." She glared at Marvot. "And you do too."

Marvot chuckled. "Isn't she delightful? No fear. I should keep her around for a while. You might learn something from her."

Guillaume scowled. "I don't like her."

"You see? You've learned something already. Jealousy." He smiled down at Frankie. "It gets cold here at night. If you asked my son's pardon, I might give you a blanket."

She glared at him.

"Suit yourself. Come along, Guillaume."

"May I come again?"

"If you're a good boy." He glanced back at Frankie. "You should really be smarter about the battles you choose, little girl. I've noticed lately that Guillaume has a cruel streak. . . ."

They were gone.

Frankie drew a relieved breath. Jeez, she was scared.

They were bullies and she mustn't be afraid of them. That's what they wanted.

She had known bullies at school, and Mom had said that if you backed down they'd keep coming after you.

She wouldn't back down.

But she hadn't been tied up in a creepy place like this stable before.

Don't be scared. Try to get these ropes off her wrists.

Don't be scared. . . .

I can't tell you how happy I am to see you." Marvot smiled as Grace was brought into his office. "I always had a hunch that we'd be together again. You were really very naughty to keep me waiting this long."

"Where's my daughter?"

"She's not been hurt—much."

Grace's heart jumped. "Much?"

"Well, last night she was trying to get out of the ropes and chafed her wrists raw. She almost made it. If one of my guards hadn't checked on her early this morning, I might have had nothing with which to bargain. One of the sentries would surely have shot her."

"I want to see her."

"You will."

"Now."

He shrugged. "You're very demanding. I should remind you that I call the shots here." He rose to his feet. "But I can understand that you're overcome with maternal concern. Come along. We can talk while we walk down to the stable."

"I want to see Frankie."

"I heard you. Your daughter is in a stall in the stable. After her bad behavior with Hanley, I decided that she should be treated like the animal she acted like. Hanley approved wholeheartedly." He was leading her down the path toward the stable. "She's not made her case any better by her defiance. She's even antagonized my son, Guillaume. I believe he'd like nothing better than to have me throw her into one of the Pair's stalls."

"That doesn't surprise me. Not if he's *your* son. Blood-thirstiness must run in the family."

"Was that supposed to annoy me? It does run in the family. I'm not ashamed of it. My father and my grandfather were both men of power, and blood is the coin of power. All through history, no conqueror has made his mark without being willing to shed blood. Napoleon, Alexander, Julius Caesar."

"Attila the Hun, Hitler, Saddam Hussein."

He chuckled. "Even better. Ultimate power without worrying about civilized consequences."

Yet he didn't look like a barbarian, she thought. Marvot was in his forties, with close-cut graying hair and handsome features. His strongly built body was clad in expensive white trousers and a loose white shirt that gave him an air of casual elegance. "Your heroes?"

"No, they all made stupid mistakes." He opened the stable door. "An error of judgment is acceptable. Stupidity is not. For instance, I thought Kilmer had forgotten about his defeat at my hands all those years ago. An error in judgment. But easily enough rectified." He waved her into the stable. "First stall."

She ran past him.

Oh, God, Frankie.

She stood there, staring at her daughter. Dirty, hair matted, bound, and tossed in all this filth.

"Hi, Mom." Frankie scooted up to rest against the wall of the stall. "Don't look like that. I'm okay. Honest."

"The hell you are." She knelt beside her and grabbed her close. "But you will be, baby." She rocked her back and forth, tears stinging her eyes. "I'll fix it. I promise. I'll fix it."

Frankie whispered, "He's a real bully. We have to be careful."

"I know." She looked over her shoulder at Marvot. "You bastard. Did you have to treat her like this?"

"Yes, I thought it would carry the point home. You're going to be much more amenable now, aren't you? But I'll be generous now that I've had the impact." He looked down at Frankie. "I'll even let you clean up those wounds on her wrists before they become infected in this filth."

Grace was looking at Frankie's wrists, and she could feel the fury tear through her. The wounds were shallow but already filled with the dirt and manure of the stall. "Get me some water and an antiseptic."

"I'll send someone after we've come to an understanding. You work with the Pair until they're docile. Agreed?"

"They'll never be docile."

"Then until they do what's needed."

She nodded jerkily. "If you leave me alone to do it my way."

"Of course. I have the utmost respect for your abilities. And I've no fear that you'll drag your heels. Such a pretty little girl . . ." He turned away. "Now I'll leave you alone with your daughter so that you can see how well I've treated her. Well, comparatively well. Come up to the house when you're finished. I'll be in my office and we can discuss details. You'll be allowed to move freely around the grounds, but naturally you'll be closely watched."

Grace waited until he was out of the stable before she asked Frankie, "Are you sore anywhere else?" Her hands were running over Frankie's body. "Did they bruise or hurt you in any way?"

"That man Hanley slapped me." She added, "After I bit him."

Grace could see the faint bruise on Frankie's left cheek. "Anything else? How about the wreck? Did you hit your head?"

She shook her head. "I'm okay."

"You're not okay." She looked down at Frankie's torn wrists and the fury flooded back to her. "They hurt you."

"I did that. You always told me that I had to fight the bullies, and I couldn't do it with my hands tied."

"I've got a big mouth. I shouldn't have—"

"But you were right." Frankie frowned. "Honest, I'm

214

okay, Mom. I got a little cold last night, but that's all. And I was so busy trying to rub those ropes through that I didn't notice that much." She lowered her voice. "But they scare me. I think we've got to leave here soon."

"We will." Grace sat back on her heels. "But it's going to be tricky and you have to help. You have to obey orders without question. You can't argue—not with me, and not with any of these people. Can you do that?"

She scowled. "I don't know. They're bullies. You said that—"

"I know what I said. The situation is different. It will make it harder for me if I have to worry about you fighting with them. Will you do it?"

She hesitated and then nodded. "If they don't hurt you. I think they want to hurt you."

"They won't hurt me as long as I'm giving them what they want."

"The Pair . . . Jake told me about them. Am I going to see them?"

"I'll try to arrange with Marvot to have you working with me. It will be safer for you that way. That's why you have to make me that promise. If he sees that you're getting in the way instead of helping, he'll take you away from me."

"You think he'll let me do it?"

She hoped to God he would. Sometimes opportunities for escape came unexpectedly and out of the blue. If she saw an opening, Frankie had to be with her. "I'm going to do everything that I can to see that he does. But I have to be able to trust you, Frankie. The Pair can be pretty scary, and you can't cry or scream even if you think they're going to hurt me."

She was silent a moment. "But they won't hurt you, will they? They'll be like the horses at home. You can talk to them?"

Grace drew her back into her arms as she saw that Frankie was shaking. She was obviously trying not to let Grace know how upset she was. "They won't hurt me." She added, "But it's harder to make them listen. It's going to take a while. The Pair have been used to having their own way for a long time."

"Remember when you had to break that stallion for Mr. Baker? He thought he was mean, but you said he was only scared. Maybe these horses are scared too."

"Maybe." She stroked Frankie's hair and tried to think of a way to distract her. "And I think it's time we stopped calling them the Pair. They're not two cogs in a machine. They're individual horses, and I have to deal with them separately. Let's name them."

"They're both white? Do they look alike?"

"Very close. One is a mare and the other is a stallion. They both have blue eyes, but one is a little smaller and has a darker mane. The stallion is bigger, more powerful, and has a small scar on his side. I think it was caused by a spur."

"See? They probably are scared of being hurt."

"Names," she prompted.

Frankie frowned. "It's hard. . . ." She thought about it. "Maybe Hope for the mare. Because that's what we're doing, isn't it? Hoping that they'll like us?"

"Oh, yes. We're definitely hoping that. And for the other horse?"

Frankie shook her head. "What did you think about when you first saw him?"

Death and fear thundering toward her. "I guess I was too distracted to think much."

Frankie was silent a moment. "Let's call him Charlie."

"What?"

"I want to call him Charlie."

"Frankie, this horse isn't anything like Charlie. He's very wild."

"But I loved Charlie. It will be easier for me to love this horse if I think of Charlie every time I see him. Maybe it will help you too."

Grace tried to smile. "Maybe it will." She cleared her throat. "Okay, Charlie it is."

* * *

"Don't be absurd," Marvot said. "The child will not
be permitted anywhere near you. She'll be kept locked up,
and if you're cooperative, you may be allowed visits."

"Why? You must know that Frankie has done work with
the horses at the farm in the past. She could help me." She
paused. "Or do you doubt that your security guards could
keep us from escaping? I suppose that's a big worry. You
haven't done very well keeping Kilmer and his men in
check."

"Was that supposed to sting? It doesn't. I've corrected
that problem."

"I don't need to worry about my daughter when I
should be concentrating on the Pair. It's going to be hard
enough. If you don't have valid concerns, then let me have
what I need."

"You're saying that the child is going to help you tame
the Pair? How interesting."

She stiffened. His smile was just a little too malicious.
"I'm saying that she'll be of value to me."

"Then I should let you try. Naturally, I'd expect her to
ride one of the Pair within a reasonable amount of time. I'll
even let you choose which one."

Christ.

His gaze was searching her expression. "No?"

The idea scared her to death. But he was obviously going to turn her down cold unless she agreed. Perhaps she
could stave him off until she could find a way to escape. "It's
possible."

"No, it's certain." He chuckled. "And I decide the reasonable length of time. Guillaume and I will pay you
frequent visits to see how you're progressing. I can't wait
until Guillaume sees her on the horse's back. He doubted
that I'd treat her as I would you, and it will be a good
lesson."

"If you hurry me, I won't be able to do anything with the Pair."

"I can be patient. Unless you annoy me." He paused. "Or Kilmer annoys me."

"Kilmer's out of this." She changed the subject. "I want a cot for me and one for Frankie set up at the stable."

"Really? I was going to give you slightly more comfortable quarters."

She shook her head. "I want to eat and sleep with the Pair. They have to get to know me. I'm sure you'll see that we're well guarded."

"I'm sure too." He shrugged. "Whatever you like. There's a shower in the stable, and the guards will bring you food when you ask. I expect rapid results, and I'll give you what you need to get them. As long as I see things going my way. If I don't, I'll be very angry and make sure that they do."

"You'll get your results." She turned, left the office, and walked down the polished tile hall to the French doors that led to the path to the stables. Everything in this palatial Mediterranean-style villa spoke of the luxury and power that was meant to intimidate all comers. She wouldn't be intimidated. He might have the power, but power could be broken.

But, Jesus, what had she gotten herself and Frankie into? Frankie was good with horses, but she was a child. There was no way Grace wanted her anywhere near the Pair. She'd hoped that she would be able to keep Frankie near but on the outskirts of the training.

It wasn't going to happen. Okay, accept it. It made it more difficult to keep Frankie safe, but they'd find a way.

She saw Frankie waiting at the door of the stable and forced a smile. "Hi, I talked him into it. We're going to be together. Isn't that great?"

* * *

They heard the outraged neighing and stomping of the Pair as soon as they came into the stable.

"They sound angry," Frankie said. "And loud. Why didn't I hear them last night?"

"They were probably in the paddock. They don't like to be confined and they make their dislike known. The stable boys are afraid of them and only bring them in occasionally. Well, actually they open the gate and stable door and run them in. It's quite a production. When I was here before, I had to make them take a stone out of one of the Pair's hooves."

"Which one?"

That's right—she had to remember not to refer to them as the Pair. "The one you call Charlie."

"They're beautiful," Frankie whispered. Her eyes were shining as she caught her first sight of the horses in the two stalls. "I don't think I've ever seen horses this beautiful. Have you, Mom?"

"They come pretty high on the list."

Hello, guys. It's been a long time. Has it been bad for you here? I hope not. I imagine you gave as good as you got. She drew closer. *I'm going to try to make it as easy for you as—*

"Good God!"

Frankie looked up at her in alarm. "What's wrong?"

"The mare." She headed for the house phone on the post. "Look at her." She picked up the receiver and pushed the main-house button. "Why didn't you tell me?" she asked when Marvot picked up the phone. "And how do you expect me to work with her when she'll be edgy as a machete?"

"I expect you to do what I brought you here to do. And she's always edgy."

"She's not always in foal."

"No, it's the first time for her. I've been careful to make sure that they were separated when she's in season. I didn't want anything to interfere. Unfortunately, I was away from the farm this time and my stable men made a mistake. They'll never do it again."

"When is she due?"

"Any day now."

"And do you have a vet on call to deliver?"

"I understand there's a decent vet in the village thirty miles from here. If you run into trouble, I'll call him."

"If *I* run into trouble?"

"There's no one I would rather entrust the mare to than you. Surely you've had experience with this kind of thing?"

"Yes. We stopped breeding horses at the farm four years ago to concentrate on training, but naturally I was present at a number of births before that. But I've always had a vet present."

"I don't want any outsiders here. You do it. My only demand is that you make sure the mare lives. I don't care about the foal."

"I do."

"Then you'll have to work hard to bring them both through safely, won't you?"

"Look, the mare will be erratic as hell. I might need to wait until she's given birth before I start working with them."

"Not acceptable." He hung up.

Grace replaced the receiver and leaned wearily back against the post. And she had thought the situation was tough enough before.

"The mare's in foal?" Frankie asked. "I know you think it's bad right now, but I love the babies."

"I know you do. Baby horses, kittens, puppies. But this is a little different, Frankie." She straightened and smiled with an effort. "But we'll deal with it. I'm glad you called her Hope. We're going to have to do a lot of hoping she'll cooperate." She gestured to the other horse. "And that's Charlie. Are you sure you don't want to change his name?"

Frankie shook her head. "No, it's . . . right. What do we do now?"

"We let them free. That's why we left the stable door and paddock gate open. Get out of the way."

Frankie moved back as Grace unfastened the stall door. "Is this far enough?"

"Farther. Charlie's been known to rush anyone in the vicinity." She swung open both doors and jumped back just in time to avoid the horses as they rushed out of the stalls. She tensed as Charlie hesitated, glaring at Frankie. But the open stable door was too tempting. He turned and dashed from the stable after Hope.

"He doesn't like me," Frankie said. "I thought—"

"He doesn't like anyone," Grace said quickly. "And he doesn't have to like us. If he tolerates us, that will be fine. Come on." She followed the horses out of the stable. "We have to get to work." Her gaze wandered over the stable yard. Three guards with rifles were standing at points in front of the stable, and they looked like they knew how to use them. She hadn't a doubt that there were guards all over the horse farm. "The horses have to get used to us." She went into the paddock and closed the gate. "Or me. We'll introduce you after they become accustomed to me invading their territory." The horses were already aware of that intrusion. Hope and Charlie were staring at her with the wariness and ferocity she remembered. She stiffened, bracing herself.

Come on, get it over with. Show me how strong you are. I don't care about being boss. I'll settle for being a friend. You don't know about that yet. Let me teach you.

"Mom!"

They were streaking toward her.

It's not going to work. I can't let you hurt me.

She stood still, waiting.

They weren't going to part in their charge as they had all those years ago. It was too soon. But she had to show them she wasn't afraid, and that meant waiting until the last minute.

"Mom, get out!"

A few more seconds.

Now.

She leaped for the top bar of the paddock and swung up to straddle it.

Hope crashed into the fence where Grace had been standing seconds ago. Charlie followed, rearing, breaking the third rail of the fence.

Then they were gone, running across the paddock.

She drew a deep breath, watching them as they raced away.

First encounter. It won't be the last. I'll give you a little time but I'm here to stay.

She glanced at Frankie, who was staring after the horses. "Scared?"

Frankie nodded.

"Good. That will keep you out of the paddock until I'm ready for you." If she was ever ready to put Frankie in the same paddock as Hope and Charlie. Their ferocity was every bit as extreme as she remembered.

"I want to help," Frankie said. "What can I do?"

"Watch them. I have to know which one is leading when they attack. And I need to know if anything triggers them besides my presence in their territory."

"Can't you tell?"

"I'm a little distracted at that point," Grace said dryly.

"You worked with them before. Didn't you find that out then?"

"I wasn't interested in riding them. All I needed was for them to permit me to lead them into a horse trailer so that we could get them away from here."

"But you have to ride them now?"

She nodded. "I think so. Unless we can get away from here right away."

Frankie gazed over her shoulder at the guards and shook her head.

"It's possible," Grace said. "But we'll assume that we

need to work with the horses. Now, tell me. When they charged me, which one made the first move?"

"I don't remember. I was scared."

"So was I. Try to remember."

"I think it was Hope." She nodded. "Yes, it was Hope."

"Really?" Grace looked back at the horses. "But that shouldn't surprise me. Ordinarily, I'd have bet on Charlie, but Hope is completely unpredictable now. Her aggressiveness is probably multiplied."

"Because of the foal?" Frankie thought about it. "Hope looked . . . nervous. Maybe she's scared too."

"Maybe." She smiled at Frankie. "See, you're already helping. You don't have to go into the paddock to do that."

"I don't want you to go in either," she whispered. "They want to hurt you."

"Because they don't understand we don't want to hurt them. Hope and Charlie aren't really any different from other horses I've broken." That wasn't true. The Pair had a history of years of success that empowered any animal. And Hugh Burton had spent the horses' youngest years teaching them the ways to resist and conquer. "Together we'll do it." She got down from the fence inside the paddock. "Now I'm going for a stroll. I believe the horses have had time to get over the first flush of success. I have to let them know that it didn't discourage me."

"Will they charge you again?"

"Yes." She started walking along the fence line. "Keep an eye on them to see if they do anything unusual. . . ."

Besides trying to trample her to death.

You expect me to help you, Kilmer?" Sheikh Ben Haroun shook his head. "My tribe lost one of its best horse trainers to Marvot's men. Karim liked Burton and was trying to protect him from that bastard Marvot."

"Then I'd think you'd want revenge, Adam."

"I told Burton that he was on his own if Marvot caught

up with him. I told my people the same thing. I wasn't about to sacrifice any of them so that Burton could keep his wonderful engine safe." His lips twisted. "It's all very well to try to advance civilization, but we nomads are a dying species, Kilmer. Our culture is fading more with every step civilization takes into the Sahara. In a few decades we'll go the way of the dinosaurs."

"I can't argue with you. I wish I could. All I can say is that I've lived with your people and I know they wouldn't choose to let Marvot win."

The Sheikh was silent. "Perhaps you're right. But we don't have the weapons that Marvot has. We breed horses, not fighters. That's why I didn't go after Marvot when he killed Karim."

"I can provide the weapons and the men. And I'll try to keep you out of the actual fighting."

"But then you'll take the engine and go away."

"Yes. But not until I know you're all safe." He paused. "And it's not only the engine. Marvot has my child and her mother. They'll die if I don't get them free."

The Sheikh stared at him and then smiled faintly. "Ah, so it's not revenge."

"It's revenge. I want to castrate the son of a bitch for taking my family."

"At last we meet on common ground." He smiled. "I understand about families. I consider all my tribe my family."

"Then tell me that you'll—"

"Enough." The Sheikh held up his hand. "Don't push me, Kilmer. I'll think on it and we'll talk again."

"We may not have much time."

"Then do what you have to do. I won't be hurried."

Kilmer could see that he wasn't going to make any more headway. He rose to his feet. "What if I just ask for reconnaissance and a safe haven if I need it?"

"I won't be hurried."

Kilmer nodded jerkily. "Sorry." He left the tent and stood outside, trying to overcome the frustration surging through him. He couldn't blame the Sheikh for not wanting to take a chance. Keep calm. He hadn't been given a definite no yet. The Sheikh could still give him the help he needed. Adam Ben Haroun's mother had been half English and he'd been educated in England, and that undoubtedly had an influence on his thinking. He and his entire tribe were unusual. Most nomadic tribes were Touareg in the Sahara, but Adam belonged to one of the few tribes of Arab descent.

Kilmer stared out at the desolate gold sand dunes that surrounded the encampment. He'd enjoyed his stay with the tribe over a year ago. He'd found them both kind and intelligent after he'd broken through that wall of reserve and distrust. He didn't want to put them in danger, but, God, he needed that help. Getting Grace and Frankie away from Marvot was only the first step. Even if Grace was able to give Marvot what he wanted, Kilmer was certain Marvot would still kill them.

It was only a question of when.

15

Interesting day," Marvot said. "But I didn't see much accomplished."

"I did." She didn't look at him as she closed the paddock gate. "Toward the end of the day the Pair had two chances to rush me. They didn't do it. Come on, Frankie. Let's get cleaned up and have something to eat."

"Day one," Marvot said. "And I didn't see much participation on the child's part."

Bastard.

"She was helping. It was mostly observation and seeing what would work today." She nudged Frankie ahead of her. "You can't expect much."

"On the contrary, I expect everything. I can't wait to see her on the back of one of the Pair. Have you chosen which one yet?"

"No." She led Frankie quickly back toward the stable. She could feel Marvot's gaze on her every step of the way.

Frankie was silent until they reached the stable. "What

was he talking about? Am I supposed to ride one of the horses?"

"That's what he wants. That doesn't mean you'll have to do it."

"Why does he want it?"

"Because he knows it would worry me. He says it would set a good example for his son, but I don't think that's it."

"Guillaume," she said thoughtfully. "I wonder what it would be like to have a father like him. I didn't like Guillaume, but maybe if his father was nicer, he'd be nicer. Do you think so?"

"I think you shouldn't worry about Guillaume. We have enough on our plates."

Frankie nodded. "I'll try to ride one of the horses if you like."

"I don't like." But it had been on her mind all day. The chances of her keeping Frankie at her side depended on her being able to validate the argument that Frankie was helping. She hadn't been surprised to see Marvot. "But if he saw you do it once, it might take the pressure off. How do you feel about it?"

"Scared." Frankie made a face. "Heck, I was scared of jumping Darling the first time."

But Darling was a pussycat compared to the Pair. "You told me three times today that it was Hope who was starting the charges. Would you like to try to ride Charlie instead?"

Frankie shook her head. "I like Hope. I feel sorry for her."

"Even if she's more aggressive right now?"

"I like her," Frankie repeated stubbornly. "I think if you'd take her away from Charlie she might like me. She doesn't need anyone but Charlie when she's with him."

"We tried separating them when I was here before. It didn't seem to have any effect on them."

"Could we try?"

Grace nodded. "Tomorrow."

Frankie smiled. "Good. I won't be nearly as afraid once

we get to know each other." She paused. "It's harder for me than for you. I know you always make fun when I try to talk about it. But Charlie told me that horses really do understand you, that some people just have a sort of . . . magic."

"I'm not a magician. Don't be silly."

"But Charlie said that you—"

"I'm good with horses. That doesn't mean that I—" She stopped. She'd always wanted Frankie to live in the real world, and this talent was undoubtedly a bit weird. Yet they were in this hellish situation together and she should be honest with her. "I'm no horse whisperer or Doctor Dolittle, but from the time I was your age I've felt as if horses understood me and I understood them. I've never hidden that from you."

"My age? How did you find out?"

"I was staying on my grandfather's farm and there was a horse who was sick. The local vet didn't know what was wrong with her, but I did."

"She told you?"

"No, I just knew." She shrugged. "But he called it a guess."

"And horses do what you tell them, don't they?"

Go for broke. "Sometimes. And sometimes they don't pay any attention to me. It just means that it's easier for me to deal with them than it is for other people."

"I think they pay attention. Darling never balked with you."

"He stopped balking with you too. He just needed to know that there wasn't anything to fear."

"After you told him."

"You're the one who told him, remember?"

"Mom."

She hesitated and then nodded. "Okay, maybe I reinforced it a little. But if Darling hadn't trusted you, then he'd never have gone over that barrier."

Frankie grinned. "Mom, don't feel bad. It's okay. I guess

228

I always knew it. I don't know why you're not proud of it. It's kinda neat having a mom who can talk to—"

"I told you, I'm no horse whis—"

"Yeah, but I'll feel better riding Hope now that I know that she'll listen to what you say."

And maybe that was a good thing, Grace thought. Confidence never hurt any situation, and they needed all the weapons they could muster. Screw reality and practicality. "You can be sure I'll put in a good word for you. But forget Hope and Charlie and what's going to happen tomorrow. You need to eat and get to bed."

"You too?"

"Sure." She entered the stable and gazed at the Pair, who had already been brought in and were being fed by two very nervous stable boys. "If Hope and Charlie will be quiet enough to let us sleep."

Charlie and Hope weren't quiet. It was lucky that Frankie was so tired that she slept right through the noise they made. Grace lay on her cot, listening to the uproar until she was sure Frankie wouldn't stir. Then she quietly got up and went outside to stand in the doorway of the stable. The guard on duty a few feet away straightened and changed his grip on his rifle.

"I'm not going anywhere. I just want some air."

The guard stared at her without speaking, but he was smiling insolently.

She ignored him and gazed out at the darkness of the woods surrounding the farm. Was Kilmer out there? She was feeling very lonely and isolated at this moment. She wanted to *see* him. Strange—though sex was such a big part of their relationship, when she'd thought of Kilmer since they'd left the ranch, it wasn't of him leaning naked over her in the barn. It was a memory of him laughing down at Frankie as they rode together through the fields.

In spite of what she had told Marvot, it had been a discouraging day. If the Pair remembered her at all, it wasn't obvious. Any progress she'd made with them all those years ago was erased and she was starting fresh. But maybe she was wrong. She'd see in the next few days.

But how many days would Marvot give her? She wouldn't put it past him to try to nudge her along by taking Frankie from her. That mustn't happen, dammit.

And there was no use staring at the trees like some medieval maiden waiting for a hero to rescue her. She was the only one she could count on for rescue. She could trust Kilmer to step up if he found an opening, but in the end it would be she who would shoulder the responsibility.

And it was time she got back to work instead of standing out here being depressed and letting that guard ogle her.

She turned and went back into the stable and down the aisle toward the stalls. When they saw her, the ruckus increased.

Okay, you're not pleased. I invaded your space. Get used to it. It's going to happen again.

She sat down across the aisle from their stalls and leaned against the wall.

Get used to me. I'm not going to hurt you. I'm as much a prisoner here as you are. I know that you've been hurt before, but if you team up with me, you'll never have to worry about anyone else trying to ride you. And I'll do it as little as I can to keep you fit and well.

Were they listening? If they were, was it making any impact? She knew that she was able to communicate with some horses, but she never knew on what level or to what extent they understood her. She could only hope that they sensed what she felt.

But the violence of her reception was not encouraging.

You don't want to hear what I'm saying. I can understand that. But I have to keep saying it because it's true and because the man who is your enemy is also mine. So I'll be here every night and every day until we can get together. Tomorrow you'll be separated for a while, but don't be afraid. We just want to get to know you better. It won't be for long. Then you'll be together again.

If anything, the horses' reaction was becoming even more violent. It could be that was a good sign. At least she was getting through to them. Maybe.

My daughter, Frankie, is with me. You saw her today. She's young, only a filly, and she'll be very kind to you. I promise she's no threat at all.

She had to keep repeating those words. Frankie was no threat. Frankie would be kind. Over and over until they believed it. She had a chance. As far as she knew, the Pair had never been approached by a child. Marvot's son was fascinated but afraid of the horses. Horses sensed fear and responded with aggression.

Frankie was afraid too. Well, then Grace would have to try to eliminate that fear or at least lessen it.

She's chosen names for you. You're Hope and you're Charlie. Not very grand, but she liked them and they meant something to her. Did the first man who raised you give you names? I don't think I would have liked him. He let his bitterness hurt you.

No abatement in the disturbed behavior.

Keep talking. Anything that came into her head. The only thing she had to continue repeating was the bit about Frankie. Over and over and over . . .

W̲hat do I do now?" Frankie asked as she stood before Hope. "Do I try to stroke her?"

"Not unless you want to lose a finger." Grace smiled. "Just sit here and talk to her. I'll go into the paddock with Charlie and see if I can comfort him for the loss of his buddy."

Frankie sat down on the floor. "What do I say?"

"Whatever you like." She started down the aisle. "It's between the two of you. I'll be back in a couple hours. Stay out of the stall. If you need me, come to the paddock."

"Okay."

Frankie was very uncertain this morning, Grace thought. Who could blame her? She was moving tentatively herself.

She stood at the fence, looking at Charlie, who was glaring back at her.

I told you this was going to happen. She'll be back in a few hours. I know it sucks to feel helpless, but it's only going to be for a little while. Frankie needs to get to know her. The man who's your enemy wants to hurt her, and she can save herself if Hope will help her. I know, you don't care. But maybe you will someday.

That last was a little dumb. Charlie didn't care about tomorrow. Today was the only thing of any importance.

She opened the paddock gate. "Now let's see if you hate me as much as you did yesterday. . . ."

She barely got the words out when he charged her. She ducked, dashed to the side, and leaped for the fence.

She felt the brush of Charlie's head against her thighs as he thundered past her.

But he didn't turn and try to savage her. He pranced to the middle of the paddock, every line of his body full of pride, arrogance, and defiance. He glanced at her as he turned, and she could almost see his satisfaction in his triumph.

She drew a deep breath and tried to suppress the hope and exuberance that surged through her as she got down from the fence. Too soon. Much too soon.

Not quite as much venom as yesterday. But you definitely showed me where I stand. Now can we calm down and stay together without all this jumping around? I'm tired. Neither one of us got much sleep last night.

It seemed they couldn't. Charlie reared and then charged her again.

She jumped for the fence but didn't quite make it to the top.

He nipped her ass and then tore away from her.

Damn, that hurt. She rubbed her buttock and carefully turned to face the blasted horse.

My God, he was almost smirking.

Playing?

She stiffened and hope soared through her.

Yeah, now you're happy. That wasn't nice. I should leave you by yourself. You know I won't, but there's something you should know. I might not be such a fun playmate if you do that again. I'm not as strong as you and I can be hurt. I don't think you want me out of commission.

But maybe he did. Maybe she was wrong.

She slowly got down off the fence, her gaze fixed warily on Charlie.

He charged her again!

She's very stupid," Guillaume said. "The horse is going to kill her, and it will serve her right."

"Hush." Marvot's gaze was fixed on Grace. He'd been watching her for over an hour. The rush of the horse, the dodging of the woman, was almost like a deadly ballet. Only for the last few minutes he'd become convinced the ballet was not as deadly as it first appeared. "She's not stupid. And I don't think he's going to kill her."

"Oh."

Marvot glanced down at his son. "Disappointed? Why?"

"I don't want the Pair to be tamed. I want them to stay the way they are. This way they're mine."

"They were never yours. They're mine. And they're of no use to me the way they are. I don't tolerate objects that have no use to me. Eventually they'd have to be destroyed."

Guillaume was looking at Grace. "And she has use to you?"

Marvot nodded, watching Grace slowly approach the stallion. He was standing still and she was getting closer to him every time before he rushed her. "Yes, she has use." He suddenly chuckled as he looked back at Guillaume. "But nothing is forever. I haven't a doubt that you'll still get your wish."

* * *

How is it going?" Grace asked Frankie as she entered the coolness of the stable.

"Not so good." Frankie made a face. "I think she's ignoring me. I don't think talking to horses works for anyone but you."

"At least she's becoming accustomed to your voice. Are you ready for lunch?"

Frankie nodded and tilted her head as she got to her feet. "You look . . . happy."

She nodded. "Charlie was a little more responsive than Hope. I felt as if I was slogging my way through a swamp, but I was getting somewhere." She squeezed Frankie's shoulder. "And that's all we can hope for right now. It's only been two days. It's early in the game."

"How long do you—" Frankie sighed. "I'm sorry, I know you can't know. I just want it to be over."

"I've no idea how long it will take." But there wasn't any question she'd spend every waking moment—and also every moment when she should be sleeping—trying to hurry the process along. "But if you're afraid I'll force you to ride Hope, it's not going to happen. If I make good progress with Charlie, it will have to satisfy Marvot."

"What if it doesn't?"

She should have known Frankie wouldn't accept without questioning. "We'll worry about it then."

Frankie was silent a moment. "Do you suppose Jake will try to help us? He helped Donavan."

"I'm sure he'll try."

"But there are a lot of men with guns around. He'd have a hard time, wouldn't he?"

"A very hard time."

Frankie smiled. "But he knows all the steps. You told me he did."

"I believe we'd better depend on each other. Jake will just be a splendid surprise if he manages to get to us."

"I think he'll do it." She sat down on the cot. "He likes us."

"Stay here." Grace headed for the door. "I'll have one of the guards go and get our lunch."

After she'd sent the guard to the house, she stood and stared at Charlie grazing in the paddock. He looked lazy and unaware, but she knew he sensed that she was near. "Two hours, Charlie," she whispered. "Get ready. I'm coming back."

He lifted his head but didn't look at her.

Her gaze went beyond him to the woods. It was funny that Frankie had mentioned the possibility of Jake coming. She'd deliberately not spoken about him to her since she'd arrived here. Frankie was discreet, but she was a child, and Grace didn't want to burden her with the knowledge that Kilmer would certainly figure in any escape attempts.

Charlie neighed and was trotting over to the fence.

She smiled. "Don't rush me. You'll have your chance after lunch."

It was close to sundown when Frankie ran out of the stable and called, "Mom, come quick! Something's wrong with Hope."

Grace closed the gate and ran toward the stable. "I'll be right there. What's happening?"

"She's lying on her side. She just kinda looked funny and the next thing I knew she was down."

"Anything happen before that?"

"She was restless. She was pacing and nipping at her tummy. Is the foal coming? Should I have called you before?"

"No, you did fine." She was standing before Hope's stall. "I couldn't have done anything."

"Is it the foal?"

235

"I think so. I noticed her udders were full all day yesterday. That's usually a sign it's close."

"Why is she lying down?"

"Her water's probably broken. A mare usually lies on her side with her legs extended after the water breaks. She's getting ready for the birth."

"That's right, I should have remembered. But I haven't seen a foal born since Darling, and that was three years ago."

"A slight loss of memory is understandable. You were all of five then."

"What do we do to help her now?"

"I'm going into the stall. The foal should come within about twenty minutes. Go to the guard and tell him I need a bucket of warm, soapy water, cotton towels, strips of cloth for tying up the placenta, and two percent tincture of iodine for the navel stump. Have you got that?"

Frankie nodded and flew out of the stable.

"Okay, Hope." She slowly opened the stall door. "You don't like me and you don't trust me, but you're in no condition to put up a fuss. I'm here to help you get through this."

Hope lifted her head to glare at her.

"Don't get stressed out. It's not good for you." She sat down beside her. "I'm not going to do anything until I see I'm needed. I'll leave it up to you. Do what your body tells you to do."

Hope's head fell back and she spasmed as the foal began to come.

Ten minutes passed and there was no sign of the foal.

"Come on, Hope," she whispered. "Let's have a nice normal birth. I'm not a vet. I don't know how good I'd be if we had problems."

"I've got it, Mom." Frankie was carrying the bucket of warm water. "It took a while. They didn't understand what I needed until one of the stable boys showed up. How is she?"

"Okay, I think." Grace breathed a sigh of relief. "Here

come the head and forelegs. Thank God. Come on in here, Frankie. She's too busy to try to hurt you."

"Look at the foal's head," Frankie said in wonder. "She's still got the sack. Shouldn't it have broken by now?"

"It will break in a minute and let the foal breathe." But the amniotic sac wasn't breaking. She waited and then said, "Okay, little guy, let's give you some help." She carefully ruptured the membrane and the foal drew its first breath. "Now keep on coming. Give your mom a break. . . ."

"He's not moving. He's only half out." Frankie knelt beside the mare. "What's wrong? Is he stuck?"

"No, he's resting. Remember? A foal usually rests for ten to twenty minutes before the rest is delivered. We mustn't break the umbilical cord. We have to let the mare do it herself."

"It must be pretty uncomfortable." Frankie stroked Hope's shoulder. "It's going to be okay. It will be over soon."

Hope wasn't reacting aggressively to Frankie's touch, Grace realized with surprise. Maybe she was too exhausted.

Ten minutes later the foal emerged and Hope began thrashing around. The cord broke and Grace said, "Quick. Bring me the tincture of iodine before she gets interested in her foal." She dipped the navel stump in the iodine to dry it up and then had to roll out of the way as Hope began searching for her offspring. "Come on, Frankie, let's get out of here. It's bonding time."

"It's a colt. Isn't that super? Are we done?"

"We wait for the placenta to be expelled, but that can take up to three hours." She closed the stall door. "Now it's up to the colt and Hope."

"He's so cute." Frankie leaned on the stall door, her gaze on the mare and the colt. "Look, she's licking him."

Hope was nickering softly at the colt, not attempting to rise.

"Bonding." Grace smiled as she looked at the colt. There wasn't anything more gangly or awkward or completely adorable than a newborn. Even now the rascal had rolled onto his chest and was attempting to stand. "Keep an eye on him for a minute while I call Marvot. When the mare decides to get up, we have to make sure she doesn't step on him."

"I'll watch out for him."

Grace shook her head. Frankie was clearly besotted with the colt, and who could blame her?

She picked up the intercom phone and dialed the house.

"I was waiting for your call," Marvot said. "I trust the mare is in good health?"

"Yes, and so is the colt. I need you to get ivermectin from the vet by tomorrow morning. It's necessary to deworm a mare after the birth."

"I'll send for it." He hung up.

She replaced the phone and went back to the mare. Hope was standing and the colt was clumsily trying to suckle.

"Can we help him?" Frankie asked. "Just in the beginning?"

"No, he'll get the hang of it." She put her hand on Frankie's shoulder. "Pretty wonderful, isn't it?"

Frankie nodded. "Wonderful. But he's so little. May I take care of him, Mom? When you don't need me to do anything else?"

"I think that's a great idea. It will prove to Marvot that you're of value. It might even get you closer to Hope. She seems pretty mellow right now."

"I've thought of a name for him. What about Maestro?"

"That's a pretty big name for such a little guy."

"But I can see he's going to be special. Look at the way he's lifting his head. He has a sort of . . . flair."

And how could Frankie see that in this bumbling colt? "Then Maestro is a fine name." She squeezed her daughter's shoulder and turned away. "I'll be back soon. I'm going out to the paddock."

Frankie nodded, her gaze never leaving the colt.

A few minutes later Grace was leaning on the paddock fence.

You're a father, Charlie. He's the cutest colt I've ever seen, and Frankie's in love with him. I wonder what you'll feel when you see him. . . .

Any word from your sheikh?" Donavan asked when Kilmer picked up his call.

"He's not my sheikh," Kilmer said. "He's independent as hell and he's kept me waiting for six damn days."

"No answer?"

"Not even the twitch of an eyebrow to give me a clue." He paused. "How are things there?"

"The same as yesterday. Well, maybe not quite the same. One of the horses let Grace stroke him this afternoon."

"Damn. Which one?"

"I don't know. I can't tell them apart from this distance. She's been separating them for several hours every day and then letting them be together in the evening."

"Have you seen Frankie?"

"Only a couple times in the past few days. She stays inside the stable with the colt except when they bring him out into the paddock. But she looks fine."

"And Grace?"

"She looks like she's lost a little weight. It wouldn't surprise me, considering that she's working with that horse from sunrise to sunset." He paused. "You didn't have me here nine years ago when she was working with the Pair. She's extraordinary. I think she's reading that horse's mind."

"Don't say that to her. She gets very annoyed at any comparisons to horse whisperers."

"Still, it's fascinating watching her. Half the time I think that horse is going to stomp her to death and the other half I'm wondering why she doesn't hurry up and try to ride him."

"She's that close?"

"Close enough for me to tell you to get your ass in gear. You told me Marvot would only wait to take them to the Sahara until the horses could be ridden. He comes every day and checks out her progress."

"Is he treating Grace and Frankie well?"

"As far as I can tell. I see the guards bringing them food and they keep their distance. But there are enough guards around them to keep the crown jewels safe. You were right, it would be difficult as hell to get to them here."

"Then it has to be the desert."

"That's my guess."

"How are you doing?"

"I'm almost a hundred percent. All this lying around watching El Tariq is like a rest cure. I'm jonesing for some action."

"I've got a hunch it's going to come pretty damn soon. I can't wait any longer. I'm going to try to light a fire under the Sheikh. As soon as I get a commitment, I'll come there and take your place. I'll call you tomorrow." Kilmer hung up.

Shit. Frustration was boiling through him. If Grace was getting nearer to riding the horse, then Marvot might be bringing her here any time.

He strode across the encampment and into the Sheikh's tent. "Okay, I've had it. I'm sick of this inscrutable bullshit. I need an answer."

"You have it wrong." He smiled. "The Orientals are the ones who are supposed to be inscrutable. And you're not being courteous. After all, it's you who have asked the favor of me."

"Yes or no?"

"You're tense. Do you need a woman? I'll arrange it. Fatima enjoyed you when you were here last. She told me that anytime you—"

"I don't need a woman. Answer me."

The Sheikh's smile widened. "That annoyed you. I was only setting an example in courtesy. You clearly need it."

"Time's running out. I let my friend stand in for me at El Tariq. I need to be there."

"I've been thinking about it," the Sheikh said. "It's not a problem that's easy to solve. Do I risk my people to satisfy some sense of vengeance? Or do I stand back and watch Marvot run over you and get what he wants?"

"If you don't make up your mind, you're not going to have a choice."

"Oh, I've made up my mind. I fear I'm not as responsible a leader as I could be."

"And that means?"

"Why, that I'm going to skewer the bastard."

The stallion was standing straight and still in the paddock, staring at her. The moonlight shining on his coat turned it to silver, and he looked like an animal from a world of myth and wizardry. Grace could feel the excitement surge through her as her hands tightened on the top bar of the fence. Charlie wasn't a creature of myth. He was flesh and blood, and she'd soon see if her own flesh and blood would survive him.

I'm turning Hope out to see you in a few minutes. She's getting to like Frankie since Maestro was born. She can see how kind and loving she is to the colt. And she knows that my daughter is no threat to her. Just as you know I'm no threat to you.

I'm going to ride you tomorrow. Not early in the day. It will be about this time of night. I don't want our enemy around when I'm doing it. I won't put a saddle on you, because I know that would hurt your pride and remind you of all those other people who hurt you. Riding bareback will make it harder for me. You can throw me and, if I'm not fast enough, you can kill me. If you want to do that. I hope you don't.

"Is it time, Mom?" Frankie was standing behind her. "Hope's getting restless."

"Yes, it's time. Open the stall door." She got down from the fence and unfastened the gate. "Let them be together."

A moment later she watched Hope rush into the paddock to be greeted joyously by Charlie. It was in moments like this that the term *the Pair* took on new meaning. Tonight it was easy to forget the brutality and savageness the horses had displayed throughout the years. The affection between the mare and the stallion was obvious. Two against the world . . .

Something like the bond that was between her and Frankie.

She fastened the gate. *Tomorrow, Charlie.*

16

I'm going out to the paddock, Frankie," Grace said.
"Take care of the colt and Hope."

"Should I bring Hope and Maestro out to the paddock?"

"No, and don't send Hope unless I call you."

"Can't I come with you for a little while?" Then Frankie tensed as she saw Grace's expression. "You're going to do it," she whispered. "Tonight?"

"I'm going to try. It's up to Charlie if I actually do it."

"I want to come and watch."

"I'd rather you didn't. I may end up in a heap in the dirt."

"I've seen you do that before." Frankie's lips were trembling. "That's not why you don't want me to watch, is it?"

Grace hesitated. "No, that's not the reason."

"You're scared Charlie is going to hurt you."

"It's a possibility."

"Then don't do it."

"Frankie . . ."

"Wait until you're sure of him."

"I may not be sure of him until it happens. The past three days I've made progress, but who knows if it's enough."

Frankie's jaw set. "I'm going to be there. You may need me."

Grace gazed at her for a minute and then gave her a quick hug. "If I'm down, don't come into the paddock. The guards will be watching and they'll come and pull me out. Marvot doesn't want anything to happen to me." She fervently hoped that was true. Everyone here was terrified of the Pair and they might drag their feet until it was too late. "But I don't want to make you think that will happen. It will probably be fine."

Frankie drew a deep breath and then turned away. "Then let's go and do it."

Holy shit," Kilmer murmured. He shifted on the high branch of the tree, his grasp on the infrared binoculars tightening.

She was going to do it.

There was tension in the way she was walking toward the stallion, a spring in her step as if she were walking on land mines.

And it might well be as explosive as walking on a land mine if she got on that stallion.

She was standing before him, talking to him.

The stallion wasn't moving.

She was inching around to stand beside him, still talking.

Jesus, she was nuts. The horse wasn't even saddled.

She stood there, her hands reaching out to entangle in his mane, talking, talking, talking.

Kilmer could see the guards gathering outside the fence, watching.

Stop her, dammit.

She was on him!

The horse stood absolutely still.

She leaned forward and Kilmer could see her lips moving.

One minute.

Two minutes.

Three minutes.

Then the stallion exploded, gyrating in a series of bucks that twisted Grace like a puppet.

Then she was off, lying in the dirt. The horse was rearing above her.

Kilmer grabbed his rifle. He was probably too far away, but maybe the shot would—

Grace heard Frankie scream as Charlie's hooves landed only inches from her head.

She rolled away, but Charlie was rearing again. Closer this time.

But not touching her . . .

"Mom!"

He was rearing again. She started to move frantically to get out of the way.

And then she stopped, freezing as a thought occurred to her.

You're bluffing. Okay, get it out of your system. I did what I had to do and now you're showing me that you don't like it. But you don't hate it enough to kill me.

Out of the corner of her eyes she saw the gate opening. The guards. "No! Don't come in. I'm fine." She forced herself to lie still as the stallion reared again. Christ, she was crazy. Those hooves could crush her skull in a heartbeat.

Dirt flew in her face as his hooves hit the earth.

He neighed angrily, whirled, and galloped across the paddock.

It was over.

Now.

She slowly got to her feet and walked toward him. She was sore from the fall and shaking with reaction. Ignore it. It was crunch time. She couldn't let it go until he accepted her.

It's going to be a long night, Charlie.

Stay on him.

Two times around the paddock.

He knows how tired you are.

And you know how tired he is.

Gray light of dawn filtered through the trees and she could see Frankie's pale face as she passed her.

She should have sent her to bed hours ago. But she'd been afraid to leave the stallion for even a minute.

Two times around and we call it a draw, okay?

Charlie's pace quickened, and for a moment she thought he was going to charge into the fence as he'd done innumerable times tonight.

His pace slowed again.

One time around.

She was almost dizzy with weariness. Don't slump. Keep your back straight.

Please don't buck, Charlie. It will be too hard on both of us. We're almost there. We're going to stop when we get to Frankie. I'll get off and then we can both rest. Next time it will be easier. You'll know I'm not going to hurt you. I'll know you're not going to hurt me—much. This riding business won't happen often, but you have to let me do it when I need to. Believe me, it was easier for you than for me.

God knows that was the truth.

Frankie was just ahead, sitting on the fence.

She lifted a hand to wave at her.

We made it, Charlie.

She slipped from the horse and caught herself on his mane as her knees buckled.

To her surprise, he stood unmoving until she got her

balance. Then, as she staggered toward the gate, he turned and trotted away.

Frankie was opening the gate, launching herself into Grace's arms. "You should have waited," she muttered as her grasp tightened like a vise around Grace. "I was so scared. You should have waited. . . ."

"I couldn't wait." She gently ran her fingers through Frankie's curls. "It was time."

"It took so *long*."

"I couldn't leave him. I would have had to start over tomorrow." She glanced at the lightening sky. "Today."

"Nice job."

She stiffened and swung to face Marvot. "You think so?"

"Exceptional." He was staring at her with cool appraisal. "You look a bit frazzled, but I was impressed."

"I wasn't trying to impress you. I didn't even know you were here."

"I wasn't until a few hours ago. My men are sometimes fools. They didn't want to wake me." He smiled. "But this show was worth the lack of sleep. I really wasn't sure you could tame him."

"I didn't. I don't believe anyone could tame him. I just managed to come to an understanding with him."

"Close enough. Can you ride him?"

She nodded. "It's iffy, but I think he'll let me stay on his back. Can I tell him where to go and have him pay attention? Not likely."

"Not even if you use a bit?"

"I won't use a bit. I've seen his mouth. Whoever you had trying to break him should be shot."

He shrugged. "It healed. I had to try everything I could. It was only the one time. It was obvious it wasn't going to work and the stallion would die before he'd let himself be broken."

Son of a bitch.

"Except with you." He inclined his head. "I commend you. And I also commend myself for my intelligence in bringing you here. It's not really necessary for the stallion to take your orders. I want him to lead you." His gaze narrowed on her face. "That didn't surprise you. When Kilmer stole the map, I thought he must have an idea why the Pair were important. I'm sure he was disappointed when he found that it was so vague."

"I'm only surprised that you think the Pair can lead you to the engine. They're only horses."

"I believe in the power of revenge, and Burton wanted his revenge. I can see him taking malicious pleasure in letting me steal the key and then making sure it would break off in the lock." He turned away. "But I've been patient and now I'm going to get my payoff. We leave for the Sahara tomorrow."

"No," she said. "Give me another day."

He looked back at her. "Are you stalling?"

"I need to be sure of the stallion."

He shrugged. "One day."

"Are we taking the mare?"

"Of course. I've tried to separate them before when I've taken them to the oasis. It doesn't work. They won't budge from the corral. At least when they're together, they'll let us take them into the desert."

"And the colt?"

"It's not necessary."

"It's necessary. The colt is nursing and he'll get sick."

"I couldn't care less."

"If you take away the colt, you'll upset the mare, and that will upset the stallion."

His gaze shifted to Frankie. "Are you sure it's the mare who would be upset?"

She didn't answer. "Take the colt."

"Suppose we leave your daughter here to take care of the colt?"

"No!"

He smiled. "Give me one reason why I should take the little girl."

"You want me to concentrate on making the horses do what you want them to do. I couldn't do it if I was worried about Frankie."

"Flimsy. But we'll take the child. I may need her on-site to spur you onward."

"And the colt?" Frankie asked.

He shrugged. "There may be some truth in what your mother is saying. I don't want anything to disturb the possibility that I'm seeing at last. He can go."

Grace watched him walk away. She had gotten what she wanted and that was good. But that didn't change the sudden chill assaulting her. When they reached the oasis, it would be the signal for the action to start. Kilmer had had no opportunity here, but he'd have no choice but to make an attempt when they reached the Sahara.

"Why are you frowning?" Frankie asked. "We get to take Maestro."

"I guess I'm tired. You must be tired too." She started for the stable. "Let's see if we can get a few hours' sleep before we have to start the day."

"First I have to check on Hope and Maestro," Frankie said as she ran past her. "I'll see you in a few minutes."

Grace didn't hurry after her. She was stiff and sore and dead tired. Maybe she should have let Frankie stay here. She'd be in the middle of the action once they reached the oasis. She could have relied on Kilmer to choose a good man to protect her here at El Tariq.

What was she thinking? It would have driven her crazy to risk Frankie with anyone else. One phone call from Marvot and Frankie could be dead.

No, there were no good choices. She just had to do the best she could.

Christ, he was sweating.

And sick to his stomach.

Kilmer leaned his cheek on the branch and closed his

eyes. It had been one hell of a night. He'd probably have nightmares of that stallion rearing over Grace's body.

A sudden flash of anger tore through him. Why the devil hadn't she given up? What idiocy had led her to keep after him?

He wanted to kill her.

And he wanted to grab her close and shelter her from crazy stallions and murderers like Marvot and the whole damn world.

And he wanted to tell her how proud he was of her.

And most of all he wanted to keep himself from going down to the horse farm to get her and ruining everything she had fought for last night.

Mom, are you okay? It's ten o'clock."

Grace slowly opened her eyes to see Frankie's worried face before her. "Is it?" She sat up on the cot and shook her head to clear it of sleep. "Sorry. I must have been more tired than I thought. When did you get up?"

"Two hours ago. I checked on the colt and then I came back here. I thought you'd wake up any minute."

"I'll be right with you." Lord, she was stiff. She felt like she could barely hobble as she started for the shower. "I have to clean up and then eat something. I collapsed when I got in here. Will you dig in the knapsack and bring me something to wear?"

"Sure. Anything particular?"

"Jeans." She went into the stall and started to strip. "And the khaki shirt."

She's wearing the khaki shirt," Kilmer said into the telephone to Donavan. "That means she's trying to warn us of a change."

"What kind of change?" Donavan paused. "Escape attempt?"

"I don't think so. Not with all these guards hovering around her. No, I think they're moving out and coming your way."

"Why would they— My God, she rode the stallion?"

"Last night."

"Hot damn. I wish I'd been there."

"So do I. It nearly killed me. It took her most of the night."

"Shit, I'm proud of her."

"She's trying to give us warning. Don't waste it. Get things ready there. I'll join you as soon as I verify that they're heading for the oasis."

"I'll be as ready as I can get." He hung up.

Kilmer put away his phone and raised the binoculars to his eyes again. Grace was in the paddock, and the interaction between her and the stallion seemed to be a repeat of last night.

No, not really. He was letting her mount him.

She stayed up for only a few minutes and dismounted. Then she walked away from him and climbed the fence, talking to him.

Fifteen minutes later she went to him and mounted him again.

Shit, I'm proud of her.

Donavan's words came back to him. No more proud than Kilmer. Now that some of the terror in the interaction between the stallion and Grace was abating, he could let the fierce pride come to the forefront. Strong and brave and smart. What a woman she was. . . .

His woman.

His? If she could read his mind in that moment, she would probably cut his nuts off. Yet he couldn't banish that surge of possessiveness he felt for Grace. He had been part of the creating of the woman she was now. Nine years ago he had taught her things she didn't know, but she had no idea how much she had taught him in return.

Enough. No matter how much he wanted to stake a

claim in the making of the exceptional person who was Grace Archer, when all was said and done she was her own woman.

And he had to make sure that woman and his daughter stayed alive during the next few days.

They arrived at the oasis at four this morning." The Sheikh made a face. "With a caravan of RVs, horse trailers, and trucks filled with Marvot's private army. He's a blot on the landscape. Do you remember when I told you that we were being pushed out of our habitat? This is what I can expect everywhere in my desert in the next few years."

"Maybe not," Kilmer said. "Marvot is a criminal, stampeding his way through life. Anyone else has got to be less intrusive."

"But the intrusion will still exist. And there will always be Marvots in the world, just as there will always be evil to balance the good." The Sheikh unrolled a map on the worn leather-covered table. "He's already sent out sentries to try to locate anyone who might get in his way." His lips tightened. "As if he could find us if we didn't want to be found. We know this desert. But we're breaking camp in an hour, so let's get this over with." He pointed at a spot on the map. "This is the oasis. It's the one that Marvot uses as base all the time. He had a corral and a lean-to built when he first started to bring the horses there. There are several large tents at the camp, but Marvot occupies a fine air-conditioned RV." He stabbed his finger at a spot in the center of the camp. "Here."

"And surrounded by the army you mentioned. How many?"

"My man counted twenty-seven. Where is the map you stole from Marvot?"

Kilmer pulled the pouch from his pocket and drew out the map. He spread it next to the Sheikh's map. "Where does Marvot usually go when he takes the Pair into the desert?"

The Sheikh pointed out a quadrant on the map. "Here. It's mostly dunes except for a small deserted village. But two miles north you start running into the foothills of the Atlas Mountains." He pointed at a spot on the map. "There's water in the village, so your Grace might stop to water the horses." He smiled crookedly. "The horses should be right at home in the village. That's where they were taken out of the trailers and that's where they stayed. Marvot couldn't make them budge."

"Is there a possibility that the engine was hidden in the village?"

"No. Marvot tore the village apart looking for it. The Pair were just too stubborn to move."

"Or too well trained."

The Sheikh shrugged. "It's possible. Burton was a total fanatic about the training of the Pair. He took them away for seven months and I don't know what he did to them." His lips tightened. "Maybe I don't want to know. But they were totally obedient to him when he brought them back to the camp."

"I'm not sure the Pair were any better off with him than they are with Marvot." Kilmer glanced down at the village on the map. "Any place here we can set up a meeting with Grace?"

"A few. But Marvot will send his men in ahead to scout it out. He always does."

"We can avoid them. As long as they don't trail along with Grace."

"Not unless Marvot wants to blow any chance he has of the horses cooperating. The reason he brought her in was because the horses were totally uncooperative around his men. One hopes he's learned his lesson over the years." The Sheikh paused. "But she'll be observed all the time from a distance. Binoculars, telescopes . . . She'll be like a bug under a microscope. If she disappears for a minute,

Marvot will be on the move. You bring in a helicopter and he'll be all over you."

"I know that. I might have to take out his base camp. Do you know where he's keeping Grace and Frankie?"

"A tent on the outskirts of the oasis. A very well guarded tent. And do you know what will happen if Marvot believes he's going to lose Grace?"

"I know. It's not going to happen."

"That's what I said when Marvot stampeded over my encampment and killed my trainer."

"It's not going to happen," Kilmer repeated. "Grace and Frankie have to be away from the oasis when the attack takes place."

"I agree." He sat down and stared thoughtfully at the map. "Not easy. But there may be a way. . . ."

"What?"

"Let me consult with Hassan. He gave me an interesting bit of news this morning."

"What news?"

"There is going to be a sirocco sometime in the next few days. We may be able to work with it."

"A sandstorm? How the hell does he know? Sandstorms are unpredictable as hell."

"He knows this desert. He's eighty-nine years old and lived here since the day he was born. A sandstorm is a great danger to my tribe. We have to know when we can move with safety. Hassan doesn't often fail us."

"But it does happen?"

"It happens. He's not a seer, after all. He can only feel it coming, smell it." His brows lifted. "That doesn't surprise you?"

"No. Grace has that kind of instinct. She could always tell when rain was coming."

"I believe I'm going to like your Grace." The Sheikh smiled. "Then she'll believe you when you tell her that she'll have cover if she can manage to get your daughter out of that encampment?"

"Can you get a message to her?"

The Sheikh shook his head. "I won't tell any of my men to go into Marvot's camp and contact her. It's up to you."

"Can you at least tell me when that sandstorm is supposed to strike?"

"He thinks maybe day after tomorrow. Usually Hassan knows more the day before it hits."

"That's comforting. And how's Grace supposed to delay Marvot until Hassan is certain it's a go?"

"That's your problem. And a woman who can tell when rain is going to come should be clever enough to block a slimy toad like Marvot."

"He's not stupid."

"True." He paused. "I'll tell you. I'll send a distraction to Marvot this evening if you want to try to get information to her."

"How?"

"There are caravans of tradesmen coming through the oasis occasionally. They've visited Marvot before when he was there. It won't be too suspicious if a small caravan appears. I'll give you a lookout and appropriate clothes so that you can blend in. You won't have much time before Marvot throws them out, but it may be enough." He tapped the tent again. "Remember the guard at her tent."

"I'm not likely to forget him." He turned toward the tent entrance. "And I'd appreciate it if you'd keep on Hassan to narrow down that window of opportunity. You haven't given me much to tell Grace."

"Kilmer."

"What?"

"You haven't mentioned the engine. Have you given up on it?"

"Hell, no. I won't let Marvot have anything he wants," he said curtly. "But I won't risk Grace and Frankie to take it away from him. There's always another day."

"Very wise. I hope you get them away from Marvot safely. And I hope you find your engine."

"Because you don't like the oil cartel?"

"Partly. Have Fatima stain your face and body before you dress tomorrow." The Sheikh grinned. "She'll enjoy it."

"I'll do it myself." Kilmer left the tent.

Donavan straightened when he saw him. "When do we move? How much help do we get from him?"

"Not a hell of a lot. I think we can count on him when we need him. Until we go for the push, he's not risking anyone." He grimaced. "But he's donating the services of his tribe's weatherman. So I guess I shouldn't complain."

"Weatherman?"

"I'll explain as we walk back to my tent." He looked at the sky. It was crystal clear and dotted with stars. No sign of a cloud or any hint of a disturbance. "I hope to hell this Hassan is as good as Grace at weather predictions. . . ."

17

Charlie's trying to break down the corral," Frankie said as she ran into the tent. "And the colt's scared, Mom."

"I'll be right there." Grace threw down her washcloth and ran out of the tent.

Frankie was right. Charlie was screaming with rage, and his hooves were striking at the wooden bars. One was already broken, and the mare was becoming agitated. In a moment she'd be joining in the destruction.

"Stop him." Marvot was striding toward the corral. "He'll hurt himself. I didn't go through all this trouble to have him break a leg."

"Your consideration is heartwarming." Grace was already unfastening the gate. "I'll stop him. Keep your men away from him. He probably thinks he's been betrayed. He recognizes this place. I could see it when I took him out of the trailer."

Another board broke as Charlie's hoof struck it.

Stop it. You're not helping, Charlie. It's not what you think.

No one is going to hurt you or Hope or the colt. We have to pretend to play their game for a while. It will be the last time, I promise.

Another rail splintered.

Charlie . . .

She went into the corral and started toward him. His eyes were glittering wildly as he reared. Then he was running toward her.

She stopped and waited.

He swerved just in time.

I promise, Charlie. Just give me a chance. We can work through this together.

He ran toward the fence where Marvot was standing.

Marvot took an involuntary step back as Charlie skidded to a stop.

She smothered a smile. *Good for you. At least you know the target. Now calm down and get some rest. We may need it.*

He kicked in one more rail and then trotted to the far side of the corral.

Good. But don't kill any stable hands when they're trying to repair the corral. I don't want any of them trying to hurt any of you. You may be strong, but the colt is weak.

She turned and left the corral.

"You'll have to do better than that tomorrow," Marvot said. "You didn't exhibit much control."

"You're not dead, are you? He was just toying with you." She fastened the gate. "Tomorrow? We're going to set out in the morning?"

"There's no reason for waiting."

"The horses need to rest. They're stressed."

"They'll survive." He turned away. "The jury's still out on you and your daughter."

She stared after him as he walked toward his RV. The jury wasn't out. Marvot had already made up his mind when he'd brought them to El Tariq.

"Mom, may I go into the lean-to and see Maestro?" Frankie asked.

She nodded absently. "But stay away from Charlie."

"I will. He doesn't like me."

"He'll learn. But this isn't the time. He's nervous."

Frankie said dryly, "Yeah, I can see it by the way he tried to hammer down the corral. I was sorta nervous too."

Grace watched her carefully skirt the area where Charlie was reigning and hurry over to the lean-to, where Hope and the colt were huddled. There was no question Frankie would be fine with them. She'd been accepted by Hope, and the colt practically thought of her as a second mother.

She turned and walked back to her tent.

Bells.

Shouts.

Clang of metal on metal.

What the hell?

A guard was suddenly in front of her. "Into your tent and stay there."

"What's happening?"

"A caravan of tradesmen." He pushed her forward into the tent. "You're to stay in the tent until they're gone."

She glanced over her shoulder and caught a glimpse of an RV, several riders on horseback, and, for God's sake, camels.

The guard pulled down the flap of the tent, leaving her in musty dimness. A caravan? Too much of a coincidence? Marvot would surely suspect any intrusion into—

Hands clamped on her shoulders from behind. "Don't cry out, Grace."

Kilmer!

She tore away and whirled to face him. "You idiot! I was just thinking that this was suspicious. Marvot will catch you and hang you out to dry."

"I missed you too."

She threw herself into his arms. "Get out of here. You can't help us now. There are too many guards and the—"

"I'm going to get out of here." His arms tightened around her. "If you'll shut up and let me talk to you."

She buried her face in his shoulder. She wasn't about to

let him go yet. My God, she had missed him. She hadn't realized how alone she'd felt until she'd touched him. He smelled funny. Like suntan lotion and walnuts and something sweet. . . . "Talk."

"When are you supposed to start searching with the Pair?"

"Tomorrow. If Charlie doesn't break a leg trying to tear down the corral."

"Charlie?"

"That's what Frankie wanted to call the stallion. The mare is Hope."

"You need to stall. We have to have another day."

"May I point out that I don't have much choice? Why?"

"There's going to be a sirocco day after tomorrow. It will make it easier for us to get you and Frankie away."

"I can see that. But how the devil do you know there's going to be a sandstorm? There's nothing more unpredictable. Siroccos come out of nowhere."

"That's what I said. But Adam has his own weatherman guru in the tribe. According to him, if Hassan says it's going to happen, it will happen."

"When? What time?"

"That's where it's a little iffy. Hassan thinks it's going to be in the afternoon."

"And if it's in the morning then I won't even be able to start out."

"Then we'll think of something else." He paused. "How's Frankie?"

"Wonderful. You'd be proud of her."

"I am proud of her. And of you." He let her go and stepped back. "I've got to get out of here. Adam said I couldn't have more than a couple minutes."

She didn't want him to leave. Jesus, she was frightened for him. "Any idea how I'm going to delay Marvot?"

"Yes." He reached in his pocket and handed her a packet. "It will make you sick as hell for twelve hours. Vomiting. Diarrhea. Stomach cramps. It will be clear to Marvot that you can't function."

"Gee, thanks," she said sarcastically as her hand closed around the packet. "I guess it beats a cyanide pill."

"You may not think so tomorrow." His lips tightened. "I don't like giving it to you. If you can find any other way, do it."

"I will." For the first time she noticed his native dress and stained skin. "You look like something from 'Ali Baba and the Forty Thieves.' " She wrinkled her nose. "And you stink."

"I thought a bit of pot would add an authentic touch. Though Adam's people aren't allowed to touch it." He was heading for the opposite end of the tent, where he'd loosened the ties to crawl under the tarp. He glanced back at her. "It's going to be okay, Grace. Just try to get him to let Frankie go with you. We'll be able to scoop you both up at one time."

"And if he won't let her go?"

"We'll have to send another group to come and get her. Since he won't be sure that we've got you, it will make it easier."

"As long as this miraculous sirocco blows up out of the blue."

"It will." He was lifting the tarp. "I think we deserve a miracle."

Fear shot through her. "Have you got someone outside the tent keeping watch? Will you— Of course you do."

He smiled. "Of course I do."

He was gone.

Her nails bit into her palms as she listened. She wanted to run out and see what was happening. All she could do was stand here and strain her ears to hear every sound to try to tell if Kilmer was in trouble.

A shot!

Oh, God.

Laughter. Bells. Marvot's voice.

He wasn't shouting. He only sounded annoyed.

Another shot.

She ran to the tent opening and threw aside the tarp.

The guard who had pushed Grace into the tent was pulling a struggling Frankie behind him.

"Mom, tell him. I have to get back to the colt. All that shooting scared him."

Grace ignored her to ask the guard, "What's all the shooting about?"

He shrugged. "They're trying to sell us their guns. Very poor quality. Some are so old they were used in the Iran-Iraq War. They are going soon. They were only permitted to stay because the guns interested us." He thrust Frankie at her. "She has no respect. If she were my child, she would be beaten until she could not stand."

"I'm sure." She pulled Frankie into the tent. "Tell us when they've left and we can go back to the horses." She dropped the flap and held up her hand as Frankie started to protest. "Be quiet. You don't have to cosset the colt every minute. We need to keep a low profile for a little while."

"Why? The colt is—" She stopped, sniffing. "It smells . . . strange."

"Yes, it does. And it's your job to get that smell out of here as soon as they let us open those flaps. Use anything you can find to fan it out of here."

"But what is—" Her eyes widened. "Jake?"

Another shot.

Dammit, why were men so like children when it came to weapons?

"Jake." Grace crossed her arms against her chest to keep them from shaking. "But he can't help us yet. We have to wait."

"How long?"

"I'm not going to tell you that. It's not that I don't trust you. I just want your reactions to seem genuine no matter what happens. Do you understand that?"

She nodded slowly. "I guess so. What do I do?"

"Take care of the colt and Hope." She paused. "And you may have to take care of Charlie too."

"Why? I told you, he doesn't like me."

"I don't want anything to happen to him. I don't trust the guards to take care of Charlie."

"But you'll be here to— No?"

"I'm going to be pretty sick for a little while. I may not be able to help you."

"You mean pretend sick, right?"

She shook her head. "No pretense." She knelt in front of Frankie and took her hands. "I'm going to make myself sick, baby. But it will only last a day and then I'll be okay."

"Why?" Her hands gripped Grace's tightly. "I don't want you to be sick. What if you don't get well?"

"I'll get well."

"How do you know?"

"Because Jake gave me the medicine to make me sick, and I trust him. You have to trust him too."

Frankie shook her head. "No, not if he makes you sick."

"He wouldn't hurt me, Frankie. Any more than he'd hurt you." She wasn't getting through to her. Frankie was terrified, and who could blame her? The worst fear a child could experience was the terror of losing a parent. "He cares about us, Frankie." Oh, what the hell, tell her. "Do you know why we have to trust him?"

"Because he's a good guy?"

She drew a deep breath. "He's your father, Frankie."

"What?"

The shock on Frankie's face sent a surge of apprehension through Grace. Was it a mistake? Should she have waited? Should she have told her at all? "It's the truth."

"He didn't . . . want me?"

"No, that's not true," she said quickly. "He did want you. But he wanted to keep you safe, to keep us both safe."

Frankie's gaze searched her face. "Honest?"

"Honest." She hadn't realized until this minute that she did believe what Kilmer had told her. "So you have to trust

Jake because he loves you very, very much." Grace hugged Frankie close and then pushed her back to look into her eyes. "And he'd never give me anything that would make me sick if I couldn't get well."

"Like that movie we watched. The one in the tomb."

At first, she didn't understand. "Oh, *Romeo and Juliet.*" She chuckled. "Yes, I'll definitely come back to life in twelve hours. But you'll have to hold down the fort until I do."

Frankie nodded. "And I'll pretend to be scared when you're sick."

"I don't think you'll have to pretend." She kissed her on the forehead. "But don't be too scared. It will make me feel worse. Okay?"

"Okay." She moistened her lips. "When?"

"I'll take the medicine in the middle of the night so that I'll be sick most of the day tomorrow." She stroked Frankie's hair back from her face. "And there's nothing you can do for me except take care of the horses. It's going to hurt you to see me like that, and you'll have to be brave."

"Maybe the medicine won't work."

"It will work. Because Jake said it would. Now let's get something to eat and see if they're going to let us go back to the horses. I haven't heard any more shots, have you?"

"No." Frankie was shaking. "I've been thinking, and I don't like this, Mom."

"Neither do I. And I'm going to like it less tomorrow. But it's our chance, Frankie. We have to grab any chance we can." She got to her feet. "Now let's go soothe your Maestro."

Grace carefully tucked the blanket around the sleeping Frankie and moved quietly toward the tent flap. The next moment she was outside and being intercepted by the guard.

"I'm not trying to escape," she said wearily. "I just have

to check on the horses again. Marvot wouldn't mind me doing that, I assure you."

"It's three in the morning," he said suspiciously. "Go back into the tent."

"Look, I'm not feeling so well and I don't want to argue. Do you want to wake Marvot and explain that you kept me from doing my job? He won't be pleased."

The guard hesitated and then stepped aside. "I can see the corral well from here. Stay in full view. I'll give you ten minutes."

"I won't need that long."

Charlie was standing on the opposite end of the corral but lifted his head as she approached.

I'm not here to bother you. I had to tell you that I won't see you tomorrow. Frankie will be here, and she'll be scared and worried and I'd like it if you'd not be a complete shit to her. I'll try to see you tomorrow night and we're going into the desert the day after. It's not going to be like it was before. I don't care if you take me to find anything. If you want to wander around all day, that's great. But just help me and I promise that you and Hope will be free of the enemy. Okay?

He stared at her and then looked away.

That's encouraging.

She turned and started back to the tent.

Charlie neighed.

She glanced back at him. He still wasn't looking at her.

What the hell? Did she expect him to chatter like Mr. Ed in that old TV series? She didn't even know how much he understood. If anything. Since childhood she'd believed that at times she'd been able to tap into that comprehension. That strong bonds could exist between horses and people if you cared enough. But right now she was discouraged enough to wonder if she was only fooling herself.

Well, forget it. She could only do what she could do. It wasn't as if she—

Charlie neighed once more. And when she looked back

at him again, it was to see that he'd come to the place where she'd stood by the corral and was staring after her.

If you do understand me, just be good to Frankie. Help her.

She hurried back to the tent and passed the guard without even glancing at him.

Frankie was still sleeping.

So beautiful. Don't wake her until it was necessary. She was going to be disturbed soon enough.

She glanced at her watch: 3:45 A.M. It was time.

She took out the packet and got a cup of water from the bucket beside the bed.

Don't think about it. Just do it.

She swallowed the powder and then the water as a chaser. She quickly tore up the tiny packet and tucked it into the bottom of her knapsack. She had to work fast now. She didn't know how quickly the powder would take effect. She put the metal cup back by the water bucket, lay down, and pulled the blanket over her. She had done all she could. She had prepared the way by telling the guard she wasn't feeling well. She had taken the powder at the logical time. If the powder made her ill the full twelve hours that Kilmer had told her it would, then she wouldn't be able to function until late in the day.

She didn't feel sick. Maybe Kilmer had given her the wrong—

Trust him, she had told Frankie. She smiled ruefully. How bizarre to have to trust him to give her a dose that would—

She gasped with pain.

Her stomach was clenching, twisting in agony.

She barely made it to the water bucket before she threw up.

Y ou look terrible." Marvot was frowning as he looked down at her. "The guard says you've been throwing up for an hour. What's wrong with you?"

"How do I know?" She closed her eyes as waves of nausea rolled over her. "Did you poison me?"

"Don't be an idiot," he said curtly. "I need you."

"That would make a difference. Then maybe it's food poisoning or flu or . . . maybe a bug bit me. I don't know. You decide." She staggered over to the bucket again. "I'm busy."

She retched, but there was no longer anything in her stomach to come up. Dear God, she felt sick. "I feel a little better than I did an hour ago. Maybe the worst is over."

"You look ghastly." His lips curled distastefully. "And this tent smells of vomit." He headed for the door. "This business doesn't please me."

"Me either." She was cold and shaking from reaction. Jesus, Kilmer, did you have to do this good a job? Yes, he did, or it wouldn't have been convincing. "Do I get a doctor?"

"Hell, no, I won't have outside interference. This isn't Geneva conventions." He looked at Frankie, who was huddled in the corner. "Maybe it will spur your recovery if I remind you that without you I have no use for her."

"Give me a little time." She bent over the bucket again as a new wave of nausea washed over her. "Just a few hours . . ."

When she raised her head again, he was gone.

"I didn't think it would be like this, Mom," Frankie whispered. Her eyes were huge in her pale face. "Are you going to die?"

"No, I told you . . ." She had to close her eyes again. "It will be over after today. I'll be fine."

"Jake shouldn't have made you this sick."

"Yes, he should." It was hard to argue with her when her body was agreeing wholeheartedly. "And you shouldn't be in here with me. You can't help. Get out and go take care of the horses."

"I don't want to leave you."

"Get out of here, Frankie. It's harder for me with you sitting there worrying."

Frankie slowly got to her feet. "May I come back soon?"

"Four hours. Just so you can check and see that I'm all right. Then you go back to the horses."

"I don't want—" She broke off and turned away. "I don't like you to be sick. There should have— I don't like it."

But she left the tent, and Grace was grateful. It was bad enough to be this sick without having to comfort Frankie. Even though she'd warned her, she'd known that Frankie wouldn't be able to handle her illness with any degree of composure. She was too loving; their relationship was too close.

Oh, God, she was going to be sick again.

Just get through it. The hours would pass and the pain and nausea would stop.

But if that sandstorm doesn't roll in tomorrow on schedule, I'm going to murder you, Kilmer.

By noon Grace's diarrhea and vomiting had stopped, but the chills remained. By three the chills had gradually faded away, leaving her weak and totally exhausted. By five she was able to drink a little water.

At five-thirty Marvot paid her another visit. "You're well?"

"I wouldn't say that. I could use another day of rest."

"You're not going to get it," he said curtly. "You've wasted too much of my time. You start out at eight in the morning."

"But you claim you have so much patience."

"It's at an end. I'm getting too close."

"Very well, eight o'clock." She paused. "I want to take Frankie with me."

"No."

"She gets along well with the mare. I need the help."

"She's never ridden her. You have the stallion and you can lead the mare."

"I'd have a better chance if I—"

"No." He smiled grimly. "I'm quite sure you'll concentrate wholeheartedly on the search if the child is in my loving custody. Because if I don't have either a concrete find or at least a hint of where that engine is located, then I'll shoot that colt in front of the little girl. I don't believe you'd like that."

Grace could see the terror the threat brought to Frankie's face.

Bastard. She said through her teeth, "I'll do my best to give you what you want."

"I know you will," he said as he left. "I only have to press the right buttons."

The death of the colt. Perhaps the death of Frankie.

"I won't let him do it," Frankie said fiercely. "I won't let him hurt Maestro."

"It was a threat, Frankie."

"He'd do it. I know he'd do it. I won't let him."

Frankie was angry and scared, but no more frightened than Grace. She'd desperately wanted Marvot to permit Frankie to go with her.

Keep calm. Kilmer would know that Frankie was being left at the camp and that they'd have to adjust any plans to include the development.

But it would have been easier if Frankie had been with her so that Grace could make sure she was safe.

"Listen, Frankie, Jake will be coming for you, and you mustn't let the colt keep you from going with him. Marvot won't shoot the colt unless he has something to gain by it. If you're not here, he won't be able to hurt us by doing that."

"He might." Her eyes were glittering with tears. "And it would be my fault. I won't go without Maestro."

She gazed at her daughter helplessly. "Frankie, it wouldn't be— Okay, we'll find a way to get Maestro away from here. Just be ready."

Frankie nodded. "And I'll have him ready too."

And how the devil were they going to get the gangly colt away from Marvot?

Play it by ear. It was all they could do when they couldn't plan anything with certainty from minute to minute. "You do that." She sat up, then closed her eyes for a minute and fought the dizziness. "But right now I need you to do something much simpler. Would you go ask the guard to get me a bowl of meat broth of some sort? I have to get my strength back before tomorrow morning."

"Sure." Frankie jumped to her feet. "Anything else?"

She shook her head. "I'll try some solid food later." She wrinkled her nose. "And then I'll clean up and we'll wash this tent. The odor's terrible. It makes me feel sick again just smelling it."

"Right." Frankie ran out of the tent.

Grace struggled to her feet and followed her to the flap and gazed up at the sky.

White clouds, blue skies. No wind stirring.

They were banking everything on the sirocco that was supposed to strike tomorrow, and there was no sign that would happen. Well, if it didn't, then they'd go in a different direction. Kilmer would have an alternative plan. She had to have faith.

Marvot was becoming impatient. His threat against Frankie had teeth.

Then she'd deal with him. She'd find a way to stop him until another plan was in place.

But, dammit, she wished there was a breath of wind, a stirring of the sand dunes to indicate a disturbance in nature.

Nothing.

The horse trailers and two RVs left the oasis at eight-thirty the next morning. They reached the deserted village of Kartal an hour later.

Blockman slid down the side of the dune to where

Kilmer and Adam waited five minutes later. "They've just unloaded the trailers. Frankie isn't with her."

"Damn." Kilmer turned to Adam. "We'll have to split up the team. We'll get Grace and I'll send Donavan to get Frankie."

Adam nodded. "You'll have to move fast." He turned. "Now I'll go and see where Marvot is setting up surveillance of your Grace. When the storm hits, we'll want to know where he is so that we won't stumble over him."

"If the storm hits."

"It will hit today. Hassan says his teeth ache. It's a sure sign."

"Great." He started to crawl up the dune. "Let's hope he doesn't just have a cavity."

G̲o *away*. All of you." Grace took a step nearer Charlie. "You're making him nervous, Marvot."

"We're leaving." Marvot got back into the RV. "Actually, he's amazingly calm. Usually by this time he's tried to run over any stable hand within ten yards of him. I'm impressed."

"It doesn't mean that he'll be trotting along to Burton's cache." She put her hand on Charlie's mane. The stallion was tense but he didn't shy away from her. "Which probably doesn't exist. He probably destroyed it so that you couldn't get your hands on it."

"It exists. Burton had a giant ego. He wouldn't give up his chance of becoming a worldwide household name. And it's somewhere in that area. If we hadn't been forced to kill the bastard, he would have told us the exact location." He stared her in the eye. "You start out right away and we'll come back and set up a base here. Come back at the end of the day and we'll pick you up. I've had this entire area scoured by my men, and Kilmer's nowhere around. But there will be someone watching you all the time. Don't try to get away or I'll be heading back to the oasis to see your daughter."

"How would I get away with two unruly horses and a desert to cross?" She turned and went over to Hope. The mare seemed much calmer than Charlie. She'd been much more settled since the birth of the colt. "I'd have to have a genie in a bottle."

He nodded. "And Kilmer's no wizard." He drove off with his entourage of vehicles following him.

She patted Hope and then went back to Charlie. "Well, we're on our own, boy." She looked out at the desert and shook her head. The dunes were enormous, and the sun beating down on them would be scorching hot in a few hours. In the distance she could see the foothills of the At-las Mountains, and they looked cool and inviting compared to the stark barrenness surrounding her. She had read somewhere that there was a giant dune in the Sahara the size of Rhode Island. Looking at these dunes, she could believe it.

Kilmer's no wizard.

Kilmer's nowhere around.

But Marvot was wrong. She'd worked with Kilmer and knew that he could be a wizard on occasion. If he didn't want to be found, he wouldn't be found. He would be there for her when she needed him.

"Here we go." She pulled herself onto Charlie's back and started to gather Hope's rope. Then she stopped as she looked at the mare. This rope was totally stupid. It wasn't as if she could control the mare with it. Hope would follow Charlie without a rope, and it might get in the way. She released the mare. "Come on, Hope. Let's get this over with so that you can get back to your colt."

Hope neighed and came lunging toward them.

"Charlie?"

Would he move? Would he refuse to budge as he always had before when brought here?

Charlie, dammit. Go. It doesn't matter where. Just move.

The stallion took a step forward, then another.

We'll still be here when Marvot comes back if you don't get a move on it. Personally, I don't want to see him again anytime soon.

Charlie started to walk and then trot.

Hallelujah. Her legs tightened around him.

Now just amble around and have a good time until Kilmer comes for us.

But the sky was still crystal clear, a blue so intense that it hurt her eyes to look at it.

And Kilmer wouldn't come until the storm came.

18

"Where's that damn sirocco?" Kilmer growled as he wiped the sweat from his brow. "She's been out there for hours and we can't make a move."

Adam shrugged. "Soon. Be patient."

"Tell that to Marvot. It's clear that those horses aren't traveling to a set destination. They're just wandering around. If he thinks that Grace is of no use to him, he'll kill her without batting an eyelash."

"Perhaps he'll give her another day."

"Another day? You said that the sirocco was going to happen today."

"Hassan may be wrong. I told you he was only ninety percent correct."

Kilmer muttered an oath. "Adam, this is—"

"Wait." The Sheikh lifted his head. "Do you feel it?"

"What?"

"Wind."

"I don't feel anything."

"Then maybe I was mistaken. I don't feel it any-more. . . ."

You're going around in circles, Charlie." Grace took a swallow of water from her canteen. "I know damn well we've seen this dry creek bed before." In the last two hours he had wandered closer to the foothills of the Atlas Mountains several times. Hell, maybe he was searching for water. "Thirsty?" She got down from the stallion and poured water into the container she'd brought with her. "I shouldn't complain. You've done a good job of keeping moving. Sorry it may be for nothing. I think that sheikh's weatherman is nuts. Looks like we may have to talk Marvot into trying again to—"

Charlie had lifted his head so quickly he'd spilled the water in the container. He neighed and reared.

"What the hell?"

Hope was rearing too, her eyes glittering wildly.

Scared. They were scared.

And Charlie was looking to the west.

Her gaze flew to the western horizon.

Darkness.

A moment before it had been clear. Now the horizon was a haze of darkness.

Sirocco.

Moving fast, a veil of sand stretching as far as the eye could see. It would be on her in a few minutes.

And she'd be hidden from Marvot and his men.

"Come on, Kilmer," she whispered. "Come and get us." She quickly took off the blouse she'd worn over her T-shirt and the scarf with which she'd tied back her hair. With any luck Kilmer and his men would be here within a few minutes, but that sand would be a smothering blanket if inhaled by either her or the horses. She tore the shirt in two and dampened both sections. "You're not going to like this." She stepped close to Charlie. "But you've got to trust me with this one. I think Hope will let me do it, if she sees you. If you want to save her, you'll have to let me do it."

The sand was already stinging her face and the storm wasn't even on them yet.

Charlie was backing away from her.

"You've got to let me help you, Charlie." She could hear the desperation in her voice. "Trust me."

He kept backing away.

She stopped and drew a deep breath. "I can't make you do it. But I've never lied to you. I've never hurt you. I won't hurt you now."

He stopped, staring at her. His mane was lifting with the gusts of wind and his muscles were bunched.

She took a step forward. "Please. I'm going to put this over your eyes and nose so that you can breathe better. And then we're going to stay together until help comes. Okay?" He'd let her come close. She slowly put the cloth over his eyes and nose and tied it. "You're fine," she said soothingly. "Nothing to be afraid of. Now I'm going to do Hope and bring her to you. I'll loop the rope over both of you so that you won't wander and lose each other, and I'll hold the rope so that it won't entangle you. Be still now."

Miraculously, he shifted uneasily but didn't bolt. In seconds she had the cloth over Hope's eyes and muzzle and stood between them.

She couldn't breathe. There was sand swirling all around them, striking exposed flesh like tiny knives.

She tied the scarf over her face and put an arm around each horse, burying her hands in their manes. "Please don't panic," she whispered. "It's going to be all right. Just hold on and don't be scared." She tried to turn them so they weren't facing the wind that was blowing with gale force. She had to hold desperately to the horses to keep from falling. Talk to them. Say anything. Just keep them from running into that storm and breaking a leg.

She talked. She sang. She quoted nursery rhymes.

Kilmer, where are you?

Dammit, where is she?" Marvot's grasp tightened on the binoculars. "I can't see the bitch."

"Sirocco," Hanley said. "Sandstorm."

"I know it's a sandstorm," Marvot said sarcastically. "I want to know when it's going to be over."

Hanley shrugged. "An hour. A day. A week. As far as I know, there's no way of telling."

"Fuck. Tell Capriano to go after her."

"If he can find her. Those horses are going to panic and—"

"Get her."

Hanley nodded and tried to open the door of the RV. The wind slammed it shut. "Shit." He forced the door open again. "I'll have to—" His cell phone rang and he accessed. "Hanley." He listened. "Son of a bitch. If you let them take the kid, you're dead meat." He hung up the phone. "The base camp at the oasis is under attack."

"Kilmer."

"That's my guess," Hanley said. "Maybe he doesn't know Archer isn't there."

"And maybe he does. Maybe he's out there with her now." Marvot sat there, thinking. "The bitch may have played me for a fool. We're pulling out and going back to the oasis. Tell the men to forget about the woman and get back to the base."

"You're leaving her?"

"Do you think she won't go back to get the kid? We focus all our firepower on keeping control of the base. Then we only have to wait for Kilmer and her to come after her daughter."

"And then use the kid as a hostage?"

"Oh, yes. But no one makes a fool of me." He started the RV. "She's going to get a surprise when she gets back to the oasis. We'll see how the bitch likes having a daughter who's missing a few fingers."

Gunfire!

Frankie huddled closer to Maestro in the corner of the lean-to.

"It's okay, boy," she whispered as her arms tightened around his neck. "I won't let anyone hurt you."

The colt nickered softly, uneasily.

Was he coming?

I'll kill the colt.

And he would, Frankie thought in anguish, he would.

No, he wouldn't. She wouldn't let him.

More gunfire. What was happening?

Mom . . .

The sky was darkening and she could see a shadow, a man moving, outside the corral.

Marvot?

Come, Mom. Come, Mom. Please, come.

The sirocco was increasing in force.

And Charlie was beginning to rear again, almost jerking Grace from her feet.

"No. Just a little longer." Her voice was shaking. "I promise, it will be—"

"Let him go."

Kilmer. Relief poured through her. She jerked down her scarf and saw him through the stinging barrage of sand. He was only a shadowy figure, but he looked like something from another planet. He was wearing a scuba mask and oxygen tank, the mouthpiece dangling around his neck.

There were several men behind him, but they were too far away to recognize in the storm.

But whoever they were, they were disturbing Charlie and Hope. "Tell them to get back," she shouted. "You too."

Kilmer made a motion and the men faded back. "I'll get out of your way in a minute." He was buckling a scuba mask on her.

"Frankie. Did you get Frankie?"

"Donavan and Blockman had orders to attack the base camp the minute the sandstorm hit. The horse trailer's about thirty yards to your right. If you can get the Pair in the trailer, the Sheikh's men will take care of getting them back to his camp."

"Get away." She took a deep breath of the oxygen and tugged gently on the rope. "We're going blind, Charlie. Just for a little while. Then it will be over."

Would he go with her or break free?

Charlie reared. Hope reared.

Shit.

She tugged again, then abandoned the rope and wound her hands in both their manes and pulled.

He took a step forward.

One more, Charlie. Take one step at a time.

It couldn't have taken more than a few minutes, but it was the longest thirty yards of her life.

She led Charlie into the trailer and then went back and led Hope up the ramp. The blowing sand was still bad in the trailer, but the horses would be able to breathe. Best to leave the cloth masks on, though. She patted them. "We're going to get you out of this and take care of you. I promise you'll be safe. . . ." She ran out of the trailer and motioned the two men at the end of the ramp to close the doors.

Kilmer grabbed her arm. "Come on. We have to get to Frankie."

Fear iced through her. "You said Donavan went after

her." She ran beside him toward the SUV. "Hasn't he reported back?"

"No, but he probably couldn't get through in this storm. The sirocco hit here first, and it hadn't gotten to the oasis when I talked to him last. It's like a blanket hovering over a hundred feet. You know how good Donavan is. He'll get her out."

"I don't know anything." She jumped into the SUV. "And neither do you. So stop making comforting noises and let's get to her. Can you see in this storm?"

"No, but I covered the engine and rigged a GPS setup for the oasis." He started the SUV. "I didn't have any doubt that you wouldn't wait for Donavan to bring her to us."

"And you would? Bullshit. You would have gone without me."

He nodded. "You're damn right."

Donavan got through to Kilmer when he was only a few miles from the oasis. "We've secured the camp. We had to beat off an assault by Marvot and the goons he took with him to keep an eye on Grace. They didn't go after her as we all hoped. But we had a strong enough foothold here."

"Frankie?"

"She's not here. We've searched every tent. She's not here."

"What? She's got to be there." He paused. "Unless Marvot had her taken to another location."

"She's gone?" Grace whispered.

Kilmer nodded. "Any sign of Marvot?" he asked Donavan.

"No, he took off when we repelled his attack. But I questioned a few of his men a bit forcefully. They said the little girl was in her tent."

"Don't get in a panic," Kilmer told Grace. "Marvot isn't there. The guards thought Frankie was still in her tent."

"Don't tell me not to panic." Her voice was shaking with fear. "He could have called and given the order to kill her. For all we know she could be buried in the sand somewhere."

"Donavan and Blockman moved in fast the minute the storm struck. The action was over in minutes. There wouldn't have been time."

Maybe. That thought was too unbearable and she tried to think of an alternate scenario. "Tell Donavan to go and check the colt in the lean-to. See if he's still alive. Marvot threatened to kill him."

"Right." Kilmer relayed the message to Donavan.

Five agonizing minutes went by before Donavan came back on the line. "No colt. I looked everywhere."

"No colt," Kilmer repeated for Grace's benefit.

"My God," Grace said. "She took the colt."

"What?"

"She was afraid the colt would be killed. The gunfire must have scared her and she ran away with him."

"Into this storm?"

She nodded jerkily. "She loves that colt. Tell Donavan to try to track—" She ran her fingers through her hair. "Jesus, there wouldn't be any tracks. Not in this storm. She could die out there."

"We'll find her, Grace."

"Yes, we will." She couldn't bear to think anything else. "She's a smart girl. She wouldn't go out there without being prepared even if she was scared. We just have to think of a way to track her."

"As soon as the storm lets up a little more, we'll get the helicopter and scan the—"

The windshield shattered as a bullet plowed into the leather of the front seat.

"Shit! Duck!" He stomped on the brakes and rolled out

the driver's door. "Stay here." Which direction had the bullet come from?

Another shot kicked up the sand in front of him. The shot was too accurate. Whoever was out there was in a protected area and could see to shoot. An RV or SUV? And Marvot's men wouldn't be shooting without his orders.

"Did you think I'd be beaten, Kilmer?" Marvot's voice. "Only a temporary setback. I knew you'd be coming to rescue the child and all I had to do was wait. Listen, Archer, we can still work out an agreement. Do you think you're safe, that the child is safe? You'll never be safe. Give me what I want and the child will live. If you don't work with me, you'll both die and then the child will die. I promise it on my father's grave. It's only a matter of time."

"Time's up," Grace murmured. She was lying beside him, a rifle cradled in her arms. It didn't surprise him. Grace wouldn't hide in the SUV. "I can't see anything, can you?"

"No." Then as the wind shifted he caught sight of the RV. "There's our target. At three o'clock. I don't see any other backup for him. I'll keep him busy. You work your way around and shoot a hole in that gas tank. I want to see the bastard roast." He didn't wait for her to answer but got up and started to zigzag across the dunes.

Bullets.

Close.

Very close.

Get behind the RV.

Grace crawled on her hands and knees, sliding up and down the dunes on her belly.

She could hear the sound of the bullets.

Run, Kilmer.

But how could he run in this thick sand? She could barely crawl. She was sinking and sinking and the—

"Got him, Hanley!"

Marvot's voice, harsh, triumphant. And terrifying, because it was Kilmer they were talking about. One of those bullets must have struck Kilmer.

Then a string of obscenities. "No, he's still alive. He's up again." Another bullet. "How the hell— Where's the woman?"

Behind you, bastard.

She took careful aim at the RV gas tank.

Behind you, son of a bitch.

She pressed the trigger.

The RV exploded into a fiery mass of metal!

She buried her body and head in the sand as the shrapnel from the explosion flew in every direction.

When she looked up, the flames of the wreckage were already being smothered by the lack of oxygen caused by the storm. But there was no doubt the explosion had killed Marvot and whoever else was in that RV. No one could have lived through that inferno.

"Nice shot." Kilmer was limping toward her. "But I could have wished you'd gotten into position a little sooner."

Relief surged through her. "I was afraid— You should have—" She stopped. "He's dead. Marvot's dead."

"Good. Too bad it wasn't drawn out a little longer. Like thirty or forty years."

She closed her eyes as the realization hit home. All those years of hiding and fear were over. Banished in the time it took that RV to explode.

No, not over. Because Marvot's deeds lived on. It was because of him that Frankie was wandering around in this sandstorm. He might still reach out from the dead to kill her. "Frankie."

"Yeah, I know." Kilmer was limping back toward the SUV. "We'll go on to the oasis and round up a search party to go after her."

"Wait." She caught up with him. "Sit down and let me put a pressure bandage on your leg. Is it bleeding?"

"Not much." He kept on going. "No time."

"If it's bleeding at all, it has to be bandaged. It will only take me a minute."

"I told you." He had reached the SUV and was awkwardly trying to get into the driver's seat. "It's not important."

"It's important." She pushed him toward the passenger seat. "I'll drive." She got into the driver's seat and grabbed the first-aid kit from the backseat. "Stop being a martyr. It doesn't become you." She cut his pant leg and spread it to reveal the wound. The bullet had gone through the flesh, but it was bleeding more than he'd claimed. "You'd blister any one of your team for ignoring a wound."

"I have to get to Frankie." His lips twisted. "I'm surprised you want to waste even a minute on me."

"It's not a waste." She put on the pressure bandage. "You're not a waste, Kilmer."

He went still. "No?"

She finished the bandaging, turned, and started the engine. "No."

Donavan came out of the tent to meet them when the SUV pulled into the oasis. "No Frankie. I sent Vazquez and Blockman to look for any track. Nothing. We don't even know what direction she took." He looked at Grace. "Sorry. God, I'm sorry. If she'd just stayed put, we'd have scooped her up with no problem."

"She was scared for the colt." She jumped out of the SUV. "We have to find her, Donavan."

"I've already organized another search party." He looked up at the sky. "I issued Blockman one of those GPS beacons Kilmer brought, and we'll know if he finds her. The storm's slowing down, but we still can't chance a helicopter. Dammit, did Adam's weatherman tell you how long it was going to last, Kilmer?"

"No." Kilmer got out of the SUV. "But if I can get

through, I've got to call Adam and get him to bring his men here to help." He headed for the tent. "I'll ask if Hassan's toothache is going away."

"You're limping," Donavan said. "Did you run into trouble?"

"Marvot," Grace said. "And he needs that leg cleaned and rebandaged before he takes off again."

"Marvot," Donavan repeated. "And may I hope that you took the bastard out?"

"He's dead. Grace blew him to kingdom come." Kilmer went into the tent.

"Excellent," Donavan said to Grace. "At least something's going right."

At the moment she couldn't see anything right in the world. Why didn't this storm stop? "You're sure none of Marvot's men saw Frankie leave?"

"I guarantee they would have told me. If the storm lets up enough, we'll put that helicopter in the air and we'll be able to find her."

"We can't wait." Grace's hands clenched into fists. "She's just a little girl. She could die out there."

"I know. I know. We're going out again in another direction as soon as the team gets back to camp."

And probably find nothing, she thought in agony. The desert was huge. Yet in this storm Frankie and the colt could be only a few miles away and they wouldn't see them. Think. There had to be a way.

She stiffened. Perhaps there was a—

She headed for the tent into which Kilmer had disappeared. "Let me know when the search team gets back."

The search team arrived back at camp twenty minutes later.

Frankie wasn't with them.

Grace stood watching the practically unrecognizable, bedraggled men come toward the oasis. It was what she had expected, but it still caused the panic to soar. How long could Frankie survive out there?

"Adam's here, Grace," Kilmer said from behind her.

She turned to face him. "Did he bring them?"

"Yes." His lips tightened. "It's crazy. It won't work."

"It could. I can't think of anything else to do. The storm's lessening, but it's still stopping and starting every ten minutes or so. I don't want to wait for that damn helicopter." She turned and started walking toward the group of men gathered by the corral. "Which one is your sheikh?"

"I'll introduce you." Kilmer had caught up with her. "Grace Archer, Sheikh Adam Ben Haroun."

The man who turned to face her was tall, dark, and somewhere in his late thirties. He had an interesting face that looked more Western than Middle Eastern. He bowed. "I'm delighted to meet you. I regret that it's in such sad circumstances. My people will do everything possible to find your little girl."

"Thank you." Her gaze went beyond him to the horse trailer. "And thank you for bringing the horses."

He shrugged. "My handlers were delighted to be rid of them. They were puzzled as to how to get them out of the trailer. It's not that my men aren't skilled, but these horses are . . . different."

"I'll get them out of the trailer."

"And why?"

"I'm going to let them have a try at finding Frankie."

"In this storm?"

"It's not quite as bad now. It's stopping and starting. Did Kilmer ask you about the protective hoods?"

The Sheikh nodded. "You were right. Since we live in the desert we've had to use specially constructed devices occasionally to protect the horses' eyes and other orifices. Though we prefer not to travel at all during this kind of weather."

But his was a nomadic tribe, and it was natural that

there'd be circumstances when it was necessary. It was the answer she had hoped for. "And you brought two of them with you?"

"Yes, but horses don't like the device. It causes them to sweat. They'll probably panic and you'll lose them too."

"They won't panic. I'll work with them. I'll be with them." She hoped she was telling the truth. The horses had been very close to panic before she'd gotten them into the trailer. "It's a chance I've got to take. My daughter has the mare's colt with her. I'm hoping that instinct will lead them toward her colt. I've heard of it happening be-fore."

"Them?" Kilmer asked. "You're taking both of them? All you need is the mare."

"That's what I thought at first, but they've been to-gether all their lives. They're the Pair. The mare is nervous without him. I can't be sure how she'd react if I turned her loose by herself." She opened the trailer door and pulled down the ramp. "I can't stand here and talk. I have to get them ready to go. Thank heaven, the sand's not so stinging now."

"I'm going with you," Kilmer said.

"No, you're not. You're a stranger to them. I told you that the horses are going to be nervous enough. I want them to focus on Frankie and the colt. Give me a GPS bea-con and you can zero in on me when I've found them." She started up the ramp. "In the meantime Donavan and Robert can go out with another team and try to find her. We need to explore all the avenues we can."

"And I'm supposed to twiddle my thumbs? No way."

"Do what you like. You're not going with me. Even if you didn't have a bum leg, you'd be a handicap." She went into the trailer. Jesus, how much she wanted to have him with her. She was scared and he always made her feel stronger. She was tired of being alone. She was tired of being without him.

Well, she was alone in this. Except for Charlie, except for Hope. So get to it.

She gently stroked the stallion's neck.

Hello, Charlie. I didn't expect to see you this soon, but we have a problem. . . .

19

The wind was picking up again. It was hard to breathe.

How long had she been out here?

Hours?

Probably not. They might not have been gone from the oasis for long. It was hard to tell. It seemed as if she was in a time warp.

Charlie's breath was laboring through the clear plastic mask over his eyes and nose. The bottom was open to allow air circulation, but the air was still thick with sand. Hope seemed to be doing a little better.

Charlie stopped and lifted his head.

Keep on going, Charlie. Where the hell is that wonderful instinct? We have to find them.

Charlie suddenly started forward. Then turned in another direction and struck out at a faster clip. Hope fell in behind him.

That's not the way it's supposed to go. Hope is supposed to be leading this time. She's the mother, dammit.

But Hope was used to following Charlie. Grace could only pray that she would assert her dominance when that maternal instinct kicked in.

The sand was thicker on this dune ridge, but she was disoriented and couldn't tell how close they were to the slope of the dune.

Charlie slipped, skidded, and caught himself. Grace barely managed to keep from falling off him.

Hope neighed uneasily.

I'm scared too. It's like being lost in hell. But if I'm this scared, what must Frankie be feeling?

Charlie was going down, straight down the dune, slipping, skidding, jolting.

On the third jolt she catapulted over his head.

Darkness.

She shook her head to clear it and nearly threw up.

"Charlie?" She couldn't see him. She couldn't see anything but sand and darkness that came and went. Get to the signal beacon in her pocket. Press the button. Tell Kilmer where she was.

She nearly screamed when she tried to move her right arm. Something was wrong with her shoulder. . . .

She fumbled with her left hand until she found the beacon and pressed it. Come and get me, Kilmer. I fouled up. It's over to you. You have to find Frankie.

"Charlie!"

There he was, only a few feet away, with Hope a few feet behind him.

She tried to sit up and then fell back down as pain surged through her. She drew a deep breath and waited for the pain to subside. She couldn't leave the horses alone and helpless when she was helpless herself. They might panic and hurt themselves. The storm had subsided enough again so that the sand was a stinging annoyance but not a blinding threat. She crawled over to Charlie and slowly got to her knees. In another minute she managed to get to her feet.

She checked the security of the plastic mask over his head and then did the same for Hope.

You're on your own. Go back to the corral, Charlie. Take Hope home.

He didn't move.

Go back to the corral. What are you waiting for?

He neighed and didn't move.

Go on!

He turned and in another moment he and Hope had vanished behind the veil of sand.

She sank back down in the sand and buried her head in her left arm.

"Okay, Kilmer, where are you?"

And, Frankie, baby, where are you?

G race!"

"Here." She struggled up on one elbow. "Here, Kilmer."

He was suddenly there, kneeling beside her. "What happened?"

"I screwed up. I was stupid. I fell. . . . You'll have to find Frankie. Search this area. Charlie acted as if he'd zeroed in on a direction right before I fell. Hurry."

"Donavan and Blockman and the team are right behind me. Where are you hurt?"

"My shoulder, I think. Did you see Charlie and Hope? I sent them back to the oasis. Charlie's smart, and I hoped that he'd understand and—"

"I didn't see them. Which shoulder?"

"Right."

He was feeling her arm and then her shoulder. "I don't think there's a break. I'd bet it's out of the socket."

"Then put it back in the socket and let me go find Frankie."

He shook his head and got to his feet. "I think I'll leave that up to Donavan."

She stared at him in disbelief. "What?"

"You left me at that camp and went off on your own. I let you do it because your argument made sense. But that argument's gone down the tube. I'm not letting you hobble around the desert in pain when I can search as well as you can." He started up the dune. "I'll tell Donavan I found you and I'll let you know when I find my daughter." He glanced over his shoulder. "*My* daughter, Grace. I'm not being cheated of my chance to save her. She belongs to me."

"Damn you, Kilmer. Fix my shoulder."

He didn't answer. He was already halfway up the dune.

"Damn. Damn. Damn." She could feel the tears sting her eyes. She was going to murder him.

"Donavan!" she shouted. "Donavan!"

Kilmer ran into Donavan at the top of the dune. "Grace has a dislocated shoulder. Put it back into the socket, but take your time about it. She's going to be in pretty bad pain, and I want to find Frankie before she goes through that hell." He turned to Blockman. "Grace thought there might be a chance Frankie was in this area. You go east with Vazquez and I'll go west."

"I'm the one who's going to go through hell," Donavan called after him. "She'll know that I'm stalling."

"Probably. Deal with it."

"Bastard." Donavan paused. "Good luck, Kilmer."

"Thanks."

Luck. He'd need all the good fortune he could beg, borrow, or steal. Such a little girl to have such a powerful hold on all of them. Anything could have happened to her in this storm, and he'd never been more frightened in his life.

No, that wasn't true. When he'd seen Grace lying hurt in the sand, it had scared the living hell out of him.

Forget Grace. She was safe.

Think of Frankie. Find Frankie.

Grace had said she might be near. He hoped to God she

was right. The storm was now a thin veil of grit and sand, but he could still miss her.

Call her. Keep on calling her.

He took off his face mask. "Frankie! Frankie, answer me!"

No answer.

"Frankie!"

Frankie!"

God, his voice was cracked and hoarse. How long had he been shouting her name? Fifteen minutes? Thirty minutes? His throat was dry and sore from inhaling sand.

"Frankie!"

Maybe she couldn't answer. Maybe she was hurt or—

"Frankie!" he shouted desperately. "It's Jake. Answer me."

No answer.

"Frankie!"

A faint sound came through the whistling wind.

He stopped still. A cry?

"Frankie?"

The sound came again, to the left, down the dune.

And it wasn't a human cry.

It was a neigh, a horse's cry.

And Frankie had taken the colt.

He stumbled down the dune, slipping and sliding.

Why hadn't Frankie answered? If she was conscious, she must have heard him. He'd been right on top of her. Maybe it wasn't Frankie. Maybe the colt had wandered away from her. Christ, he didn't want to think about that.

"Frankie!"

Then he saw the blanket-covered heap in the sand at the bottom of the dune.

"Shit!" He was down there in seconds. He tore off the blanket.

Frankie was curled up next to the colt, her arms around

him. Her face was pale and crusted with sand, her eyes tight shut.

Alive?

Her eyes slowly opened. "Jake?"

God. His throat was so tight with emotion that he couldn't talk. He nodded jerkily.

She hurled herself up into his arms. "I thought it might be Marvot. He wants to hurt the colt."

"I know."

She wriggled. "You're holding me too tight. I can't breathe."

"Sorry," he said unevenly. "I'm new at this. And I've been a little worried about you. So has your mother. We'll have to get you back to her right away."

"She's okay? I was scared that Marvot would—"

"Marvot won't bother us any longer. And your mother is fine. She hurt her shoulder a little searching for you, but nothing serious. Now let's get you out of here." He pressed his beacon. "Is the colt okay?"

"Fine." She made a face. "But Maestro's not too bright yet. He wouldn't stay under the blanket. I kept telling him that we had to hide, but I guess he didn't understand. I was wishing that Mom was here."

The colt was trying to get to his feet.

"See?" Frankie said in disgust.

"At least he was bright enough to let me know you were down here."

"Oh, that wasn't the colt. That was Charlie."

"Charlie?"

"Charlie and Hope. They're over there." She nodded to the left. "They came over an hour ago. Did they run away?"

"No, they didn't run away." Now he could make out the Pair through the haze of sand. The driving wind had practically disappeared, thank God. "They were looking for you."

"You know, I thought maybe they might be. Charlie kind of stood there in front of us like he was standing guard. And he doesn't really like me. But maybe he was taking care of the colt. He's his sire, you know. I guess it makes a difference."

He stood her up and began to dust the crusted sand off her. Not that it was going to do much good. "You can bet on it."

Donavan's beacon went off while he was finishing up Grace's sling. He stiffened and looked down at it. "That's Kilmer. He must have found Frankie."

Grace threw his hand aside and struggled to her feet. "Let's go."

He nodded. "But he's going to have all kinds of help. Every man in the team and a good many of Adam's men will be pouring across these dunes when they see the beacon."

"Let's go."

"Just thought I'd tell you." He tried to help her up the dune, but she shook him off. "Even though you're in no mood to listen to me."

"I'm not in a mood to listen to anyone but Frankie."

"He'll bring her to you, Grace."

She knew that, but she was in an agony of worry. Frankie had been found, but was she hurt? She wouldn't think past that possibility. "He's not going to have to bring her to me. I'm going after her."

"Then let me help you."

She'd been angry and frustrated with him, but none of that mattered now. Not when she had to get to Frankie. She nodded. "Yes, help me get to her, Donavan."

Ten minutes later she saw Frankie.

She heard her first, and then a few minutes later she appeared through the haze of sand. She was riding on Robert Blockman's shoulders, her mouth and nose covered by a scarf. Kilmer was walking beside them.

"Hi, Mom." Frankie waved at her. "Robert is taking me for a ride. I told him I could walk, but he said I must be pretty tired."

"And she didn't have the forethought to bring a horse she could ride." Kilmer grinned. "But Blockman will do well as a beast of burden—lots of brawn and no brains."

Robert laughed. "At least I didn't get shot like you did this time."

They were joking, Grace realized in wonder. She was so overwrought that she felt as if she was going to fall apart, and they were laughing.

"Put her down, Blockman." Kilmer was watching Grace's face. "Take a break for a minute or two."

Blockman carefully set Frankie down. "I have to go and check to see if the horses are following us, anyway." He strode back in the direction they had come.

"Yeah, but Maestro seemed fine with coming along, and I think Charlie will keep him in line." Frankie suddenly frowned as she caught sight of Grace's bandaged shoulder. "You okay, Mom?"

Grace flew across the distance between them and fell to her knees in front of Frankie. "I'm great," she said huskily as she enfolded her in her arms and buried her face in Frankie's hair. "Now. You scared the life out of me. You should never have run off like that."

"I had to protect the colt. You told me when he was born that it was my job to take care of him." She hugged Grace tightly and then stepped back. "I took a blanket and we covered up and hid out. The colt was pretty skittish, but I managed to talk him down." She wrinkled her nose. "Not like you. But he knew I loved him, and I think that helped."

"It usually does." She looked over Frankie's shoulder at Kilmer. "She's not hurt?"

"She's a little dehydrated but that's about it," Kilmer said. "Except that she's tired. I think she'll sleep well tonight. The SUV is parked on the road. Let's get her there and take her back to the oasis. How's your shoulder?"

"It's not great," Donavan said. "And neither was her temper." He smiled at Frankie. "You may have to put a good word in for me. How about it?"

"What did you do wrong?" Frankie asked.

"I was too slow with her bandage. She wanted to go after you."

"Jake found me, Mom. He heard Charlie."

"Charlie?"

"She said that Charlie stood guard over her and the colt," Kilmer said. "She thinks that he was really standing guard over Maestro because he's the sire. I told her it was possible." He smiled. "Fathers have a special feeling for their offspring."

"Found them." Robert reappeared. "They're following. But that colt is taking his time."

"He's little," Frankie said defensively. "Can we take him in the SUV?"

"I don't think that would be a good idea," Grace said. "There wouldn't be room. And he probably wants to stay with his mother."

Frankie frowned. "Then I'll walk back with him. He's my responsibility."

"No, you won't," Grace said. "I want you out of this desert and back at the oasis."

Frankie's jaw set. "When the colt is out of it."

"Frankie . . ."

"I'll send Blockman to escort the horses back to camp," Kilmer said.

"Who, me?" Robert grimaced. "I can try, but maybe you'd better get Vazquez to help."

"I have to take care of Maestro," Frankie repeated.

"How close are we to the camp?" Grace said.

"Four miles," Kilmer said. "Too far for her to walk it after all she's been through. We're two miles from the road. We can bring back a horse trailer as soon as we reach the camp."

"I wasn't thinking about Frankie." She smiled at her

daughter. "You're right, the colt is your responsibility, but Charlie and Hope are mine. I brought them into the desert to find you, and they did their job. I couldn't leave them out here with no one they trust to bring them back to the corral."

Frankie nodded. "Then we'll both stay."

"It's kind of silly for us both to stay. You can check out the trailer when you get back to the camp and make sure it's okay. That would be a big help."

Frankie shook her head.

"Frankie, you've done your job. You made sure Maestro was safe. Now it's time to make it easy for all these men who've been looking for you and the colt. They'll worry until they know you're safe at the camp."

"But I don't want to—" She sighed. "Okay. I'll go and check out the trailer. But I'm coming back with Jake." She turned to Kilmer. "You send someone with my mother to help her. They won't be able to handle Charlie and Hope, but I don't want her to be alone."

"Neither do I," he said quietly. "Will I do? Donavan could take you back to camp and get the trailer."

Frankie gazed searchingly at him for a moment. "You'll do."

"Excellent." Kilmer gave her a quick hug and turned to Donavan. "Then the three of you get going. It would be great if you could have that trailer at the road by the time we get there." He went back to Grace as Blockman, Donavan, and Frankie started out. "Is there any way we can hurry those horses along a bit?"

"Probably not. They're most likely thirsty and every orifice is stinging. That means their tempers will be stinging too. Did Blockman check those masks I put on them?"

"I did. Very cautiously."

"Then I'll check them again." She looked up at the sky. "I think the sky looks lighter. Is it finally clearing?"

"Hard to tell. But the wind is a hell of a lot calmer." He glanced back down the road. "I think I see the Pair."

"Charlie and Hope," she corrected.

"Whatever."

"No—they found Frankie. Calling them the Pair makes them . . . anonymous. They don't deserve that."

He glanced back over his shoulder and smiled. "Charlie and Hope, then."

"You're still limping. You should have left Donavan with me and—"

"No, I shouldn't." He looked her directly in the eyes. "This is exactly where I should be."

Jesus. She couldn't pull her eyes away.

He nodded and shifted his gaze to the horses walking toward them. "They don't look like they're in any hurry. Why don't you have a chat with them and tell them we are?"

"They don't always listen." Her voice sounded breathless even to her. "And they've had a rough time."

"We all have." He stopped as Charlie reared when he saw him. "Hey, I'm not going to hurt you." He grimaced. "That's fairly ridiculous, isn't it? He could crush me like an elephant would a beetle. Okay, you tell me what to do."

"Let me handle them. You look out for the colt."

"How humiliating. Relegated to the nursery." He glanced at the colt. "But cute. Very cute. Come on, buddy."

Grace took a step closer to Charlie and stroked him. He twitched and shifted from side to side. As she'd said, the horses had gone through experiences that day that would have shaken more placid animals. It was incredible that they were as tranquil as they were now. "Calm down. It's almost over. Just a little while longer and we'll have you out of this." She whispered, "Thank you, boy . . ."

Mom," Frankie said softly. "It's daylight and the storm is over now. Not even a whisper of wind. May I go down to the corral and check on Maestro?"

Six-thirty A.M. Grace yawned. "It's barely daylight. We all

pretty much collapsed after we got the horses settled last night. The colt needs his sleep too."

"I just want to see him. After yesterday . . . I was so scared." She lifted her shoulders. "I just want to see him."

Because she'd been afraid she would lose the colt. Just as Grace had been afraid she'd lose Frankie. "I know." She held out her arms. "Come here." She pulled Frankie into her embrace and rocked her. "Hey, did I ever tell you how much I love you?"

"Don't be mushy." But she still buried her head in Grace's shoulder and tightened her arms around her. She stayed there for a few moments. "I was scared about you yesterday too. But I remembered everything you told me about trusting Jake. He did it, didn't he?"

"Yes, he did it." She hugged her again. "And you did it. And I did it. It was a joint operation."

She smiled. "And wasn't it funny how Charlie called Jake to come and get us?"

"Charlie's very smart."

Frankie nodded. "Like our own Charlie. I was right to name the stallion after Charlie, wasn't I? Maybe Charlie liked it too. What do you think?"

"I think Charlie would have been proud that a stallion that helped save you was named for him."

"You know, when I was lying with Maestro in the sand, I was thinking about Charlie. And I kept hearing his music in my head. It made me feel kind of . . . warm. Not scared anymore."

Grace swallowed to ease the tightness in her throat. "That's good, Frankie."

"And when Jake came, I knew everything was going to be all right. It wasn't because you told me he's my father. Because I've met some of my friends' fathers who are real losers."

"How do you feel about Jake being your father?"

Frankie shook her head. "I don't know. It's kind of . . . weird. I'll have to get used to it."

"Do you blame me?"

Frankie looked at her in surprise. "Why should I? I like Jake, but you're my mom. I love you. And we got along just fine without him."

Grace chuckled. "Just asking." She stood up. "Go on and check the colt. I'll be down to the corral as soon as I get dressed."

The Sheikh was standing at the corral looking at Charlie and Hope when Grace got there forty-five minutes later. "They don't seem any the worse from being out in the storm."

Grace nodded. "Your plastic-mask apparatus helped a lot. But you were right, both horses were sweating excessively. Frankie and I cleaned them up and washed out their eyes when we got back last night." She made a face. "It wasn't easy."

"I'm surprised you could do it at all."

"So was I. They must have learned a little trust under fire."

"Exceptional horses," he said. "I remember thinking how beautiful they were when Burton was training them, but I'd forgotten how wonderful they are. What do you plan on doing with them?" He grinned. "I might be persuaded to take them off your hands."

"You're too kind." She smiled back at him. "I suppose Burton's descendants have a right to them, but they're not going to get them. They've had a rough life and I'm not going to take a chance on them being put through any more hell."

"I'm very kind to my horses."

She shook her head. "I promised Charlie I'd take care of him. I'm going to do it."

The Sheikh nodded. "I can understand that. Responsibility." He turned away. "And I'd better go back to my camp and assume responsibilities of my own. It's been a pleasure meeting you. I hope to see you and your daughter again soon."

"You've been very kind, but I believe Frankie and I will want to stay away from this part of the world for a while."

"Memories fade, and I can show you a desert so incredible that it will stun you."

"That sandstorm stunned me."

"True." He chuckled. "But give us a chance."

She watched him walk away.

"He meant it, you know." She turned to see Kilmer coming out of the lean-to. "Adam never says anything he doesn't mean. He's very proud of his desert, and he realized you had a bad experience."

She shook her head. "I want to go home."

"Charlie's place?"

She nodded. "Frankie needs a normal life again. And I need to say good-bye to my friend Charlie. I never really did that. If his friends haven't set up some kind of memorial service for him, I'm going to do it."

"Okay, that's understandable." He looked back at the horses. "Where does that leave me?"

"What?"

"I'm not letting you go. Not you. Not Frankie."

Heady joy and then fear cascaded through her. "You don't have a choice. Neither of us belongs to you."

"Then I'll work and pull out every trick in the book until you do." He looked back at her. "Frankie's not going to be that hard. She's willing to give me a chance. She just told me that you told her I was her father. Why?"

"It seemed the thing to do at the time." She moistened her lips. "She took it okay. How was she with you?"

"Very matter of fact. No tears or hugs. I think I'm on probation. That's fine with me. I don't expect anything else. All I want is a chance." His voice lowered. "A chance, Grace."

"I told you I'd let you see her."

"A chance with you, Grace. A chance to build."

She shook her head jerkily. "We don't have anything to build on. Oh, sure, sex. But that's not enough."

"It's a hell of a good start." He paused. "And I think there's a hell of a lot besides sex going on. Respect, liking . . . maybe love. At least on my part. I care about you. Let's give ourselves the opportunity to find out what else is there." He smiled. "I promise I'll make it entertaining for you."

She felt a rush of heat tingle through her as she looked at him. "I don't want to be entertained."

"Yes, you do. Right now you're remembering how good it was for us. I don't have to remember. It's with me all the time."

She shook her head. "I can't deal with this now. I don't know how I feel about you. I don't know if I want to risk having you as part of Frankie's and my lives."

His gaze searched her expression. "I can see that. I'm rushing you. Okay, I'll back off and give you some time." His lips tightened. "But not much time. When do you want to go back to Alabama?"

"As soon as possible. I have to arrange transport for Charlie, Hope, and the colt."

"That's going to take time. You don't have papers for the horses, and it's not easy to arrange transport to the U.S. from a foreign country."

She frowned. She hadn't gotten around to thinking of the logistics. "Damn."

"I'll send you and Frankie back to the U.S. tomorrow. I'll ask Adam to send some of his people to help take care of the horses while I make arrangements to ship them to you. Is that good for you?"

"Yes, thank you."

"Don't thank me. I want to take care of you any way I can. I've got nine years to make up." He gazed directly into her eyes. "And until I'm able to get those horses to you, I'm going to be in contact. Every night I'll call and we'll talk, we'll get to know each other. Maybe if we're not within touching distance, it will be easier for us to communicate on a cerebral level." He turned and started back to the tents. "I'll get moving on it right away."

"Kilmer."

He looked back over his shoulder.

"What about the engine? Do you still want it?"

"Hell, yes."

"Even if you find it, do you think the CIA will let you keep it?"

"If I can find it fast enough to get in and get out. Possession is nine-tenths of the law." He grinned. "And I took out insurance over a year ago. I contacted Burton's two legal heirs and bought out all their future rights in Burton's estate. I offered them a hundred thousand dollars and ten percent of anything I managed to salvage. They thought I was crazy to believe in a pipe dream, but they took the money, signed the papers, and ran."

"Very clever."

"It was fair. I took the risk, and that ten percent could make them rich beyond their wildest dreams." His gaze narrowed. "Why are you asking about this now?"

"You might go back to the area where I was wandering around with Charlie yesterday. Somewhere near that rocky gully on the other side of the dunes."

"Why?"

"He kept going back there. I wasn't paying much attention. I wasn't sure that I believed Charlie and Hope could take anyone to Burton's hiding place anyway. I thought he was just going around in circles."

"Maybe he was."

"But last night when we were searching for Frankie, he seemed to know where he was going and he did find her. Instinct was working. Maybe instinct was working yesterday afternoon too. Instinct and memory."

"Possibly. It's worth a shot." He held her gaze. "Instinct and memory can be a hell of a good foundation, can't they?"

It was a moment before she could pull her eyes away from his. "Sometimes." She forced herself to turn away. "Like you said, it's worth a shot."

"Exactly," he said softly. "That's just what I said, Grace."

EPILOGUE

Six months later

T hey're here, Mom." Frankie came running into the stable. "I see them coming around the turn in the road."

Grace stiffened and then turned away from Darling. Her heart was beating hard and she could feel the heat flush her cheeks. "Why don't you go to meet them? I'll be right with you."

"Hurry." Frankie ran out of the stable.

She didn't want to hurry. She closed her eyes and tried to compose herself. It wasn't as if she hadn't known this moment was coming. Kilmer had called her last night and told her they'd be here today.

But knowing hadn't prevented her from lying awake all night or from being in a fever of anticipation. And it didn't keep her from wanting to run down the road like Frankie.

She drew a deep breath, turned, and walked out of the stable. Blockman, Donavan, and Frankie were opening the gate and letting Charlie, Hope, and the colt into the paddock. Cosmo brayed and trotted toward them.

And Kilmer was walking toward her. "You've got some new livestock. I hear you need a stable hand."

God, he looked wonderful. "You're overqualified. I like my help to stick around for a while."

"I'll stick around. Try me."

"You told me you found that engine. Wasn't it what it was cracked up to be?"

"Yes, the preliminary tests are astonishing."

"Then you don't need a job."

"I need it. I need you." He smiled. "Think of your status in the horse community. You'll be the only owner with a billionaire stable hand."

"The idea has its merits." He was close enough to touch. Jesus, she wanted to touch him. It had been too long. "You know how I've always prized my social status. Of course, I'd be willing to give you fringe benefits."

"I'm counting on them. I'm anticipating them. I can't do without them."

"Neither can I." It was time. She couldn't wait any longer.

She took a step forward and was in his arms.

The Second Coming of the Church

JOHN KILLINGER

ABINGDON
Nashville • New York

THE SECOND COMING OF THE CHURCH

Copyright © 1974 by Abingdon Press

Library of Congress Cataloging in Publication Data

KILLINGER, JOHN. The second coming of the church.
1. Christianity—20th century. I. Title
BR121.2.K49   209   73-22118

ISBN-0-687-37280-1

MANUFACTURED BY THE PARTHENON PRESS AT
NASHVILLE, TENNESSEE, UNITED STATES OF AMERICA

With love to
Mary
who is the kind of
sister-in-law
everybody should have

Contents

Introduction

Can the church hope to survive its own institutional success in the world? Is it able to deal at all creatively with both its traditions and the pressing needs of the day? Can it retain its propertied status and still cope with the militant spirit of the Third World? What about dissension within its own ranks—the schism between the fundamentalists and the liberals, the biblicists and the critics, the orthodoxists and the humanists? How can an organization which in many areas is still dogmatically pre-Darwinian continue much longer to speak to the minds of people in a society which is post-Freudian and postnuclear?

These are questions which haunt many of us today. Ironically, they are most often voiced by clergymen themselves, who seem to feel that they have been called upon to man a leaking ark. There is great unrest in their ranks. At least half of them one meets appear to be wondering what the future holds for the church, and whether they have not elected to serve the world from the wrong place.

I remember the consternation of a young priest who had spent four years at Vatican II and had gone to Paris to attend a meeting of bishops and theologians. The meeting was held in one of the comfortable hotels of the city. Its purpose was to discuss the geometrical design of the pall, the little piece of cloth (sometimes it is cardboard covered with cloth) which is used in the Mass to cover the chalice. The disquisitions were laboriously learned, said the priest, and they went on and on.

One day there was a great deal of noise in the street outside the hotel, so that the eminent churchmen were having difficulty concentrating. One of the bishops rose and went to the windows and began closing the great wooden shutters. Soon the room was insulated from the noise, and the conferees were able to resume their work as before.

"Do you know what that noise was?" asked the priest. "Do you know what the clatter was coming from? It was the student revolution of May 1968!"

It can hardly come as a surprise when I say that the priest is highly critical of the structures of his church and wonders how they can survive the crunch of the next few decades.

Recently I spent a weekend with a friend who is the senior minister of one of the most widely known and respected parishes in the United States. I had not seen him in the five years since he went to the post, and I was soon struck by the apparent changes in him. His voice was noticeably deeper. The rhythms of his speech were both smoother and less natural, as though they proceeded more from the professional necessity of having something to say than from the heart of the man I had known before. There was an air of gravity about him I did not remember. It seemed to say, "I represent this important congregation and I am always on call to it." I had an uncomfortable feeling, as though I were talking to a stranger who had imprisoned my friend inside his body.

"Bill," I said, "when you get up to preach on Sunday morning"—he is especially noted for his preaching—"how much pressure is put on what you say by the enormity of this church and the size of the budget that is required to keep it operative?"

"Oh, a man always feels responsible to the organization he represents," came the reply. "I try to think of this need and that need."

"I mean," I said, "how much does thinking about the building debt and some of the big givers in the congregation skew what you would otherwise say in a sermon? How conscious are you of the need to pull your punches on such questions as race, war, and poverty?"

He lowered his head a minute. When he looked into my eyes I could see that he was impaled. "I know what you mean," he said. The tone of my old friend returned. "It's a hell of a dilemma. If you say what you think ought to be said, you know it will alienate a lot of people who make the style of this church possible. If you don't, you sort of lose touch with yourself. You just have to work out the compromises as you go. And besides, these rich S.O.B.s need somebody to minister to them too."

It was my turn to understand, now that I had my friend back again. I did understand. A harsh, uncompromising prophet would probably have blown that church to pieces in a matter of months. I have seen it happen. My friend was probably taking the only course he could take, the one I would have to take if I were in his shoes and he in mine. He had to hold things together and try to bootleg the gospel any way he could. Maybe he could do it better as the head of a prestigious church like that than he could if he were the outspoken pastor of a small church or a professor in some seminary.

But the reason I knew his situation so well, and could probe precisely where the pain was, is that the situation is so universal. Almost every minister I know is faced by it. He must temper everything he says and does in the light of institutional needs and organizational management. If he does not, if he is reckless and speaks forthrightly as an individual, he will bring the whole, delicately poised machinery of the church down upon his neck. His family will suffer. He will go from one bad situation to another, his past pursuing him like a chain of falling dominoes, until he either cannot get a position at all or cannot get one that will support the daily needs of his family. In bitterness or in brokenness he will eventually leave the ministry.

It is no wonder that the Grand Inquisitor, in Dostoevski's story, kissed the returning Christ with his bloodless lips and told him to go away. The people were tranquil in his memory and did not need his disturbing presence again.

Christianity is of course not entirely dependent on the church for its continued progress in the world. Thank God for that! Just as Luther and Calvin had to invent a theology of the "hidden" church in order to account for the survival of true belief both in and alongside the medieval church whose errors they protested, there is considerable talk today about the latent or invisible church which goes on doing its work even when the church on Main Street has become hopelessly moribund and irresponsible. From the Jesus groups to the secular religionists, there are countless ways in which the leaven of Christian teachings is continuing to permeate society.

But *is* the church hopelessly moribund? Can the church not somehow regain its perspective and integrity so that its word counts for more in the human community? Is the church so ridden with the very evils and inadequacies it seeks to root out that it can get no leverage at all on the human condition, and must therefore be content to be another weak voice crying in the wilderness of the world's pain and confusion? Is the church so much in need of the gospel that the gospel is put to shame every time the church tries to speak of it? Can the church which has talked so egregiously of salvation these many centuries now hope to be saved?

This book is my attempt to say that it can. The leaven at work in the world is also at work in the church. I suspect that it has come back into the church from the world, fulfilling the old saying about bread that is cast upon the waters. It is even at work in the church of my friend who says he must think of the budget when he prepares his sermons. It is at work in encounter groups led by one of the associate ministers. It is at work in a continuing effort on the part of a few people to sharpen the social consciousness of the church through interracial meetings, seminars on politics and ethics, and missionary placement of medical teams in isolated South American villages. It is at work in the zeal of the young people who, on the Sunday I was in the church, sang Avery and Marsh's anthem, "I Wonder Why?" which ponders in a very contemporary idiom why society always tries to silence its messiahs.

But if the church is to be saved—if it *can* be saved—it will be according to the same rule that goes for all of us as individuals. That is the rule of true repentance. To turn the church's own language upon itself, it must earnestly desire to be saved. It cannot dictate its own terms of surrender. On the contrary, it must prostrate itself before its Lord in utter brokenness and humility, and accept in sincere readiness whatever is given as its role and status in the time ahead. It is in no position to quibble or remonstrate. It must be open to whatever future is assigned it. It must become a glad beggar again, a servant whose only joy is in serving. That way there will be no counting of the cost, no worry over property or possessions, no concern about status. The load will be lightened, and the way will not seem hard. The dreams will be good again, not troubled, for they are dreams of the wholeness of mankind.

All of which is to say that if the church as we know it is to live and thrive in the days ahead it may not be the church as we know it. It may be utterly different. Its shape, its form, its ministry, its modes of self-perception may have undergone such changes that it may not even appear to be the same institution. But this is relatively unimportant. It is life itself that counts.

Sometimes it is hard to remember this. We forget that form is only the shell of substance, the crystallization of an idea. Form follows the substance or idea, and has no special merit in and of itself. To be hung up on form is, well, it is sometimes to lose the life it once gave shape to. In the case of the church, it is to lose the Spirit. It is a twist of irony that this should ever happen to the church, which was born at a time when Judaism was caught in traditionalism and unable to follow the movement of the Spirit. But it can—and has.

Maybe the church is able to contemplate something new today because it is already broken and humiliated.

The sense of failure and desperation so widespread at both denominational and local levels could well be a necessary prelude to radical reformation. Nothing is quite so effective as destitution for evoking the innate desire to venture, to gamble, to become creative.

If this is true—if we are ready to take some chances—there are no limits to what can happen in the coming church. The future is wide open. And that is what this book is about.

Patterns in the Mind

There is an ancient and venerable tradition about an unusual figure—Wandering Jew, Ancient Mariner, or blind soothsayer—who encounters people and reveals extraordinary insights to them. A recent experience of my own confirms the validity of the tradition, but the holy man in my case, with proper deference to Women's Lib, turned out to be an attractive young career girl smartly attired in a knit suit, sandal pumps, and a pair of oversized sunglasses.

It was on a jet bound from Atlanta to Boston. I was 18-D and she was 18-E. The little freckle-faced girl behind the checkout counter had innocently arranged our fateful tryst with a grease crayon. I wonder if she suspects what tricks of destiny she plays midwife to every day, just with a flick of the wrist and a smile.

"Excuse me," said the voice under the dangling brown hair. One hand was on the seat in front of me, the other clutched an arm-styled briefcase, and she was sort of pointing with an inclined head and torso. "I believe that is my seat."

By the time we were airborne we were already both at work—I on a paper I was to read in Boston and she on a sheaf of materials extracted from her briefcase. The two or three furtive glances I stole toward her lap revealed some sketches that looked like floor plans, and pages of figures which she appeared to be checking. Occasionally she circled a numeral or crossed out something. She seemed to work swiftly, like a highly efficient data screener.

When the stewardess brought us our dinners, there was a necessary lapse in our labors.

"Designer?" I inquired.

"Mmmm, architect," she replied.

Trained at Auburn and now employed by a firm in Birmingham, she was on her way to consult on a design for an office tower to be erected in south Boston.

Did she find being a woman a handicap in the business world? Not really, at her level of assignment. It was only at the uppermost ranks, she said, that women encountered real resistance. Men were uneasy about working for women as supervisors or employers. She planned eventually to have her own firm; then she would face a new order of problems.

What did I do? she asked. Was I in government?

No, I explained, I was a professor. Maybe the paper had thrown her off. I was preparing it as a lecture for an audience of clergymen and theological students.

"Oh," she said.

There seemed to be an element of disappointed surprise in the way she said it. I couldn't tell whether it was really there or I just imagined it because I expected her to react that way.

I proceeded somewhat awkwardly at this point, I am afraid. "What church do you stay away from?" I inquired.

It was a gambit I recalled from one of my teachers, and I mentally cursed myself as I uttered it.

"All of them," she said.

This time *I* said, "Oh."

She offered no apologies, as most people do when seeming to slight the practice of piety. The firmness of her answer had conveyed a kind of self-assured decisiveness, with no trace of rancor. It wasn't a touchy subject.

"Have you had a bad experience with the church?" I asked.

"No," she replied, holding an onion ring aloft between thumb and forefinger and biting it neatly in half. "Not necessarily. I just find all of them hopelessly . . . *antique.*"

Apparently she had wanted another word but could not find it in time.

I smiled, first at her and then at the stewardess who had just brought our coffee.

Almost involuntarily she reached for her papers and began to rustle through them again, as if she were going to re-enter the privacy of her work. Then, hesitating a moment, she put them down again and took a cigarette from her purse.

After a deep breath and an exhalation of smoke, she asked, "What are you going to say to them?"

"To —?"

"To the churchmen in Boston."

I felt uneasy trying to answer. It was difficult to frame in a few words, I said. I was going to talk about theological style in our time—about games theory and its application to the understanding of human life.

"Why don't you really tell them what the church could

be like?" she said, obviously having dismissed my explanation before I had even gotten into it.

I waited, knowing she would continue.

"I mean," she said, "why don't you simply forget the church as it is, which always weights any discussion unfavorably in the past, and let your mind free-float to the future? I do it all the time in my work. Can you imagine architecture today if no one had done this in the past twenty years and all our buildings had been mere restatements of what we had known before, with maybe a few amendments in the facades?"

I could see her point, but if I smiled a little it was more at her sudden aggressiveness than at the idea she was championing, which was not entirely novel to me.

"Do you see my point?" she pressed as if she had half read my mind. "All the really great strides in human achievement come from an absolute freedom from the past and the way things have always been done. The imagination must soar without limits! Chagall—you know, the artist—Chagall once said that he wanted his studio to be a place where the impossible could happen. And it did! It happened because he refused the limitations of what had gone before. He simply shut his mind to what had been done by other painters. He allowed himself to fantasize without restriction."

"But doing it on canvas is one thing," I said. "Can you do the same in a building?"

"Oh, there are always limits," she said. "I know that. Even for Chagall. A kind of inner gravity or inertia you can't escape. But the important thing is to try to forget them at first. You have to come back to them before you're through, but you mustn't succumb to them in the beginning, before you start. If you do, they spoil everything. They rule with complete tyranny. Freedom isn't absolute. It never is. But it is crucial to dream, to fantasize as wildly as possible, in order to expand our horizons. Otherwise we would always live imprisoned in the past, in our own traditions. Traditions would become sealed off, like graves, instead of being open and dynamic."

I thought of Nietzsche and the grave of God.

"Suppose you were imagining the church of the future," I said. "Maybe thirty or forty years from now. Not as it probably will be in most places, but as it might be. What do you see?"

Her cigarette had burned down as she talked. She lit another, thinking as she did.

"Okay," she said. "To begin with, I see a church that is physically different from any I see today. I guess that's natural for an architect. The dominant feature of the present buildings is a sanctuary, a large room capable of seating a crowd of people—fixed pews, choir loft, pulpit, chancel, all that. But that is already out-of-date, a hangover from the days when people were uneducated and the ministry did everything for them.

"Now there is a need for particularity. There is a pluralism of spiritual needs just as there is a pluralism of everything else in the world. The church of the future, therefore, will abandon the huge room it calls a sanctuary, in favor of many smaller spaces where only a few persons can do their thing together. Maybe, in some cases, people will do their thing alone, without anybody else."

"Without even a minister?"

"Yes. I'm thinking of an art house I visited once on a university campus. It had a crude sort of computer in it

21

which anybody—or a small group—could program with his own tastes in art and music. Then the computer would pull out certain slides for the projectors and certain tapes for the sound deck, and they would enjoy a multimedia experience designed more or less personally for them."

"Fascinating," I said.

"Imagine what it would be like to worship the same way," she said. "I think the reason I stopped going to church was that it so often constituted a rape of my feelings. I would go in a happy mood, and the minister would be in one of his 'down' moods; or I would go with a sense of depression, and he would be having one of his jolly days. I would go away angry and resentful, even though he had no way of knowing where I was in my thinking and feeling."

"But in the new church—"

"—in the new church each of us could go to whatever room he felt like going to, or to whichever group, and could program whatever he wanted. Maybe we wouldn't just seek experiences that were in phase with our own moods all the time. Maybe we'd even program contrapuntal experiences sometimes. But the important thing is, we would be free of conformity to the large group and what it was doing."

"Or what it was being *forced* to do by the minister and whoever else planned the service."

"Exactly."

"But what about preaching and praying?" I asked. "Would they simply pass out of existence?"

"Not necessarily, I think," she said. "There might be brief tapes of either done by a minister—maybe even videotapes—which would be part of the canned repertoire. I can imagine that their quality would be considerably higher than that in the average church today, because they could be done by the best ministers and then circulated among the churches. There might even be some longer sermons, as there are today, especially for older persons nostalgic for them. After all, their needs would have to be met too."

I had to confess that I was slightly bothered by this notion. It struck me much the way tales of canned services in funeral homes have in the past.

"I always thought that the best preaching, and maybe even the best praying, depended on some kind of reciprocity between the minister and the congregation immediately before him," I said.

"That is probably true," she said, "for some people. But if it is, then the ideal environment for such preaching is not in a large auditorium where the feedback the preacher can measure is very diffuse and meager, but in a small group setting where there is a maximum of give-and-take among all the persons present."

"You mean—," I interjected as she crushed out her cigarette.

"I mean," she continued, "that the preacher's skills will necessarily entail more than they have in the past. Along with his theology and whatever else he gets in school now, he will need to be a competent small group leader, or at least a good participant in the group. He will need to listen better than he does in most instances now, and be able to pick up on what other people are saying, both overtly and in all the secret ways we have of talking."

"Like body language and significant pauses."

"Precisely. He must do this in order to say whatever

23

it is he has to say to the particular person or persons in the group. He can't prepare his sermon in advance the way most preachers do now. All he can do is prepare himself, so that when the time comes he has something to share with the other pilgrims."

"Implying that he himself is a pilgrim."

"Yes, of course."

"I can imagine," I said, "that this would take a lot of weight off the minister's shoulders. He wouldn't have to appear as an authority figure all the time, dispensing 'correct' religious answers for every occasion."

"I think so," she said, "though it wouldn't mean he would need to be less of an expert. In fact, he would need all the skills he has now, plus the skill of a counselor and group participant, and that isn't an easy skill for some people to acquire."

By this time the stewardesses were clearing away the dinner trays, and we paused momentarily as ours were stacked and removed. I secured the folding trays in their original positions, and she lit another cigarette.

"I don't think there would be any denominations," she said, smoke curling around her dark hair. "Not as you have them now, anyway. People would choose their churches on the basis of how agreeable they found the leadership and facilities."

I admitted that I thought it was largely this way now with many people, especially those who are more transient in our society. Few people really know the history of denominational origins or understand the finer doctrinal positions which once marked ecclesiastical boundaries.

"When you speak of 'leadership,' " I said, "what are

you thinking of? How would the church of the age to come be organized?"

"Functionally, I suppose," she replied. "Maybe they would be run by local theological councils or something like that, with diverse kinds of ministering talents represented there. The idea would not be to enforce a certain image of the church, as is often the case today, but to stimulate the imagination about how best to serve people, and then to give some practical reality to what is imagined. The emphasis in the whole church would be on sensitivity to the theological dimension of all of life, not on conformity to a particular moral code or doctrinal outline."

"But I am troubled by one unpleasant question," I said. "Will people really pay to operate such a church? Surely you have observed that it is the strictest and narrowest churches that tend to thrive in the financial or physical sense. People who are more liberated in the manner you suggest seem to be liberated also from financial responsibility for organized religion."

"I suppose that is true," she laughed. "But the church I am talking about really doesn't need much financial support. Its property needs are very small—nothing like maintaining a terrifically large plant such as stands on half the street corners today. Because of its functional nature, its housing can be relatively small and inexpensive, depending, of course, on the size of the membership served. In most cases, an old house could be converted into a very adequate church building. There would need to be rooms for various worship experiences and group meetings, and these could double as counseling rooms and committee rooms at other times. And, with the old notion of a Sunday-morning congregation put behind us, people would not all swell into the building at one time. They would come at the time or times during the week most convenient or meaningful to them."

"That would be true especially if there were computerized worship experiences available at all times for individuals to operate, wouldn't it?"

"Yes. And it also occurs to me that many churches in the future will probably operate on something other than a voluntary financial basis. Maybe like a neighborhood club, with dues assessed to members on the basis of income and ability to pay. People who wished to belong would simply expect to meet a stated annual obligation."

"That would certainly solve a lot of problems," I said, "if it worked." Frankly, I had some doubt as to whether it would, but I couldn't think of a very good reason why it wouldn't. So I introduced instead another negative feeling I had managed to formulate in my mind as she talked.

"I admit that I am fascinated by your thinking on all these matters," I said. "You would certainly shake up a few things if you were to get on a big church council or were elected pope or something. But I find myself unable to quell a kind of uneasiness about one question. If there were no denominations, no standardized church buildings, and no uniform hours of worship with stated sermons, prayers, and such, what could provide the church with a sense of identity? How would belonging to your future church differ significantly and crucially from belonging to a neighborhood improvement club, say?"

Characteristic noises from the depths of the plane indicated that the pilot was throttling back in preparation for landing. I think I expected my attractive young seer to show signs of attentiveness to this, shrug her shoulders as if in recognition of the approaching termination of our conversation, and thus beg the question. But she didn't. She looked deeply serious for a moment. Then, adjusting her seat belt and bringing the seat back into place as the No Smoking sign appeared on the overhead racks, she gave her answer.

"Identity," she said, "is for many people something conferred from without. But in its highest form it is something recognized from within. It is true that the ideas I have been entertaining would frighten many persons, because to those persons they would appear as utter anarchy. But Christ had to do with freedom, didn't he? Not absolute freedom, of course—the freedom to become birds or the freedom not to be mortal—but freedom from being or remaining subhuman, freedom from traditions imposed by the past, freedom to live life openly and joyously and creatively. I don't say it will work for everybody, but maybe the best kind of identity for Christians occurs when they identify themselves as persons who do the kind of work he did. That is, when they live genuinely and responsively as he did, when they reject the tyrannies over men's bodies and souls he rejected, when they are even willing to endure enmity and crucifixion in the pursuit of the things they are inwardly sure to be right and good in life.

"Part of my rejection of the church," she continued, "stems from the kind of conformity it imposes on people —the necessity to seem to be something they aren't. I always feel there is something false about a huge congregation and the way it sits disguised in fine clothes and tolerant smiles while a paid minister stands in the pulpit and talks about the virtues which supposedly support a

27

godly community. There is so little opportunity for people to say who they really are, to expose themselves, with all their doubts and faults and crimes, to the others. They simply come, subject themselves to a certain manner of speech and song, and go away."

The wheels screeched on the runway, and we braced ourselves for the sudden reversal of force our bodies expected.

"I would like to be part of a church someday," she continued, "in which all the particularities of myself and my experience are accepted as important, if not to other persons, at least to me. A church that provided wide open group discussions in which I could say 'Jesus is a green frog' if I wanted to without some minister making a note to talk to me afterwards about my conception of Jesus and bring me into line.

"I don't mean there shouldn't be any instruction in the history and understanding of the faith. Such instruction is important. But it ought to be oriented toward the future—toward *my* future, not toward the past, toward the Jews and Greeks. It should exist to help me make sense of my world by understanding who I am and how I function as a human being, not merely by referring me to an institution which desires to be my alter-parent. It should start with me as a person, as a member of the human community, and ask how I can realize my personhood and my membership in the community, not how it can subvert my individuality and indenture me to its own system, language, and ends.

"I think it should provide me with training and instruction for being a more effective member of the total community, instead of alienating me from that community by promising redemption from it. I would like to see the church developing task forces of various kinds for coping with community situations and trying to improve them. For example, it could actually recruit and train people to bring political power to bear in local elections. It could mobilize members to combat various social problems such as poverty, racism, drug abuse, and ecological imbalance or pollution. By using such techniques as role-playing and information saturation, it could help persons like myself to become effective agents in the restructuring of the environment for human existence. Isn't that the work of Christ? Doesn't that produce and sustain a free society?"

These last sentences had come in a torrent. It was obvious that my companion on the journey was not so entirely dispassionate about the church as her initial coolness would have indicated. She seemed somehow a little less remote, even less immaculate, than she had when I first saw her. I was less afraid of her. She had become real in the course of her description of a future church. She was a creature of flesh and blood—hot blood—I now realized.

I thought of her as I rode in a taxi out to the university where I would give my paper. If the dream of a church could produce a girl like that, I wondered, what would the real church, her dream incarnate, do? I didn't let myself think about the paper I carried in my briefcase until I took it out to present it. I didn't dare, because I felt it would bore me out of my mind.

Once, as I studied my shoe and half-listened to the words of introduction which preceded my going to the lectern, I had a moment's impulse to abandon my carefully prepared typescript and talk about the church of the

29

future. I wished that I were sure my audience was ready for such freedom, but something told me it wasn't. I was afraid the consequences would be disastrous and dismissed the impulse as absurd.

There was warm applause after the paper, and I was quoted fairly accurately in two civic newspapers, a little less accurately in the university paper, and erroneously in a subsequent alumni bulletin. None of it mattered, for I didn't really feel present anyway. I was tracing patterns in my mind—an architect's drawings—of the church to come.

March 7

Dear John,

    I hope your conference or whatever went well. Better, at least, than my meeting. We finally lost the contract.

    I didn't consider the trip a total washout, however. I have thought a lot about the things we talked about. Could it be that I have copped out on the church? I realize, when I think about it, that it is still one of the few institutions in the world <u>theoretically</u> dedicated to the nonprofit improvement of society.

    If only it could be moved off dead center!

        Hopefully,

        M. W.

Dear W. W.,

Thanks for your note. I'm sorry you lost the contract, but I'm sure it won't be the last building in the world.

I agree about the church. For all its problems and failures, it is still the church, and there is something magic in that. Think of it! All those companies, all those wicked and/or ignorant leaders, all those commitments to faulty ideas or erroneous doctrines. Yet the church has consistently produced men and women of magnanimous spirit to make the world more habitable. It's a miracle, however you look at it.

I guess what I wish most is that I knew how to help the church to become its best self today. The poor thing heaves and tosses like a net full of fish, flashing out here and there, but basically unable to get coordinated and act with any unanimity of spirit or understand- ing. The conservatives are paranoid and liber- als are half-hearted. Everybody fights every- body else. Why can't we quit looking sideways and just look ahead at what we could be doing for the world?

You shook me up some, I want you to know. I had a hard time concentrating on my lecture that day in Boston. I kept thinking about your future-think trick. You're some gaf--and ob- viously a product of the church.

Let's not let go. Maybe we can still resurrect the church--or put ourselves in an attitude where God can resurrect it.

Faithfully yours,
John

Dear John,

I've had a bad trip, and you are to blame. Partially, anyway. After your letter I decided that I was going to give it the old college try again. So I picked out a church and went to worship last Sunday.

What a disaster! It's a wonder I can even write about it. The minister was such a cute bore. He was on stage nearly the whole hour, except for a terrible old organist and a few sickly romantic hymns about the Hour of Trial and the Beauty of Holiness and the Rewards of Piety. I honestly thought I would puke.

The worst part was the way all those people just sat and took it. How do they do it? And I'm sure they do it each and every week. I almost wondered who was crazy, me or them.

It's as bad as I remembered, maybe worse, because it hasn't changed.

But you know, I had a funny feeling the minister knew it was all a game. Maybe I only read it into him because I knew it. But I could swear he was ready to shout out some horrible oath just to break the spell, only he managed to control himself for one more Sunday. Imagine, if I'm right, what it would be like to live that way week after week after week.

Anyway, it was all simply terrible. I don't know where this leaves me. I'm really confused. I feel as if I've started down a road and can't turn back, yet am repelled at the very thought of going further.

Help!!!

Desperately,

M. W.

May 1

My dear M. W.,

What can I say? Your experience is simi-lar to the one I have had over and over. You wonder what it is that binds the people in a church like that together, and enables them to subsist for years on a diet of scrambled homilies, tasteless music, and misconceived Christian education. Why don't they all drop away? What strange power keeps bringing them back, Sunday after Sunday and year after year? It is a mystery to me.

The kind of minister you describe is what drove one friend of mine out of the mainline churches into the Society of Friends. He said he found the practice of meditation and silence so much more true and creative than the inces-sant talking in other churches.

But you mustn't give up, oh can't, as I gather from your letter. I am enclosing the address of another church and directions for reaching it. It is about thirty miles from where you are, but I think it would be worth your checking it out sometime. I've never been there myself, but I've heard about it from two or three sources.

Sincerely,
John

May 19

Dear John,

I haven't yet visited the church you suggested. One weekend I was under the weather, and last weekend I had loads of work to catch up on after a three-day trip. But I do intend to try it.

Feeling better,

M. W.

June 12

Dear John,

I finally made it. On the whole, I guess it was a good experience. Maybe it was a bad Sunday, but things didn't really seem to catch fire. I don't mean in a revivalistic way. There just didn't appear to be any great enthusiasm at the center of what was happening. No tongues of fire on people's foreheads and all that. I suppose it was constructive enough, especially for people who are involved in the weekly programs. I hadn't bought into anything but the worship hour, however, it didn't do too much for me. Maybe I'll try it another time.

M. W.

P.S. I've been reading one of your books,
Leave it to the Spirit. Tell me, have you
ever been examined for possible schizophrenia?

June 15

Dear W. W.,

What kind of darn fool question was that?

J.

The Making of Future Ministers

Having had the experience of meeting my young architect on an airplane, I continued for several weeks under its spell. I found, in fact, that my clairvoyant friend's observations about the church, delivered so casually and almost naïvely, grew in importance to me until they nearly became an obsession.

It was during this period, when my mind could turn to little else but would automatically revert to our discussion of futuristics, that I had a strange and wonderful dream.

In the dream, I found myself transported to a seminary campus several decades hence, visiting with the future ministers and teachers of the church my architect friend had envisioned.

As in most dreams, what is reasonable and what in fact exists stood in no opposition to each other. Nor shall I, in relating what I can remember of the content of that dream, be at any pains to separate them. I shall simply report, as adequately and accurately as I am able, what I saw and heard on that unusual campus.

I should say at the outset that my impressions of the campus itself are rather hazy. Although I saw many things in clear detail, items of panoramic magnitude were often less than precise. I distinctly recall, however, a constant sense of amazement at the aesthetic pleasure afforded by the general environment. There was a feeling of tranquillity everywhere, in the buildings as well as on the grounds, though not of idle tranquillity, for much seemed to be happening at all times.

I believe there was a very agreeable use of space in the buildings, so that I never experienced a feeling of either crowdedness or loneliness. Often I begin to remember green plants growing indoors, providing a sense of freshness and serenity, though when I try to focus on them in any particular setting I am unable to do so. The same elusiveness occurs when I attempt to recall the plush carpeting which I associate with the rooms and hallways. The moment I concentrate on it, I become unsure and wonder if the floors were not hardwood, brought to a beautiful, clear sheen, with occasional rugs of bold Danish or modern Persian design.

My guide through the extraordinary campus (I confess that even he came and went according to my mode of perception) was both a student and not a student there. That is, he appeared to identify himself with all the others who were there, yet transcended them in some ways, as though he had already progressed through all the stages of learning and were now beyond the scene. He shall remain nameless to the reader, as indeed he did to me in the entirety of the dream.

Perhaps, in the light of the foregoing paragraph, I should say a word here about the character of the students in this seminary. As I was told by my guide, they were neither admitted nor graduated by the tedious recording processes at use in former times. They simply came, when it was time for their seminary experience, and left, when the time was ripe for them to do so. Only, having left, they continued to return as often as they felt the need or the ability to profit from doing so. Being told this, I noticed that many learners present appeared to be in their middle or later years, some even approaching senescence. There seemed to be no artificial divisions among them—all were engaged in the activity of learning and growing, regardless of age.

My guide said that most ministers in the church of that time found it useful and normal to return to a seminary for at least a month a year to re-engage themselves in various problems at a more intense level than was often possible in the parish. There was no literal specification that they must do so and no rule regarding their absence from the churches. They merely came and went as the need arose, making whatever arrangements were necessary at the time.

Didn't the church members complain of the looseness of this arrangement? I inquired of the guide. No, he said, they regarded it as important to them as well as to the minister, and besides, the churches were structured in such fashion as to make the regular attendance of the ministers unnecessary. The idea of the clergy as enablers, so widely discussed in the sixties and seventies, had become widely accepted in the churches, and now the laity did much of the actual ministering work of the parishes, leaving the clergy free as sort of experts-in-residence.

This is as good a place as any to introduce the curricular structure of the new seminary, for it will help to explain how ministers occupied in churches for most of the year can return to the seminary and enter with any integrity into the ongoing theological program. Perhaps it will be of interest to those who have been vitally interested in upgrading methods of continuing education in seminaries but have always had the desperate feeling that even the best continuing education programs are mere adjuncts or stepchildren of the regular programs.

Let us begin with the cinemetronics labs, which I found to be a fascinating area of the future campus. I had seen many rooms where earnest discussions appeared to be taking place, but had seen nothing which I identified as formal classes in any of the disciplines so familiar to me when I was in seminary. Accordingly, I inquired of my host about the lectures in church history, Bible, and theology, assuming that it would be very interesting to enter among a few of them and remark how they differed, if at all, from what I had known.

At that he laughed good-naturedly and ushered me into a section of the main building whose appearance resembled that of the language laboratories presently found in many universities. There were perhaps forty or fifty desks or console tops, each mounted by a set of headphones, a small switchboard, and an assortment of viewing screens, the largest of which might easily have been a television screen.

At my guide's invitation, I sat at one of the desks and fitted the headphones to my ears.

"Now," he said, consulting a small manual which lay on the surface of the desk, "name a period or person in theological history that fascinates you."

I believe my first impulse was to name Augustine or Luther, but, fearing that either would seem an obvious and unsophisticated choice, I pronounced the name of Thomas Bradwardine. I had once had a church history professor who had written a thesis on Bradwardine, and he had spent more time on him in classroom lectures than on any of the popular reformers. Now I could recall almost nothing of the man or his thought, so considered him a reasonable choice on which to test the machinery before me.

The guide found the proper reference in the manual, adjusted a few switches on the console, and instantly I was not only hearing about Bradwardine and Gabriel Biel and the whole nominalist controversy in the late medieval church, but was seeing a movie on the screen as well, depicting scenes in which the eminent theologians of that day argued and contended for their positions.

I was amazed. In quick succession, I tuned in to depictions of the councils of Nicaea, Chalcedon, and Trent, the controversy between Augustine and Pelagius, Henry VIII's proclamation of the Act of Supremacy, and John Wesley's experience at Aldersgate. "What a way to learn history!" I remarked as I removed the headset.

"Don't get up," said my mentor. "There's more."

He pressed a button and another area of the console lit up.

"How's your biblical Greek?" he asked.

"Atrocious, I'm afraid," I said.

"Then we'll start with simple verb forms."

An uncomplicated sentence in koine Greek appeared on an oblong screen.

"Translate it, if you can," said the guide.

"The man is . . . throwing . . ." I couldn't complete the sentence.

The guide pushed a red button.

". . . a javelin," read the screen. Then the words vanished and new ones appeared, again in Greek. This time I could read the entire sentence. It said: "The javelin throws the man."

A machine with a sense of humor!

"Almost all our basic teaching," explained the guide, "is programmed for machine instruction: history, Bible, languages, even sociology, ethics, anthropology, psycho-mythology, and theology."

"But how?"

"How can theology be programmed? Of course it can't be, completely. But the history of theology can be, and students can be required by the machines to respond creatively to certain theological puzzles which have perplexed men for ages, utilizing where possible the insights of Spinoza, Schleiermacher, Tillich, and other giants of theological discussion. When the student has been through a full regimen of tapes with one of our machines, he is a pretty competent theologian himself, at least as far as he can be equipped out of the theology of the past. Then he is ready for his *real* work."

The real work, as I was to learn, came in the small group sessions which were considered the heart of the new theological training. But that is getting ahead of my story. My guide had one other trick to show me at the console.

This time flipping a blue switch, he explained that I was now to witness something I was very likely unprepared for in my own theological training. Actually, as it turned out, it was not theological at all, but had to do with the improvement of creativity and originality in thinking.

"This is one of the newer concepts," he said, "and we have one of the two systems now being pioneered in this country. The developers of the system believe that one of the greatest impediments to free and creative theological work is the tendency of the mind to idolize old conceptualizations and forget that they were once only tentative formulas. The system is therefore programmed to disrupt fixated thinking by various visual and linguistic playgrams. For example . . ."

As he talked, he pushed a combination of numbers, and the oblong screen lit up with these words: REDIMMED BY THE BLOAT OF THE LIMB. When I fitted the headphones to my ears, a taped voice said: "This is an exercise in word-play. Please recognize the traditional religious phrase disguised under the mutated logogram. Silently form the logogram on your lips. Enjoy the freedom of the new formulation. Now we shall proceed to another phrase."

The former phrase vanished and a new one appeared. The voice on the tape provided instruction as before. One after another, the phrases came and went: THE KLANDOM OF GOD, THE BRIGGING OF GOAT NOOSE, THE ZONE OF GOAD, DEBT ON THE GROSS, THE THROWN OF GOT . . . .

I was fascinated, but also disturbed. "I don't know," I said to my host. "This is intriguing. But something inside me feels uneasy, as if I were blaspheming or something."

He laughed.

"Not really," he said. "Quite the contrary. Words and phrases become blasphemous themselves when fastened upon. They lose their transparency, their sense of discovery. Then it is necessary to disunite ourselves from them in order to proceed to new discoveries.

"The same is true of visual images. Therefore the system presents alternate and quite opposite pictures of such abstract concepts as God, messiah, faith, love, and so on. For example, God may be represented by such various images as a gull flying over a rocky shoreline, a gleaming supercomputer, or even an empty screen with no picture at all. Love may be seen as a mother cradling an infant, as a government employee working late at his desk, or as a killer standing over his victim. The viewer is forced to recognize the infinitely wide range of instances in which love assumes different forms, even hatred and aggression.

"There is one wrinkle in the system I would like to show you but can't because we're having some mechanical problems the engineers haven't cleared up yet. See this little instrument—"

He handed me a metal object similar in shape to a ballpoint pen.

"This is a laser pen. It writes with light, and can be used to alter patterns on the video screen. Certain exercises are provided in which the student is asked to perform his own mutations directly on phrases and drawings flashed before him. The machine then responds by further altering the phrasings or configurations, and requests the student to follow suit. I have seen a clever, imaginative student make up to nine or ten 'plays' with the machine before it moves on to a new problem."

I had to admit that I felt two emotions simultaneously, one a sense of awe and excitement at the sophistication of the process (despite the mechanical breakdown), and the other a feeling of having been cheated by not having such practice in my own experience.

My host generously reminded me that persons have used similar methods for centuries, and that the machine had merely refined the mechanics of them. Playfulness and creativity have always been intimately allied, for it is only in play that the mind breaks its customary circuits and explores new territory and new combinations of data.

Sitting in this mechanical Shangri-La, I could not forbear inquiring about the reading of books. I had seen no library at all, and the library was once a central feature of any seminary or university campus. Didn't the students read as they had in my day?

"Not very much," replied my guide. "We have largely made the transition to oral and imagistic learning with little emphasis on linear training. Our students are all rapid readers, of course, and have been since they were five or six years old. But much of their reading is done at television consoles, where the entire collection of the World Information Center is at their fingertips. That includes art, drama, movies, and so on, as well as ordinary printed materials. And, for those who desire them, of course, there are still the old pobs, though there is little need for them anymore."

"Pobs?"

"You didn't have pobs? I'm sorry. I didn't realize when they came into use. 'Pob' is an anagram for 'printout book.' It's a looseleaf book of chemically treated plastic leaves capable of receiving phototelegraphic images from a master printer at the WIC. They were the rage for a while, but now it's even getting hard to obtain maintenance for our transmitter. Occasionally we get a student—usually an older one—who still has a strong linear attachment and seems to require a pob. But there aren't too many anymore."

I don't know whether it was the amazement I felt or what in a dream might pass for fatigue or hunger, but at this point my host suggested a change of pace. He led me into what appeared to be a relatively smaller version of a gymnasium, where a number of men and women together were participating in various kinds of recreational activities. Some were working on parallel bars, some were doing group calisthenics, and some appeared to be taking part in some kind of yoga exercises. I felt immediately more comfortable at being in what was at least a more familiar setting.

"Was much emphasis placed upon sports and play activities in your seminary?" inquired my host.

"Very little," I said. "We played tag football on the lawn, and got together occasionally for basketball or tennis. But only on a voluntary and scattered basis."

"Physical training is an integral part of our program," he replied. "Our therapists are as important to us as any staffers we have. I don't know what we would do without this aspect of our training. I can go away for a week, and, if I don't continue my exercises faithfully, I feel myself becoming sluggish and inert, mentally as well as physically.

"We don't have any requirement of a specific number of hours to be spent in the gym or pool, of course, any more than we have other sorts of requirements. But I can't imagine that anyone spends fewer than ten or twelve hours a week here. Some friends of mine are probably here thirty to thirty-five hours. It's amazing what it does for their total personalities as seminarians. They're probably the best students here."

My smile tried to mask an inward wince. I thought of all the times I had refused a tennis or handball invitation because I had been "too busy" to take part at the time.

But something my host had said about requirements intrigued me. "You mean there are no requirements of any kind?" I asked.

"None whatsoever."

"But how can you operate like that?" I asked. "Surely there must be *some* rules. How do you know when a student is ready to graduate?"

This time it was my host who smiled. "We gave up admission and graduation requirements years ago," he said. "We finally admitted, in the case of the former, that we were only accidentally correct in some of our admissions, and were often wrong, because we simply could not test many of the intangible factors related to seminary training. And as for the latter, graduation. . . . Well, I guess you might say that we abandoned that to remove the false notion that one really ever completes his education.

"Our students remain here until they feel that it is less fruitful to be here than in a primary involvement situation. Then they go out to work somewhere else, in a church or school or other form of employment.

"But of course they rarely stay away. Most return frequently to work on specific problems confronting them or simply to put a new edge on themselves. As I explained earlier, what you once called 'continuing education' has become a way of life for us, not a mere adjunctive program."

"But," I questioned, "how can you assess a person's performability for a prospective employer or for other educational environments? We always depended heavily on grades and quality-point averages and the like."

"Oh, that's no problem," my host assured me. "Each student is simply rated, when necessary, on a quality chart by his fellow students. We have found this to be much more adequate than former assessments by teachers, whose angle of vision on the student tended to be vertical and not horizontal, as the case is with both fellow students and the people with whom the person will be working outside."

I had to admit the idea was feasible.

By this time my host and I had jogged around the elevated track several times, and he led me through an air-screen door into a large room where there was a swimming pool. We splashed into the water and swam the length of the pool several times, then crawled into one of the swirl baths adjacent to it. As the warm water whirled pleasantly around us, my guide continued his introduction of the new seminary program.

One of the things we discussed during this pleasant interval was the use of chemotherapy in the new program. As yet, said the guide, it was in the experimental stage, but showed great promise. An outgrowth of the earlier usage of LSD and marijuana as perception-altering aids, the present concern was to find harmless drugs which could be used under controlled conditions to restore balance to impaired personalities and induce consciousness-expanding practices which would subsequently become automatic in students who habitually exercised too much restraint over their imaginations and emotions.

"Hasn't there been objection to this from puritanical church people?" I asked.

"Some," he replied, "but the experiments are not highly publicized, and they are being conducted on only the most promising respondents, with extremely capable supervisors. I have heard some reports, perhaps exaggerated, that within a decade every seminarian will be routinely checked by computerized chemical analysis and will be provided with daily supplies of the additives required by his system. It may sound preposterous, but I am prepared to believe it, in the light of other remarkable innovations in the past few years."

From the bath, my host led me into a carpeted dressing room, where each of us received a deep massage from the student attendants. Apparently I fell asleep on the table, or perhaps my dream was temporarily interrupted, for when I resumed my inspection of the seminary I was with a different guide, a woman of more mature years, though presently a student in the seminary. We were sitting in a small, comfortably furnished room with nine or ten other persons.

I suppose I simply intuited that she was my hostess, as no exchange had thus far passed between us, and we were both involved in the procedures of the entire group.

I had been in a similar group before, I thought, as this one appeared to be functioning as a sort of sharing or sensitivity group. Very personal things were being spoken in a most open and casual fashion, as though those present were accustomed to live candidly before one another at all times. No topic was too intimate for serious discussion, and, in the space of what must have been two hours, various persons aired feelings of emotional distress, occupational uncertainty, sexual difficulty, and attraction or hostility toward other group participants. My hostess spoke of her sense of frustration at having entered the ministry rather late in life, after the loss of her husband, and of having less time ahead for her vocational fulfillment than many others had. I thought her very graceful and beautiful, and wondered how she could ever experience negative feelings about herself.

Afterwards, as we strolled through the neatly manicured grounds and sat on a bench in an alcove surrounded by a semicircle of boxwoods, she talked of the importance of the therapy sessions to her. I conjectured that they must be extremely meaningful to all who are involved in them. How many students, I wondered, availed themselves of such personal growth experiences?

"All that I know," she said. "It is not a requirement, of course. But who would want to miss it? It is a marvelous opportunity. Besides, how would one proceed as a leader in a church without first having had such experiences?"

It now occurred to me, as it had not before, that this was the new seminary's method of developing group leadership—not by rote teaching procedures, but by actual participation in growth groups. I asked who were the leaders in these groups.

"I'm not really sure," she replied. "You see, we don't always attend the same group. Circulating is encouraged to develop an ability for 'instant immediacy.' Even leaders circulate. It is entirely possible that groups meet occasionally without any leader's being present.

"The truth is," she said, "leaders are awfully hard to

identify here. I suppose it has to do with the whole leadership system."

I confessed that I knew nothing of the system. It now struck me that, while I had seen some persons who appeared to be discussion leaders, I had seen no one whom I would really have taken for a professor.

"Oh," she said, "we don't have professors. Not for years now, I understand. They're all at the GTC. We have only advanced students or facilitators—what they called 'fellows' when I was an undergraduate years ago."

"Wait a minute," I pleaded. "It is all too fast for me. What is GTC?"

"I'm sorry," she said. "GTC is General Theological Center. There are two in this country, you know, one in the East, in New York, and the other in San Francisco. And there are several others around the world. Western Europe has one in Geneva. They are sort of theological think tanks, I suppose you would call them—societies of elitist scholars and terribly creative persons who interact with one another and do their work and then communicate the benefits of it to the various seminaries."

"You mean you never see them? You don't have professors here?"

"Well, it really isn't a problem. We do have the Telly-coms—that's Telecommunication Conferences. They are regular multichannel sessions in which various topics are discussed by all the professors who are concerned with them. Students are on the video too and can enter the discussions. They're often very exciting, especially when one of the facilitators who is especially keen challenges the position of one or more of the professors. Of course that's the way they get to be professors. Only the brightest and most articulate persons are chosen."

"How are they chosen? By a committee?"

"No. They are proposed and voted on by the entire population of students in all the world seminaries."

"Wow."

"Excuse me?"

"I'm sorry," I said. "I was just thinking about how radical that would have sounded when I was a theological student."

"I suppose so. The radicals today are those who insist that the power of selecting professors ought to be vested in the laity of the church. They accuse the seminaries of exclusivism, and of operating too independently of the constituency."

"How do you feel about it?" I asked.

"Oh, I don't know. I suppose I am old enough to be excited by the way things are now. But I have great respect for the arguments of the more radical voices in the church."

"Tellycoms. I must remember that when I wake up," I recall having thought. It seemed such a practical way of reducing overhead by simply avoiding unnecessary duplication of function and labor. And facilitators. I liked the word. I was also fascinated by the global dimension the church and its training centers had apparently adopted.

"Is there considerable unanimity in the world church," I asked, "to enable the various seminaries and centers to conduct profitable joint discussions?"

"Oh, yes," replied my hostess. "Or perhaps the profitable discussions help to provide the unanimity. But, either way, there is a great functional harmony in world

Christianity. Much more than when I was younger. It isn't a unanimity of opinion, you understand. Only a willingness to pursue certain basic goals, with absolute freedom regarding the routes to be taken. There isn't the parochialism of interest there once was. All the issues now—everything from education and agriculture to urbanology and politics—are genuinely global issues."

"Is this a common attitude?"

"I would say it is. The church doesn't get the credit for it, of course. I think people just finally realized that we couldn't inhabit the same terrestrial space any longer without thinking of the whole world and planning for everybody. The church just sort of tuned in on what everybody knew, or at least on what they suspected."

"You mentioned the global issues," I said. "How do the seminary and the church relate to those?"

"I'm sorry—?"

"I mean, how is theology done in relation to all the issues?"

"Oh, I see. Yes. Well, you must understand that theology is no longer regarded as a language unto itself. No respectable theologian, even at the facilitator level, is competent in theology alone. Most are trained in several disciplines, including psychology, sociology, and the various arts. Usually it has to do with personal aptitude. But there are none of the artificial boundaries I remember having encountered as an undergraduate. All disciplines are regarded as tools or techniques for the study of life itself—and the fuller the tool kit the better!

"This philosophy is implemented in the GTCs and in seminaries by involving professors and facilitators whose principal work has lain outside theology per se. They

52

know enough to be conversant theologically—indeed, today even the children in the churches are—but they are really experts in fields such as social engineering, pharmaceutical therapy, and psychoanthropology."

About this time we were interrupted in our pleasant conversation—I had no idea of the time—by my original host, who appeared before us and said that he really wanted me to attend the daily case study with him. I thanked my lady friend, who had entertained me most graciously, and we walked along the curving pathway to a sort of open building where the participants in one of the preannounced case studies were already gathering.

Here, explained my host, we were at the most vital part of the seminary undertaking. All other aspects of the students' training—technical, physical, therapeutic, and even devotional—came into play in these sessions. They were central to the understanding of how the seminary functioned.

A young woman of Oriental descent sat near what I presumed to be the head of the room, there being a large videoscreen on the wall slightly above and to the right of her head. She began the session by addressing the rest of us—perhaps twenty in all—who were seated casually in a sort of oval or circle.

"This is Study Section 18-A," she said. "Our situation for today will now be shown to you."

At once the screen behind her was filled with angry faces, and loud, nearly hysterical voices broke the quietness of the setting. It soon became evident that we were witnessing some kind of political demonstration.

As the film progressed, the story that unfolded went something like this: A city council in a town of approximately two hundred thousand inhabitants had just voted to cancel univehicular service—a kind of centralized transportation service—to an outlying suburban district on the grounds that, federal appropriations having failed to materialize, the city treasury could not afford to continue operations in the area. The enormity of the situation for the residents of the district became apparent to me when it was pointed out by my guide that individual vehicular transportation was no longer permitted within city boundaries, and that nearly three thousand, five hundred men, women, and children would suddenly be left without locomotion for traveling to schools, offices, and commercial destinations within the center of the city. Some would travel by bicycle, very possibly, but many would find the withdrawal of services a severe inconvenience indeed. The persons whose faces had first flashed on the screen were residents of the district who had walked several miles in a march on the offices of the city council and were engaged in a vociferous protest. Two persons were finally arrested, and one woman had to be hospitalized for exhaustion and hypertension.

Now, broadly put, the case study question for the day was: How should the churches of the affected district respond to this emergency in the daily lives of their parishioners?

As discussion proceeded, several facets of the question were delineated.

First, what reaction should be made to the real situation, i.e., the loss of vehicular service? What political force was available in the churches themselves, both the churches within the area and sympathizing churches outside, for redressing the problem? Could legal action be instituted against the federal government, the city government, or both, to restore the service which had been interrupted?

Second, what immediate help could be provided to the inconvenienced persons in the area? For example, what arrangements could be made for delivery of necessary food and other provisions? What emergency measures could be drafted for the continuance of the children's education?

Third, what kinds of forums, if any, should be arranged to provide an airing of the people's grievances? What speakers in the city should be asked to participate in such hearings?

Fourth, how did any of the teachings of Christianity assume particular relevance in this real crisis? What kind of social and personal growth might be aimed at in the solution of the problem?

Soon the group had subdivided into smaller, more manageable units to grapple with the aspects of the situation. The division did not occur haphazardly, but with what appeared to me to be a high degree of orderliness and intelligence—persons having special legal, social, psychological, or other qualifications being deployed to the units where their skills might prove most useful. Almost at once the groups were eagerly at work in various parts of the room, producing a great buzz of argument and conversation.

My host soon fell to discussing the whole plan and merits of the case study system with me, and thereby prevented my following the present topic to its final disposition. But what he had to say proved very enlightening, and I could hardly grieve at having missed any-thing.

There would be much more to the present case than a mere analysis of the factors which had been outlined, he explained. Before they were through, there would prob-ably be some role-playing, in which the most enthusias-tic opponents of the city council's action would be asked to take the council's part, and maybe even a liturgical or homiletical design period, in which the subgroups would cooperate in preparing means of worshiping and celebrat-ing Christian communion which took into full account the problematic situation. There might even be some mini-lectures by any facilitators present on how to improve social, therapeutic, or liturgical skills demonstrated dur-ing the course of the case study.

By this time I was so overwhelmed by the thoughts of such a total learning experience that I am afraid I had very little presence of mind for asking helpful questions.

I did inquire whether there was any connection between this case study method of education and the whole prac-tice of field work as we had known it when I was in semi-nary, to which my patient host replied that field work had long ago been abolished as a second-rate rival of this approach within the seminary itself. It was decided, he said, that the on-the-job experiences, often poorly super-vised, lacked not only the concentrated intensity of the case studies but the important setting of collegiality as well, within which students would be stimulated and in-structed by the display of their friends' imaginations and expertise. Whereas a student in a field-work situation might proceed through three or four major experiences a year, with only sporadic or uneven treatment in a seminar setting, he might reasonably have as many as sixty or seventy such experiences annually in the case studies program.

Briefs of the daily studies, I learned, were circulated among the students several days in advance of the public hearings, so that there was opportunity for research and reflection before actually becoming involved in the sessions themselves. The subjects for the studies ranged widely. Generally they had to do with parish response to such situations as the alarming consumption of sexual pornography by the young; the death of a nonbeliever; the divorce of a prominent parish couple; the defeat of a particularly worthy candidate for political office; the bombing of a small African city by UN containment troops; a devastating flood that had left thousands of tenement families homeless; public indifference to educational method; and subliminal patterns of prejudice on government television channels.

It was primarily for the case studies, which were constantly being changed and renewed, that most of the ministers and laymen returned to seminary once they had left. A month's worth of these sessions, declared my mentor, and they go back to their parishes like new persons!

Many of the case studies, I learned, were brought to the seminary by returning students. Some represented actual incidents which they had had to face in the line of duty. Others were the fruit of imagination and speculation which resulted when the students reflected on the relationship between various life situations and certain theological teachings or positions. All in all, it meant that there was little place in this modern seminary for purely abstract thought or belief. The religion inculcated there was a *commando* religion. Belief was constantly being challenged by real situations.

I could not but concede to my host that it was the most incomparable system I had ever encountered.

But did it mean, I asked, that students never entered upon church vocations during their seminary training? And, if it did, how were their educational expenses defrayed? I remembered the high proportion of students in my day who had to work at some financially gainful employment in order to support themselves and their families.

"Oh, they may work in our local parishes," I was told, "and many in fact do. But not in any remunerative arrangement. They are supported on a *pro rata* basis, according to the size of their families and any other special needs, by the World Church Seminary Fund. It isn't a grand salary, by any means. Like military pay, it isn't enough to attract many persons not seriously interested in the style of life. But it is adequate, is given with no strings attached, and offers the freedom necessary for anyone to become a better servant of the church.

"While here, a person's primary commitment is to life as a student. Hence the student lives in common housing and receives a nominal allowance. Student families are even given special training, for they will be engaged in the same problems and situations. Couples are expected to receive special marital therapy, and children too are exposed to carefully designed programs leading to fuller self-understanding and general awareness. Everything conceivable is done to assure a fuller life-style for those who will try to communicate such a style to other persons. It is all seen as part of the mission of the church."

I heard these last statements of my host with a somewhat troubled consciousness, for I had the feeling that the dream was coming to an end. I think he said other things which I wish I could recall, but the sense of interruption was predominant. It was as if I had been tuned into one radio wavelength, and another were beginning to gain the ascendancy over it.

With a desperate effort to hold on, I thanked my host for his extraordinary kindness to me, and assured him of my genuine pleasure in all that I had seen and heard. I did not hear what he said in reply. His lips moved, I am certain, but at this point the other wavelength took over completely.

I woke that morning to a day of remarkable luminosity, though with a sense of some disappointment that what I had witnessed had been only a dream. Later, after a light breakfast and an animated report to my family of what I had dreamed, I carried my heavy briefcase down the familiar old corridor of my seminary. Somehow what had been familiar now seemed strange to me. I thought of the video consoles and the happy, enthusiastic seminarians at work in the pleasant rooms of my nocturnal imaginings. Wistfully, I placed the briefcase by my desk and began to review a lecture I was scheduled to give at nine to a class of men and women who were counting the days until they were out of seminary and more or less permanently settled in new jobs. Suddenly, even though it was early morning, I was tired. It would be a long day.

But someday—maybe—

July 5

Dear John,

Something wonderful seems to be happening to me. I hate to use the language, because it's so reminiscent of a lot of bad religion that has gone under the bridge for me, but it's like I'm about to be born all over again. Don't ask me how. I just feel it.

Why I can tell you. I've gotten involved in that church that I wasn't too impressed by the first time. I'll write more about it later. Tonight I've got to finish some sketches that are long overdue. The client is flying in tomorrow.

I just wanted you to know.

Love,

M.W.

July 10

Dear M.W.,

I'm hurt. After all my trouble to write down my dream about the seminary of the future, you haven't even mentioned receiving it. Didn't you like it?

I'm kidding, of course. Honestly I'm glad for your sense of excitement--and maybe a little jealous that whatever it is is happening to you and not to me.

Affectionately,

John

July 14

Oh John,

I'm so sorry about your paper. Of course I read it with interest. It was just that I was so absorbed in this other. No, I have to be honest with you. Somehow I couldn't find much enthusiasm for the dream seminary. I thought many of the notions unusual and interesting to consider, but it all seemed so remote from the present situation.

Perhaps my involvement in the church group has blunted my appetite for speculative Christianity. Earlier I might have entered the dream as though it were reality. But now even the most prosaic aspects of this real church situation are more exciting to me than my fantasy world ever was.

Did I tell you I'm on the liturgy committee? For three or four months the committee has been reviewing the history of worship and talking about principles. Well, last week we got down to the business of trying to develop some new liturgies with our particular congregation in mind.

We have this one little old woman who is charged with being our critic. Her name is Norma. I wish you could know her. Norma is supposed to blow the horn whenever she catches us lapsing into mere traditionalism for traditionalism's sake. She's really incredible. A _tiny_ woman, with wiry gray hair which never looks as if it has been brushed. And the most _unreal_ voice. It's sort of shrill and labored, as though she never learned how to make sounds properly. But she has this fantastic gift for just sitting and listening until wham! all of a sudden she spouts off and begins taking apart everything you're doing and telling you what's wrong with all of it, right down to the smallest points.

The first thing we asked, in trying to design a particular liturgy, was what we wanted to do in the service. We were all pretty well agreed, I was surprised to find. We wanted to have a good time. I guess we'd all had it up to here with serious religion. We wanted something that would be fun, that would lift us out of our routine approach to worship and make us really glad we had come. We wanted to do something that would cause people to go away saying, "Gee, that was great. I feel tons better. I feel re-created inside."

Okay, the next question was _how_. What would accomplish this? Games? A _slide_ show? Music? Dancing? Norma interrupted us a couple of times when we were verging on mere gimmickry. Whatever happened, it had to be contextual with the people's inner natures, not something they would be put through the way a dog is made to jump through a hoop.

In the end we decided that rhythm--the natural pulsing of the body--would be essential to what we hoped to achieve. If we

could get people physically involved we would
be halfway home. So we agreed to have a good
combo--drummer, bass, guitar, and maybe a sax-
ophonist. We would use some contemporary mu-
sic--maybe some of Ed Summerlin's jazzy things.
It turns out we've got a couple of hip compos-
ers in the congregation, and someone suggested
that we involve them in doing two or three
pieces. It would be fun to have some original
stuff.

We almost rejected the idea of having any
kind of sermon. We put together some litanies
and other readings using both Scripture and
contemporary things. But Norma held out feet
to the fire on the sermon. We teased her and
said she was the traditionalist. But she was
right, of course--Christianity has always set
some kind of "message" at the heart of its
worship.

So we decided to do a different kind of
sermon. We would videotape the first half of
the service, with the music and rhythm and
all, and then play it back for everybody to
watch. Someone could then give a little meditation on rhythm, being natural, being open
to the world, and so forth. We even made up
a story to go with it, called the Parable of
the Turtle. This turtle, see, lost his shell.
I don't know how he lost it. Maybe he was
taking a bath, and when he came out of the
creek it was gone. Anyway, he was so embar-
rassed about it that for days he wouldn't
leave his hiding place under a tree. But he
finally had to go out to get something to eat,
and was spotted by a frog, a rabbit, and a
chipmunk who were sitting at a toadstool playing cards. He thought he would die of morti-
fication! But the frog, the rabbit, and the
chipmunk liked him without the shell. They
said they felt it was easier to get close to

him. The shell, they confessed, had always
made it hard for them to experience any
intimacy with him.

Norma voiced what I'm sure was a legitimate fear that a lot of people would feel
that they hadn't really been to church after
such a service. So we tried to deal with
this problem by planning an interruption
in which someone would be primed to speak out
and ask what all this has to do with religion.
Then someone else would be ready to respond,
"Everything! Jesus tried to tell us that religion is made for man, not the other way
around. We're trying to be human. We want
to find ourselves and one another. Maybe
sometimes there's too much religion around
for us to do that!"

I could go on and on. We talked about
much more, of course. Anyway, you get the
gist of it. We hope to "perform" the service
the last Sunday of next month. We're going
to try to break the congregation into looking
forward to something new at least once a
month for now, and maybe more often a bit
later.

I wish you'd react to some of this, John.
It should be down your alley.

M. W.

Conversation at the Breakfast Table

Wife: John, did you see that Dalmatian elephant that just walked across our patio?

Me: Mm-hmm.

Wife: Your nose is on fire.

Me: Hmmm?

Wife: What are you preoccupied about?

Me: Who, me? Oh. Sorry. Have the kids left for school?

Wife: Fifteen minutes ago. Didn't you feel the breeze? What are you thinking about?

Me: I wasn't preoccupied.

Wife: Mmmm.

Me: Well. . . . Actually I was thinking about this lecture I have to prepare on the religious education of children and what it ought to be like in the future. I can't figure how to organize it. There are so many strands, so many separate little notions, that I want to incorporate in it. I haven't been able to figure out how to outline the thing to get them all in without simply resorting to a numbers scheme.

Wife: Would it help to talk about it?

Me: I don't know. Sometimes it does.

Wife: What do you want for our own children?

Me: I don't know.

Wife: But you can dictate how it ought to be for somebody else's?

Me: No, no, I don't mean it that way. I mean, there's so much I want that it gets very complex in my mind. I don't know how to begin.

Wife: Well, try this. Why don't you feel it important that our boys go to Sunday school regularly now?

Me: You know why not. We've been through that a thousand times. Because the teachers don't know what they're doing. They aren't in touch with themselves. They don't know anything about theology. They don't know how to evoke anything in the kids. They parrot the lessons. They manipulate the kids. The kids are turned off. The whole thing's a washout. But I don't want to get hung-up on that. That's the negative side, the situation as it is. I want to think about how it ought to be.

Wife: Well, it bothers me that the boys don't know very much about the Bible. At least we learned the Bible in Sunday school, even if we swallowed a lot of prejudices and incorrect ideas too.

CONVERSATION AT THE BREAKFAST TABLE

Me: I guess so. But sometimes I think it would be better not to learn any Bible than to learn it in the crazy, half-baked way we did. It has taken me years to get free of a lot of the claptrap I was saddled with, and I know there's a lot I'll never get free of.

Wife: That's probably true. But does that mean that you wouldn't want children to be taught the Bible in the future?

Me: No, I don't mean that. It is too bound up with our history, with who we are and how we feel and dream, to be left out now. But there has to be a new approach. Maybe teachers could be sent to a special training school for a few weeks and given an immersion course in how the Bible came into being, what our attitude toward it ought to be, and how to impart a proper attitude toward it to the children. I want the boys to understand it as the record of an ancient people's struggles with religious and ethical problems, not as the final statement of what we should believe and how we should live today. They could do worse than live up to the Bible, to be sure. But I don't want them indentured to its systems. I want them to understand its achievements in terms of freedom from bondage, whether that bondage is being trapped in the self or being trapped in a religious system. I want them to see it as a launching pad, not a landing platform.

Wife: Freedom is awfully hard to live with. It has put its strains on us.

Me: Yes. But maybe it won't be so hard for them if they grow up understanding it. We had to learn that you pay a price for nonconformity, that many people are afraid of the very appearance of freedom and try to eradicate it, often going out of their way to do so. But maybe, if we had been taught this as children, if our teachers had talked about the Cross in terms of Jesus' choice of manhood and death over conformity and permission to go on living, we would have grown up hardier and wouldn't feel the strain so much.

Wife: They're good boys.

Me: We've spent a lot of time on them. What I would like to see in the churches is an educational process that would take part of the load off the parents. No, not that, I guess. What I mean is, I wish the churches could be counted on to supplement what we do, which would make our burden easier. And there are a lot of homes where the parents make little or no effort at training their children morally and spiritually. What the kids learn is often wrong and perverse. They become entangled in the same twisted mess that snares the parents.

Wife: Maybe ours do too.

Me: Yes, I thought of that as I said what I did. How do we know that we are teaching our boys the right things? Maybe a good church program would serve as a guarantee or an antidote or something like that.

CONVERSATION AT THE BREAKFAST TABLE

Wife: I hear you saying two things: We have to educate the children in the home, but we can't do it all; there needs to be some kind of systematic approach by trained Christian educators.

Me: Right. I'm sure we could educate our children in a secular fashion in the home—reading, math, languages, and all that. But not nearly so effectively as they do it in school. Kids need peer groups, learning models, study motivations, visual aids, and lots of other things which we can't provide as well as the schools. And the same goes for religious education. We're only limping along now. The church of the future has got to take its educational program more seriously, the way the schools do. One reason the boys give for not going to Sunday school is that it's not up to their weekday standards. Teachers unprepared, rooms dull and messy, lessons irrelevant and unexciting—the whole thing.

Wife: I remember how thrilled both boys were last summer with their Christian day camp experiences. Do you remember how happy they were to go off every morning? Krister's group erected a tent and lived as if they were biblical characters, eating raisins and nuts, and even making themselves shepherds' costumes.

Me: And when the teacher said they could all pick biblical names for themselves . . .

Wife: And Krister said he reckoned "God" would be all right with him! That little bug! And Eric was in seventh heaven out on the farm, fishing crayfish out of the stream, eating watermelon, and talking about God and nature. They were so elated. Why can't church school be like that all the time?

Me: You're right. Then they would want to go. We wouldn't have all the Sunday morning hassles over whether we ought to go to Sunday school or not. Which may be the handle I'm looking for, a way into my lecture. I'd like it to convey something of the excitement that good Christian education could generate. A lively learning process always stimulates people. We like to learn, because to learn is to grow. It's the stagnation we can't handle—the stagnation and repetition.

Wife: What kinds of things do you think would make church school exciting in this way?

Me: Well, first, teachers who've had some training and know what they're doing. I don't think paid teachers is the answer—if teachers can grow along with their students, I think they'll find it worth their while on a commitment basis, without financial reward. Second, I think place is important. Nobody wants to go sit in a dingy little room that smells of mold or old choir robes. More thought should be given to the architectural context for Christian education. Little children, for instance, would love rooms of molded plastic like the inside of a whale. Third . . .

Wife: Do you remember the night we went over to the Randolphs' and had a happening with the children? Dave and Davie blew up that plastic balloon in the backyard, and we all crawled in. The Ochsen-riders were there too, and he played his guitar and we sang. And we talked about Jonah and the whale, and the children made finger paintings of what they thought about during the story, and then we put them on the topside of the balloon facing down so we could look up at them? That was a memorable experience. The boys talked about it for weeks.

Me: Exactly. And we enjoyed it too. How often does that much imagination go into planning a church school class? But you could even have fixed architecture that would be more exciting than what we have now. Why, teen-agers would love a molded cave with psychedelic lights and posters for their meeting place. It would create the kind of ambience they enjoy.

Wife: I interrupted you. I'm sorry. You were going to say "third."

Me: No matter. The word "create" is the key to it anyway. I think it is important to make church school a place where creation is taking place constantly, where the children are involved in making, thinking, and doing. Most church educators persist in the old "I've got the information, you open your hatch and I'll pour it in, then you repeat it back to me so I'll be sure you got it" game. But we've got to get to the place where we understand that what the children have to offer is important too. Maybe play theology will get us to the point someday where we'll realize this.

71

I don't think Rousseau and Wordsworth—and Jesus—were entirely wrong in their opinion that we can learn from the children. Maybe we don't listen to them enough. I think a good teacher listens as much as he or she talks. Children should be allowed to vent their fantasies without having them shot down like clay pigeons.

Wife: I hope our children never lose their sense of inventiveness. I think it is amazing what they draw and write, the little plays they make up, the things they invent . . .

Me: For example, they should be permitted to draw their own images of God and then talk about them. They have a sense of God. I know they do. It just isn't so refined and dogmatic as ours. It is probably much more physical and inarticulable than ours—which may mean it is actually superior, for they can feel it more deeply. Drawing pictures of God, as an example, would be an experience in shaping their thoughts about him, in struggling for articulation. Maybe a child would represent God as a peacock, with lots of eyes that watch over him, or as a tree with strong branches that shelter from the sun and rain.

Wife: The important thing is that no teacher should jump over those attempts at early recognition and identification and simply go bingo! here's the answer, God looks like this, with every hair in place!

Me: That's right. Learning is a meeting. It is the junction where what a person feels and is only beginning to conceptualize within him suddenly touches and forms a bridge to what is out there in the world. This is a process that ought to go on continuously in all of us. The meetings should always be tentative, never finalized or crystallized. They may be only preparatory to other meetings which are more significant. If we fixate on the first meetings, we abort the later ones. Which, I am afraid, is what most doctrinaire Christian education does. It forecloses the options by trying to pass on the answers it accepts as the final ones.

Wife: If we had open-ended Christian education in our church schools, wouldn't it affect what happens in the entire church—in worship, for example?

Me: Yes, I think it would. Maybe for the better. We might be more in the mood for celebration when we worship, because we would be making new discoveries all the time. Revelation wouldn't be something sealed and settled centuries ago. It would be going on in our midst, and we would feel like shouting hallelujah.

Wife: Or eureka!

Me: Right.

Wife: Have another cup of coffee.

Me: Okay. But let me go on a minute. I don't mean that we shouldn't have any structures. Learning doesn't take place in a vacuum. I only think there should be more options, more freedom for the learners to expand at their own rates—that sort of thing.

Wife: You mean optional classes?

Me: Yes, that would be part of it, only with options within the classes too. I think children who have reached a certain age and are exercising choices in secular school settings should have the same kind of opportunity in the church. We do it for adults, but I haven't noticed its being done much for the youngsters.

Wife: I've noticed in Eric that interest in a subject varies from time to time, and he does well in proportion to how interested he is.

Me: Maybe I could devise a sample offering of courses. There might be some straight Bible courses for those who wanted them, arranged either by book or by topic. By topic I mean such subjects as "Young People in the Bible," "The Cities of the Bible," "The Teachings of Jesus for Young People," and the like. Then there could be a variety of other courses, such as "How to Deal with Parents," "How to Recognize Your Inner Self," "What to Do with Spare Time," "Working out a Value System" . . .

Wife: "The Christian and Drugs," "The Christian and Sex." I see what you mean. I can imagine Eric if he were confronted by a range of choices like that. He wouldn't know which door to go in at first, he would want to go to so many.

Me: I think a lot of kids would even be interested in courses in church history. They have learned a lot about the world by the time they're in fourth or fifth grade. Maybe they would be ready for some serious study in the way the faith moved through the ages. They could do imaginative things like sit around the table and role-play their way through a creed-writing session, as if they were the Council of Nicaea or Chalcedon. It would help them to understand that creeds are partly political contrivances, arrived at by debate and compromise, not divine decree. Then, when they said the Apostles' Creed in church, they would know what they were doing.

Wife: Maybe. But it sounds a bit heavy to me. They have a lot of that during the week.

Me: I don't mean it should be done in a dull, methodical way. Learning is tedious only when we become conscious of it as something we have to do. For instance, they love films. But how many times do they see good films in church school? They love writing plays and acting them out. How many times do they do that in church school? You know how they will take down the *World Book* and research a point for hours if it's for something they're caught up in. Well, I think Christian education could live the same way if we could only reconceive it on a rather massive scale and implement a new way of doing it.

Wife: I like the role-playing idea you mentioned a minute ago. I think they would enjoy that. They could also prepare art exhibits. And they love music. Why couldn't they compose songs and sing them, or even have a combo and beat out some new music?

Me: That's the point. As long as they are involved in
the creating, in what is going on, they're happy.
And they learn far more that way than by sitting
in a chair and having a lesson drummed into them.
What we're talking about is a new attitude in the
church toward its mission in education. A lot of
these innovations we've mentioned are already
being tried sporadically around the country, and
with a fair measure of success in most places.
But we've a long way to go in terms of total
church attitude. We have to see that our job
isn't just transmitting a body of data, more or
less intact, from generation to generation. We do
have something to transmit, I believe. But it's
just as important to let what is transmitted interact
with the new context, so that faith becomes a joy,
not a burden, a thing that lives and breathes in
us, not a bundle of musty sayings out of the past.
We can't be afraid of the results. The process
must be free to go where it will. If we try to
program the ends or goals, the whole game is
rained out. We've got to let it happen.

Wife: There's one other thing I wish our children would
get in church school, partly because I feel so in-
adequate to deal with it myself.

Me: What's that?

Wife: I wish they would get some real help in dealing
with human crises like illness and death and betrayal. As it is, we usually learn to cope with these
things when we have to. We blunder through
somehow, if we're lucky. But it seems to me there

ought to be a way of preparing children to face them, so that when they occur the children rise to meet them as naturally as they rise to meet new demands in science or English composition.

Me: It sounds like a good idea to me. Probably one reason we haven't done it is that there aren't many adults who have really learned to cope with crises. But that's only another argument for initiating the children and giving them some honest-to-goodness training before the actual situations arise. I'm afraid we have been far more interested in social control—you know, thou shalt not steal, thou shalt not kill, thou shalt not commit adultery —than we have in equipping people to meet the inner strains and demands.

Wife: And I don't mean giving them pat little answers for these problems, like holding out heaven as the compensation for death. I mean really working through an understanding of grief and what is involved in the loss of a loved one. Children can grasp such things. Maybe they don't become real until someone actually dies, but the ground work would be there.

Me: I remember that Toffler said in *Future Shock* that schools ought to depart from the old trivium-quadrivium arrangement and offer courses in contemporary subjects as well. What you are suggesting is that the church do the same thing.

Wife: Exactly. If our theology has nothing to do with these questions, then it is worthless anyway. But if it does have something to do with them, I'd like to see it fleshed out in them.

Me: Which is precisely the idea of the incarnation.

Wife: I didn't mean to divert you or take over the conversation, but there is one other thing you haven't mentioned, and I think maybe it's important too.

Me: What's that?

Wife: You haven't said anything about time. Do you think the present Sunday morning arrangement is sufficient to undertake the kinds of things we're talking about, or would we have to rethink the whole matter of schedule?

Me: Well, I wouldn't say it isn't important. It is possible to do a lot of innovating within the present structures. But McLuhan has driven home to us how important the media are and how they often speak louder than any message that's being programmed through them. As time is a medium, I guess a lot is said in our society by the fact that our kids spend five days in school and maybe an hour in church classes on Sunday morning. It isn't any wonder that they have the feeling religious education isn't important.

Wife: I wonder if they would feel the same way about secular education if the situation were reversed and they spent five days a week in church and one hour in school.

Me: I guess I'm not prepared to say how we can alter the time schedule we now have. There are several possibilities of course. Released time from daily classes is one of them. Evening sessions at the church is another. Saturday mornings is another.

Wife: What about summers? Why couldn't churches do a lot more with the summer months than they do? I think the kids would be glad for something to do after about two weeks at home.

Me: That's also a possibility, though it may not be for long if the twelve-month school programs being experimented with in some places catch hold. I suppose I am more concerned at this point about the nature of what takes place in religious education than I am about the calendar or the clock. Even with the present arrangement for meeting an hour or two a week, it seems possible to me for us to better utilize the time as an integrating factor in children's total schedules. As it is, we now ignore most of what our children are doing in weekday schools when we plan their learning experiences in Sunday school. I mean, we simply add another segment to their fund of knowledge, without trying to pull together and build upon what they have already done.

Wife: I think I'm following, but go a little further.

Me: Why couldn't our curriculum planners incorporate into the experiences in Christian education more of what our children are doing during the week? For example, Eric is now studying Africa and Asia in his social science class. He's excited about it. He does extra assignments on tribal customs, dress, and so forth. Why not coordinate church activities with that so as to take advantage of it? He could study African and Asian religions and learn how they reflect or help to shape the cultures they represent. Through comparative methods, he would also learn a great deal about the Christian faith he does not presently know or understand.

Wife: And even math and science could form the background for discussions of how we know our world, how the knowledge affects us, how it changes our lives . . .

Me: And how it changes our religion!

Wife: Mmmm. That's something to think about. It's a little frightening, but it's also exciting.

Me: It may also seem discouraging when you think how far it is from where we are now in our practice of Christian education. Yet it's in line with what I think should be the general aim or purpose of Christian training.

Wife: What is that?

Me: I think Christian education ought really to put a person in touch with himself and with the world he lives in, and do it in such a way that the history and meaning of the faith are seen as being characteristic of in-touchness. It should help the person to feel more at home in the creation, and, reciprocally, to become more responsible for it. This would mean assisting him to become more secure in his relations with other persons as well as more knowledgeable about the larger society and environment. I know we have much overused the word *celebration* in recent years, but I think it is still applicable. Christian education should evoke a sense of loving relationship between the individual and everything that impinges on his life, excepting evil, of course, so that he learns to live in a mood of discovery and celebration.

Wife: We always had a much more evangelistic emphasis in our training.

Me: Yes, but this is evangelism too, of a very high sort. It is good news when a person gets in touch with himself. It is good news when he gets in touch with his world.

Wife: But that's so much less tangible than Jesus Christ as the good news. Do you think the majority of church people will ever buy it?

Me: That's a hard question. I think more and more are buying it now.

Wife: Maybe Jesus means sensitivity.

Me: I'm sure he does, among other things.

Wife: I'm sensitive to one thing.

Me: What's that?

Wife: You won't get your lecture written if you don't get up from this table and go to your office.

Me: You're right. And dear—

Wife: Hmmm?

Me: Did you notice what happened while we were talking?

THE SECOND COMING OF THE CHURCH

Wife: No, what?

Me: A hippogriff laid an egg in our birdbath.

October 3

Dear John,

It has been so long since either of us has written.

I hardly know where to begin. I guess it's best to start with the biggest news first. I'm going to build a church! Our congregation has grown so much that we've decided to acquire new property and erect a suitable building, and I have agreed to do the plans as an offering to the church.

I'm so thrilled! We have a large committee at work now trying to factor out the theological and practical dimensions before we decide how to plan the space. It's time-consuming--I guess we met for a total of twenty hours last week. But it's a great experience.

Our monthly innovative services have been a huge success. Last month we did something inspired by Zen Buddhism. We had some Oriental music and a short explanation of Zen by a local religion professor. We tried to meditate for a few minutes, concentrating on the void out of which all of life's illusions rise. We even had some Zen mondos, alternating with brief sayings of Jesus, read as part of the sermon. It's amazing how Oriental the words of Jesus seem when given a setting like that.

A lot of people have suggested we go to a 2/2 plan, with two traditional and two novel services each month, but we frankly couldn't come up with more than one well-planned thing a month. Besides, I think most of us want the newness to remain and are afraid that too much of it might erode the novelty.

I'm with a new firm now (note stationery!). Better position, more pay. I don't enjoy the general tone as much, but it's improving. And there is less travel involved, which I like, especially now that I have this whole church building to do by myself!

Do write. I miss our correspondence.

Cordially,

M. W.

October 8

Dearest M. W.,

I apologize and will try to do better. I've been trying to finish a book and have been busy with students. Time has simply flown.

Congratulations on the new job and on tackling your own church building. It must really put pressure on you to do a building for the congregation you worship with. You can't just walk off and leave it afterwards. You'll have to look at it every week.

How do you feel now regarding what you said that time about flexible space? Has your experience in this church confirmed what you projected about the need for small, intimate rooms, or are you going for a large corporate space?

You know, I've always wished for a sanctuary where the seating was tiered in a cone, with the table and place for the Liturgist or preacher down in the vortex and the people gathered around facing one another. I think it would symbolize the unity of the congregation as well as serve the practical purpose of really putting persons in eye-to-eye contact with each other.

I'm glad you're finding your church so fulfilling. I'm still looking, but I hear of many interesting things happening here and there across the country. Maybe church is coming back, only differently. I hope so.

Blessings,

J.

October 20

Dear John,

I do think church is coming back, only differently, as you put it.

I have a theory that there is a kind of lag between where the culture is and where the church is at any given moment. The forward-thinking Christians are always complaining about this, and the others are glad for it and try to delay the closing of the gap as much as possible.

I used to think I couldn't tolerate the church because the second group always seemed to have its way. But I see it differently now. I think the church invariably pursues the times, whether we help it or not. The secular consciousness eventually invades it

even though people try to stop it. The conservatives usually lose in the end.

Maybe I'm wrong, but at least thinking
this way has made me more tolerant of the
people who are less open to change. I feel
sorry for them, and sometimes I want to stand
in front of them and fend off the changes that
frighten and disturb them so.

I do think the church is coming alive in
our time again. It may not be avant-garde or
anything like that. Maybe it can't be, with
all sorts of people in it. But there do seem
to be evidences of a spirit at work, don't you
think?

Hopefully,

M. W.

October 27

Dear M. W.,

By all means! Maybe what you are experiencing is the second coming of the church.
There is always a lot of talk about the second coming of Christ. If the church is his
body, as Paul said it was, then why shouldn't
there be a second coming of the church?

Sincerely,

John

The Modern Saint

How do I see the saint of this new age?

I will tell you.

He (or she) is not a pietist in the old sense.

He is not especially submissive to any order or system.

He is not straining to get to heaven.

He is not looking for any awards or certificates. Neither does he lust after headlines, TV interviews, nor praise from his associates.

He is not automatically opposed to strong drink or drugs, and he is no more chaste than others are. In fact, his morals are often questionable to those who put great stock in such things.

He does not care greatly for college degrees, ecclesiastical titles, or job security. He probably does not believe in saints and might laugh in your face if you called him one.

It is possible that he doesn't believe in anything very strongly, or at least will tell you such. Not even in God the Father, God the Son, and God the Holy Ghost. And not even in Truth with a capital T.

In fact, the new saint is sometimes hard to tell from a lot of people you know. He doesn't wear a long white robe or a look of beatific surrender on his face. And he doesn't carry a sign that says "saint" in Old English lettering.

This is a Zen trick, of course, saying what something is by saying what it is not. The *roshi* or Zen master often deals with questions about the nature of Zen the same way. "It is not this . . . or that . . . or the other." Sometimes it is effective. The disciple will be driven to discovering for himself what Zen is.

But I shall not leave you dangling—on one condition. You must not hold me accountable for everything I am about to say. Instead, you must weigh what is said against what you know of saints in the modern world. For you may already know more than you have realized.

One thing is sure: There will be ambiguities in the portrait, areas of patchiness and shadow where we cannot draw the lines clearly. There may even appear to be contradictions which cannot be understood apart from a deeper knowledge of some particular saints. You would suspect something if it were otherwise, for everything in the world is unclear today.

But no matter. Life itself is a hazard.

For a beginning, let us say that the saint today is a person in touch with himself and his world. Even before he is in touch with God he is in touch with himself—his body, his feelings, his patterns of behavior, his carnality.

This is important, for it saves him from gnosticism. When he hears someone say that God became flesh he knows what God became because he knows the flesh. He does not recoil from it as though it were inferior to spirit. He does not try to escape from it as though it were his enemy. He knows it is his friend, or will be if treated properly. He has little use for those grotesque portraits of sainthood which survive in caricature from the Middle Ages—gaunt, haggard figures emaciated by fasting and discolored by time spent in dark chapels and other tombs of prayer. The world is good in his theology. The body is good. He does not need to save either by telling beads in a closet.

This philosophy of life is closer to that of Father Zossima, the old monk in Dostoevski's *The Brothers Karamazov,* who said: "Love to throw yourself on the earth and kiss it. Kiss the earth and love it with an unceasing, consuming love. Love all men, love everything. Seek that rapture and ecstasy. Water the earth with the tears of your joy and love those tears. Don't be ashamed of that ecstasy, prize it, for it is a gift of God and a great one; it is not given to many but only to the elect."

Where did we get the idea that a saint is one who moves through the world as though not seeing it, in whose eyes is the image of some distant city not made with hands? Were we betrayed by the words of men who faced death daily as martyrs and needed some prop for their loyalty? Did they teach us that being religious means wearing blinders so that we will not be tempted to enjoy the world our Creator has made? Would they say the same thing now if they were here and if no noose were around their necks?

To be sure, a saint sees what will be, or can be, as well as what is, and disciplines himself for the sake of his children and future generations. But he knows better than to mortgage the present always to the future, the future that never comes, the future that has a way of clinging to the horizon. Life is more than vision, even though there are times when vision sustains life. There is a balance in these matters, and the saint is careful that the fulcrum not be adjusted too much in favor of what is to be, slighting what is.

The cynic, it has been said, is a person who knows the price of everything and the value of nothing. Perhaps a saint is one who knows the price of nothing and the value of everything.

I remember the story a friend told me about Clarence Jordan, the missionary-preacher who founded Koinonia Farms to help the blacks in Georgia, and was, for his troubles, cursed, beaten, shot at, and burned out more times than he ever bothered to count. The friend had gone down to Americus to pay his final respects a few days after Jordan's funeral. Making his way through the piney woods on the back side of the farm, my friend arrived at the clearing where the body of the dead man lay beneath an unmarked mound of red clay earth. He found two girls, apparently the daughters of farmers, stretched out on the mound, sunbathing in the nude. "I couldn't help thinking," said the friend, "how delighted Jordan would have been!"

It is a picture I treasure, for it says much of the man's humanity. I warm to him, even though I never knew him, for he obviously loved life and all its incongruities.

Maybe it is a care for the incongruities that first identifies the modern saint. He sees the humor in what God has made, perhaps as an extension of the Creator himself, and there is always a twinkle in his eye or the trace of a smile on his lips. The love of the Creator has become incarnate in the face of a man beholding what the Lord has made. It is etched in the wrinkles that tell of joy and laughter.

THE SECOND COMING OF THE CHURCH

Picasso was a kind of saint. He celebrated the world for a long time. He painted ducks with no feet and tables with no legs and women who look like no women men ever saw. He made us grin at what we had been seeing almost forever, only now it was as if we were seeing for the first time. He distorted almost everything he touched, in order to make the visible truly visible, and, in so doing, delivered back to us the world we almost lost.

That is what I meant by being in touch with the self and the world. When God appears, it is not in spectral formlessness, but in what he has made. We love him by loving his earth. We celebrate him in the joy and laughter. And the Jordans and Picassos become our votary priests.

By the same token, the contemporary saint is also a realist. Because he sees the world as it is, without blinders, he deals with it as it is. This is not to say that he holds no vast prophetic templates in his head, no imaginative visions of what the world might become with a little help or a little force in the right places, only that he does not expect God to bring in the Kingdom without a struggle in the undramatic but most desperately real places in all creation—in congresses and parliaments, in the offices of newspaper editors and petty politicians, in voting booths and schoolrooms and hospital corridors and television studios—in short, wherever human life is bought and sold or human opinion formed and manipulated.

He knows, our saint does, that there is no victory without many victories—maybe countless victories, indistinguishable victories, so small and thankless as to seem meaningless in themselves. Therefore he is more a particularist than a universalist. Instead of clasping his hands and talking, talking, talking of the cataclysmic end of things when God will see to it that the last become first and the first last—as preachers have been wont to do—he rolls up his sleeves and pitches in to elect better candidates, build better schools, enact better legislation. . . .

But you get the picture. He is something of an activist. It is not that he has not dreamed of a heavenly city, the New Jerusalem, as we all have—only that, having dreamed it, he is at work to build it up, stone by stone, instead of waiting for it to descend out of the blue, as earlier saints sometimes did.

This is one reason he is no moralist. He believes, and convinces me, that moralism was made for man, not man for moralism. In this sense I was wrong in saying that he knows the price of nothing but the value of everything. He does know the price of everything, and he is usually willing to pay it, if the value is right too. He is not crippled by allegiance to mythical codes of honor which owe their existence more to the novel of manners and prewar Hollywood than to either biblical religion or genuine piety.

For the moment, at least, he appears to be something of an anti-institutionalist. Like the Spocks and Berrigans and Angela Davises, he senses that the forms of government itself have gone awry, and are less than satisfactorily responsive to the needs of individuals and minority groups. Perhaps it isn't that government and other forms of bureaucracy, including ecclesiastical hierarchies, have grown worse, becoming more sordid and putrescent with age, but only that the saints have become more sensitive. The experience of the Bonhoeffers and Niemöllers makes us wary: Suppose complacency towards the concentration of power and corruptness in high places is actually a manifestation of the demonic in our world. In that case, eternal vigilance *is* the price of freedom, and the saint does well to be distrustful of any amalgamation of forces over his life and the lives of others. It is here that his realism becomes most apparent. For, while he loves the earth and daily celebrates its basic goodness, he nevertheless appreciates the power of the unruly and demonic to distort and render painful the normative modes of human existence. Biting the end of his cigar and looking much less heroic than an out-sized John Wayne, he settles back with a child in his arms and rests a machine gun on one knee, waiting for the greedy killers who he knows will be coming after the child's legacy.

It is in this sense that our saint is also radically—Is the phrase Bonhoeffer's?—a man for others. There is no heroism implied in that. He is not consciously a martyr. Others may make him one, though that comes later. He merely has an innate feeling of involvement in, and commitment to, the society he lives in.

Maybe, if phrases have a way of bringing the world around, it was John Donne who is largely responsible for the unconscious acknowledgment of the idea that "no man is an island" and that whatever affects a single person in this world affects all the others too, however subtly and immeasurably.

The modern saint knows this. He knows it without asking or thinking about it. It is in his bones to know it. In this sense he is not just man but Man. What is done to him in Pakistan or Vietnam or Biafra affects him in Paris, Auckland, or St. Louis. When an infection attacks one part of his organism, he knows he will feel it all over, or, if his feelings are not refined enough, that he will suffer from it all over without knowing why he is suffering. Therefore he does not ask whether starving people must be fed in this place, or political oppression stopped in this, or health services provided in this. It is no question. There is no such thing as sacrifice. There is only a need and the reflexive action to meet it.

Again at this point our saint feels the inadequacy, the sometimes hopeless awkwardness, of institutional agencies in relieving distress. He sees golden pipelines being laid to provide a trickle of moisture after men have died of thirst. He cannot wait, and bolts ahead to carry the water himself, or, if he cannot carry enough, to organize smaller, more efficient bucket brigades to do the job that must be done now, not ten years from now. It is not that he does not appreciate the importance of building for tomorrow and all the tomorrows after that; he pays taxes for that. But his love of life has bred in him a sense of immediacy. He knows that some people can't wait. They are living now . . . hurting now . . . dying now. Therefore he charters an airplane, when refugees are dying of starvation in an African nation, loads it with foodstuffs, and cuts the red tape by flying an unauthorized mission of mercy, or he donates a month's salary to some revolutionary organization whose personnel he may not actually like but whose ends he approves and believes ought to be facilitated for the sake of some people he has never met whose skins are a different color from his and who speak in a language he could not begin to understand. He is not always right in his judgments, and probably contributes sometimes to the wrong causes, but he can never be faulted for his impulses, which are invariably humanitarian and, therefore, in the best sense of that word, godly.

It was the late Thomas Merton, who, as a product of the church trying to mediate between former and more recent understandings of saintliness, said in *Life and Holiness* that the best way to know the will of God is to ask: "What is best for the people around me?" That, to me, makes eminently better sense than retiring to one's closet and trying to make a decision about which way to go by insisting of the Lord that he reveal the answer. As one who used to try the latter way, I confess that it usually produced more heat than light. That is, it generated a great deal of anxiety in me about whether I was doing the right thing without providing the genuine guidance which I needed and desired. But to draw aside and ask, "Lord, what is best for the others?"—*that* I have found to be singularly instructive, and the answers that have come to me thereby, when I have followed them, have always seemed to me beyond impeachment, even years afterwards.

It may be recalled that Simone Weil, that remarkable Alsatian woman, drew from just such a principle her strength not to join the church. She said in her letters to a priest that she had wanted very much to become a part of the visible body of Christ, but could not because it would cut her off from those she loved and wanted to help.

This is perhaps hard for some Christians to understand, yet it is very much a part of the ambiguity of the contemporary scene in which persons become saints. The church, no less than the government, lapses into mere officiality and institutionalism. Worse, the church in its instinct for institutional survival unconsciously supports

existence that he prefers to postpone the beatific vision of the deity until his beatific picture of creation has been more nearly approximated.

It was Rilke, I believe, who wrote that God is too difficult for us, and that we must defer him for the present in order to do slowly the long work that separates us from him. That is the essence of our new saint's thinking.

I have said nothing of his relationship to Christ, the archetypal saint, the Holy One of Israel. I have purposely omitted this part of the discussion until last, thinking it would not be so easily grasped until now.

We are accustomed, ever since Paul's time, to speak of the saint as a man in Christ. I do not say there is anything wrong with this. The phrase "in Christ" expresses what the fellowship of all saints is about. It bespeaks the feeling of unity among those whose lives count together against whatever imprisons the spirit of man. The Roman centurion who ministered to the prisoners in his care, the copyist who spent his life tracing out the Scriptures in his own language, the abolitionist who died in what was for him a war of principle, the missionary who labors to bring education to an illiterate people—all these and millions more are gathered up in the notion of a mighty sainthood, a collective body of those who have seen the example of Jesus and having seen have become followers in the way.

Yet we seem to be witnessing a new phenomenon in our time: a saint who thinks of himself not so much as a disciple or follower but as a lonely individual who does what must be done. In other words, he is not *in* Christ, he *is* Christ. This is not to say that he is arrogant or pretentious; on the contrary, he manifests a spirit of humility and self-reflection. But he often acts with the feeling that there is no one else in the world to know or care what he is doing—indeed, that there is not even a cloud of witnesses to cheer his sacrifices or cure his isolation.

Perhaps it is only the deep sense of alienation that has settled over our culture generally. Most of us today suffer at one time or another from the Kafka syndrome. We feel cut off—from history, from family, from intimates, even from reason and meaning. We have a sense of what the German philosopher Heidegger calls *Gewörfenheit*—the experience of being cast onto an empty stage without any script or cues. In such a culture, the saint naturally feels cut off too, even from God. The God most spoken of is the God of history. And if ours is a time different from all others, and therefore anti-historical, the most sensitive figures of the age cannot fully accept the traditional God. The saint must wait in what Nietzsche called the time between the times, when neither what was nor what will be is quite clear or embraceable. He is almost, in that sense, a saint without God. Not really or ultimately, but practically.

When he steps into the fray, then, when he goes forward to die, it is without the kind of universal assurance which saints of earlier ages appear to have experienced. He is not buoyed up by the hope of a heavenly compensation, of legions of angels rushing forward to lay garlands on his neck. On the contrary, he is smitten with the same existential loneliness we detect in the accounts of Jesus himself, culminating in the famous cry of dereliction from the Cross. If anything, he is even lonelier than Christ, for the disjunction between himself and the body of religious truth is even more pronounced, and the enterprise of faith more desperate. Belief has worn thin. There are moments when not even the work of Christ himself appears to have been vindicated, when the accounts of such vindication—as the Resurrection was intended to be—seem tarnished by the possibility of fabrication or wishful thinking. The pressure of history in such moments becomes negative and suggests the futility of every righteous act or intention.

All the more reason to view this person as saint. He embodies the holiness, he sanctifies us, because he behaves as he does in the face of apparently overwhelming odds, and without vindication. Who is to say he is not Christ, or Christ is not a succession of Christs? Perhaps the *kenosis* or self-emptying of the eternal which Paul spoke of in Philippians was not a one-shot affair, as we had assumed, but a continuing activity of God. Where is it most likely that we are to see the spirit descending today? In the spiritual aristocracy, which is a direct extension of the New Testament events, i.e., the scribes and Pharisees of Christendom? Or, again as before, in the unlikeliest candidates, the stones our contemporary builders would reject? The saint is, after all, the residence of the holiness of God in the world. And the holiness of God— well, it is that which produces tensions between the lower and higher parts of our selves, or between the evil and the good in our world. Thrust into our midst like a catalytic finger, it electrifies us and produces crisis. We are judged forever—affected hereinafter by how we respond. The saint is the bringer of this electrolysis. We are damned or saved by his presence.

THE SECOND COMING OF THE CHURCH

Who would want to be a saint? No one in his right mind, surely, for it is painful to be the catalyst. The self is exhausted in the work it is put to. Moreover, the saint is often abused by the very persons he helps the most. It is even possible that his effectiveness as saint or sancti-fier exists in inverse proportion to the alienation he experi-ences. Kierkegaard understood this, and wrote of how he would provoke his enemies into killing him, if necessary, in order to redeem them.

But the remarkable thing is—I am convinced of this —there is more willingness among people to be saints today than ever before. Even to be saints without God. In a day when the very word *God* is too much preempted by Christendom, so that it is associated with all that is tyrannous and manipulative in the structures of human existence, it may be necessary to be saints *in spite of* God—*that* God, at least—and the image of Promethean-ism is once more very strong in the earth. Certainly it is a fact which we should celebrate, for it must obviously gladden the heart of the transcendent One who, when-ever his name becomes too familiar among the peoples of the world—so that it is spoken both in jest and in vain—takes another, vouchsafed only to a few prophets, them-selves unwelcome in the homes of men.

All this is to say that the church today may have much to hope for in its future—but not where it is most likely to look for hope, in the forms and images by which it presently recognizes itself. The work of God in Christ—in *all* his Christs—goes on continuously, reclaiming its anonymity as it goes.

In the final consummation, if we may speak thus con-fidently of something we shall probably always experience only in part, God is expected to put all evil under his feet and under the feet of his Christ, whose name is to be called by every man, woman, and child in creation. But we may well be surprised at those who appear then as Christ—the unexpected saints and saviors of the world.

No eye has seen, nor ear heard, the joy that will then be felt by all.

November 20

Dear John,

Thanks for letting me see the ms. Yes, I am glad for you to use my letters if you want to. But please disguise my name if you will. I am not ready for any kind of fame just now. It might destroy my credibility as a modern saint!

I liked many of the things you said about saints today. I tried to reflect on that essay in light of your comment in the letter about the second coming of the church.

Seeing all these pieces and letters together, way back to our original conversation on the plane, gave me a new perspective on my local church experience. What I understand now that I didn't before is that the diffusion of the church in the world is as much a part of the second coming as what goes on inside the church itself. It's as though the aura of Christianity, and even its main teachings, had escaped from their original container and were loose everywhere.

When you do find a good church, then, as I have, it's as much a reflection of the Chris-

tianity at work in the world as it is of
what has been preserved in the church.

I like this discovery, for it gives me
a real sense of the grace of God underlying
everything. He takes care of the church even
when we think it's about to die, and, lo and
behold, it comes back stronger than ever!
Send me a copy of the book, and I'll
send you pictures of the new church. By that
time, there should be something to photo-
graph.

Faithfully,

M. W.

P.S. (On the back of the envelope) The one
thing that seems to be missing from the ms.
is a discussion of the new theology. I only
now realized that, after reading the letter.
Can you talk about the church of the future
without saying something about its beliefs?

November 29

Dear M. W.,

You are too sharp! Of course, you are
right about the church's being revived by the
world--it is another instance of bread cast
upon the waters returning to bless its source.
Maybe that is why it is so hard to talk about
theology and why I avoided it.
Surely the theology of tomorrow will be
as much informed by the world as the more
"practical" aspects of the church will be.
This does not imply a pusillanimousness on the

part of the church--smashing more of the wil-
low than of the oak, as one old churchman put
it--but an openness to truth from whatever
source it comes. If we are secure in our central belief, that God is _for_ man, then we can
hang loose to a great number of other things.

I do think--or hope--that we will come
out with more unanimity of spirit on the other
end of the long tunnel we have been in. Ration-
alism's effect on the church was inevitable,
and it has done much to divide us in the past
few centuries. I don't know which is worse,
to be pre-Cartesian and cling defiantly to
orthodox patterns of thinking or to be post-
Cartesian and dismiss those patterns as in-
fantile. I myself have gone through both
phases.

Maybe a softening of positions will occur.
I hope so. I don't think the time will ever
come when there will be unanimity of opinion.
Not even the small early church had that.
The New Testament is rife with references to
their numerous points of conflict. But it
would be wonderful if we could ever reach
a stage of mutual tolerance and respect for
the feelings and ideas of others.

Along that line, you might be interested
in a little parable I picked up somewhere.
I'll try to remember to enclose a copy. Perhaps we could include it in the book as a
kind of postlude.

I'm looking forward to seeing your
church building. I have the feeling that
it's part of the future, just as the congregation is. Let me know how the work goes.

Warmly,

John

The Parable of the Statue

I will tell you a story, O best beloved, knowing your delight in such contrivances, and knowing also that they are often a boon to your understanding and enlightenment.

Once upon a time, O best beloved, which is the proper tense for all mythical happenings, there was a small but very impressive piece of statuary, fashioned, no doubt, by a primitive but nonetheless competent maker of such things. Cast in the form of a man bent beneath some heavy but invisible burden, it seemed to exude a double spirit of agony and joy, and, overall, a sense of deep humanity.

As the years went by and the statue passed into various hands, someone—we are not quite certain who it was, O best beloved—someone apparently decided that the nobility of bearing in the figure called for a more upright posture. And so an overlay was fashioned and attached to the form, raising it somewhat in height and adjusting the inclination of the posture until it was quite erect. Trained eyes could still see the molding line where the new material joined the old, but most people who saw it never guessed that the amended statue was not in fact the original one as it had been intended by the first artist.

Some more time elapsed—again we are uncertain of the more precise details, O best beloved—and someone was inspired with the notion that such a handsome piece of statuary was fitted for far more than the base metal in which it had been cast. So this person suggested that the figure be gilded, to set off its finer qualities. As the suggestion was bruited about, a committee of responsible citizens—meaning, O best beloved, that they had money —undertook to carry out the idea, and soon the remarkable piece of artistry glistened with a new kind of overlay.

Probably it was about this time that a fear arose regarding vandalism or the possible theft of so valuable an ornament. Therefore measures were taken, O best beloved, and the statue came at last to rest in a famous museum where it could remain at all times under the watchful eyes of guards especially trained to ward off attempts at appropriation.

For years then, even centuries, O best beloved, people from far and wide would arrive at the museum very early in the day and queue up before the famous statue, hoping for even a glimpse of it to bring sunshine into their otherwise dull and ordinary lives.

At some point—again, O best beloved, we are mocked for want of a more careful history—a viewer, who had on the several occasions of his visits to the shrine of the statue been moved to an act of extraordinary piety toward it, presented to the authorities an exceptionally rare and beautiful jewel, together with the wish that it might be incorporated into the statue in such a way as to enhance its already legendary attractiveness. The authorities, being men who understood not only the motivation for the gift but the value of the offer, accepted at once, or

107

almost at once, O best beloved, and had soon contracted with a most skilled lapidary to have the precious gem set in the very forehead of the figure.

When the statue was returned to its pedestal in the museum, the crowds coming to view it, O best beloved, were larger than ever. In fact, it was soon necessary to move it to more commodious quarters, and eventually to charge a price of admission in order to reduce the number of visitors. Only this last maneuver was notably unsuccessful, as it only whetted the appetites of people to see it so that the crowds grew larger and larger by the year.

For years, O best beloved, even for centuries, the bejewelled and gilded statue was adored in this way, with hardly ever a remission in the attention paid to it, either among potentates or the common people.

But one day, O best beloved, there was a great scandal. Someone who had made many visits to the shrine of the statue—and who had become quite familiar with every detail of its workmanship, for he was a renowned aesthete, O best beloved—startled the entire populace by announcing that the statue as they then admired it was not in its original form at all. And what is more, O best beloved, he demanded that all the trappings—beautiful trappings, you will agree, O best beloved—be forthrightly removed, restoring the object to its former self.

You can imagine—oh, you can imagine, O best beloved—the hullaballoo that was raised among the populace. Wailing and screaming and gnashing of teeth. Some, O best beloved, even cried for the poor fellow's head! What he had proposed, they declared, was—why, O best beloved—it was even blasphemy against the nature of God!

But I must not be sidetracked into narrating the miserable events in that poor creature's life thereafter. Suffice it to say, O best beloved, that his words found lodgment in a few stout hearts, and that eventually there was enough support for them among those who came after him to lead to an open debate on the merits of stripping the statue of its overlays and returning it to its earlier state.

Finally, O best beloved, some of these stout hearts organized a clever raid upon the museum where the statue was displayed—you will find this hard to believe, O best beloved—and held the place against the criers of alarm and threatening policemen until the experts among their number had performed the necessary operation upon the figure. When at last they surrendered to the dismayed authorities, the original statue stood on its pedestal, looking, O best beloved, rather plain and crude for such a gilded setting. The agony and the joy were once again visible, and the nobility of the demeanor had returned.

Again I must not be derailed from my purpose, O best beloved, by detailing the trials and future outcomes of those involved in this incredible raid. It is all surely written in the history books somewhere.

But for years, O best beloved, something seemed to have gone out of the spirit of the people. They continued to speak of the statue, and many even continued to come to the museum to view it. But it was not the same, O best beloved. One could easily see that it wasn't. A mood of dejection—some might even call it despair, O best beloved—had set in. It pervaded the entire culture. Crimes of violence increased in number. The suicide rate rose. People began to wonder what had happened to common decency and order.

Finally someone realized it was the statue. Yes, O best beloved, the statue. The mood of the people had changed when the statue was denuded of its gold and jewel, when, O best beloved, it lost its upright posture.

The case was put to the people. Should the statue remain in its starker form, as it was originally cast, or should the overlays be returned? The people, O best beloved, clamored for the return of the statue they had come to know and love, even if it meant covering up the original masterpiece beyond all recognition. And this will surprise you, O best beloved, even many of those who had been party to the raid and the desecration of the gilded statue gave their consent to the refurbishing of the figure. Those who had not committed suicide, that is, or were not in mental institutions. The consensus was—and this is the important point, O best beloved—that not all figures are best in their original form, however important the earlier conceptions were. For human life being as it is, O best beloved—which is to say fluid and dynamic in character —it stands to reason that tastes and aesthetic requirements change too. And in a case like that of the figure, what is of paramount importance is that the needs or requirements of the newer ages be met, not, O best beloved, those of the age which gave birth to the figure in the first place.

What, O best beloved, you wish the story explained? O best beloved! To explain the story! O beloved! O foolish beloved! O impossible beloved!

But very well, beloved. If I must ruin the story by explaining it, then I shall ruin it.

The statue is Jesus of Nazareth, who, a noble human being indeed, was bent beneath a sizable burden. The look of agony and joy was his. Early on, of course, his